Other Books by ARCH WHITEHOUSE

HERO WITHOUT HONOR

HERO
WITHOUT
HONOR.

Arthur George Joseph

~~Arch~~ *Whitehouse*.

DOUBLEDAY & COMPANY, INC.

Garden City, New York

1972

fiction

6.95

ISBN: 0-385-02725-7
Library of Congress Catalog Card Number 70–186050
Copyright © 1972 by Arch Whitehouse
All Rights Reserved
Printed in the United States of America
First Edition

HERO WITHOUT HONOR

1

The war-scarred, storm-stained RMS *Trigantic* thrashed her nineteen-knot course off the Great Circle route and turned her bow for the less choppy Straits of Belle Isle. With Belle Isle, a misty mound ten miles or so ahead, her crew and passengers hoped for a respite from the violent weather of the North Atlantic. For most, the voyage had been a turbulent anticlimax to a war that had seen too many blood baths, dozens of bayonet charges, clouds of suffocating gas, shattering artillery barrages, terrifying air combat, and hours of terror or boredom. At last they were on their way home, laggard returnees of what was left of a mighty overseas force when the Armistice brought an end to the twentieth-century Armageddon.

The *Trigantic* had been launched ten years before, a ship of grace and elegance. There had been luxury in her cabins and salons, and Blue Ribbon speed in her screws. Transatlantic trippers had considered her their very own when crossing from Montreal to Liverpool on their periodic visits to the Old Country. Today, she was besmirched with the same smutty exterior of any service vessel. More than four years of military transport duty on the Herring Pond, and several emergency runs through the Mediterranean to supply troops in Salonika and the Suez battle zone had left their mark. She had evaded U-boat packs, thanks to her speed, and more than her share of luck. Midsummer hurricanes and midwinter blizzards had stripped the gloss of her prewar glory, and brazed the gleam from her superstructure. The residue of half a dozen patterns of camouflage still crisscrossed her hull, leaving indistinct patches of gray, murky greens, and rust-stained blues.

Trigantic had served through a dirty war—and showed it. She was delivering home her final cargo of khaki-clad warriors where they hopefully might pick up the ragged ends of an earlier civilization and renounce the Armageddon that had disrupted their lives. The manifest included a number of ashen convalescents with the dull gleam of hospital routine in their eyes, and the stragglers of that last contingent of men who had volunteered to fight their war in the skies. To fill out her makeshift cabins, she had also accommodated a handful of men and women of the special services who had "done their bit" to sustain those who had fought in the trenches or on the high seas. Coincidentally, *Trigantic's* future represented the prodigal abandonment of the times. She had logged her service, done her stint, and when she had discharged this cargo of discards, she would be towed off to the breaker's yard where her plates, keel, and machinery would be reduced to scrap. After all, of what use was an aged troopship in a peacetime world?

The war was over.

A young man in undress uniform hunched over the forward rail, contemplating the choppy waters below. He was pondering moodily on his future, for at this point it all seemed behind him. His prospects of civilian life in no way related to the general impression that "our boys couldn't wait to get home and enjoy the comfort and sanctity of their homes again." He was aroused by the raucous cry of a gull gliding nearby, quoting the prospects of the ship's waste scoop. He looked up, and with a professional eye admired the built-in aileron control the feathered flier employed to keep station with the troopship. He wondered whether the bird was related to the gannet or the tern, and the meditation aroused a memory of the day he had shot down a gaudy Fokker triplane.

He had been cruising over Hallouin at S.E.5 altitude, hoping to fill out his score of fifty Huns before going on leave to London. The Jerry pilot had been tootling about with the same unconcern as the gray-white gull, satisfied with the idea of padding the time in his logbook. The S.E.5 had height and plumb-bob diving power, but the pilot knew the ropes and made certain the Fokker was not stooging about, acting as bait for a flight of Albatri he had noticed a short time before.

The instant he was certain of his prey the stalking pilot went down like a bolt. He reveled in the whiff of hot oil, the odor of the interrupter-gear pump, and the tang of ammunition snaking up from the box. The Hun tried to get away, and made the mistake of striving to outdive the S.E.5. When a short burst took out a section of his engine cowling, he attempted to zoom. The move was murder. The instant the Fokker topped its climb, the Britisher steadied with his rudder, put the triplane into the Aldis sight, and sent another burst dead into the center-section struts. The Fokker floundered, and the mid and upper planes flipped away, as if carelessly discarded. The Jerry fuselage, with a dead pilot at the stick, went into a flat spin and began to smoke. The stress and strain accumulated, and another, quite unnecessary, burst shattered the tail assembly. Then the lower airfoils cranked up and slapped together over the cockpit.

Zooming sharply to avoid the storm of debris, Maxwell Kenyon checked the sky and saw an Albatros C-III two-seater plodding on toward the lines, presumably to carry out an artillery shoot. Kenyon made the most of his ailerons and worked his way to below the tail of the Art-obs bus to keep clear of the rear gunner's weapon. That unfortunate was too absorbed in reeling in his wireless aerial to notice what was going on below. Kenyon moved into position skillfully. Then, flying a parallel course some fifty feet below the artillery machine, he drew down his Lewis gun from its bracket on his top plane, tilted it slightly and fired a short burst dead into the mud-streaked belly of the C-III. He saw the gunner's arms swing outward in supplication, and then a gout of the flame ran along the lower longerons. The Albatros went out of control and, dragging a long, greasy scarf of smoke, whip-snapped back and forth until a great belch of flame rammed it into a straight glide. Kenyon used the torch as a target until there was little left to perforate.

It was typical of Maxwell Kenyon. He never gave a foe a chance on the presumption no Jerry would ever concede him quarter. It was a profitable mode of operation, but not always considered in the best of taste. Had taste and sportsmanship been a factor in his makeup he would never have been awarded the Victoria Cross, but he might have become a more popular hero. He had estimated early on that one couldn't have everything.

The reminiscence concluded, Kenyon felt he would like to have a word with the sea bird. In fact, he would have been grateful to speak to anyone who appreciated the mechanism of a precise aileron control. So far during the trip there were few fellow passengers who indicated the faintest interest in him. Many of them had stayed in their cabins, wretched and inert, for the voyage had been unseasonably turbulent. There were some flying men aboard, but those he had casually encountered were obvious Quirks with little, or no, active-service time in their logbooks, and certainly with no impressive ribbons below their wings.

Many of the male returnees had already discarded their uniforms and were wearing civvies, bought with their gratuities, from noted Bond Street tailors. Obviously, they had been in the war only a short time, not long enough to appreciate it was a way of life. Already, their talk was of business, their return to previous jobs, and in many instances there were snobbish references to picking up college courses where they had left off. The Army types, regardless of rank, had no eyes for this young man who wore a double row of decorations—all of them for distinguished conduct or bravery in the field. Kenyon had not put up any of the several campaign ribbons as he felt his decorations explained he had been in the thick of the fighting somewhere. The campaign ribbons were for those who simply had to prove they had been overseas, and it was disconcerting to see a young man in his early twenties flaunting field rank *and* the blood-red ribbon of the Victoria Cross.

Maxwell Kenyon was almost twenty-four, and in repose looked five years younger. Of medium height, his years of campaigning had kept him slimmed down to a point where he complimented his uniform. His hair had once been corn-stalk blond, but with adult years it was becoming a glossy nut brown. He still subscribed to the short military cut, but in the past few weeks had conceded to a longer forelock which, to his quiet satisfaction, had revealed the pompadour wave of his teens. His eyes were smoky gray, his nose small and perky. When he smiled his mouth reflected his basic friendliness. The day he was commanded to appear at Buckingham Palace, everyone admitted he was the beau ideal of the Royal Flying Corps. That is, he was to women. For reasons he could never understand, men seldom took to him. Most disliked him on sight. He wondered about that, but because he was Maxwell Kenyon he could not comprehend anyone else's viewpoint. Sometimes he wondered if it was because he was an only son. If so, that was none of his fault.

Kenyon turned his back to the rail and became aware he was being approached by a young girl in an unfamiliar uniform. She was neat and petite with a coronet of auburn hair that was becoming an oriflamme in the fingers of the wind.

"Well, hello!"

"Excuse me, sir." The girl produced a Kodak box-type camera. "I . . . I don't know your rank, but I recognize you from articles in the newspapers. Would you mind if I took a picture—a photograph of you to take home to my parents?"

Maxwell Kenyon was delighted with her approach and evaluated its possibilities. "Of course. Glad to. I'm a squadron leader." He glanced down at the rank braid on his sleeve. "By the way, what's that dress, or smock, you're wearing?" He expertly took in the attractive curves of her breasts.

"It's not a smock. It's the uniform of the American YMCA," she corrected, and then remembered her finishing school training. "I'm Nancy Bradford, and I've been working in a hut near Tours, but I so wanted to get somewhere near the British front. My parents are English," she added as if that explained everything.

Kenyon was intrigued with her voice and its tonal qualities which he recognized as the cultured speech of New England. He also wondered where this young goddess had been throughout the voyage. "Same here," he said. "My dad and mother came from Manchester which is how I joined up early in the war, long before the United States came in," he explained almost wistfully as though trying to remember those early months of 1914. "Now we're all going home to take up where we left off."

She stood studying the ribbons below his wings. "You don't sound very excited. Aren't you glad it's all over?"

"I'm not sure. I wish we had finished the bloody war—properly. We haven't, you know."

She nodded somberly and forked a lock of hair from her eyes. "I've heard that opinion from so many flying men. It's hard to understand. As for me, I shall be glad to get back to school."

"School? Oh, I suppose you mean college. You're too young to be a schoolteacher . . . and too attractive," he added as a trial straw.

"I'm going back to Vassar for my last year . . . and the daisy chain." He looked puzzled. "Graduation ceremony," she said, and laughed. "Now will you stand over there where there seems to be a fair amount of light? What do you plan to do when you get home?" she asked as they moved away from the rail.

"I have no idea. I'm not even sure I have one to go to. We were always a poverty-stricken lot, in and out of the gutter. I've never seen the inside of a high school, and I have no trade or profession. I've been tossed out of my service with only the ability to fly a scout plane and fire a machine gun. Not much future in any of that today."

The young woman stared, took hold of his sleeve. "You shouldn't worry about a formal education. Four years in the war must have taught you many things—and you have the Victoria Cross."

He'd never forget that day outside Buckingham Palace. That was the stunner. "Decorations are only important during a war," he said solemnly. "My V.C. won't mean much. I can't wear it with civilian clothing, and I doubt whether it would be recognized in . . . in the United States. Going home means I have to start at the bottom again—somewhere."

"Don't be downhearted. You'll make it. I know you will," the girl said cheerfully. "Now what about this picture? Would you stand over there in front of that piece of machinery? My parents will be thrilled when I tell them I met and photographed Squadron Leader Kenyon of the Royal Air Force," she chattered on.

He enjoyed her youthful gaiety and looked over her uniform again. The coverall-type dress which buttoned from the shoulder to the hem had interesting possibilities. Three buttons down and four buttons up should establish a strategic working area. "You want me to pose against the donkey engine? Now there's a symbolic background for a discarded flying man."

"Discarded? What do you mean?" the girl said with concern. "Your parents won't consider you a discard."

"I've been discarded. I wanted to stay in for a twenty-one-year pension. I like flying, but they wouldn't keep me on for peacetime service."

"They wouldn't take a man with all those decorations . . . and after all you've done?" she quaked in disbelief.

"Only men with good university backgrounds, or certain administrative qualifications, I was told. There are thousands of young lieutenants who can fly scouts. Lieutenants come cheap."

"It doesn't seem right," the girl concluded and polished the lens of the finder with a corner of her handkerchief. "Well, I'm lucky I caught you before you discarded your uniform. Will you turn your left shoulder forward so those ribbons show up?"

The preparations attracted a few after-breakfast deck walkers who gathered in a half circle behind the American girl. Kenyon began to enjoy this unexpected prestige and looked forward to improving the promising acquaintance. This was more like old times . . . before the Armistice.

The YMCA lass turned to look up at a faint gleam of sunshine. Satisfied, she peered into the finder and prepared to flick the shutter. Suddenly there was a bellow of officialdom from the bridge, and an irate ship's officer clattered down the companionway to the deck. The girl jerked her head up, startled.

The officer was short and wide, and carried his hands with the open claw-like attitude of a man who has long been familiar with hawsers. He tugged his service cap down hard, glared with piercing eyes and knuckled the ends of his tobacco-stained mustache. He wore four rings of Mercantile Marine braid on his sleeves and a greasy clutter of campaign ribbons high on his jacket. The Old Man was not in a chummy mood this morning.

"That woman there! You can't take photographs. Put that camera away, at once!" he bellowed and thrashed his way through the onlookers.

Miss Bradford flicked an auburn lock from one eye, still startled by the interruption, and then looked to Kenyon for an explanation. The airman was equally surprised and a jolt of reality warned once more that his days of glory were over.

"May I ask what's wrong, sir?" he inquired and saw that the fourth ring of gold braid was new, indicating the officer had recently been given this command. If so, he would be facing the same future as Squadron Leader Kenyon. Possibly, this would be his last trip as skipper of a first-class troopship. In a short while he, too, could be discarded and left high and dry on the beach.

"No one can take photographs aboard the *Trigantic*. This vessel is on military service as a British troopship. You should know better than that. You're supposed to be an officer—of some sort, aren't you?" the ruddy-faced man in wrinkled blue barked.

The onlookers began to whisper their comments with a Serves-him-right! look in their eyes.

"It's only a Kodak . . . for a snapshot," the YMCA girl interceded. "This . . . squadron leader is one of Britain's greatest airmen. He was awarded the V.C."

The Navy man wagged his head like a poleaxed bull. "I don't

· 7 ·

care who he is. You can't take photographs on the deck of a military transport. I shall have to confiscate the film."

"But I haven't taken a picture yet. We were just . . ."

"Don't lie to me. I saw you aiming the camera."

Kenyon tried to explain with his best "temporary gentleman" voice. "I assure you, sir, she did *not* snap the shutter."

"I'm not taking your word for anything. I'm master of this vessel and there will be no photographing of important details of my ship under any circumstances." He snatched the camera from the girl's limp hands.

"But the war has been over for several months."

"Has it now? Perhaps for you flying men, but *we* are serving under the terms of the Armistice, or haven't you been advised?" He rammed his thumbnail into a nickel-plated slide of the black box. "The Peace Treaty has not yet been signed." The back of the box dropped on its hinge, and the outraged Navy man hooked a forefinger behind the black paper shield and snatched out the strip of yellow film. A metal spool trickled across the deck, and the camera was tossed after it.

"You're being most unfair, sir," Kenyon remonstrated, and bent down to pick up the offending instrument. "No pictures had been taken."

"How do you know?" the officer raged, tossing the curling film over the rail. He leaned over to watch it flutter down into the broadening wake of the ship. Turning back, he glared at Kenyon. "If I see you encouraging this young woman to use that camera again, I'll see that the bloody thing goes overboard, also. You may be a squadron leader in your ragtime Flying Corps, but aboard my ship you're only a passenger," and with that denunciation the apoplectic skipper returned to his post on the bridge. Naval discipline, born in Nelson's day, had been upheld, and service traditions rigidly maintained.

The onlookers began to break up in small clots to quietly discuss the incident. By now, some of them were indignant at the captain's behavior, a few were unable to understand the reason for the angry business over the camera. A small knot of Canadian infantry officers exchanged glances, clearly agreeing that the V.C. bloke had it coming to him. Another one of those bloody war heroes who had been peering down his nose at anyone who didn't sport a row of decorations. The quicker he learned that he, like they, had relinquished his commission, that the war was over; the sooner he'd be accepted in present-day society.

Kenyon walked Miss Bradford back to the rail and closed the back of the offending camera. "Forget it," he said under his breath. "I have plenty of pictures in my stateroom. Some showing my S.E.5 . . . my scout aeroplane. I'm in full flying kit."

Nancy considered the offer, and then caution steadied her enthusiasm. "I've a better idea. You pick one . . . very representative of you and your aeroplane. My father would treasure that."

"I'll even autograph it for you."

Nancy Bradford reacted immediately. "That would be wonderful. "They . . . my parents will be meeting me in Montreal. I'll introduce you to them, and who knows? Papa might find a place for you in his plant. There must be something you could do there. He makes brakes and shock absorbers for automobiles," she rattled on, ideas and possibilities spilling out like fruits and ambrosia from a cornucopia.

Kenyon held his breath, unable to believe this sudden turn of luck. "I'd like to talk to him. I learned a lot about mechanics in the School of Aeronautics. I always serviced my own guns . . . and the interrupter gears," he babbled in reply.

"I'm sure it will work out. We'll all meet on the dock, and you can give Papa the picture of yourself. After that, leave the rest to me," the excited girl trilled, and hurried off.

For a few minutes Kenyon enjoyed a surge of high optimism. He had completely broken out of his dejection before the girl had disappeared along the promenade deck. This was a chance, if ever there was one. He could envision all of it. Her parents would be waving from the dock, so delighted to see their daughter again, they'd settle for anything. There would be breathless introductions, the explanation of the bar of blood-red ribbon, a quick flash of the Kenyon personality, with the rest as smooth as the aileron control of that gull. No excuses would be listened to. They'd take him home with them—for a good rest. There would be an inspection of the plant—in uniform, of course, and within a week he'd move into a cushy job, as easy as he used to slip behind the tail of Jerry D-VIIs. Nancy would insist on a church wedding and a proper honeymoon, and he'd get plenty of what he had planned the minute Miss Bradford tripped into his life.

Until now the homeward voyage had been a complete dud, but there had to be a law of averages. He had no intention of returning to that slatternly tenement he had left nearly five years before. The kitchen table leveled with a broken clothespin, the greasy plates and the tang of stale food. He dreaded going back to that degrading home from which the war had rescued him. But Nancy Bradford, a true representative of the top level of society, would complete the reclamation.

His pleasant reminiscences were interrupted by a low-toned feminine voice, purring a few inches from his left ear. "Hello, Max. Your bad penny has turned up, but I simply had to come . . . to America."

Kenyon turned his head slowly, his mind refusing to accept the words. Then, under protest, he responded, "Dido! Dido Maitland! Where in God's name did you come from?" He reached out and gripped her upper arms. "You've been aboard all this time?"

Miss Maitland trilled a light laugh, slipped from his grip and steadied herself by the rail. "I didn't know you were aboard until shortly after we sailed. I thought you had gone back to . . . that place in New Jersey. This is the first chance I've had . . ." she almost whispered.

She was a tall, slim girl with a cosmetic-ad complexion and flashing teeth. Her eyes tried to dance, but some inner listlessness slowed the tempo. She lowered her lids and shook her head gently. "I've looked for you, but I suppose you're in the Senior Officers' quarters."

"I haven't seen your name on the passenger list."

She avoided his direct gaze. "I'm supposed to be Mrs. Ralph Wallington."

He stiffened in disbelief. "You're married to Wallington? Not *Ralph* Wallington?"

"Don't you understand? I had to get to America, somehow, and find you."

"Am I supposed to understand any of this?"

"I spent weeks looking for you, but you were never where they said you were."

"You're traveling as Ralph's wife just to get across, and find me?" He tried to piece this annoying riddle together. "Is he on board? I hadn't noticed him."

"You wouldn't. He lost a lot of weight in prison camp and he's wearing civvies. He was shot down and taken prisoner."

"Is that swine still spilling that line?" Kenyon glanced around the group. "He actually deserted. Should have been court-martialed."

"I suppose so, but when he was repatriated the whole affair had blown over. He says dozens of others did the same. He's a changed man, Max."

Still pondering on the situation, Kenyon said, "So you're trying to work the old war-bride game. Are you married, or aren't you?"

Dido wrung her hands helplessly. "I had to find you. This is just a temporary arrangement. Ralph listed me as his wife before his demobilization papers came through, so we were booked together on the same ship. I had hoped when we got to Montreal we would pick up our bags and go our separate ways. That's all there is to it."

"All there is to it!" Max snapped in exasperation. "Who the hell thought up that crummy deal?"

"I did, but I had hoped to work it with you. When you disappeared so completely, I had to make the offer—suggestion—to Wallington. He was the only one I knew who was still waiting at Scampton aerodrome."

Kenyon shook his head in frustration. "I was on a loop between Cranwell and the Air Ministry in London trying to get a permanent commission. I wanted to stay in the Air Force for good."

Dido looked bewildered. "I thought everyone wanted to go home when it was all over."

"They had to call the Military Police to put me aboard this bloody ship. Who the hell wants to go home? What is there to go home for? I worked my guts out to get where I am, and now I'm supposed to throw it away and start from the gutter again."

"But everyone has to face that, Max. That's why I wanted to get across . . . to help you . . . and be with you. Don't you understand?"

He turned and stared beyond the rail. "Of all the ridiculous situations. I've been slogging to stay over there, and you . . . you're shagging your way across the Atlantic . . ."

"Forget that part. I was trying to find you."

Max looked her over again and tried to remember when she had had London at her feet. She had been a featured dancer in the long-run *Chu-Chin-Chow* extravaganza, and her meeting with Maxwell Kenyon proved to be the first false step on her path to stardom. Not only was she a fascinating figure with sensational routines, but she was a born actress who could handle lines whether she was performing her steps and twirls or trading fast dialogue with the leading man. But with the diversionary pitch of social intercourse, she began to show more interest in this "intrepid birdman" than the curtain time at the theater. The newly gazetted Lieutenant Kenyon with his impulsive gaiety, youthful personality, and love of military life, entranced her. Beginning with five-shilling teas at the Savoy, dinners at the Waldorf, supper dances at the Carlton Club, they ended up in bedrooms of Mayfair hotels. In this manner the ex-Shoreditch shopgirl who had spent the few shillings she had earned behind a Marks & Spencers counter for dancing lessons, enjoyed the segments of life previously viewed through open doorways, or during exploratory saunters through the Leicester Lounge. She could have made a fortune—perhaps gone on to Broadway, but she threw it all away for Max Kenyon.

He looked at her with compassion. "What's it like? How's Wallington treating you?"

"Nothing like what he was. Prison camp took all the fight out of him. He's a beaten man, Max."

"Well, you ought to know . . . sharing his cabin."

"Yes," she agreed faintly, "but it's not as bad as it might be. There are days he hardly looks at me . . . because he's frightened, knowing you're on board. Don't worry, it'll be all over in a day or two."

"I can't believe that about Windy Wallington."

"Put it all out of your mind. It's not too bad, considering." Kenyon soothed his frustration by scanning the deck which was becoming crowded with passengers responding to the comparatively balmy weather. Some were struggling with deck chairs. A deck-tennis game was in progress, and small groups were commenting on the evergreen background of the Labrador shore. An ex-RAF cadet, now wearing a British knickerbocker suit, was twanging a ukulele.

> *"Good Byee! Don't sighee!*
> *Wipe the tear, baby dear,*
> *From your eyee!"*

"Where's Wallington now?"

"Probably hiding in the Second Class saloon, hoping to evade you. He plays cards and drinks most of the day. He hardly notices me."

"I'd like to read the riot act to him. If only to make him treat you . . . the crummy, yellow bastard!"

"You don't have to, Max. He's frightened to death of you, knowing what you'd do. He can't wait to get down the gangplank, clear Customs and hurry home to Calgary, or somewhere."

Kenyon knew that Dido was floundering in a bottomless pit and had little chance of disembarking in Montreal. It had been a ridiculous scheme right from the start, but with an oaf like Ralph holding the reins, the worst could be but a matter of hours. He touched her arm lightly. "Did you bring any papers? You have a passport, I suppose, but you'll certainly be asked for your marriage certificate."

She turned and studied the wake of the vessel and answered as if by rote. "I have a passport in my own name. I took that out when I hoped to go home with you. I'll have no trouble there, but they'll have to accept the marriage from the manifest, or some excuse about its being destroyed in a Zeppelin raid."

"That won't work. The bomb-raid story has been worked to death."

"I suppose so. I just hope Ralph will stand by me."

"Knowing Wallington, he'll duck, leaving you stranded. You'll be classified as an undesirable and deported."

"Why do you say that, Max? I want to get ashore and be with you. Isn't that what I've been trying to do ever since we first met?"

"I had half a dozen offers myself, but the war-bride game has been played out."

Dido dry-washed her hands again. "I thought it would be easy. I heard all the Yanks and Canadians were taking girls across like this. Who wants to go back to what's left of wartime London?"

Max nodded glumly. "They were, but that was right after the Armistice when anybody in uniform was a hero and could do no wrong. Then the Canadian Immigration people began to get nasty, once the glow of victory burned out. I doubt whether you'll get through unless Wallington makes a definite stand for you, but I wouldn't trust that louse."

"Bon Soir, old thing,
Cheerio! Chin-Chin!
Naphoo! Toodleoo!
Good Byee!"

Squadron Leader Kenyon emitted a sigh, and Dido made the most of her eyes while praying for a reprieve.

"If you're stopped, you'll wind up with a moral turpitude charge, and with that you'll never get a job in New York, or London," Kenyon muttered as if trying to remember where he had heard the phrase. "Just what are you trying to do?"

There was a weariness in her eyes, but she held her ground. "I had to come after you, Max. Call it what you like. I had to be nearby. Together we can get along famously. We can't run away from our backgrounds. The war wasn't real. Neither of us were real people, and we have to start all over again with the strength we absorbed from our poverty-stricken beginnings. But you've got to face the peacetime world."

He wondered about the job Nancy Bradford had suggested, but another look at Dido erased it clean. He was silent for several seconds and then came to a drastic decision. His jaw stiffened and a white spot spread across one cheekbone. He flattened both palms on the rail and spoke quietly. "You'll never make it with Ralph, but I can't think of but one other choice." He stared about as if expecting his solution to flutter from the foremast. He turned and gripped her arms again. "You stay here. I'll be back in a few minutes. Don't move until I come back. We may be just in time," and with that cryptic remark Squadron Leader Kenyon, V.C., D.S.O., M.C., D.C.M., M.M., hurried through the clots of passengers and headed for the companionway that led up to the bridge. As he started to climb the sun came out full and gilded the foredeck in gold.

2

Maxwell Erskine Kenyon was delivered by a Polish midwife in a railroad flat of five rooms which stood in nominal decay on South 10th Street in the Hill section of Newark, New Jersey. This six-family rabbit warren had been the Kenyons' abode since Bob and Selina had escaped from Ellis Island in the spring of 1893. Young Maxwell booked in two years later at the end of the year, just as the Kenyons were getting a bit o' brass in the Howard Savings Institution. They had planned to hoard five thousand dollars and bung off back to Manchester, England, but this jolt of unplanned parenthood reduced their savings considerably—and increased their parsimony. Selina had to give up her closing-room job at Banister's shoe factory where she was paid seven dollars a week stitching the uppers and preparing them for the lasters. Robert, her spouse, who had been nicknamed Bob months before he was formally christened, had found work in the Hyatt Roller Bearing factory, a job somewhat comparable to his Lancashire occupation where he had been apprenticed to a manufacturer of cotton-weaving looms. Bob had started at eight dollars a week, but by the time his unwanted son had arrived, he had been raised to ten. Still, with the loss of Selina's "dibs" their fortunes suffered considerably, and young Maxwell was seldom given the chance to forget that period of their depression.

In those years neither Bob nor Selina had learned much about the Land of the Free, for their minds and yearnings had never withdrawn from the sooty industrial regions of Lancashire. They took no interest in politics. In fact, neither one had ever gone to the polls in Manchester. Their basic Socialism was just a subject for argument. They could not conceive their personal views having an influence on a state or national election. America was just a

country to flit to when "things got bad" in trade. When they had
made enough to go back—back they would go and pick up where
they had left off. Because of this disinterested attitude, they never
quite understood what their son was learning in school, or why he
was taught such a packet of misinformation. He seemed to know
little of the Magna Carta, Oliver Cromwell, Queen Victoria, or
Alfred the Great. Geography? The kid couldn't explain where
Manchester was, or how far it was from Land's End to John O'
Groats. In fact, the idiot seemed to have the idea Manchester was
way up in Massachusetts!

In general, Max's parents considered themselves part of a feudal
system and accepted their roles with little depth of thought. They
had always had to work hard. Their fathers and mothers had worked
hard, and from what they remembered their grandparents had
endured the same toil-blighted existence. It was the way the world
was, and it was useless to aspire to anything better. The big pots
had all the money, and the rest had to work for theirs. It would
always be this way.

On the day Maxwell could be legally packed off to school, his
mother returned to her stint at Banister's, thereby raising the Kenyon
income to its rightful level. A small corps of neighbors was deputized
to watch out for young Maxwell and see that he went to the w.c.
if he was caught scratching his privates. Amazingly, the system
worked. The youngster survived all hazards and juvenile plagues.
By the time he was nine he had learned to fend for himself, do
the family shopping, get his own lunch, and have the chief in-
gredients of the evening meal "on the hob" by the time his parents
crept in from their treadmills of toil.

According to modern psychology, young Kenyon should have
completed his education in a reform school, been in and out of
prison several times, and ended on the gallows before he was old
enough to vote. Instead, by steadfastly adhering to the doctrines of
Horatio Alger and Frank Merriwell, he avoided all gutter pitfalls
and had the pleasure of bringing himself up, thus relieving his
parents of a tedious chore. True, Mr. Rushton, Vicar of St.
Matthew's Church on South 9th Street, had played an important
role, and even offered to put Max through Newark Academy and
send him on to Princeton, but Selina Kenyon had other ideas and
instead, she applied for his working papers.

There were no schoolboy heroes in Max's day, that is, none he could identify with or emulate. The valiants of 1776 were beyond his ken, and he had no desire to become a Nathan Hale or join the Green Mountain boys. The woods and fields of the outraged colonists were beyond his scope of experience. The Civil War's heroes were all generals. How could one wait to become a general? He couldn't recall anyone of note in the Spanish-American War, except Teddy Roosevelt who had become renowned by showing his teeth and grunting "Bully!" to everything he did. Worse still, Teddy had recently become a big game hunter, but always had someone to load and carry his gun. What sort of a hunter was that?

Nor could Max identify with sports headliners. Baseball was a game played by a handful of highly touted players—Christy Mathewson, Iron Man Joe McGinnity, Wee Willie Keeler, Three Fingered Brown, Rube Waddell and, oh yes, Honus Wagner, the fellow with the German name. Football? That was a college game played with a funny-shaped ball, and since he had no hope of going to Princeton—and team up with Hoby Baker—there was no future on the "gridiron."

Where could a youth become a hero in this dull, commercial world?

Bob Kenyon's British schooling, such as it was, had omitted any reference to the American Revolution, and he had started work at Hyatt's with no idea of how the United States had attained its sovereignty. He knew Canada belonged to England because on all school maps it was colored red, but how America became non-British was a conundrum. What he did learn during a lunchtime discussion at the plant was that you could be anything, Irish, German, Italian, Polish, Scotch, or even a Swede, but not one toiler at Hyatt's would confess to being English. Didn't the English put on that massacre at Concord Bridge? Didn't the bloody Redcoats set fire to Washington? They massacred innocent people at Bunker Hill and starved the Colonials at Valley Forge. The Highlanders were never mentioned, nor were the Hessians. It was always those bloody English Redcoats.

Bob Kenyon could take no part in these heated discussions. Valley Forge? Bunker Hill? Concord Bridge? He had no idea where these places were, or what the skirmishes were about. He couldn't quite place George the Third. All that must have been a bit before his time. But Bob Kenyon knew on which side his bread was buttered. No one in Newark knew where Manchester was, and it was a simple matter to renounce England and become a Scot. After all, Glasgow wasn't far from Manchester. It was the thing to do at Hyatt's. Proclaim one's ancestry, just as one trumpeted his support of a baseball team, or the Democrats. Hyatt's was staffed with German-Americans, Italian-Americans, Irish-Americans, and even Polish-Americans, but who the hell ever heard of English-Americans?

"Ah'm a Scotsman," the Lancashire renegade protested. "I' fact, once I almost 'listed i' the Gordon Highlanders. Th' Gay Gordons they're called. But Ah wasn't quite tall enough."

When Maxwell Kenyon received his eighth grade diploma from the principal of Fourteenth Avenue School, he was ordered to apply for his working papers, and almost immediately was provided with a job at Milligan's Book Store on South Broad Street. The work was a striking contrast to his saunter through grade school. Now his day began at 7 A.M. when he arrived to brush off the sidewalk, set out the morning papers on a shop-front counter, sweep out the aisles and wash the windows in turn. By 8 A.M. two sales clerks arrived, checked his work, and lined up his morning errands. These included delivery of stacks of glossy-paged magazines to most of the lavish homes along South Broad Street, Lincoln Park, Clinton Avenue, and to many business offices up and down Broad and Market streets.

And there was no lolling in sloth on Sundays. To observe the Sabbath, Max had to arrive at the store by 5:30 A.M. to insert the supplements of the Sunday papers, and to help Mr. Pyle arrange the stacks of New York *Americans* for some twenty youngsters to deliver before the rest of the city had been aroused for breakfast. He was also honored with a select Sunday route which he delivered on his way home. However, there was a hidden bonus in this chore, for he was often able to secrete a G. A. Henry or Oliver Optic adventure book among his newspapers, and in that peculate manner begin to build up a personal library of juvenile classics.

He grew to like the work and its associations with books and, since his petty pilferings were never noticed, he became a popular employee. Now and then he was entrusted with an emergency errand to New York City, usually to pick up a few extra copies of a popular novel. Wandering through the spice-scented canyons of lower Manhattan, he sniffed intrigue and adventure. For hours, his identity and assignment would be forgotten. When he reached Broadway he enjoyed being swept north with the rip tide of humanity. Here were gay shops, entrancing window displays where antiques and romantic costumes claimed his attention. When he reached Bannerman's with its memorable offerings of dress swords, ancient carbines, battle flags, displays of medals, grapeshot, dirks, dueling pistols, and Highland bonnets, he was held spellbound, his mind churning in a delirious whirl.

On one occasion, on a March day in 1911, a fiery tragedy seared its stamp on his fertile imagination. He was an eyewitness of the Triangle Shirtwaist factory fire that in minutes of fervent agony, snuffed out the lives of 146 young women who were trapped in the upper stories of the sweatshop. Maxwell Kenyon saw and heard their terror, and knew they had no choice but to jump. He stood below, gripped in horrified fascination as their flailing bodies hit the pavement. Many of them screeched all the way through the gouts of flames that clawed from the windows. Some bodies bounded like sacks of grain—and exploded with dull thuds—but several hit metal-and-glass inserts in the sidewalk, passed clean through, leaving definite outlines of their figures in the jagged metal.

But the snuffing out of so many lives did not affect Max. He was more intrigued with the dramatic backdrop of the disaster. In this instance, death created no fear. Instead, it reinforced a juvenile belief in personal immortality.

When he got back to Milligan's all the newspaper EXTRAS were stacked on the counter, and breathless patrons clogged the doorway to scan the headlines and stare with disbelief at the smudgy halftone illustrations. But Max's eyewitness account of the holocaust was told with stark simplicity and detailed immediacy.

A far-flung war was being prepared for Maxwell Kenyon's consideration. It was being feathered, festooned, braided in gold, presented in newspaper headlines, and on the Pathé Newsreel screens. The Manchester papers which arrived every week announced the declaration of war, showed emotional scenes in the streets, outside barracks, and at the gangplanks of troopships. They published the popular cries, the swaggering songs, the calls to arms, and explained the odium of the white feather. As a result, the bugles rang in his ears, drums rolled, and visionary men in khaki bellowed, "Are we downhearted? . . . Naooo!"

Maxwell Kenyon's die was cast.

Late in that memorable August of 1914 when the BEF had landed at Ostend, Calais, and Dunkirk, when the British fleet had sunk three German cruisers and two destroyers off Helgoland; when the "enemy" had occupied Brussels, sacked and burned Louvain, young Kenyon was sent on a routine errand to New York. He had little concern for the details of his mission for the war was flaunted before his eyes at every turn. There were placards on churchyard railings. They fluttered at the waists of newsboys, were plastered on the walls and at the windows of downtown newspaper plants. All related to the ebb and flow of the bloody conflict.

In Union Square enraged men bellowed from the plinths of statuary, accusing the British of every breach of international law known to civilization. Savagery in the Boer War! Pirates of the high seas! A war for international trade! Maxwell listened from a secluded spot and wondered what his father would think of these wild harangues.

Small knots of slack-kneed men, wearing cloth caps, down-at-the-heel shoes and with grizzly chins, listened and exchanged grumbled rebuttals. One, wearing a blue jersey with CUNARD LINE stamped on the chest, edged up to the slim youth. "You one of our lot, chum?" he said from one side of his mouth.

"Me? Well, er, my dad and mum are from Manchester, if that's what you mean. Why don't the police stop this sort of thing? All those lies . . ."

"We don't want the police. We're all going to bash in and break it up. You like to 'ave a go?"

"You mean you're going to start a row, and knock them about?"

"They're arskin' for it, ain't they? Been blathering on for more than an hour. Nobody does anything about it. We're gettin' together to give 'em a taste of the old what-for!"

"Don't do it," a voice behind Max warned quietly, but distinctly. "You'll only cause more trouble. They've got a permit. They know what they're doing."

The warning came from a neatly dressed man who wore a velours hat and carried a leather attaché case. Young Maxwell sized him up and decided to take his advice. The seaman tugged at his forelock respectfully. "But look 'ere, sir. Someone ought to do something to shut up them bloody Germans. All bloody lies, what they're saying."

"Of course, but you can't do anything about it in a neutral country. You're a seaman. You ought to know that. America is neutral in this war, you know."

"But they let those bloody Germans sling their weight about like that, an' we're not supposed to do anything about it?"

"You will only wind up in a police station, and the British Consul will have to get you out. These people have a permit for a public demonstration."

"Ought to shoot the whole lot of them," Max said, enjoying the belligerency.

"I'd do it in a minute," the seaman added.

"That's the spirit." The sedate gentleman looked around in a casual manner. "You could go home and enlist. Kitchener has called for a hundred thousand men at once."

"Go home? Fine bloody chance," the brawny sailor snarled and spat. "We're over here. Kitchener's over there. Where would we get the fare?"

"That can be taken care of."

"How? Who?"

"If any of you want to go home to enlist, we can get you there with no trouble, but you have to keep it quiet."

"You could arrange free passage for anyone?" Max said in disbelief.

The mysterious stranger took Max's elbow and drew him aside. "You seem like a chap who can be trusted. I'll tell you what we have in mind. You can relay it to any of the others who are British and want to go home to join up."

Maxwell Kenyon had no objection to being elected one of the Bulldog breed. In fact, he felt a surge of anticipation. He listened carefully and promised to remember every detail. It seemed like the chance of a lifetime! Milligan's Book Store never saw him again. He conveniently forgot the thirty dollars entrusted to him to buy a gross of Christmas calendars being laid in for the holiday season. Two weeks later the money came in very handy.

On the way home Max pondered on the difficulty of explaining his decision to quit his job—and sail to England . . . for the war. He rehearsed his opening statement several times, knowing it would come as something of a shock. But anything to get away from home, and South 10th Street.

"I'm going to England . . . to join up!" he announced as matter-of-factly as he could. He skimmed his cap to a peg on the kitchen door. "Tomorrow afternoon, from New York. A lot of us are going."

Her arms akimbo, Selina Kenyon considered the announcement for nineteen seconds. "You're what?"

"I'm going to England to join the Army. It's all arranged. We get free passage across," he added with more emphasis.

Mrs. Kenyon frowned and turned her gaze on Bob. There was no general dismay, no objections, no maternal concern. Selina sniffed. "You a soldier? The Royal Standbacks, you!" she derided and turned back to the stove and put another sausage in the pan. The idea *was* rather comic. Fancy young Max a soldier!

"Don't try to stop me! I've practically signed up and there's no way of getting out of it. Wouldn't think of it. They're providing passage for any able-bodied Britisher who wants to go home and enlist. Lord Kitchener . . ."

"Britisher?" His mother jabbed the sausage savagely. "Well, that lets you out. You're an American . . . born over here. We have your birth certificate . . . somewhere."

"But I told the British Consul man my father and mother were both British." Max turned toward his father who was peering over his paper. "I didn't say 'English,' Dad. They told me there would be no question. Just to be at Pier 14 on West Street tomorrow afternoon . . . before six o'clock. There's a ship waiting there, but we have to be careful because America's neutral."

Bob Kenyon cranked slowly from his chair, folded his newspaper and squinted across the murky kitchen. He focused his myopic eyes on his son and spoke slowly, "Is this a right 'un? You tellin' the truth?"

"'Course he ain't. It's just one of his games," his mother said and took a swig from a bottle of beer.

"Absolutely, Dad! The ship sails tomorrow and docks at Tilbury . . . that's in London, in about ten days. It won't cost a penny."

Bob Kenyon pondered on the details while the greasy clock on the mantel seemed to lose some of its metallic rhythm. "Could I go?" he asked like a little boy begging for a Woolworth toy.

Max was astonished at the question. His father seemed older

than Mr. Rushton. Much older, in fact. "I don't think so, Dad. How old are you?"

"I'll be forty-three in December."

"Tell us another," Selina broke in. "You'll be forty-four. It's me who'll be forty-three. Matter of fact, I was forty-three last March."

"Forty-three . . . four?" Max tried to calculate the length of so many years. He had no idea his father was that old. "They'd never take you, Dad. Only chaps in their twenties, perhaps thirties. Besides, who would stay here and take care of Mother?"

Old Bob suddenly felt the weight of his years and tried to remember whether he was born in 1870 or 1871, but the date was seared in his memory. No one could make a mistake about being born in 1870. He looked from his son to his wife, and then dropped his eyes to the kitchen floor. His years had him trapped.

"You can go as far as I'm concerned," Selina said and put the corner of her apron to a very dry eye. "Both of you can go. I can take care of myself. Always had to, and I can keep on. Go on, both of you, and enjoy yourselves. It's what you both have been wanting for years. A fine bloody pair you'll make . . . in uniform and ammunition boots. You'll eat all their grub, and your old man will guzzle all their beer. A big help to Lord Kitchener, I must need say." She rammed the sausage into a pile of mashed potatoes and skimmed the plate along the table. "Sit down and shove that into your guts. It may be a long time before you get another square meal. Bully beef an' biscuits from now on, Lance Corporal Kenyon."

Bob peered at his son's supper and wondered how much of Selina's tirade was grim prophecy. Max sat down and began to saw at the sausage. "You're dockin' London, not Liverpool?" Bob asked.

"You ain't taking any of this serious, are you?" his wife challenged. "He ain't going, unless some chit of a girl has been trying to talk him into something."

"I don't know any girls," Max protested. "Not since I left Fourteenth Avenue School."

His father broke in again. "You're sure you're dockin' in London?"

"London. Tilbury Docks," his son said without looking up.

Bob slapped a heavy paw on the table and growled. "That's good! Bloody good! From Tilbury you can join the London Scottish. You are Scottish, remember. That's one of the best regiments . . . in England."

· 23 ·

"I don't know whether we shall have much choice. They say there'll be a color sergeant coming on board the minute they let the gangplank down. That's all I know."

"Never mind color sergeants. They'll book you for anything. They don't have to go and fight. They just enlist chaps into regiments that have been cut up. You sneak off, an' join the London Scottish. They wear kilts and go in for bayonet charges. Bloody good mob."

Max nodded his head over the mound of soggy mash, and his decision was made. In that cursory manner the Kenyons contributed their only son to the Cause. No further objection or appeal was expressed, since they both knew—or believed—their British roots ran deep, and that young Max would go no matter what obstacles or logic they placed in his path. In their grasping minds they half thought there might be a "bit o' brass" connected with it somewhere. They tried to remember how it had been worked during the Boer War.

Selina unearthed a pair of heavy woolen socks, a reasonably clean shirt, and then fingered a five-dollar bill from the teapot on the mantelpiece. Bob donated his fairly new safety razor with an extra blade, and delivered a repetitive monologue on making sure he kept his bowels open and to avoid all color sergeants.

3

The arrangements were all Maxwell Kenyon and his conrades-in-arms had been promised—and more. They found a vessel tied up at Pier 14 on West Street's waterfront. That was plainly evident, but the number of sullen men of various ages and states of physical ability who turned up took much of the gloss off the venture. Most of them were unshaven, lank-haired, hollow-chested, and wore Salvation Army charity clothing. Short lengths of cigarettes dangled from dry, mucous-crusted lower lips.

They were asked one or two leading questions at the entrance, and advised to proceed through the gloomy shed and up the gang-plank. "Don't stand about here, you'll attract attention. Get out of sight."

Several men shuffled along a few yards, took one look at the bow, identified the vessel and its ownership, did a right-about-face and crept away with the decision to await further—and more comfortable—accommodations.

Twenty or thirty less worldly volunteers with the gleam of glory in their eyes—a few wearing collars and ties—were encouraged to mount the gangplank, from where they were guided to a deal table and ordered to sign a grimy Mercantile Marine contract that was ambiguously worded to evade conflict with the precepts of the Seamen's Union. It agreed to pay them a token wage of one shilling, plus their passage, for serving as able-bodied seamen aboard the SS *Peruvian Prince*, a 5700-ton cargo vessel, chartered for the express purpose of carrying explosives from New York to London. It was highly illegal, but such measures had to be taken to evade America's neutrality.

Those volunteers who had anticipated livable accommodations were stunned to learn—too late—that no passenger staterooms were available. The freighter had been hurriedly converted for the stowage of gun cotton, cordite, gunpowder, and dynamite. These explosives were stacked and tucked in every space and locker, and in compartments that had served previously as comfortable berths. In her new configuration, crew accommodations had been set up in a narrow portion of the fo'c'sle where crude bunks had been built of standard construction timbers on which cheap straw mattresses had been thrown. Because of the scarcity of space, sleeping periods were divided into the three nautical eight-hour shifts, and the volunteers had to make the best of what was available, since a small regular crew, being paid combat-zone hazard wages, had taken over the best quarters. There were few arrangements for primary sanitation, messing, or what might be considered recreation. Anyone finding time for such foibles was immediately sent below to patrol the narrow aisles, dividing the stacks of explosives—in case of fire.

Young Kenyon knew he had bought a pig in a poke, but also realized he had burned his bridges. There was no turning back, since he wasn't a very good swimmer. On the credit side he had thirty purloined dollars of Mr. Milligan's sewn into the waistband of his B.V.D. underwear. His mother had ironed a clean shirt, and her five-dollar bill was reserved for immediate expenses.

He couldn't go back now.

While the regular crew was carrying out the necessary seamanship to get their cargo of ammunition safely past Ambrose Light, Maxwell and another youthful adventurer, named Horace Drage, decided to pal up and establish a base in one of the lifeboats.

"It's perfect," Horace Drage chuckled with boyish vigor. "We'll have plenty of room, some privacy, and if the cargo blows up some night, we'll have a lifeboat all to ourselves. I can row. Can you?"

Unquestionably, it was far better than anything available in the fo'c'sle, and no one questioned their right to unfasten one end of the tarpaulin cover and make themselves comfortable. At least it provided shelter for their few belongings, and offered some cover when the gang bosses were on the rampage.

Horace Drage, Kenyon learned, was the son of a British professor who had taken the Chair of Literature at one of the Ivy League universities, but despite his sheltered background, Horace took on anything or anybody, and laughed with ease. He was a tall, slender lad, pink-cheeked, and topped with a classic mane of oat-blond hair. Max had spotted him early, for Horace was a standout among the rabble that had responded to the Call. He wore a neat blue serge suit, an expensive flannel shirt, and rubber-soled oxfords. He also carried a small valise in which he had packed a copy of Arnold Bennett's *The Old Wives' Tale*, some extra socks, a soccer jersey, and several boxes of Nabisco wafers. These he generously shared with his boatmate.

His explanation for being aboard the "lugger" was that he was fed up with school, his overindulgent parents, the domineering attitude of college girls, and felt that since he was getting nowhere of interest, he might as well go "back home" and fight the blasted Kaiser. He could always return to his schooling again when the Huns had been properly potted.

"If parents would only let a chap grow up his own way," Horace explained as they mucked out the lifeboat, "there wouldn't be all this bother to put up with. Can you imagine me becoming a university professor? That's what Gordie keeps harping about."

"Gordie?"

"My governor! That's what he's worked at as long as I can remember. Would you believe it, he's never netted a hare, caught starlings with birdlime, or even collected butterflies." Max was even more bewildered. "Now his viewpoint on the war. He can't understand anyone wanting to stick a bayonet into a Prussian Guardsman. It's people like him who put the blight on their offspring."

"Mine are exactly like that," Max said, simply to stay in the league.

"When I said I wanted to go home and join up . . . my governor cut off my allowance, and I had to borrow ten dollars from cook to get to New York."

Max began to realize how lucky he was, having more than thirty dollars. Then Drage lowered a small-sized boom. "What was your school?" he inquired, for no particular reason.

"School? I never went to a . . . a real school. Just public school. Not even high school."

"Lucky you," Horace concluded.

"I . . . well, I could have gone, but my folks wouldn't let me." Horace squinted his perplexity.

"It was like this. Our Vicar, Mr. Rushton, took a liking to me. I

used to sing in the choir. Well, he decided I ought to go to college—that I was college material, and planned to put me through
Newark Academy . . . and then pay for my tuition at Princeton."

"*While the Tiger stands defender of the Orange and the Black!*"
Horace sang in an untrained voice.

"No, I mean it. He planned to have me stay with him at the
rectory, but I could go home on weekends. My mother had to do
my laundry, that was all."

"What the hell are you doing here?"

"Mother wouldn't stand for any of it. Didn't believe in higher
education, and she pulled me out of school when I had finished
the eighth grade. Said they needed whatever I could earn . . . to
make ends meet."

"I can see you've got a lot to learn," young Drage reflected.

For the rest of the voyage Maxwell paddled in the wake of
Horace's influence, and while never able to avoid completely all
deckhand chores, he gradually learned the art of soft-soaping the
opposition in order to be assigned to less arduous tasks. Polishing
brass or painting companionways was not too wearying, but chip-
ping rust and untangling the anchor chain in the locker, particularly
during bad weather, left the volunteers weary and wan. During the
rough days, there always were problems when the cargo shifted,
and generally it was the volunteers who were assigned to go below
and bugger-haul the boxes and containers of explosives into safer
arrangements. It not only was the physical effort, but the psychologi-
cal strain that reduced the unskilled to imbecility. To add to the
maniacal atmosphere the gang bosses always bellowed something
about not to worry, because explosives usually fizzed a little before
going off.

Once all hands had settled down and worked into a semblance
of co-operative routine, there were odd intervals of time in which
to discuss their further plans. They had little news of the war, except when Sparks, the wireless operator, mouthed short snatches
of information concerning the situation in France, one of which
was that the government had been transferred to Bordeaux. Then
there was the arrant day he reported hearing that the whole German Army had been driven back from Paris, and that it seemed to
be all over.

"Just our luck," Horace Drage said while spooning his dixie of horse-meat stew. "If they keep that up, the blasted war will be over before we get to London. Then what will we do?"

Maxwell Kenyon had no idea.

They were scotched on the iron bollards forward, staring at the zigzag wake the ship was leaving behind in its effort to dodge German submarines that were presumed to be out in great packs.

Horace put a reasonable question, "What will you do if, when we get in, we find it's all over?"

"I don't know. I suppose I'll have to work my way back again. Still, if it only lasts until Christmas, I shall have time to enlist . . . in the London Scottish, I suppose."

Horace put his dixie on the deck to denote his shock. "You're going into the London Scottish?" he squeaked in astonishment.

"It's my dad's idea. He claims the Kenyons are Scots, and that I can easily get in. Why? What's wrong?"

Horace tapped Max's knee with his soup spoon. "You listen to me. The London Scottish was the first Territorial regiment to land in France. They've probably been cut up by now. Worse than the Black Watch. I read something about them in the Boston newspapers."

"What's that got to do with me?"

"If the London Scottish have been cut up, there's no chance of your being turned down. Nine weeks is all the training you'll get with that mob."

"Well, then," Max said with some relief, "I should just about make it, with a bit of luck."

"I'm pretty certain you will," Horace said, studying a bottle that was bobbing about in the rollers. "I'll bet you'll get all the action you can take but, of course, that's what we came over for, isn't it?"

Kenyon took up the study of the bobbing bottle, and then added, "My old man was dead set on my joining the London Scottish." He slitted his eyes, and asked, "By the way, what are you going in for?"

Horace picked up his dixie, tried another spoonful, and assumed an imperious attitude. "Me? I'm going to join the Flying Corps. The Royal Flying Corps, that is."

"Flying Corps? What's that?"

Horace looked down on the insect, cleared his throat and explained, "Hopping about in aeroplanes. It's all the thing in this war." He allowed that to sink in and then resumed with the details. "They have squadrons of these aeroplanes, on both sides. Haven't you read H. G. Wells's *The War in the Air?*"

Maxwell shook his head. "Just G. A. Henty and Oliver Optic."

"Proper name William Taylor Adams," Horace corrected with a haughty glance.

"Beg pardon?"

"Oliver Optic's real name. Another blasted teacher before he started writing books for boys. Didn't you know that?"

Maxwell Kenyon took refuge in the previous subject. "What were you going to say about flying?"

"It's simple. Join the Royal Flying Corps. They teach you to fly, and you go out doing aerial patrols. For God's sake, don't you read *anything?* You photograph the enemy's positions, draw maps, and go scouting for chaps on the ground. You ought to look into it."

"But I don't know anything about flying. Do you?"

"Of course not. Who does? They have to teach everybody, I suppose. When you pass, you get a commission, and besides your rank pay you get six shillings a day, called flying pay because it's supposed to be a bit risky."

"What's a commission?" Kenyon beeped, wishing he had never brought up the subject in the first place.

"You are commissioned an officer . . . a lieutenant to start with. Then when you get to be a flight leader, or a squadron commander, there's no telling what they'll make you."

"I wouldn't fit in there," Kenyon capitulated. "I didn't go far enough in school. I'll be lucky to become a private in the London Scottish."

"Well, don't ever say I didn't tip you off about the Flying Corps. You'll remember my words when you're in the middle of a bayonet charge with your kilt fluttering up above your bare bottom. Ladies from Hell . . . hell!"

A bellows-lunged gang boss put an end to Kenyon's despair with, "All hands below! Number Three hold. Look sharp, there!"

"Blasted cargo must have shifted again," Horace grumbled. "Give me your dixie. I'll take it back to the boat."

"And you'll stay there," Maxwell muttered, and grinned. "Now who would have thought of the Royal Flying Corps?"

As luck would have it, the *Peruvian Prince* crossed the Atlantic without having her cargo detonated by a German submarine, or being swamped by foul weather, and arrived three days late at Tilbury. In their anxiety to get ashore the volunteers neglected to draw their shillings. They scurried down the gangplank the minute it was lowered into position. There were no customs or immigration officials to hinder them, no color sergeants to sign them up, no one to welcome them or provide aid or service of any kind. They might just as well have been badly bundled items of cargo, for the nearly two weeks of toil under the gang bosses had reduced their clothing to the tattered raiments of Ganges mendicants. There *was* a gaudy poster on a wall of the dock which read:

YOUR KING AND COUNTRY NEED YOU!

Evading the ragtag and rabble that had found its own level, Horace and Maxwell hurried to get clear of the docks. They had "poshed" up somewhat and both wore shirts they had managed to wash, and had knotted their neckties. Had their trousers been cleaned and pressed they would have been reasonably presentable.

"Where are we?" Max inquired with some concern.

"Tilbury is down the river from the city. We're twenty-six miles from London."

"Oh."

"We've got to get into town before we can plan our next move. By the way, do you have any money on you?"

"About thirty-three dollars, all told," Max said, suddenly remembering he had broken the five-dollar bill.

"American money! It's no good over here. Why didn't you change it before you left New York?" He considered Max with the air of a man studying a lost dog.

"But I thought there'd be a recruiting officer, or some sort of recruiting office on the dock . . . that it would all be taken care of."

"Lucky you have me with you. Let me have your bills and I'll pop into the first bank we come to. Oh, and could you let me have ten dollars? I've got to get to Farnborough. That's the headquarters of the Royal Flying Corps. After we change your money we'll find a policeman, or someone who can tell you where to find the depot of the London Scottish. That is, if you still want to fight in a kilt."

The two youths walked on in silence, each considering his own problem. Suddenly Horace darted up the steps of a grimy building that showed a brass plate at its doorway. In a few minutes he returned with a thin wad of new paper currency. "Here we are," he said. "I got just over six pounds for your thirty-three dollars." He palmed the notes and coins like a card sharp. "The ten dollars you are lending me comes to just over two quid. Let's say two pound, ten. Right?"

"I suppose so." Max folded the strange currency, feeling like an alien.

"I also found out that the best way to get to London from here is to take an Underground train to Charing Cross. There's a station just around the corner. Come on."

"Is Charing Cross in London?"

"Of course! And when we get there, it might be a good idea to get a decent meal where we can make our plans in comfort."

Horace seemed quite at home. He quickly found the Underground station and guided his new pal through the general maze to the platform. Once aboard a westbound train, he got in conversation with a stolid man in a bowler hat and a Melton overcoat. It was a rewarding contact, and in a few minutes he turned back to Kenyon who was trying to puzzle out his unfamiliar surroundings.

"I've got it all straight," Horace explained. "We get out at Charing Cross, and nearby in the Strand is a Lyons' Corner House . . . a restaurant. We can get a decent meal there for a few bob."

At this point Max felt no more like a gay adventurer than the woman with a basket of laundry who sat opposite them.

"What about the London Scottish?"

"Oh, that. That gentleman works in the Army-Navy Stores, and he says the London Scottish are probably recruiting at the Wellington Barracks which is at the other end of Birdcage Walk."

Max looked more bewildered then before.

"About Farnborough. I have to take a train from Waterloo on the Southern Railway. Your two quid will just about get me there."

"Where's this Birdcage Walk? Are you kidding me?"

"It'll be right close by. I'll explain when we've had some fodder. Don't worry. By tonight you'll be swinging your kilt in St. James's Park."

"I will if I get in . . . and pass the medical examination. If I don't, what do I do then?"

Horace pondered for a few minutes. "If it gets that bad, you can always join the Salvation Army. They'll send you out to France quick enough—to dish out tea and crumpets."

"Don't talk like that. You sound just like my mother."

Horace relented and patted Max's shoulder.

When they reached the twirling doors of the Corner House, Horace bowed with cavalier grace and said, "After you, Max, old boy. The King's men-at-arms must be nourished—and fighting men deserve the best. I suggest the London broil."

The gay gesture gave Max a welcome lift, his heart became light and music strummed through his frame. The life and color of the Strand presented a new world, new hope, a promise of manhood. South 10th Street was three thousand miles away. His parents had dissolved into a misty, unreal twilight. The dread of failure no longer disturbed his mind.

After a modest-priced spread, topped off with a half-bottle of wine, a ceremony Maxwell had not shared before, they exchanged solemn assurances they'd get together again within a week. "I'll send your money back as soon as I start drawing flying pay," Horace promised, and peered around the restaurant. "Don't worry. You'll get every cent of it."

"I'm not worrying at all. Let's *determine* to meet outside this place a week from today. By the way, where are we?"

"At the bottom of the Strand near the Charing Cross Station. We'll plan to meet at the dot of noon."

Kenyon fashioned a grin that illumined a query. "I wonder if we shall know each other in uniform?"

"Of course we shall. Up the Jocks!" Drage raised his glass.

Kenyon was so full of enthusiasm he had no immediate response. He finally lifted his goblet, cocked an eye at the heeltap of liquid, and said, "I like you, Horace. You're a good companion and I wish we were going together, but . . . I'll never see the Royal Flying Corps."

Enlisting in the London Scottish presented no problems. The road to war was smooth and paved with every aid and assistance possible. Within twenty-four hours, Maxwell Erskine Kenyon was outfitted in the border gray kilt and cutaway tunic, below which hung a hairy sporran, a clasped bag in which he could stow what few shillings he had left. On his head was clapped a green Glengarry cap, and a corporal adjusted the length of his kilt. The uniform puzzled Max, for he had expected to be outfitted in standard khaki, but the corporal assured him this was the correct uniform of the 7th Middlesex Battalion of the Rifle Brigade, better known as the London Scottish.

The kilt, itself, intrigued him, for though it was familiar in the Highland stories he had devoured, it proved to be far different from what he had expected. In the first place, it was not a skirt, but a short, pleated, wrap-around garment that contained about eight yards of heavy woolen cloth. After putting on the harsh flannel underwear and a blue flannel shirt, he found that instead of dreading the damp London breezes, he was actually sweating, particularly after he had drawn on the gray tartan stockings and white gaiters.

There were about half a dozen other volunteers in the depot supply room, all acting bewildered. They spoke in short, jerky sentences, asked inane questions, or stared at one another as if demanding to know where they were. Most seemed to be in their mid-twenties, and from their civilian clothing could have been clerks, haberdashery salesmen, or tramcar conductors. None had any Scottish background, family service tradition, or showed any particular interest in the items of uniform that were being doled out. A few questioned the order to toss their civilian clothing into a large bin for delivery to the Salvation Army. One or two were strutting up and down, learning how to make the kilt swing properly.

Within six months most of them would be buried somewhere in Flanders Fields.

By the time he had stuffed the additional gear and extra equipment into a brown canvas bag, Kenyon began to feel that at last he was a member of the London Scottish, and secretly gloried in the aura of having "come all the way from America to enlist." It was a mild distinction that lasted for several days. His personal items included a sewing kit, known as a "housewife," and a canvas holdall for his knife, fork, and spoon; a straight razor, toothbrush, comb, and soapbox were tucked in a haversack slung across his shoulder. He inquired about a dirk to stick in his hose top, but was told such items were for full-dress uniforms—not for the trenches.

"All right, then. Everybody got his full gear?" a weary-eyed quartermaster corporal creaked and glanced down at a wad of papers in his hand. "Who's Appledore?"

"'Ere I am," a squeaky voice piped up. "Over 'ere."

"Over here, *Corporal*, you bloody ignoramus. Since your name's first . . . alphabetically, that is, you're in charge of this lot."

The man who had answered to the name of Appledore was a massive chap with unruly red hair that sprouted in tufts around the rim of his Glengarry. He had a ruddy complexion, watery-blue eyes, and wore a perpetual expression of surprise. In uniform he looked like a music hall caricature of a Scotsman.

"Me, Corporal?" Appledore quaked and his great hands began to tremble. "What do I know . . . ?"

"Abso-bloody-lutely nothing! You wouldn't be here, if you did. But you can start learning. Here's the draft list, and railway warrants. You march this lot to Liverpool Street Station and get the railway transport officer there . . . to wipe your nose and put you all aboard the proper train."

Appledore appealed to the others, his great hands in pathetic supplication. "I've never marched anybody . . . not even in the Boy Scouts."

"Bloody good time to learn. All of London will be watching you. Come on, pick up your clobber and get on with it. We'll have another mob here any minute."

In that comedy of military manners, Private Maxwell Kenyon entered his training for a global conflict to be known as the Great War. He was taught to form fours, fire a .303 Lee Enfield rifle, handle a Lewis automatic weapon, salute officers—and take orders. Without knowing why, he made a good soldier, accepted military discipline as he had accepted a milder form at home and, to his quiet surprise, learned he was popular with his comrades and one or two NCOs. The regimen first slimmed him down and then put bulk and muscle where it would do the most good, and had it not been noticed that he was often caught reading a book, he might have been promoted early in his training. But book readers were suspect. They often became barrack-room lawyers, a breed that was completely anathema to the British Army.

Bob and Selina Kenyon knew little of all this, for their son had given no thought to either once he had arrived in London. During one weekend leave he mailed a postcard of London Bridge and explained that he had succeeded in getting into the London Scottish, but did not bother to include his military address. He also wasted a stamp and a sheet of YMCA notepaper trying to get in touch with

Horace Drage. But nothing came of that and neither one made the planned rendezvous outside Lyons' Corner House.

The American rookie looked for no letters and expected none, but he did receive a disturbing missive from a Miss Daphne Huddleston who worked in a Dymchurch fish-and-chips shop. Miss Huddleston was one of those curious flappers who was concerned with what Scottish soldiers wore under their kilts. The revelation had brought about her undoing, and in her letter she explained she would probably have to leave her job until something could be done about it—and did he have any ideas?

On reading the letter a second time it finally dawned on Max that the sooner he was sent out to the front, the better. He volunteered for the next draft, and by late February 1915, five months after docking at Tilbury, he was sent out to what remained of the 7th Battalion at rest a few miles north of Bethune. They were particularly pleased to have him since he had arrived with a brand-new Lewis gun, a trained gun team and some general knowledge of how to keep a machine gun firing. There were only two such weapons in the whole battalion.

4

F̲ew historians have been able to present in convincing detail the anguish and misery endured through that first winter of trench warfare. Only a small number of those who were there have come anywhere close. Once the twin festoons of mud, chalk, and clay were strung from the North Sea to the Vosges, thousands of men had to stand guard against enemy attacks in mud, slush, or intermittent snow and rain. Continued saturation brought on rheumatism, trench feet, and kindred ailments. The thud of bombardment made more motive warfare doubly welcome. The British soldier actually looked forward to the first big spring assault of 1915—the Battle of Neuve-Chapelle.

General Joseph Joffre, whose armies still bore the brunt of the action, believed he might break through the German defenses with determined attacks eastward from the Artois Plateau and northward from Champagne. On paper, Joffre's plan was convincing, but enemy defense tactics of 1915, based on the machine gun, barbed wire, and deep entrenchments, were too much for his offensive strategy. The French had no success in Artois, and after a month Joffre tried again in Champagne. There was some minor progress, but the gains were small, and 90,000 men were killed, wounded, or taken prisoner—on both sides.

General Sir John French, in supreme command of the British Army on the Western Front, felt that supporting a third major thrust could be bad arithmetic and, instead, decided on an attack of his own.

Early in March there had been spells of sunny weather, and the waterlogged country began to dry up. General French also felt that if Neuve-Chapelle could be taken, it might be possible eventually to capture Vimy Ridge, and with that swarm over the rail network on the plain of Douai. He massed four divisions in secrecy on a frontage defended by only one German division. All this had been determined by reconnaissance airmen of the Royal Flying Corps. Large-scale maps of Neuve-Chapelle, showing every trench, strong point, and supply dump, were printed and issued to the troops.

Among the four divisions moved in were the London Scottish, and a rookie machine gunner Private Maxwell Kenyon. The attack opened on March 10, and remarkable success was enjoyed at the start. The Germans, who were completely unaware of Allied plans, were quickly overrun. The Tommies who had gone over the top expecting to be cut down by the whiplash of machine-gun fire, were astounded to find themselves whole, and the enemy trenches practically deserted. There were no stoics in the sapheads on whom to hurl their jam-tin bombs.* The artillery barrage of fire and steel had dazed the Prussian troops, and those who were able to reach their communication trenches, scurried away, huddling from the heavy spray of shrapnel. In some instances the thud of artillery was so severe many of the trenches caved in under the concussion.

Private Kenyon's company was billeted in the ruins of what had once been a village not too far behind the system of reserve trenches. Views from openings that had once been windows offered an interrupted picture of devastated landscape. There were a few deracinated tree stumps, but little foliage for more than a mile in any direction. Here and there in pathetic array stood the masonry of a burial ground, and in symbolic contrast a few odorous piles of barnyard manure. Every building in sight had been battered and left with nothing but irregular outlines and chunks of crumbling walls. Some new cemetery plots were marked with rusty rifles, rude wooden crosses, bayonets with steel helmets (French) tilted on them, and at intervals simple nosegays of artificial flowers forced into the necks of wine bottles. There was no roadside crucifix or prayer shrine, for contrary to early legends, most of

* The famous Mills bomb had not been produced at this time. Jam-tin bombs were simply that. Tin cans filled with amatol or some convenient explosive, and ignited with a length of fuse. Kitchener had refused to consider the land warship to be known as a Tank, and he also believed that two machine guns per battalion were quite enough. Stokes mortars were relegated to the level of "crank inspired" weapons, and had no place in modern warfare.

them had been destroyed in Jerry's withdrawal from the Marne. One with a sense of symbolism could have regarded it as the graveyard of the world. Everything was dead—trees, villages, factories, farmsteads, and the men who had been there before. Only the frowning steel guns and the creaking transport wagons showed evidence of life.

Sheltered behind what months before had been a picturesque dairy, Kenyon's machine-gun team shuddered under the reverberating crash of two large howitzers dug in nearby. With each titanic cough, the skeletal remains of the village rocked against the concussion, and then settled back amid the melancholy of the dank morning. Odorous vapor curled up from the barnyard pile, smoke crept along with the vagrant breeze, and the tangy smell of alfresco cooking assaulted the nostrils of some and aroused animal anticipation in others.

Kenyon, Appledore, and their Number Three, a Kentish man named Denham, sat on their equipment and stared up through the gash in their roof. They were weary and unquestioning, for the march up the night before had dampened all the novelty of the action and vitality from their loins and limbs. On a dusty plank was arrayed some grayish bread, brakish tea, tins of bully beef and a saucer of unidentifiable jam. No one was hungry, but all three wished they could get a real wash and a shave. A small lard-tub of water had been assigned them, and they took turns swilling off. To Kenyon this was a new degree of humiliation, for he recalled the sterile bathroom in the rectory of St. Matthew's Church.

"I wonder what we are doing here," Appledore finally inquired as he dried his face. "I ask you, what are we doing . . . ?"

"This is known as gettin' on wiv the war," Denham said. He was a slight cadaverous man who was forever cold. He began wrapping himself in his blanket.

"I suppose Lieutenant Carlock will explain it when he gets around to it," Kenyon replied tonelessly. "That is, he will when someone explains it to him." He went to the door and listened to two other guns that were joining the deep basso chorus.

"I don't think Mister Bloody Carlock knows much about anything. It's a puzzle to me 'ow these chaps get to be officers," Denham continued, adjusting his haversack for a pillow. "Just 'ow does one become an officer?"

Appledore kicked the spare parts bag for no especial reason.

"It's easy for them. They know 'ow to talk. They've bin to proper schools, and they learn 'ow to wangle anything. It's all just talk. Blokes like us never got the chance. We just learned 'ow to apply immediate action when a Lewis gun stops firing, when talkin' ain't necessary. Mister Carlock just has to give orders. That's all an officer is supposed to do."

Kenyon decided to keep an open mind. "They must have to know something. Most of them were in the Territorials long before the war broke out. They had two weeks' training every summer, and that puts them a bit ahead when a war breaks out. Me, I'd never fired a gun of any kind before I joined up."

"Don't believe it," Appledore squeaked. "How do you account for being so bloody 'ot on the range? You passed for a sniper the first week. Fifteen-rounds-rapid . . . an' all bulls! I don't understand it."

"I remember that," Denham added, sitting up suddenly. "Then at Hythe, doing our firing tests with the Lewis, you didn't miss one of them metal targets . . . five hundred yards away! I couldn't 'it the bloody sand dunes, once that blasted gun began to shoot. Frightened me to death."

"Don't ask me," Kenyon said and tried a chunk of bully beef. "I think I just wanted to show that damn' fool sergeant—the Boer War veteran—who kept saying it took three years in the old days to make a machine gunner. He must have been thinking of those old Maxim guns he used at Spion Kop."

"I must say you showed 'im."

"We'll find out," Kenyon said and squatted on a pile of gun drums. "Shooting on a range for marks is one thing. Shooting at a guy who's looking for you with a rifle grenade is something else. I just hope we don't get any bolt-extraction trouble, that's all."

"As long as you're on the gun," Appledore mumbled, "I shan't care. I just hope you don't get plonked, leaving me to take over. I still can't do that Number Three stoppage."

"Don't worry. Mister Bloody Carlock will take over," Denham predicted with a hoarse chuckle.

"Mister Carlock can't even wind his own alarm clock. His batman has to do it for him," Appledore added with a high squeak.

Kenyon's platoon had been held in reserve until the Regulars had forced their way across the first two lines of trenches. His superior, First Lieutenant Garrod Carlock, a peacetime Territorial officer was, on the outbreak of war, gazetted to the London Scottish, although, like Kenyon, he admittedly had never been north of the border. He was a handsome man of above average height with a glossy head of hair that curled tight above his ears. He sported a neat military mustache and looked the typical Sandhurst soldier, although he had never seen the famous school. Not overly ambitious, he had a general idea of what was expected of him, but usually left important matters to his sergeant major.

"They know everything and have been trained to serve, so let them enjoy themselves," he said frankly. "Young officers can only command in the field when all the preliminary work has been done. That's how it has always been."

Lieutenant Carlock held a secret admiration for Kenyon, and knew he had volunteered from somewhere in America. That put Max a stride or two ahead of the others in the platoon. More important he knew how to handle a Lewis gun. Carlock had no idea what made the bloody thing keep firing, or how the ammunition got down from the drum and into the breech. Max had tried to explain but his cocky familiarity with feed pawls, the piston group, actuating studs and sear pins, left Carlock completely bewildered. He decided early on to let the youngster handle things on his own.

Once the enemy trenches had been cleared, the open area to the village became the objective of the troops of the 8th Division, IV Corps. As soon as the artillery had lengthened its range, some reserve trenches to the northwest of Neuve-Chapelle were assaulted. Again, there was little opposition, and Kenyon's M.G. team, along with Lieutenant Carlock, found themselves amid a motley collection of Scottish Rifles and some Middlesex infantry. The German southern flank had been turned and the retreating Jerries swarmed into the village to take assigned posts in every cottage.

However, there was some uncut wire in the area encountered by the Scottish Rifles and men, stepping gingerly through the accordion-pleated barricade, were cut down by machine guns and particularly accurate rifle fire. The small band of London Scottish went to the rescue. Kenyon looked for advice from Lieutenant Carlock but that worthy was trying to tear the first field dressing from the tunic of a Middlesex man who had been wounded in the face. Carlock was noted for his sympathy and kindness, but in this instance the man could have been turned around and ordered back to a casualty clearing station.

"No use waiting for that bastard," Denham snarled. "Let's get on with it."

Kenyon could see a low buttress from where enemy machine-gun fire was spitting. He rammed the bipod of his gun out, flopped on his stomach and glared at Appledore for a drum of ammunition. He raised the notch of the rear sight slightly, for about 100 yards, and spread his legs to get a stable position. It was the first time he would fire a shot at any enemy target.

"Don't waste any," Appledore growled, peering toward the enemy gun site.

Max felt strangely elated, and sensed no fear of the opposition. He had long objected to having to carry the heavy weapon, but this early spring morning with its tang of lyddite, burned burlap, fulminated latrines, and the revolting whiff of death, afforded a backdrop for his sudden animosity. Being Number One on a machine gun added power, stature, and a heady swirl of possibility. He had no idea whom he was shooting at. All he could see were a number of alien field-gray caps and indistinct faces bobbing about. He did not consider who they were or whether they had come from a Berlin slum, a Bavarian farm, or the Hamburg docks.

He tucked the short stock of the gun deep into his shoulder, pulled the cocking handle back twice, and took aim. When he pressed the trigger the firing pin snapped forward, igniting the detonator, and a .303 bullet spun down the rifled barrel. During the infinitesimal second after passing the gas vent—bored into the barrel—and screeching through the muzzle; cordite gases were deflected through a gas regulator set beneath the vent and directed into a cylinder. Here this pressure rammed a piston backward and a toothed rack revolved the pinion to wind a return spring. The automatic mechanism set within the body casing took up the work of directing cartridges from the drum into the breech chamber. As long as Max held the trigger back, the firing sequence would continue until there were no rounds left in the drum. And as long as this compact mechanism had ammunition to fire, men died or were crippled for life.

Over the next three years, variations of this recoil-return spring executioner would be as much a part of Kenyon's life as his heartbeat.

"That's enough!" Appledore was screaming in his ear. "You bloody near ran off the whole blasted drum!"

The Number One man came out of his rage-drugged stupor, and released the trigger.

"That's the stuff to give 'em," Denham bellowed from his position behind Max's heels. "Skittled the bloody lot. What are we waiting for?"

Kenyon got to his knees and stared up the gentle slope, and then wondered why no one was potting at him. He peered about, looking for another target, but the area offered nothing but zigzag movements of faceless men in khaki, or swinging kilts, darting back and forth as they hurled themselves prone, fired from half-kneeling positions, or crouched and encouraged others on by waving their arms. One or two had faltered, turned around and were making their way back with uncertain strides past smoking mounds of earth. Above, argosies of artillery shells were crashing over into the enemy reserve area behind Neuve-Chapelle. There were no poppies anywhere—just blobs or streaks of scarlet fluid slowly turning to deep maroon.

"Bloody good!" A young lance corporal of the Middlesex kneeled beside Kenyon. "We can use you over here. There's another bloody M.G. pit opposing my bombing team. We can't get close enough."

He was a smart, trimly dressed man with a girlish complexion, yet looked every inch a soldier. His eyes darted in all directions, and his compact jaw was firm, making him speak out of the side of his mouth. He patted Kenyon's shoulder affectionately. "If we work together, we can turf the buggers out," he said, managing a determined grin.

Still the 5.9s screeched over and exploded somewhere beyond.

Denham, with the spare-parts bag and an armful of ammunition drums, was already starting ahead. He stopped and looked back as a swarm of Mauser slugs whistled over his head. "Never mind bloody Carlock. He should have been a VAD. He's enchanted with blood—as long as it's somebody else's."

Not knowing, but more than willing to be accepted, Max shouldered the weapon and followed the Middlesex lance corporal. He was exulting in success. The Lewis no longer weighed twenty-six pounds, but felt perfectly balanced, and he had to stare at the splayed bipod to realize he had taken an active role in the excitement . . . an actual battle! He hadn't experienced emotions like this since the day he stood in lower Manhattan and watched as dozens of young women hurled themselves from the upper stories of the blazing Triangle Shirtwaist factory. At this moment he relished the thrill of involvement, but felt no dread of personal vulnerability.

"Come on! Come on!" Denham screeched with sportive gaiety in his eyes. "I can see a fold of cover over . . ." Those were the last words the Kentish man spoke. As he crouched with his load of drums and spare parts, the upper part of his face exploded and his Glengarry twirled end over end and fluttered away. His knees folded unevenly and he fell flat. In a final involuntary gesture one hand turned the loaded drums upward so no mud would jam the cartridge guides. He let out a gurgling sigh, his feet drummed in the broken earth, and one arm jerked across his face, as if to hide the ghastly exit wound from which blood spurted and bypassed his ear.

"Some bloody Jerry!" Appledore whispered, staring down at their Number Three man. "Gimme them drums, an' the spare parts. We'll copper the bastards!"

Kenyon's mouth was parched, and he tried not to look at Denham. He crouched, wondering where he had first met him. Instinct, or discipline, carried him to one fold of ground Denham had pointed out, and he dropped prone and steadied the gun on its bipod.

"Where are they?" he appealed to the Middlesex man.

"Not quite sure, yet. Telephone wire has been snipped by our own bloody artillery."

"Well, let's move off on an angle. We might be able to spot them that way," Max said, remembering some fanciful instructions while at Hythe.

"Where's your officer bloke? You had one when you started, didn't you?"

Kenyon was on one knee again, lugging the Lewis to his stomach. "He's back there somewhere, trying to help some chap who had been wounded."

"One of those guys, eh? It's all very bloody Florence Nightingale and compassionate to stay in a fold of ground and bandage up some chump who ought to be able to take care of himself. But the bastard, whoever he is, ought to be with you. Come on. Let's ease over toward that bit of broken wall."

Appledore was well on his way to the cover. Another storm of shrapnel spattered down and the Middlesex man stared at a rent sleeve. Kenyon looked back to where Carlock was still crouching beside a wounded man who lay flat on his back in the mud with one knee cranking up and down. Appledore had broken a couple of ancient bricks from the segment of wall, and Max rested the weapon in the square depression.

"Perfect," the Middlesex man commented. "I'll rejoin my bomb crew. Keep your eye on that mound with the bit of shed beside it. That's where I think the bastards are. You cover me, eh?"

Kenyon nodded and snatched at a new drum of ammunition. Appledore squeaked. "Where's that blood coming from? Anyone hit?"

"It's me," the lance corporal said. "I didn't feel anything at first, but it looks like I'm leaking somewhere." He held his hand down and a scarlet stream filled his palm. "Funny thing. I never felt it."

"Better tie it up when you get back with your mob," Max said and yanked the cocking handle back twice. "Clear off. I think I can see a gun muzzle." He pressed his trigger and sent two short streaks of fire into the Jerry shelter.

The Middlesex NCO darted away in a zigzag pattern. There was no gunfire from the enemy cover, and he reached his group with a long slithering dive. Kenyon kept up the intermittent fire until Appledore caught a signal from the bomber group. Kenyon was withdrawing the gun from its port when Lieutenant Carlock dropped beside him. He was breathless, slack-jawed, and lay staring at the thinning puddle of blood and the small pile of empty shells.

"What are you . . . we doing here? Who's wounded?"

"None of us. We're covering a Middlesex section. They're trying to get a Jerry machine gun, somewhere over there."

"Where's your other man? What's he doing?"

"Denham? He stopped one when we started across here. Didn't you see him?"

Carlock peered about. "Maybe I ought to . . ."

"No use. It blew most of his head away. He's dead. We've got to support these Middlesex chaps."

"There they go!" Appledore pealed. "They put three bombs smack in the gun pit. They're signaling us on."

Kenyon rose to his feet. Carlock grabbed at an ankle. "Where are you going?"

"They need our support . . . those Middlesex bombers. We're supposed to get into the village somehow, and drive the Jerries out. We're the only Lewis-gun team anywhere about, sir."

Carlock seemed bewildered with all the activity. "You sure our Number Three man, Denham, is dead? I may be able to do something for him."

"That's for the poultice wallahs, the RAMC blokes," Appledore said in disgust.

Another salvo of 9.2s roared over with the self-importance of express trains and exploded deep in the Jerry reserve area. A primitive biplane chugged and rattled across the smoky turbulence and fired a green Very light. No one knew why, and there was no acknowledgment, but Kenyon suddenly wondered where Horace Drage was.

"But Denham may have just been knocked unconscious," Lieutenant Carlock persisted.

"Come on, Kenyon. They're waiting for us," Appledore grumbled and started picking up the drums. "Everything's clear."

Kenyon appealed to his superior officer. "Can you take the spare parts bag, sir? We're short a man, you know."

"I think we should make sure about Denham," Carlock said as a last resort, but he picked up a single drum and the leather bag and gave Max an apprehensive grimace. "Won't we be under fire all the way?"

"No, sir!" Kenyon said, still imbued with the spirit of Oliver Optic and G. A. Henty. "They've bombed out the Jerry gun. There'll be some general rifle fire, that's all."

And in that manner Lieutenant Carlock was persuaded to scurry to where the bomb team was reforming for its next sally. A wayward shell buried its nose in the ground near the stone wall. It was a dud and went plop and sent up only a spray of loosened earth.

Working with the Middlesex group over the next half hour, Kenyon's short-handed gun team eventually made its way into a pungent stone-and-timber shelter that offered two small shapeless windows and the skeleton of what had once been a tiled roof. Through the gaps could be seen framed sections of the smoke-streaked sky, and the antics of a clackety biplane cruising back and forth over the battleground.

According to Appledore, it was a perfect site because it had openings that provided a field of fire in two important directions. Facing one was the jagged remains of an orchard, and through the other they could cover an open area that was pocked with small holes. If the Germans tried to counterattack and retake Neuve-Chapelle, they would have to skirmish across one or the other of these two open areas.

"Bloaters an' jam!" Appledore predicted with evident relish.

The attack did not prove to be as successful as General French had hoped, but there was some justification for continuing the push. During the day the whole labyrinth of trenches before and around Neuve-Chappelle had been taken on a front better than two miles, and the attackers had consolidated the new positions about 1200 yards beyond the enemy's original front line. More ground had been gained than on any other day since the Battle of the Aisne.

The thrust was resumed the next day, for it was learned that the Germans had moved in reinforcements by train and motor transport from distant parts of the Western Front, and they were being force-marched into Aubers to support the line of the Layes and the area around Biez Wood. The British artillery was expected to deal with these defensive points, but bad weather barred aerial observation and most of the field telegraph connections with the batteries had been cut. In some instances when British troops moved forward, it was impossible to advise their own artillery, and in consequence many Tommies fell victims to their own guns. The two chief points blocking the advance were the same as on the preceding day—the enemy's position at Moulin de Piètre and the bridge over the River Des Layes.

During these probe-and-parry operations, the Germans were able to bring their reinforcements into action and, supported by heavy artillery, attempted a number of counterattacks, most of which failed to regain any ground. It was during this bloody fighting that the dispersed members of the London Scottish more than earned their rations.

Kenyon and Appledore took turns standing guard while Carlock huddled in a corner and learned how to transfer ammunition from partly used drums and replenish others. At intervals, Appledore crept out through the haze and smoke to seek out dead or wounded men and relieve them of their bandoliers of ammunition.

On one foray he returned with three filled drums that had been discarded by some other gun team. There was no time to ask questions. The ammunition was more important. Scattered rations, water bottles, and first-aid kits were next on the "scrounge" list as they fully expected to be holding the shed until regimental HQ was brought up and established on the captured ground.

In that manner a few hours were well occupied, but there were not many occasions to use the gun. No enemy troops appeared in their zone of fire, and at intervals there was a chance for short snatches of sleep. When there were obscure reports brought by divisional runners, it was learned that the attack was being halted to allow fuller consolidation. At that point Crown Prince Rupprecht made his last effort to retake Neuve-Chapelle.

Late in the afternoon when the area was draped in ground fog and battle smoke, the enemy artillery opened again. This time they almost revealed a key to what was to come a few weeks later. Salvo after salvo of artillery shrapnel exploded above and drenched the area with nose and eye irritants, as well as the slugs that screeched through the streets of the battered town. Because of the cold, damp weather the effect was not immediately apparent, but it did affect the marksmanship of the machine-gun and rifle fire. Kenyon and Appledore squinted, blinked and swore, but held their own.

"This bloody, stinking smoke," Appledore complained again and again.

"What the hell sort of explosive do they use?" Kenyon grumbled and wished he could blow his nose. "Don't we have a rifle that Mister Carlock could use? He could pick off a few of the singles and we wouldn't waste so much."

"He'd probably give himself an S.I.* wound, and I wouldn't put it past him," The Number Two man said and replaced the drum.

"If you go out again, see if you can pick one up."

"There's only Jerry Mausers out there. Our ammo doesn't fit their rifles, although they—the bastards—can use ours."

"It's just an idea, to give him something to do." Kenyon took aim on indistinct figures moving through the orchard. He was about to press the trigger when an express-train screech made him cringe. There was a blinding flash and an ear-splitting explosion.

* Self-inflicted.

An indefinite period of time seemed to pass, and Kenyon found himself bundled up in a heap in one corner of the shed. There was a heavy stench of gun cotton and his nose was bleeding. He knuckled the fluid away, and then saw his gun on top of some rubble. It was bent almost double at the barrel casing, and the drum was folded together like a metal omelet. As he adjusted his vision he saw Appledore splayed out. A small puddle of blood was seeping from somewhere under his sporran, and his fingers were clawing at the dirty stone floor.

"Appo! . . . Appo!" Max mewed. "What's all that blood?"

The Number Two man struggled to his hands and knees. He wagged his head like a floored boxer. "They're coming . . . up the slope," he muttered. "We'll need another drum."

Kenyon crawled across the shed, knuckling more blood from his mouth. He clawed at Appledore's kilt and looked for wounds along his bare thighs. "Come on, Appo. Where are you hit?"

The wounded man rolled over on one side and pawed at his chest. His tunic had been slashed from shoulder to the side pocket. Kenyon shook off his faintness. "Take it easy, Appo," he begged as he fumbled for a first-field kit. "We'll get it plugged in a minute."

While Kenyon tore Appledore's first-aid kit open, Lieutenant Carlock suddenly appeared in what had been a doorway. He was shrouded in smoke, and for an instant created the impression of an animated war memorial figure.

"What are you doing?" the officer demanded.

"Appledore's been hit, sir. A shell hit somewhere over here. He has a bad gash across his chest. Where were you, sir?"

"The latrines. I had to go . . ."

"You were lucky. Can you give me a hand with Appledore?"

"I can't now. I've been ordered to guide a party of walking wounded to a nearby dressing station. You'll have to stay here and do what you can."

"It'll take only a minute, sir," Max pleaded. "Then we can join your party."

"You'll have to wait," Carlock said. He looked around and spotted the distorted Lewis gun. "I'll take this along. You can get a withdrawal chit from the next officer who comes along."

"That gun's no good, sir. A complete discard."

During the discourse Kenyon was bandaging two wads of gauze, moistened with antiseptic, to Appledore's chest. He had pulled the wounded man's tunic and shirt up over his head.

"We'll have to return it to get credit for carrying it until we were put out of action," the lieutenant was saying as he peered back into the street. "Have to follow regulations, Kenyon."

"We'll be with you in just a minute. Please wait."

As Kenyon finished wadding up Appledore's gash, he realized his own left arm was no longer responding to his will, and he had difficulty tying two square knots in the bandage. He rubbed a trickle of blood from his upper lip and looked around for Carlock. The officer had disappeared.

"He could have waited a minute," Kenyon complained. He yanked Appledore's shirt and tunic back in place and dragged him to where he could be supported in the corner of the wall. "Stay there and take it easy. I seem to have stopped something myself. Whole damned arm is numb. Funny thing . . ."

Appledore sat like a drunken man, slobbering mucous over his lip. "Get Carlock to . . . help you," he whispered. "Fancies himself a bit . . . of a doctor. An', Kenyon . . . make sure the blood ain't comin' in short jets . . . just flowing evenly."

"Take it easy," Kenyon begged as he unbuttoned his own tunic. "Be with you in a . . ." His blue flannel shirt was soaked with sweat and blood. He stared at himself in disbelief. He finally realized that a single shrapnel ball must have slashed through the open space in the roof of the shed, passed through his tilted Glengarry and pierced his left shoulder. The wound was clean enough where the shrapnel had entered, but there was no evidence that it had emerged anywhere. The initial numbness was wearing off, and a flood of pain was spreading across both shoulders.

"It's nothing . . . serious, Appo," he assured the recumbent figure. "Soon as I can get a pad on . . . the hole, we'll get away and join Mr. Carlock's wounded guys. Won't be a minute."

But Appledore had no interest in the proceedings, or the promise of rest or repair. He lay groaning and spewing up gobs of blood.

When the shrapnel wound had been stanched, Kenyon hauled Appledore to his feet. "Come on, Appo," he begged, but Appo was dead to the world and completely helpless. Max slapped him hard across both cheeks, but the blows brought no response. "Come on, Appo!" he raged and then straightened his teammate up, bent over before him and allowed the inert body to drape itself across his right shoulder. Then with his left arm already stiffening, he clutched Appledore's neck and staggered out into the street.

The capture of Neuve-Chapelle was carried out from March 10–13, 1915, with the loss of 190 British officers and 12,337 men killed—including Private Appledore of the London Scottish.

5

To this day, Maxwell Kenyon has no idea how he made his way from the eastern side of Neuve-Chapelle and found himself on a stretcher outside the casualty clearing station at Doullens. He asked about Appledore, but no one had an idea what he was saying or who he was talking about. A medical officer gave him a toothglass half full of rum and ordered him to drink it. While he was recovering from that dosage an orderly, who obviously hailed from Lancashire, gave him a terrific shot of antitetanus serum and warned him, "Eh, an' you'll 'ave three more afore long."

When some semblance of consciousness returned, he realized he was lying on bare ground. How the stretcher and blanket had been removed he had no idea. Nearby was a large tent which the Lancashire man called a "ward," and fluttering about was a tall, horse-faced woman dressed in a nurse's uniform. She came up to him, jabbed the toe of her shoe into his ribs, and said, "Well, cheer up. You'll soon be back in England—with your young lady." Then someone else came along, helped him to his feet, and walked him into the "ward."

There were hours of being disturbed, for no particular reason. They took his name, regiment, and regimental number, and tied a tag to his epaulet. He couldn't tell whether he was lying on a stretcher or a bed, but none of it mattered. He wondered about Appledore and what had happened to him. There was another antitetanus shot and a mug of hot milk. He went to sleep and dreamed he was back in Fourteenth Avenue School vainly explaining to Mr. Terwilliger why he had been absent for so long. When he roused from that encounter, he discovered he was to be transported to a Red Cross train which would take him to Étaples. Where the hell was Étaples?

But sometime before he was taken to Étaples, he was examined by an officer who wore a blood-streaked smock of some kind. "So you're trying to hang on to a shrapnel ball, eh?" he said after examining the ticket tied to Kenyon's epaulet. "Well, we'll soon relieve you of that."

His tunic and blood-soaked shirt were removed and another orderly bathed him roughly and bellowed for someone named "Chalky" to come and give a hand. Chalky materialized from somewhere, and Kenyon was hauled to an area where the stench of antiseptic almost made him throw up. He was passed from compartment to compartment until he realized he was being prepared for an operation of some kind, but before he could question the procedure, a filthy cone was rammed over his nose and the last thing he remembered was being told to "Take a deep breath."

What seemed hours—or days later—he found himself in a clean bed with a comfortable pillow under his head. His ragged Glengarry was on a boxlike cupboard nearby, and his military boots were tucked between the legs of the convenience. He noticed an unopened package of cigarettes and a bar of chocolate beside his cap. He felt unbearably thirsty, but not hungry. He wanted to call out and ask for a drink of water, but his neck and shoulders were stiff and painful. By forcing his chin down he could see about the area and decided there were other beds and other men as uncomfortable as he. Some moaned, some snuffled, some whimpered like puppies, but no one responded to their pleas or requirements.

Gradually the impact of the situation thumped into his mind. He remembered that he had been wounded. A shell had exploded when he was in . . . er, Neuve-Chapelle, and he had stopped a shrapnel ball. Mister Carlock had been in the latrines. Old Appo had been wounded, too. But where was Appo? Kenyon forced himself to his elbows and looked around the ward. There was no one who remotely looked like Appo. None with his rusty haystack hair and his brick-red cheeks. He began to worry about Appledore, and lowered himself to his pillow again.

By the time he was hauled out to the transport that was to take him to Étaples, he had learned nothing about Private Ernest Appledore. No one bothered him about anything, except to change the dressing on his back where the shrapnel ball had been taken out. He'd never known anyone who had ever been in a hospital. If it had been his mother or father, they would have taken a glass of

Duffy's malt whisky and gone to bed early. Nothing was ever more serious than that.

But it was different out here in France in a military hospital— even though it was only a tent—because he had been wounded up the line while fighting with the London Scottish. No one back home would ever believe a word of it, unless he had some sort of scar to show what he'd been through. He felt over his shoulder to make sure there was a surgical dressing where one should be. It was like a half-forgotten dream because no one else made anything of it. The orderlies were too busy, or too bored to answer questions. The nurses didn't talk to anyone but the doctors, and the doctors looked worse than the wounded. They were exhausted.

The other wounded were always asleep, or were being taken away before he had a chance to ask them anything. He wondered where they went. They never waved so-long or even looked over at him as they were carried out. Hospitals were funny places. No one in Newark would believe a word of any of this, and who could blame them?

He did not know that his parents would be formally advised that their son, Private Maxwell Kenyon, had been WOUNDED IN ACTION ON 11/3/15. Neither Selina nor Bob believed it. "There must be a mistake somewhere. Damn my eyes, it seems only a week or two ago he was sitting here having his supper."

When Kenyon was taken to the ambulance that would remove him to Étaples it was raining and felt good on his face as his stretcher was manhandled and tucked away.

"There you go," the man called Chalky said, and grinned. "You're on your way to Blighty, chum. You lucky bastard."

The train at Étaples was like something out of a child's picture book—shiny maroon with glistening windows. The top part was creamy white with gleaming red crosses painted so they could be plainly identified. The trucks and wheels looked brand new in their black paint, but Private Maxwell Kenyon had no idea it was carrying him into another chapter of his adventure. A nurse, about twenty, with a cluster of yellow curls beneath her cap, and a dark blue cape with a scarlet lining, fluttered up and asked if there was anything he wanted. Six months later he would have a saucy answer, but today he just smiled and said, "No thank you, Sister. I'm very comfortable."

"That's the spirit," she said, and stroked his forehead. It felt like the caress of an angel. "You'll be somewhere near home tomorrow."

Kenyon closed his eyes, and prayed, "I hope not."

He slept all through the trip to Calais, but was able to get on his feet, make his way off the ambulance train and follow the line of walking wounded from the platform to the boat pier. At the bottom of the gangplank he came to a halt while an officious individual of some ill-defined organization examined the tag fluttering from his hospital robe collar. The situation reminded him of his hesitancy in scrambling up the gangplank of the SS *Peruvian Prince* some six months before.

"Where do you live?"

"Nowhere." Kenyon steadied himself at the rail.

"Nowhere? You must live somewhere. You're London Scottish, aren't you? What about somewhere near London?"

"It doesn't matter where. I have no home in England." He was feeling faint and wanted to keep moving. "My parents are in America, the United States."

The officer stared at him and checked the tag again. "We like to send wounded men to hospitals near their home, but of course America's out of the question."

"I know," Kenyon nodded dumbly. "America's neutral."

"Well, you'll have to take your chance."

"What about Manchester?"

"All right, let's suggest Manchester." The officer jabbed his pencil at Kenyon's tag. "It's queer, a London Scottish man wanting to go to Manchester."

"My parents were born in Manchester. Who knows, I might run into an uncle or aunt or two," the wounded man explained wearily.

The officer managed a grin. "God only knows who you'll find in Manchester, once you get there. Up you go, then. The matron will see you are made comfortable."

So comfortable, that Max slept most of the way across the Channel, and was not too sprightly when he was disembarked and led across a pier and made snug in another ambulance train. For half an hour or so he sat and stared out the window, munching on a cardboard sandwich provided by a hawk-nosed woman who wore the coverall of some church organization. As small villages, farmsteads, gently rolling fields and grassy meadows swept past his eyes he saw that the England he had read so much about in the books pilfered from Milligan's was indeed a delightful country. Strange, he had not noticed any of these features when he was in training. But there was little time for contemplation then. It was all work, instruction, learning, and the determination to stay with the London Scottish. He had been too busy trying to be a soldier.

He wondered what would happen to him now. He had no idea of the routine wounded men went through in order to regain their regiments—or wangle a discharge and go back to civvie life. None of that had come up before. What did they do with wounded men, once they had recovered from their wounds? What had happened to Appledore, and where was Mr. Carlock? Did he ever get back with his company of walking wounded? And if so, how would he explain what happened to Denham . . . and whether anyone knew what had happened to Private Maxwell Kenyon? All Max knew was that Lieutenant Carlock had taken their broken machine gun and left them to take care of themselves. He wondered how Carlock explained that when he got back to company HQ. The war was too new for mere privates to have acquired such information or assumptions. Perhaps he'd be told when he got to some hospital near Manchester.

He looked around the compartment and saw that another man was just rousing out of a disturbed slumber. His head was bandaged, and one arm rested in a khaki sling. He managed a smirk, lit a cigarette and began to talk.

"What lot, you?"

"London Scottish."

"Get yours at Neuve-Chapelle?"

Max nodded. "Shrapnel down my back."

"Too bad. Probably get over it in no time."

"It makes my left arm quite stiff. Not much pain, though."

"Might be able to swing it for a month or so, but no more. Then back to La Belle France. La Belle buggery!"

"You Neuve-Chapelle?" Max adopted the laconic speech.

"Scottish Rifles. Bomb squad. Got mine first day, but not picked up for twelve hours."

"We supported a Middlesex bomber mob. Was Number One on a Lewis gun."

The man of the Scottish Rifles jabbed his cigarette into the window ledge. "You M.G.? Bloody lucky, you. Don't go back on a machine-gun team. Proper suicide club, that."

"I know what you mean."

"If I was M.G., I'd put in for a transfer."

"Transfer? Can anyone do that?"

"Listen, chum. You don't want to go back to the ditches, do you? You'll be light-duty in two weeks and getting a medical for fitness a couple of weeks later. Then back you go. That's the schedule these days."

"But transfer to what?"

"The Flying Corps. Don't you read regimental orders?"

"You mean the *Royal* Flying Corps?"

"Ain't no other. They're begging for machine gunners for the new battle aeroplanes. I wish to bloody hell I had taken M.G. training, but like an ass I ducked it. Everybody said it was a suicide club. But you . . ."

"That's a funny thing," Kenyon said and glanced at his reflection in the window. "I came over from New York with a kid who had this Flying Corps idea."

"New York? You came from New York? I thought you had a bit of Yankee twang. Fancy coming all that way to . . ."

"But this fellow," Kenyon went on, "was educated. Private preparatory school, and all that. Last I heard of him he was heading for Farnborough."

Scottish Rifles pointed a finger. "That's the place. Farnborough. But you won't need a la-da-dah education to be a machine gunner on a battle plane. You take my tip, chum. Don't go back to the ditches."

Kenyon repaid his companion for the information with a pack of issue cigarettes. He didn't smoke, but it broke up the conversation, giving him a chance to ponder the possibility of evading another Neuve-Chapelle and a platoon officer like Carlock. It couldn't be any worse in the Flying Corps, and who knew, he might meet Horace Drage again. He wondered if Horace flew battle planes.

Typical of diabolic routine that continued throughout the war, wounded men who innocently indicated a preference for hospitals near their homes, usually were sent as far from such a destination as the geography of Great Britain would allow. Thus, Private Kenyon who, in a moment of indecision, mentioned a family association with Manchester, was instead detrained at Basingstoke, Hampshire, about 150 miles away. However, his wound and the operation necessary to remove the shrapnel were not too painful, and after two weeks of rest and routine care, he was provided with a hospital suit, a cerulean blue serge with white facings and cuffs which, with his regimental cap and boots, enabled him to take short walks through the old town. During one of these rambles he was interested to learn that Jane Austen, a novelist whose works he had never attempted, had been born in Basingstoke, and he visited the local library where for half an hour he tried to worry his way through *Pride and Prejudice*. But the style did not interest him, and he remembered Horace Drage's reference to H. G. Wells's *The War in the Air* which the librarian soon produced. He remained so long with the story he was admonished for being late for supper. But he had absorbed enough of Mr. Wells to appreciate the creation of a Royal Flying Corps. Later he skimmed over the daily newspapers for timely information on this upstart service. Actually, there was little to learn, for the communiqués offered only scant items concerning the activities of the few squadrons that were in France. The war correspondents found nothing of popular interest in the routine observation patrols carried out by the airmen. Lieutenant Rhodes-Moorhouse had not yet made his historic flight to bomb Courtrai's railroad station for which he was awarded the Victoria Cross, and Reggie Warneford would not down Zepplin *LZ.37* until June 11, 1915, focusing world-wide interest on the men who were fighting in the skies. Still, Kenyon was intrigued with the aviation service, but realized he hadn't the slightest idea how to go about making the transfer.

Nearly a month passed, and he had heard nothing concerning his future with the London Scottish. As his convalescence progressed he lost patience with his inability to make a move to get into the Flying Corps. Then, to his dismay, while sketching some primary details of a German Albatros found in a dog-eared copy of *Flight*, he heard his name called at the door of the hospital lounge.

"Private Kenyon! Private Kenyon! You're wanted in the reception room."

A corporal in the Wiltshire Yeomanry, with one leg in a cast, stroked his crutches affectionately and shook his head in mock sympathy. "That's you, Kenyon. Two bob you're going on light duty.

I told you to keep off your feet and swing the lead more. You'll learn."

The call was disturbing, but not one the corporal in the Wiltshire Yeomanry had predicted. When Max reached the reception area he was mildly astonished to see Lieutenant Carlock talking to a day nurse. He came to an uncertain halt, not knowing how to approach an officer while wearing hospital "blues." He hadn't saluted anyone in weeks.

"Ah, there you are, Kenyon," Carlock greeted him cheerfully. "I've had quite a time tracing you. I must say you're looking fit."

Kenyon had no answer, and the nurse was no help. Finally, he mumbled, "Lieutenant Carlock. Have you come to take me back?"

It was the officer's turn for bewilderment. "Take you back? No. I'm on seven days' leave. My D.S.O. I was at Buckingham Palace yesterday. Didn't you see the notice in today's paper?"

"We don't see many papers . . . that is, London papers, sir."

"Well, the investiture was yesterday. I actually shook hands with the King."

Kenyon began to unravel the situation, and focused his gaze on the strip of red-and-blue ribbon gleaming above Carlock's left breast pocket. It was the first time he had considered these strips of ribbon as decorations.

"What did you do, sir?" Kenyon asked with youthful simplicity.

"I just stood there and His Majesty pinned the order on my tunic, and then shook my hand," Carlock explained with restrained enthusiasm.

"No, sir. I mean what did you do to get it?"

"Oh . . . that." The lieutenant stared down at his polished boot toe. "Well, you know how these things work out. I was the only one of our gun team who got back from the attack on Neuve-Chapelle, and when I showed them our gun had been . . . shattered, the colonel realized what we had been through, and put me in for the D.S.O."

Max saw in a flash that Lieutenant Carlock had staged a deceitful charade with the unserviceable weapon, but had not explained what had actually happened. It was "what we had been through" that had convinced the colonel. Carlock had, singlehanded, mounted a Lewis gun at a vital attack point until it had been shot out of his hands. And Neuve-Chapelle *had* been taken.

The nurse excused herself, and disappeared.

"I see," Max said with a lack of enthusiasm. "You showed up with the gun . . . ?"

"Never mind that." The lieutenant changed the disturbing subject. "That's not what I came for. I happened to be in the vicinity, and remembered I should explain that I mentioned you, and how we supported the bombing team. You weren't at HQ to speak for yourself."

"How could I be? The last I remember was trying to get Appledore where he could be attended to, but I woke up in some casualty clearing station. They took my name and number, but what for I have no idea."

"I made all that clear, and you got a Mention in Dispatches about how well you handled your gun until you were wounded. I put it all in my report."

"A Mention in Dispatches?" Max slitted one eye in query. "Do I get a piece of ribbon like that, sir?"

"Well, no. It just goes on your record. There's no decoration, as such, to wear." The lieutenant studied the crest on his swagger stick.

"I should have thought," Maxwell started to say, but the rank injustice of the whole affair swept over him like a cold bath. So this was how men were awarded military decorations. It had nothing to do with valor or heroics. There had to be some carefully staged theatrical climax, played out before senior officers back at HQ. The men who died or were wounded while engaged in the action were just carted away to be dumped into a convenient shell hole or ranked in rows at a casualty clearing station and patched up to fight another day. The man who returned unscathed, carrying a useless machine gun to indicate how he had stood and fought to the very end was awarded Britain's second highest decoration for valor in the field. Had he brought in an armful of broken machine guns he might have been given the Victoria Cross. The whole corrupt revelation triggered a retaliatory riposte in the mind of the young infantryman. He kept his head, however, and chose his words carefully. Maxwell Kenyon was growing up.

"Well, thank you, Lieutenant Carlock, for remembering me, and may I congratulate you on winning the D.S.O. Your parents should be very proud. Now could I ask one . . . one more favor?"

"I haven't got much time," Carlock parried, looking at his wrist watch. "I'm due back . . ."

"It's like this, sir. I don't think I should go back to the London Scottish, after what has happened, getting wounded, but coming through the Neuve-Chapelle attack. Someone might ask *me* a lot of questions. I wouldn't want them going over the records again."

"What are you getting at?"

Maxwell Kenyon was satisfied to have planted the seed of distrust, and he gave the explanation a new twist. This was Selina all over again. "I've had enough of the infantry, sir. I want to transfer to the Royal Flying Corps." He spoke with the air of a young man deciding to take a walk with Daphne instead of Diane. "I believe the Flying Corps is asking for machine gunners to volunteer for the battleplanes. I'd like that, sir, if it could be arranged."

Lieutenant Carlock studied the statement carefully, and found himself off balance. "I . . . I don't think the colonel would release a Lewis-gun man at this time. There aren't too many available, Kenyon."

"I'm not available, sir. I'm in hospital and probably will be for some time. Hundreds of machine gunners could be trained while I'm convalescing."

The commissioned man knew he had been expertly trapped. If this kid got back to the regiment he could raise a hell of a stink, for it was obvious he was not to be palmed off with a mere Mention in Dispatches. It might be a good idea to steer him into the R.F.C. A proper suicide club, the R.F.C.

"Look here, Kenyon. I'm on my way back to London. I'll drop by the depot and see if the adjutant there can take up the matter. I'll explain that you no longer care to serve in a kilted regiment, and since you came all the way from the United States, your appeal ought to be considered."

"I'm not appealing, sir. I'm requesting a transfer to the Royal Flying Corps as a machine gunner on the battleplanes," Max reiterated, clicking his heels.

"Of course." The lieutenant wished he had ignored the impulse to stop off at Basingstoke. It was reminiscent of the old chestnut about the evildoer returning to the scene of his crime. "I'm sure it can be arranged. I'd better be going. Good luck, Kenyon. All the best."

"Good-by, sir."

Private Maxwell Kenyon knew he was as good as in the R.F.C.

Lieutenant Garrod Carlock would never allow him within fifty miles of any London Scottish regiment.

That strained interview with Lieutenant Carlock took place in April 1915. The wheels of officialdom ground as slowly as the design and manufacture of first-class aircraft, and it was not until mid-May that Private Kenyon learned he had become 2nd Class Air Mechanic Kenyon and ordered to report to the Training Establishment at Farnborough.

6

The cogs of Kenyon's war continued to grind slowly, but mesh they did, and at Farnborough's School of Army Co-operation he changed his slacks and London Scottish jacket for a double-breasted tunic, breeches, and rolled puttees. His Glengarry was replaced by a cheese-cutter cap that had been devised from the Crimean War's Balaclava helmet. On those fortunate enough to have a trim physical appearance, the R.F.C. uniform was flattering. Those who tended to be portly looked more like amateur extras in a Ruritanian comic opera. Kenyon seemed to have been especially bred for the aviation uniform.

The gathering of NCO candidates for flying duties was as diverse as the group which nine months before had joined the London Scottish. A few of them were refugees from the trenches, some were discards from the officer training schools, while others had "gotten the word" from someone "in the know" and were positive Farnborough was Open Sesame to pilot training, a commission, and they would be looked upon as the elite of the fighting forces. That's the way it was portrayed in all the musical revues along Shaftesbury Avenue. They were broken up into small groups and marched off to various sheds, buildings, and classrooms to take required instruction in telegraphy, Morse code, photography, machine guns, map reading, and identification of enemy aircraft.

Since Max had booked considerable experience with the Lewis gun, he was immediately given two stripes and, to his disgust, made a machine-gun instructor.

After a month went by, he was called to the orderly room one morning and told to pack his kit and report to Number 4 hangar where a Captain Alistair Grimshaw was waiting to fly him to Sutton's Farm.

"What's Sutton's Farm?" he asked. Much of his early respect for lofty rank had begun to deteriorate.

"It's an aerodrome," a bulbous sergeant major detonated. "Gorbli'-me, what do you think it is?"

"Sounds like a hick cow pasture."

The S/M subsided a trifle. "You're being assigned to the 18th Wing as an aerial gunner. The 18th commands all Home Defense squadrons, meaning as how you'll be expected to stop the bloody Zeppelin menace," the warrant officer explained through fumes of bitter beer.

"Zeppelins?" Max sounded as though he had not heard the word before. "I'm to go up . . . after Zeppelins?"

"You transferred to be an aerial gunner, didn't you?"

"But I haven't finished my training. I've never been up in an aeroplane."

"Neither have I, but there's quids in it. Four shillings a day extra . . . flying pay."

Max asked no more questions. He couldn't think of any. He took his papers and went off to pack his gear, his mind awhirl with the glorious possibilities.

During the next half hour as he packed, he suddenly recalled the name of Reggie Warneford, the R.N.A.S. youngster who had been awarded the Victoria Cross for destroying a Zeppelin over Ghent in Belgium; how he had stalked it for nearly an hour, and had finally sent it down in flames. Just then the guttural Klaxon of a tender snapped him out of his reverie, and he was rushed out to where a B.E.2c stood on the Tarmac of Number 4 hangar. A tall, stoop-shouldered officer was pacing up and down behind the tailplane. It was the closest Max had been to an aircraft since arriving at Farnborough.

"Ha! There you are. Kenyon, is it?" The officer's voice resembled nutmeg graters in opposition.

"Er, yes, sir."

"Well, come on, then. Can't wait around all day."

"But I've just been advised, sir."

"What's that got to do with it?" The captain's face was deeply tanned, lined and marked with a shadow of a beard. He wore a perpetual frown, and when he spoke managed to show both rows of gigantic teeth. "There'll be no time for routine matters, if we are to get into the air fast enough to . . ."

"Where shall I put my gear?" Max gave the primitive biplane a closer look.

"Get along with you, dammit all! Front seat, you, and watch out for the guns. You're in charge of that department," Captain Grimshaw clacked in a higher register.

A ground mechanic came to Max's aid. "Here, chum. Give us your kit. I'll stow it for you." The captain was climbing into the rear cockpit and adjusting the chin strap of a massive crash helmet. The mechanic remained on the wing root and explained further. "You put your right foot in that stirrup hole, Corporal. Then you put your left on this bit of wood, here. That's all you have to stand on, but you can manage from there if you're careful."

Kenyon climbed up as advised, suddenly realizing he had been ordered aloft in an aeroplane. Up till now flying had been something impersonal; talked about, but never actually carried out. But here he was, one foot on the wing, the other cocked over the coaming of the front cockpit. But the heroic script was running off the roller again. He was just a passenger, not actually flying the battleplane himself. Still, he was aboard an aeroplane, and there *was* a Lewis gun mounted on a metal peg bolted to one side of the cockpit.

"Sit down, man!" the demon from under the crash helmet bellowed.

Once that order was obeyed, Max saw someone twirling the four-bladed propeller, and heard Captain Grimshaw barking unintelligible orders toward the ground crew.

Max appealed to the mechanic. "What about flying gear?"

"You won't need any for that short trip. Just pull the flaps of your cap down and button them under your chin."

"No goggles?"

"You won't need goggles. Just squat low behind that bit of windscreen, but be sure your belt is fastened. Old Grimshaw is a bugger of a stunt merchant."

By the time the engine was running and screeching in spurts, Kenyon found himself deep in a weary wicker seat with four center-section struts holding something of a shelter above his head. There were guy wires running in all directions from every strut and point of support. Ahead, he could see the cylinder heads of the air-cooled engine, and the air scoop behind the whirling propeller. There was a definite stench of petrol and lubricating oil which made him wonder if there was a leak under his seat, but he was too securely buckled in to investigate.

The engine roared again and the propeller seemed to disappear, but the battleplane rumbled off toward an open stretch of turf. Kenyon squatted even lower. There was considerable bumping below, as the engine tried to screech its lungs out. Then it all smoothed down and the machine started to climb, and suddenly tried to stand on its tail. At that point Kenyon remembered that he used to be sick on the Newark trolley cars, and wondered how he would cope with a similar situation. Ahead, there was nothing but a grayish sky, and he wanted to turn around to make certain the pilot was still in his seat, but his belt held him secure.

He did not feel ill, or too concerned, but then, to his horror, one wing went down and he had the feeling he would be tossed out and sent down the varnished slide and dropped into thin air. But again the battleplane straightened out and, after settling down again, he enjoyed looking over the machine gun at a beautiful expanse of old world countryside. There were fields, hedges, and roads, and here and there he could identify cattle and flocks of sheep grazing in the meadows. At the junction of winding lanes small clusters of houses with red-tiled roofs or dun-brown thatch could be plainly seen. Churches with square towers or sharp spires, and then small streams trickling through the countryside to finally join a broad river. He did not know that the great tortuous waterway was the Thames, and that they were heading for Hornchurch on the western side of London.

As they continued on, Max began to enjoy the flight and the colorful panorama ahead when suddenly the biplane started to pitch and roll. It went into a steep dive, snapped up sharply and went over on a wingtip again. Max wished he could twist around enough to make sure his pilot was where he was supposed to be. Another steep dive, and suddenly the earth dropped away, and again there was nothing but sky ahead. He felt he was being rammed down hard in his seat by some mysterious power. There was an instant he was positive the pilot was leaning forward and squashing his head down between his shoulders. It reminded him of the roller coaster at Olympic Park. The landscape came back and the B.E. went into a sharp climbing turn, but still circling a definite area below. This went on for what seemed hours. Then the engine stopped, or was shut off, reminding Kenyon of his helplessness. The nose went down and there was a dreadful sickening spell when he was certain the aeroplane was winding itself into a spinning nose dive.

It was, but after three or four twirls it eased out smoothly and the engine came on as they flew toward a long strip of level turf. There was a cottage nearby, some small haystacks, and the typical outhouses of a farmstead. By the time the wheels were rumbling unevenly, they were swinging in an easy curve toward a single Besseneau hangar where three other biplanes were ranked on parched turf in front of the aviation shed. Max sat staring at the scene like a kid seeing his first magic lantern show.

"That's all!" Captain Grimshaw was bellowing. "You can climb down now."

"Where are we?" Max asked when he had unbuckled his belt. He felt cold and fluttery about his middle, but was relieved he had not been sick.

"This is Sutton's Farm, near Hornchurch," Grimshaw said and laughed. He climbed out and stood on the wing root. "You feel all right?"

"Quite all right, sir. It was most interesting." Max had no intention at this point admitting he felt a trifle queasy.

"Good lad. You stood it well. Now you'll have to make the best of accommodations here, for the time being. It'll be rough, but you'll survive." And with that Captain Grimshaw seemed to disappear, but there were other figures moving about, some in khaki uniforms, some in mixtures of military garb, university sweaters, and golf stockings. It was a motley crew, and Kenyon wondered what they were supposed to be. He forced himself up from the seat, stepped out on the wing root and started to haul out his kit bag. The propeller wigwagged twice, and the exhaust let out a belch of poisonous smoke.

"Kenyon!" a voice called from the small throng around the battle-plane. A hand gripped his leg just above the ankle. "Max. What the hell are you doing here?"

As Kenyon looked down he saw, to his amazement and delight, Horace Drage. His lifeboat companion was standing with outstretched arms awaiting a mutual embrace.

"Horace!" the mere corporal cried, and then felt some explanation was in order. "Horace, I made it."

"I'll say you did, and what a show Grimshaw put on," Horace

babbled on. "Where the hell have you been? I've been trying to get in touch with you for weeks."

"In hospital, mostly."

"Yes. I heard you were wounded, but couldn't find out where you had been dumped. Get down here. I want to look at you." Horace grabbed Max's kit bag.

"What's going on here?" Grimshaw suddenly reappeared, frowning on this unmilitary fraternization. "You know this man?" he demanded of Drage.

"Know him? We came over on the same ammunition ship to join up when the war broke out." Horace grinned widely. "I wanted him to join the R.F.C. right away, but he was steamed up about the London Scottish—and got himself shot to hell."

The captain vetted Kenyon again. "You were out with the London Scottish?"

"Right! But I transferred as soon as I got out of hospital."

The captain cocked one eye sharply. "You were wounded?"

"At Neuve-Chapelle. I was a machine gunner out there."

Horace broke in. "I hope I can have him as my gunner. We're both Americans, and it would be swell if . . ."

"Oh, no you don't! This one is mine. I brought him, and if he's had front-line action, he's the boy for me. What's more, he's the first one who hasn't been sick after my stunting. You're *my* gunner, Kenyon. You remember that."

Captain Grimshaw started to pick up his gear, and then turned back. "You put up your wound stripe, Kenyon. That's an order . . . and get an observer's wing, and put that up, too. Never mind an exam, this is an emergency station and, who knows, we might be on alert tonight."

Horace tried to concoct a new appeal, but Grimshaw was striding off under the thrust of his own esteem. Max turned back to Horace and noticed he was wearing an R.F.C. jacket, Bedford cord breeches, golf stockings, and brogues. He sported the single gold star of a second lieutenant on his shoulder straps. He knew Horace could get nowhere arguing with a three-pip captain, and he quietly reveled in his own importance.

"Too bad, Max," Horace grumbled as he lit a cigarette, "but hang on. We may be able to work it later. Grimshaw will probably get a squadron and pike off somewhere else. Just sit tight."

"What is this place?" Kenyon asked, staring about.

"It's called Sutton's Farm . . . near Hornchurch. This is a detached flight of Number 19 Reserve Squadron which was organized to put up a defense against Zeppelins. It used to be the responsibility of the War Office and the Admiralty, but they soon found out that ground guns were of no use, so they decided to drop the menace into our lap. The squadron is actually dispersed around London on nine different fields."

"Have you been up after any Zeps, yet?"

"Not yet," Horace confessed. "I'm a real Quirk. Don't know how I got through. I was a dud at Ground School, but finally went on old Farman Shorthorns. What a bloody laugh! Next, I managed a couple of crashes, but eventually learned to fly tractor biplanes and wound up in the B.E.2c pool. That's how I came to be here."

"You haven't been up after any Zeps yet?" Max repeated to show his amazement.

"We don't have landing lights for night flying, and the Jerries come over only at night. We're just using up petrol in the daytime to keep our hands in."

"I see," Max said in an aggrieved tone. "Where do I bunk in?"

"I don't know. The officers are down at the White Hart until suitable accommodations can be built here," Horace explained and looked disturbed. "Too bad you didn't join up with me. You'd probably be commissioned by now. As it is, you'll have to make the best of a bunk in the hangar, sleeping under the aircraft until they erect some bell tents."

"I don't mind any of that. It was worse out in France," Max said stoically. "I just want to get into the air where I can get a shot at something . . . a Zeppelin preferred. But I'll settle for anything where I can get credit for what I do."

"Now don't start thrusting. You'll have all the chance in the world to get action. This night flying can be a . . ."

"I know. Suicide club. I've heard that a hundred times, but here I am!"

"Well, take it easy."

"I'm through being a pushover. Let me tell you what happened when I was wounded at Neuve-Chapelle. I stayed with my gun until I was the only one left, but I didn't let any Jerries get through. All I got was a hunk of shrapnel down my back—and a Mention in Dispatches. You know what my officer got—and he was hiding in a trench latrine—a D.S.O. I got Sweet Fanny Adams, and a lousy Mention in Dispatches!"

The young second lieutenant couldn't believe what he was hearing and was shocked at how his boatmate had changed in the past months. His boyish grin was gone, and his speech had become the jargon of the London guttersnipe. One major engagement had made him a tough, unreasoning pot-hunter. He wasn't satisfied with getting out of the action at Neuve-Chapelle with his life; he wanted a medal to prove he had been there. Well, he would get all the pot-hunting he wanted with Captain Grimshaw. They would make a bloodthirsty team, if they lived long enough.

Max was still ranting. "I'm going to get one of those gasbags, if it's the last thing I do. It should be easy. I was surprised, flying up there. Nothing to it—just fun. I sat there imagining I was pouring a couple of bursts into a Jerry Zep. I'd like to shoot one of those big bastards down in flames. Jees, that would be great!"

During the next few weeks Corporal Kenyon was more than satisfied with the activity at Sutton's Farm. He had been provided with a short leather jacket, hip-length flying boots, gloves, helmet, and goggles, and was taken aloft every morning by Captain Grimshaw and given the opportunity to handle a gun in the air. They would go up to about 3000 feet and practice immediate action on gun stoppages, and take aim against imaginary Zeppelins or enemy Rumpler *Taube* aeroplanes that were believed to be threatening East Coast cities.

The gunnery prospect was not too enticing and Kenyon soon realized he had assumed a particularly difficult task. He wondered what he would do if he got a chance to put a burst of bullets into something hostile. Where he sat he felt completely entangled with a complex of center-section struts, braces, guy wires, control cables, and such impedimenta germane to biplanes. It was a position where it was difficult to swing the observer's gun through even a limited angle of fire without the danger of shooting away something important in the construction or control of the aircraft. By much the same token, Captain Grimshaw's weapon was fixed at an angle outside his cockpit, allowing it to fire past the tips of the propeller. Thus, in order to shoot at any enemy target, the B.E. had to be flown crabwise to get bursts of bullets anywhere near an objective.

Despite these difficulties, Max was given the experience of firing on a ground target laid out on one of Farmer Sutton's fields. In this exercise Grimshaw would circle the target very low, and when the aircraft was in a steep bank, Max would risk a burst or two through the tangle of guy wires and interplane struts. When the firing period was over, his pilot would hoick back upstairs and put on another of his stunt shows which always brought out the mechanics and other pilots to see "old Grimmy pull his wings off."

Fortunately, Grimshaw flew well enough to carry out his display with the least possible strain on the wing structure, and after a few days Kenyon looked forward to the playboy exhibitions. But the days and nights crawled by with no promise of action or a change of scenery. No Zeps appeared, no alarms were sounded, no more Victoria Crosses were won, and the newspapers were particularly drab—unless there was any truth to the report that a French airman, Roland Garros, had devised a scout plane from which the pilot could fire bursts of bullets through the whirling propeller. But, of course, the whole idea was ridiculous.

Max complained of the inactivity to "Taffy" Morgan, a Welsh-man who did most of his flying with Lieutenant Drage. Taffy was a short compact man with a face that more than justified Darwin's theory. But he was a skilled observer and had been through the complete training course at Farnborough. He knew his way around, was conversant with the mechanics, and kept his ear to the ground.

"You're getting in flying time, aren't you?" he growled. "Be satisfied you're getting flying pay—for joyrides."

"I want to get a shot at a Zep. At least I'd like to see one in the air. That's what I transferred for."

"We'll never stop any with the machines we've got," Taffy proclaimed, and screwed up the other side of his face. "More than likely get shot down by our own ground guns. It has happened."

"I'd be willing to take the chance, just to get one good burst into a gasbag."

"You listen to me. This bloody war will be on a long time, and I just hope I can last it out," Taffy said in his singsong tone. "I started out all Land of Hope and Glory, but I'm getting sensible."

"I didn't come three thousand miles to kite about all night and lose a lot of good sleep for nothing."

"Don't worry. None of us will be here much longer. All the gunners are to be shoved over to France."

"What are you talking about?"

"Them gasbags can rise faster than we can climb. They're already up there when they're first spotted. We have to get aboard, get off the ground, and reach their altitude. We have a hell of a time getting to ten thousand feet. By that time they've dropped their bombs and are on their way home. We're just burning petrol."

"But suppose one of us is already up there?"

"There's no such luck in this war."

"But just suppose . . . ? Max continued.

"You a telegrapher?"

"No. I was kept on gunnery instruction. I never got to the telegraphy class."

"Well, then, you'll never get a flash from the ground to tell you where they are. I'm a telegrapher . . . was one in civil life. I could use the set we have in one of the buses and find out where the Jerries are. But, again, it's all luck, and I don't have any."

Max gnawed on his knuckle, pondering on that. "I see what you mean. But why will we be sent over to France? What's that about?"

Taffy moved in to get cozy. "Here's what will happen. Our pilots will fly without gunners. Machine guns will not torch Zeps. Not with the ammunition we're using. They'll carry Hale grenades, carcass bombs, and incendiary darts. See those ammunition boxes over there? That's what's in them. Bombs and grenades."

Kenyon glared at the crates just inside the hangar.

"Our B.E.s will be flying without gunners, and will climb faster. All the pilots have to do is fly over the gasbag, drop the bombs, grenades, or the darts, and Boom! It'll be money for jam."

Another pipe dream of Kenyon's was shattered. "But what will they do with the gunners?"

"I bloody well know what they'll do with me," Taffy muttered. "A bloody telegrapher, me. I'll be shipped to France with my dots and dashes to do artillery observation. You know, spotting for the artillery. Barging about just over the Jerry trenches, taking all that ground muck, trying to tell our gunners where to drop their shells. Art-obs blokes last about six weeks at that bloody game. I wish I'd never heard of telegraphy."

Kenyon glared at the bomb crates again.

"Three patrols a day," Taffy concluded, "and all the medals you can wear. Who the hell wants medals? The pawnshops are full of 'em."

"Are you sure about all this?"

"Want to know what will happen to you?"

"Let's have it . . . you bloody Jeremiah."

"You're just a gunner. You'll be transferred to a two-seater squadron. Sopwith 1½-Strutters, they call 'em. I heard old Grimshaw saying he might be given a Sopwith squadron—and you know who he'll take with him. You'll be on two-seater fighters, you lucky bostid!"

Kenyon held his tongue, wondering what he had stumbled into now.

"You are lucky, you know," Taffy was saying. "These new Sopwiths have the gunner's cockpit behind the pilot's seat, and the gun is mounted on a new ring so it can be swung in any direction. The pilot's Vickers is bolted down and geared to fire through the blades of the propeller, just like the Fokker scouts that have been causing all the trouble."

Little of this made sense to Max. He knew nothing about gun gears or fixed guns that were timed to miss hitting the propeller blades, but if Captain Grimshaw was trying to get in a Sopwith two-seater squadron, there must be something special about the aeroplane. He decided to make a few careful inquiries when a chance arose.

As luck would have it, or perhaps as an example of the idiocy of coincidence, an alert was sounded that night. Captain Grimshaw, with Max as his gunner, was the first to get away. Drage and Morgan were on stand-by, while Lieutenant Westley and Air Mechanic Cockburn were simply ordered to be on call at their quarters.

"We ought to find this one," Grimshaw confided. "She's not too high, and it's a clear night, so far."

The reference to altitude dampened Kenyon's spirits, but he hoped for the best and asked, "Excuse me, sir, but is there such a plane as a Sopwith two-seater?"

Grimshaw glanced over his shoulder. "You mean the Sopwith 1½-Strutter? Where did you hear about that?"

"It seems to be talked about by some of the other gunners. A new Sopwith of some kind."

The pilot settled himself in the cockpit. "You content yourself with a B.E.2c for now, Corporal. I'll tell you about it after we have a go at this bloody Zeppelin." Grimshaw allowed his face to break into a crooked smile.

"Yes, sir."

It was a beautiful night when they took off just after eleven o'clock. There were a few scarfs of cloud here and there, and enough light from the stars—and the subdued glare from the city of London—to enable the pilot to make a clean take-off without the aid of ground flares. The early autumn night air was crisp and invigorating. That is, it was until the engine began to discharge its petrol and oil fumes. They climbed to 10,000 feet during the first hour, and then set out to patrol toward Joyce Green. By that time more clouds were gathering below.

Well after midnight Kenyon saw the thin blades of three searchlights flashing back and forth some distance southwest of Woolwich. He pointed them out, and Grimshaw banked hard and took up the chase. More clouds gathered, but Kenyon loosened his belt and paid some attention to his gun, and made sure it was loaded. The activity warmed him a trifle, so he continued to wriggle back and forth from one side of his wicker seat to the other.

"You see anything?" Grimshaw said over the primitive Gosport tube communication connected to Kenyon's helmet.

"Only the searchlights," the gunner bellowed back. He was not connected to his pilot's earflaps.

"Keep your eyes open. There must be one in the vicinity somewhere."

The spectacle was nothing like the newspaper illustrations, drawn to show what a Zeppelin raid was like. The gunner, anxious for action, sensed nothing but the biting temperature, the false drama, and lack of movement, except for the ceremonial swaying of searchlight blades. Even the engine seemed to hold its breath, and Kenyon felt it all was a military fraud. But below, nearly ten million human beings crouched and huddled in nameless dread. Most were spellbound, the rest ran in senseless courses, seeking they knew not what. The vitriol of massed terror spurted through their veins like the flow of petrol to an engine that twirled a great propeller.

At that point anxiety and anticipation took over and both air-men thought they could see Zeppelins in every quarter. There were instances when they were positive a dirigible was within shooting distance, but after darting about in pointless pursuit, new clouds appeared and the phantom Zeppelin faded into nothing. They searched at various levels until a number of gunfire blasts slapped yellow splotches against the sky. But the instant they turned in their direction, an inverted tripod of searchlight blades splayed up in another quarter. Grimshaw swore and warmed his gun again. Kenyon tried searching where no glare or explosion daubed the night.

"We're getting nowhere," the pilot growled. "Have to start back soon. Running low on fuel."

Kenyon who wanted to hear none of that, got to his knees and turned to look over at his pilot's panel. He had no idea which was the fuel gauge, or whether there was one to consult. Grimshaw poked a gloved finger at the watch.

"We've been up long enough. May not be able to get back to Hornchurch. No luck, Kenyon."

Max resumed his seat and then noted considerable gunfire well east of the London area. He sat watching the display and wondered what it meant. He pointed it out to Grimshaw who studied the explosions, shrugged his shoulders and headed back to Sutton's Farm. This was how it would always be, Max reflected bitterly. All the sweating effort and nights wasted looking for some phantom airship, some tableau of ghostly glory. They had been shown bombs, cutaway drawings of bombs and been told the explosive content of bombs—but they never dropped any, on anything!

War was a bloody fraud!

When they arrived back at the field they noticed considerable activity. A series of Very signals were being fired, and the landing flares were unusually large and illuminating. Kenyon turned to look at his pilot who shrugged his shoulders again and stared down at the pyrotechnics. "Something must have happened," he concluded.

As they glided in the display increased and Very signal flares of all colors arched up and spluttered all over the field. Max fastened his gun and leaned over to see what the obvious cele-bration was about. The figures of men were running in all directions. One standing near a ground flare waved his arms wildly and tossed his cap into the air.

The B.E. bounced once, switched her tail, bounced again, and seemed to drop to her knees. The propeller screeched and threw segments of her four blades into the sky, which fluttered away through the glare of the ground flares.

"Christ Almighty!" Grimshaw swore. "What a bloody awful landing!"

Kenyon had been slammed against his belt, but still almost went through the center section. His gun snapped from its clip, swung on its pivot and the short shoulder stock cracked him across the elbow. It was a terrific clout and he sensed his arm or elbow had been broken. Then he passed out for a few minutes. When he came to, he felt himself being lifted out of the machine which was standing on its nose. "You'll be all right," someone was saying. "Don't struggle like that. It's just a bad landing."

"My arm! My arm!" Kenyon screeched and almost fainted again. "Let go my goddam arm!"

There was a tender chugging nearby and he was helped into the front seat. Grimshaw was nowhere to be seen. Another tender was trying to pull the aeroplane down to something resembling a flying position.

"Take it easy. You'll be all right. God, that must have been a thrill!"

"Thrill? Crashing on your own aerodrome is a thrill?" Kenyon babbled.

"No! Shooting that blasted Zeppelin down. It just came through on the telephone. The bloody thing is down in the Channel."

As Max tried to ease the pain of his arm, he mumbled. "The Channel? We were nowhere near the Channel. Just around Woolwich."

"Well, somebody from Hornchurch finished it off. We thought it was you and old Grimshaw. We *thought* it was you," the driver explained.

"Who else was out?" Max asked hollowly.

"Mr. Drage and Taffy Morgan. It must have been them. Strike me blue, but won't they get decorated."

"Let's get somewhere where somebody can take care of me," Max groaned.

7

Corporal Kenyon was taken to a small cottage hospital in Horn-church where X-rays disclosed he had a broken arm—a clean break above the elbow. He was soon back in hospital blues once more fuming with discomfort, frustration and berating his continued ill luck. The crash landing was an anticlimax he could well have done without, but there it was and there was nothing he could do about it.

Late in the afternoon of the third day Captain Grimshaw came to inquire how he was getting on. He was in a smartly pressed uniform, polished boots, and carrying a walking stick that had been fashioned from the propeller of a previous crash. He was very posh, pretentious, profoundly concerned about his gunner, and glutted with news—of sorts.

"How are you?" he asked, poking pleasantly with his stick. "Broke your arm, they tell me. I suppose it's bloody painful, while its lasts, what?"

"What happened?" Max took in his pilot's sartorial elegance, noting for the first time that Captain Grimshaw did not have one decoration, or even a wound stripe. He wondered how he had collected so many stars on his tunic.

"It was all my fault—and yet it wasn't," the captain began, squatting on Max's bed with a thud. "For one thing I was too bloody interested in the Very pistol display. Never noticed that we'd run completely out of petrol. So the engine conked. We were going into a stall, fell off and then I think a tire blew. That's all we needed. She veered, and that was that. You got yours when she tried to stand on her nose," Grimshaw clacked on until he seemed to make the ward shake with the thunder of his words.

"I mean, sir, what was all the celebration about?"

"Oh, that. Didn't you know? Drage and his chap . . . Morgan, were sent off about an hour after we left. They must have gotten lost, for they were nowhere near their assigned area, but they did find a Zep that had been hit by ground gunfire. It was losing height and floundering home. Drage caught up with it, flew alongside for a time and, er, Morgan poured a whole drum into the blasted thing, and it finally went down off the Dutch coast."

"Did Morgan set it on fire?"

"No. He must have shot all the controls away, according to Drage, and the bloody hulk flopped into the sea. They won't get full credit, of course, since it was the ground guns that had really put her out of action. Morgan just finished the job."

"Too bad it didn't catch fire, sir."

"Ah, bad luck, that. Still, they have both been put in for decorations. Drage will get the Military Cross and his gunner will probably get a Distinguished Conduct Medal, er, posthumously, of course."

Kenyon squinted, and finally said, "What does that mean, sir?"

"Posthumously? Oh, I didn't explain. Morgan was hit—rather badly while he was raking the Zep. Drage said they had a gun turret mounted on top of the thing, and Morgan didn't live to see the bloody gasbag go down. He was dead long before Drage could fly back and land."

"Morgan's dead? He'll get a medal but won't see that either," Kenyon said, and began to scratch his shoulder.

"Poor devil," the captain added and used his stick like a fencing blade. "He wins a medal, but will never wear it. Well, that's war for you." He slapped his boot leg and got to his feet. "I must pop along. Don't be in too much of a hurry to get back to the squadron. I have other plans for you."

"Are they really going to dispense with aerial gunners, sir?" Max asked mournfully.

"They're going to dispense with me. I'm to leave Number 19 and organize a new squadron."

"With Sopwith two-seaters?" Max brightened.

"That's it. We'll be known as Number 70, and as soon as we can get machines, pilots, and gunners, we'll be posted to France—in time for the next spring push, I suppose," Grimshaw said, inspecting his nails. "I shall indent for you, of course, so you'll still have to put up with me."

"Thank you, sir. One other thing. May I put up another wound stripe . . . for the crash and being in hospital again?"

The captain looked puzzled, but finally rose to the occasion. "Oh, no. Wound stripes are awarded only for wounds suffered in action against the enemy. This affair was—just an accident."

"Yes, I suppose so."

"It's not too important, is it? But rest anyway, and don't become impatient. I'll put in for you as soon as I get somewhere to hang my hat," Grimshaw said and clattered off.

Recovery took Max Kenyon through many days of despondency, boredom, personal discomfort, and disappointment over what he had hoped would be a second wound stripe. He was only mildly affected by Taffy Morgan's death, for he was becoming inured to a sudden and violent end, as do all fighting men. But he was concerned that Drage's companion had been killed by a machine gun mounted on the upper side of the Zeppelin framework. He had not realized that dirigibles were armed at all. It was something to remember. But the fact that Morgan was being awarded the Distinguished Conduct Medal, when he had so recently expressed his low opinions of decorations for valor, was truly ironic. He realized that Taffy would never know he had been recommended for the honor. It was all such a waste, since, as Grimshaw had said, he would never wear it. If it was sent to his next-of-kin, what would his parents, still mourning his loss, do with a bauble like that? Probably tuck it away in a bureau drawer, and forget it. Or, as Taffy had foretold, they might pawn it and buy a pint of whisky.

With the reduction of the numbing pain and a desire to move about the small comfortable rooms of the temporary hospital, Max's ennui and loneliness dissipated. He made a few friends among the other patients and gained the interest and passing affection of the VADs who ran the convalescent home. When he could move about with his arm in a sling he enjoyed short walks into the town and basked in the motherly interest and concern of women he met on the streets.

Hornchurch was chiefly residential, but being served with three trunk roads and as many rail routes, there was plenty of commercial activity along its High Street that by 1915 was developing into a modern shopping center. Years later, several streets of Hornchurch's New Elm Park commemorated the names of many World War II pilots who had scrambled from what had originated as Sutton's Farm to fight in the Battle of Britain.

In due course, Kenyon was discharged from the Hornchurch Hospital, given his uniform, and two weeks of convalescent leave. He packed his haversack with a pair of filched hospital pajamas, extra socks, a khaki shirt of civilian cut, and his holdall, and took the Underground for London.

"Where will you be?" the matron inquired. "I understand you do not have a home in England. Where can we get in touch with you?"

"The Ensign Club on Waterloo Road. That's a service hostel," he explained, and winked at a passing VAD.

"Oh, of course. All you boys from overseas go there, don't you? It's a lot cheaper than hotels, isn't it?"

Kenyon considered that. "I don't know. I've never been to a hotel."

The matron looked puzzled. "Not even on a Christmas holiday?"

The Ensign Club was popular with English troops who were paid less than a lascar seaman. At this famed hostel on Waterloo Road they could obtain wholesome meals, refreshing teas, and clean beds on dormitory floors for a nominal sum. There also were theater tickets for the many London revues and musical comedies, dramas, motion picture shows, and sporting events.

Max registered on arrival, showed his leave warrant, and stowed his gear in a locker beside a bed on the third floor. After a wash-up and a hair-comb, he brushed his tunic, and descended the stairs ready to take on all comers, especially if they were of the opposite sex. And there were a number of such on the staff of the Ensign Club.

After a mug of tea and a Bath bun, he sauntered over to the Accommodation Desk and looked over the board that displayed what theater tickets were available. He had no intention of wasting his first evening. The offering was not too promising, as there were tickets only for a few stodgy dramas, a Gilbert & Sullivan operetta, and something called a mystery play. He was pondering on that when one of the waitresses moved along from the food counter and asked if she could be of any assistance.

"I was wondering if . . ."

"You're lucky," the waitress said with a sly smile. "I have just one for *Chu-Chin-Chow*. That's the most popular musical in London. But I have only one. You can have it, if that's your style."

"I'll take it. I love leg shows."

"'Ark at you!"

That complimentary ticket to *Chu-Chin-Chow* at His Majesty's Theatre was to play a significant role in the career of Corporal Maxwell Kenyon, for it led him, quite deviously, into his initial acquaintance with Miss Dido Maitland, a featured dancer in the memorable extravaganza.

On his return to Farnborough, he found plenty of flying and associated training, although Grimshaw, now a major, had only two flights of aircraft. As a result, Max was again teaching commissioned men the intricacies of the Lewis gun. There were only three other aerial gunners, two of whom had already been out on B.E.s, and been wounded. One gunner, Bert Laidlaw, had been awarded the Military Medal for staying with his Morse key long after he was wounded on an artillery shoot in front of Douai.

A gangling youth with a wry expression and carrot-colored hair, Laidlaw was still a 1st Class Air Mechanic, although he had put in nearly three hundred hours of front-line patrols. He was friendly, talkative, and explained, after he learned Max was an American; that he came from the Midlands, but offered no details. His Military Medal ribbon interested Kenyon.

"What's that ribbon you're wearing?" he asked after treating Laidlaw to a malted milk in the dry canteen. "I've never seen one of them before."

The Midlands youth glanced down at the red-white-and-blue decoration and sniffed contemptuously. "This is what was thought up so as not to give out too many D.C.M.s. It's called the Military Medal. It ranks with the Military Cross being palmed off on officers who should have gotten the D.S.O."

Max wagged his head. "At least it's better than a Mention in Dispatches. You have something to show."

"I'd sooner have ten quid and about seven days' leave. Christ! What I could do with a couple of fivers. A tart on me arm, and seven nights to put her over the jumps. They can have their bloody medals. I'll take mine in trade."

"Wouldn't you like to have a Victoria Cross?"

"Don't be a chump. You have to get killed to win the V.C.

We've had two in the Flying Corps, Warneford and Rhodes-Moorhouse, and where are they? Under the daisies."

Max looked pained. "But if you got it and came home . . ."

Bert Laidlaw pinched his nostrils together and then sniffed. "No one wins anything in this war, except the bloody profiteers. The blokes who do the fighting can't win." He gave Max a quizzical glance. "What made you come over here to join up? The billboards and old Kitchener sticking his finger at you?"

"There was none of that in America. My folks are from Manchester, although I was born in the States, and I got to thinking . . ."

"Thinking what? That you could come over here and get a chestful of medals?"

"No, not quite like that. But it seemed like a good idea at the time. I wasn't contented at home, and I wanted another outlook on life and a chance to better myself. Chiefly, I wanted an education, but I was deprived . . ." Max heard himself saying.

Laidlaw toned down a chuckle. "You certainly came to the right place. If you get through this mess you'll be a very bright cove, but don't go pot-hunting for medals. You can come unstuck."

"You're a pessimist," Max said, but managed a smile.

"You listen to me. We can't win this war, but we mustn't lose it, either. We can drive Fritz all the way back to Berlin, but we still won't win. We've already lost it, if you consider all the good blokes who have been killed. Just think of the thousands from the best families who joined on the outbreak. They're just names on wooden crosses, or painted inside church doors for remembrance. Nice gold letters and brass plates, but they're gone, lost, and they took all their good blood, their educations—and England's future with them. Then there're all the young girls who had hopes of a honeymoon and a houseful of rosy-cheeked kids. They'll have to settle for a second, or third best . . . and many of them will have to marry some of these bloody Belgian refugees, or even worse. Can't you see what they'll whelp from that scum? That's England's future, chum."

Kenyon looked morose. "There's something to what you say, perhaps, but we still have to drive them back to Berlin, don't we? That's what we signed up for, isn't it?"

Bert evaded Max's eyes. "You speak for yourself. I signed up because I was out of work. None of that King and Country twaddle.

I'd been haunting the Labor Exchange for weeks and there was no summer holiday in store. The Flying Corps was a godsend. I knew enough about motor mechanics to get in, and I was in clover, or so I thought. Then, when we went to France I found myself taking a course in telegraphy—anything to duck the infantry—and as soon as I could receive and send six words a minute, I was on Art-obs. The flying pay was good as long as I could spend it, but it's only cigarette pictures when you're in hospital. The bloody poultice wallahs steal everything."

Max went to replenish their drinks. When he came back, he put on a wry grin. "I can see your point, of course, but I'll take a medal, if I think I've earned one."

"Every bloke out there has earned half a dozen, but how many of them get them? The whole bloody medals and decorations game ought to be abolished. The whole bloody war ought to be abolished, if you ask me."

"Drink up. You're in the doldrums." Kenyon gripped Laidlaw's wrist. "Tell me about flying out there. Did you ever torch a Jerry?"

"On a B.E.2c? Not a chance. You're so bloody busy spotting artillery bursts and sending corrections for the next round, you never get a chance to see whether there are any Jerries about. I can't remember getting a shot at one . . . that is, until the last time I went up."

"When you won your Military Medal?"

Laidlaw became thoughtful, and then shook his head. "I didn't win a medal. I was just trying to save my own skin. I didn't even think about Mr. Condit, my pilot. Self-preservation, I think you'd call it. I just hoped Condit would stay alive long enough to get me back on the ground. After that, he could snuff it, if he liked. That's what any of us gunners ever think. Bravery has nothing to do with it." Laidlaw became thoughtful again. "When you suddenly see a bloody Hun spraying sparklers all around you, there's no time to play Sir Galahad. I drove the bastard off, but he'd put three beauties through my thigh. Funny thing, they didn't hurt too much at first, and I kept on with the shoot until I began to feel queer—sick. I'd lost some blood, so I had to tell Condit I was wounded. Didn't occur to me before. You put all that together and read it off a paper and it comes out that I was very brave and carried out my duty although painfully wounded. That's what it said in *Comic Cuts*. Brave be buggered! I was scared to death!"

Kenyon sought solace in his malted milk. "But if you drove him off from the front seat of a B.E. you must have done a damn good shooting job. I know what it's like to fire a Lewis through that tangle of wires, struts, and braces."

Bert nodded in agreement. "The swines in the War Office who keep sending those bloody B.E.s out to France ought to be strung up along Whitehall. They're not fighting aircraft."

"Well, what about these new Sopwiths, and the two-seater fighter business? Will they be any better?"

"They'll be honey-and-jam after B.E.s," Laidlaw said with a new air of confidence.

"Much faster than B.E.s?"

"That's not important. What I like is having the gun behind the pilot's seat on a mounting you can swing in all directions. It will be easier for a gunner to get a good bead on a scout pilot who is trying to get his nose on the two-seater. Their guns are fixed and they have to use joystick and rudder to aim the whole aeroplane. Don't forget that. You can put two or three bursts into him before he can get you anywhere in his sight. You just have to see him first, and take action. He'll stay away from you."

This professional information and advice aroused new spirit in Max. "How soon do you think we'll be going out as a complete squadron?"

"Christ, but you're a firebrand! Let's have our Christmas first. I wasted the last one in France." He gave Max a penetrating glance, took another sip of his drink, and prophesied, "You know, chum, you're probably going to make a bloody good soldier . . . airman. That is, if you live long enough. I just hope you never become an officer. You'll drive your whole bloody squadron up the greasy pole!"

Max couldn't conceive himself holding a commission, so he said, "I think we should try our best to win this war."

Bert doused his cigarette with a savage gesture. "You're the kind who will . . . if anybody can, but it's probably the only thing you will do. War's one thing, you know, and what you do when it's all over is something else, chum. I can recall several 'heroes' who came back from the Boer War. They all wound up on the same muck heap."

8

Long before they were reasonably prepared for active service Major Grimshaw's two understrength flights of Number 70 Squadron were posted to France during one of the early spring days of 1916. They took off, displayed a ragged formation, but finally scrambled across the Channel and found their way to a fairly new field adjacent to a hamlet known as Fienvillers, a few miles west of Marieux. It will do no good to search for Fienvillers in any modern atlas or gazeteer, and it has been totally ignored by Herr Baedeker and the publishers of all Michelin Guides of the period. Most so-called aerodomes of the Great War were simply spreads of open meadowland, acres of level pasture, or smoothed-over plowed fields; in fact, any approachable area that afforded sufficient space for portable shelters and strips suitable for take-offs and landings. Once such a primitive establishment was occupied, it usually was named after the nearest village—seldom for a town to be found on any military map.

Fienvillers consisted of a dusty crossroad, one slaughterhouse, a few scattered cottages, an abandoned church, a roadside shrine, and the ubiquitous *estaminet*. The aerodrome itself had been laid out on what had been three small farms which had provided pasture and pickings for a few sheep, pigs, dairy cattle, and flocks of clucking poultry. Most of the sheds or barns were quickly demolished if they blocked the proposed landing strips. What were retained were adapted for storage, workshops, armament shelters, or cover for motor transport. Ancient haystacks were either burned or gradually salvaged to fill paillasses for bedding for noncommissioned ranks. Portable hangars of the Besseneau type, Adrian hutments, and bell tents (later called pyramidal tents by the Americans) created an appropriate background and enabled approaching airmen to recognize the layout for what it was intended. Nissen huts, those most efficient prefrabicated habitations invented by Lieutenant Colonel P. N. Nissen of the Canadian Army Engineers, were not yet available. A circular lime-washed compass-swinging base, and a wind sock floating from the peak of one of the hangars assured the aerial wayfarer that this indeed was an aerodrome, but unless there were recognizable aircraft out on the cab rank, he would have little idea whether he was gliding into hostile or friendly territory.

After their arrival at Fienvillers, Major Grimshaw had everyone scurrying hither and yon to set up housekeeping, and become familiar with their military area. It turned out they were part of the Ninth Wing, commanded by a man affectionately known as "Stuffy" Dowding who, twenty-four years later in World War II, became Air Chief Marshal Hugh Dowding, head of Fighter Command of the Royal Air Force. Also included in the Ninth Wing were Numbers 21 and 23 Squadrons, saddled with artillery-observation or photoreconnaissance, and Grimshaw was immediately advised his new two-seater fighters were to provide close escort for all patrols carried out by either squadron.

"I have been given to understand that Number 23, in particular, is to complete a photographic mosaic of the whole Somme area," he explained to his pilots and observers. "This mosaic will provide maps and information required for a spring push. I take it, too, this offense will be undertaken mainly to force the Germans back far enough to breach their line and allow our cavalry to go through. Well, that's the general idea."

Airmen who had recently transferred from infantry regiments began to whistle softly, probably in unconcealed joy, knowing they no longer were gravel crushers.

Major Grimshaw caught the sibilation, and smirked. "I know what you mean, but Number 23 will have to carry out many contact patrols when the troops begin to move. I should remind you, contact patrols provide the liaison between the front line and the battalion and brigade headquarters. It is important to keep in touch during the inevitable disorganization of other means of communication during the various phases of the attack. But airmen patrolling at low altitude can easily see red flares fired by the infantry—signals to indicate their position, or the extent of the advance, if any. In such cases the observer will mark down the positions of the flares on his map, write down the co-ordinates on a slip of paper, put it in a weighted bag and, swooping down over any HQ, deliver his report. As the attack progresses, the positions of the flares can be given hour by hour. But contact patrols will have to be protected at all times. In other words, gentlemen, we are in for a long stretch of difficult, but most important escort flying."

Kenyon, Laidlaw, and another aerial gunner, Eddie Dougherty, who had been permitted to sit in on this discussion, huddled together in a remote corner of Major Grimshaw's office. Gunners were seldom included in such high-level briefings. Their opinions were never asked, and if tendered were seldom considered.

Grimshaw continued, "Tomorrow, if enough aircraft are serviceable, I intend to take you out, flight by flight, for a general look-see up and down our balloon lines. It will give you an idea of our sector, and help you find your way home again. It will be 'A' Flight at nine o'clock, 'B' just before noon, and 'C' if any of them turn up in the meantime, in the afternoon. I want all observers—and gunners—to make the most of this first show. Keep your eyes and minds open. Is that clear?"

After dismissal everybody scattered to arrange for his comfort. The aerial gunners, with their combined knowledge of how to cope with active-service conditions, took over a slatternly shed which had been a wagon shelter. In a few hours it was converted to a habitable cabin, complete with beds contrived of discarded wing spars, chicken wire, and straw-stuffed paillasses. Engine crates, ammunition boxes and loose lumber were scrounged to make cupboard space and seating arrangements. The aperture that had once been an open window was covered with a sheet of oiled linen in which extra guns had been wrapped for transport.

A discarded domestic stove was cleaned up, dragged in and set in the middle of the compartment. By the time the orderly officer was free to make his rounds, the gunners' shack was a veritable home-from-home, and Dougherty was tacking up pictures of dogs clipped from an ancient issue of *The Sphere*, and admiring his handiwork.

The orderly officer made a cursory inspection and complimented them on the comfort of their abode. When he left, Laidlaw turned on the interior decorator. "Now look here, Dougherty, we don't mind pictures on the wall, but don't bring in any more than one . . . and he sleeps under *your* bed. I know you bloody dog lovers."

"What's all that about?" Kenyon asked as he put his loose gear away.

"You're senior man, Kenyon," Laidlaw explained. "We had one of those dog blokes in our squadron. They're unbearable. In about a week he had collected a hunting pack of the damnedest mongrels you ever saw . . . in our bell tent! These chumps never know when to stop, and not only that he'll expect us to share our rations with them."

Dougherty, a lean, stoop-shouldered man, cringed like a criminal about to hear his sentence. "But dogs don't get anything to eat . . . out here at the front," he pleaded with poignant earnestness.

"Let 'em go up the trenches and chase rats. That's where they belong," Laidlaw bellowed.

Dougherty appealed to Kenyon.

"One. Just one, Eddie, and not a big one, either," Kenyon decided.

"Thanks, Corporal. Just one . . . under my bed," Dougherty replied as though finishing a prayer.

Most of the pilots were out early the next morning, chiefly to give the new Sopwiths another inspection. During the organization period at Farnborough both pilots and observers had had to make the best of anything that would fly, in order to get in air time and some formation practice. A few early Strutters, as they were known, were eventually delivered for organizational flying. One or two bore Scarff rings for the gunners, and some were provided with simple peg mountings. Several had a fixed gun for the pilot that used a Vickers-Challenger synchronizing gear, while others came through with the Sopwith-Kauper system. There even was one Strutter that carried a Lewis gun, mounted on the center-section in the earlier Nieuport manner. Only one model was delivered with a dual-control gear for the occupant of the back seat although, later on, various versions were supplied for in-air emergencies. In general the observer-gunner could take over control by inserting a tubular handle into a pivoted socket located on the right-hand side of the cockpit. With this lever he could actuate the elevator but not the ailerons. For rudder control, a short length of doweling was bolted to one of the rudder cables, and by moving it backward or forward, lateral direction could be acquired. The engine control was a simple lever pivoted on the left side, and was connected to the pilot's throttle.

The Strutter with the dual-control gear had been commandeered by Grimshaw, and since Max expected to be the CO's gunner if Grimshaw led any patrols, he decided to learn something of the device. "Let's have a look," he suggested to Laidlaw. They both climbed up on a wing root and peered down into the depths of the gunner's cockpit.

"How do we work a dual control?" Max asked.

"How the hell do I know? We never had dual control on the B.E."

"But suppose we *have* to use it . . . just in case?"

Laidlaw climbed inside the Scarff ring and gingerly fingered the equipment. "If we get in trouble and have to take over? What a laugh!"

"Well, I mean . . ."

"Now let's suppose your pilot stops a packet." Laidlaw made up his instruction as he went along. "If that happens, he'll probably fall forward on his stick. That would put the bus into a steep dive, and you'll know something's gone wrong. First thing you do is to yank him off his control, somehow, and keep him from falling forward again. Then you fumble about for your stick, get it out of the prongs, stick it in its socket and pull the bloody ship out of its dive. If you panic and yank too hard, you'll pull the blasted wings off, and the rest won't matter. But if she comes out properly, you then have to decide in which direction you're flying and get her turned around toward our lines. That you do by tugging one way or the other on this rudder-cable handle. That's all there seems to be to it."

Kenyon had a suspicion Laidlaw knew more about dual control than he was willing to admit. "But suppose the pilot keeps falling on the stick?"

"Yank the bugger back and fasten him where he belongs with your flying-coat belt . . . to something. Not to the Scarff ring here. You won't be able to swing your gun, should you have to." Laidlaw climbed out and Kenyon took his place on the fold-down seat. He peered over the gun mounting and tried to imagine going through all those motions. "But what about getting down and making a landing somewhere?"

"That lesson will be continued in our next edition." Laidlaw grinned. "You don't for one minute believe this bloody tackle works, do you? Nobody could ever fly a Strutter down to a safe landing with that jumble of old iron. If he did, he'd bloody well *earn* a Victoria Cross." With that conclusion, Bert stepped off the wing root and strode away.

Max sat pondering on the problem. He hadn't the slightest idea how an aeroplane was landed, or what means he should take to keep it from crashing. In all their weeks of organization this possibility had never come up. Still, the cockpit and its primitive equipment fascinated him, and for several minutes he went through a self-taught routine for self-preservation. He was thus engrossed when Major Grimshaw climbed up beside him.

"Morning, Kenyon," his CO clacked. "Getting acquainted with all the works? I shall want you for today's training flight. Better collect your flying kit."

"I was looking over this, er, dual control, sir, trying to figure it out."

"Forget it. None of it is worth the space it takes up. You concentrate on your gun, and our tail. It isn't likely any gunner will have to worry about bringing a wounded pilot back. The whole idea is ridiculous. You'd have to have a complete flight-training course to use it. But don't worry. I'll always bring you home, or die in the attempt." The major displayed his broken crockery grin.

"But couldn't we be given a chance to use it now and then, just in case, sir? I mean, like when we're coming home from a patrol."

"Damn your eyes! Don't you try it when I'm up front! I don't want my controls tangled up with all that ironmongery. Make certain you put it all back out of the way."

"But suppose, sir . . ."

"We've no time now. Better get into your kit. We'll be taking off in a few minutes."

"Yes, sir," Kenyon replied, but felt ticked off and wished the major had a little more confidence in the dual control.

When he was down on the turf again, Grimshaw slapped him on the shoulder. "I want you to be particularly alert on this show. It's supposed to be restricted to our balloon lines, but I might go over a mile or so to get the new pilots used to seeing and hearing

Archie fire. You know, antiaircraft bursts. They'll have to get used to it, and the quicker, the better."

"We'll be going across the lines?" Max pealed in anticipation. The problem of dual control was immediately erased. "Are we likely to see any Fokkers, or anything like that?"

"Who knows? That's why I want you to keep your eyes open, and let me know what's going on all around us. That's one of the chief jobs of the leader's gunner. I shall be relying on you. We're not practice-flying over Farnborough now."

Corporal Kenyon was more than delighted, his earlier pique forgotten.

It was a ragtag collection of Strutters that were warmed up for the first instruction flight from Fienvillers, but the late spring morning might have been ordered. The air was scented with the early wild blossoms that fringed the hedges of the field. The sky was azure blue with only a scattering of languid clouds to give height and distance to the welkin. To the east rose a dark backdrop rung up by the guns and smoke of war, but, nearby, nature was doing her best to welcome the new squadron, and the local world was in song and plummage. In fact, it was hard to believe the war was only a dozen or so miles away. The practice flights over Hampshire had provided more concern than this trial foray over the picturesque valley of the Somme.

The airmen gathered in small groups. Those slated to go were dressed in their new leather equipment, and were adjusting chin straps or the tops of their hip-length boots to the belt that supported their breeches. Those who would have to wait their turn readily helped, or chain-smoked Capstan or Gold Flake cigarettes. The pilots were called to Grimshaw's aeroplane and given a final look-see at his map spread out on the lower wing of his biplane.

"This is where we shall be patrolling," he began. "We'll take off, one by one, circuit the field and get into formation at about five thousand feet. We'll try to maintain a tight show most of the time, but as long as we stay on our side of the line—above our own balloons—we can fly relaxed and make a good study of the area."

Kenyon edged into the select group and saw that the major was pointing to the towns of Maricourt, Mametz, and Thiepval. His finger also traced the long straight road that ran from Albert to Bapaume. He had almost forgotten the general details of the

Allied front as he had known it, and he wished he had a map of some kind so as to keep up with the officers. But aerial gunners were not expected to show that degree of interest or intelligence.

"Well, there we are," Major Grimshaw concluded and folded the chart with finality. "Let's get off and form up at five thousand feet. All clear?"

The leather-clad figures flipped their cigarettes, tightened their coat belts, and plodded off to their mounts. Mechanics in dun-colored coveralls, but still wearing their uniform caps, scurried about the aircraft, pulling the propellers through to loosen up the engines, fussing with the wheel chocks, or fastening the Lewis guns to whatever mount was available.

As Kenyon climbed into his cockpit he noticed two strips of green canvas fastened to the elevators. This was something new, and he called an armorer over to make an inquiry. "What are those bits of . . . whatever it is, tied to our tail-plane?"

The mechanic looked puzzled, and then grinned. "Them? They're your streamers. Major Grimshaw is the leader, so he carries two of 'em. The subleader—that would be Captain Bolithow—will be carrying one."

Kenyon wanted to give himself a boot for being so dense.

"It's like this. If you and Grimshaw are shot down, Bolithow will take over, and the others will form up behind him. Didn't they tell you about that? Cool!"

"All right. I understand. No need to make a Sunday school lesson of it."

The major was saying, "Switch on. Petrol on," and then the prop was snapped over and the Clerget engine began to pop, hiss, and gradually work into a regular sequence of power. Kenyon swung his Scarff ring back and forth, checked his ammunition drums, and finally sat down on the folding seat to await his introduction to military aviation.

Major Grimshaw had no further words for his gunner, and gave all his attention to taxiing out for his take-off. He waited at the end of the strip to make certain the five other Strutters had their engines running and would join the parade. Kenyon, also, assumed the task of making sure they'd have a full formation.

Then suddenly, the Strutter seemed to stiffen from engine cowling to rudder, the Clerget rotary screamed, and Max had to pull his goggles down against the slip stream. The whole aircraft shuddered, and the basic stench of gasoline and oil was brushed away as they roared across the field. The gunner was suffering an unfamiliar tenseness and stress. It was strangely like the first time he dared to swim under water in the pond in West Side Park. It was nothing like the flights at Farnborough. Yet he could not explain this strange concern. That's what it was. He realized, with some inner shock, he *was* concerned . . . frightened, for he had no idea what his pilot was taking him into. It was nothing like the day in front of Neuve-Chapelle when he knew what he had to do and had a gun team to help him do it. On the ground he could pick his cover, his target, and if it proved too hazardous, he could make the decision to lay low or move elsewhere. Here, he was confined within a metal ring, blasted with the slip stream of the propeller, and hurtled through the air at more than a mile-a-minute speed at a height that increased minute by minute. At Farnborough he would sit and study the Hampshire countryside, fire his gun at a fabric target fluttering from a kite balloon, or watch the various panels of control flip up or down. That's all there was to do, unless by luck he could get a gun camera and try his "laying-off" sequences against another Strutter. No one fired back at him, and the aircraft were all the same—that is, they all wore the British blue-white-and-red roundels. He wondered what he would do if they came across something, er, different. Some aeroplane with black crosses on it! Just what was he supposed to do? He'd been told what Fokker monoplanes and Albatros biplanes looked like, and there was something called an Aviatik, and another known as a Rumpler. He was certain he could recognize any of them, especially if they were marked with Iron Crosses, but what was he supposed to do if they came across one? As far as he could remember, no one had ever been explicit about it. He'd been shown how to fire a machine gun and keep it firing. He'd been told about German planes, but he couldn't recall anyone telling him exactly what action to take.

He came out of his disturbing reverie to realize all the aircraft of the flight were already in beautiful formation. He squirmed around in his seat and caught the fluttering streamers on their tail. That prompted him to glance about for a Strutter with a single streamer, which would be Captain Bolithow's plane. Someone in the back seat was waving at him and he decided it could be Laidlaw. So Laidlaw was flying with the subleader.

Ahead and below was spread the cocking main that was to endure the Battle of the Somme. Since Roman times it had provided the stage for dozens of attacks aimed at Paris from the north. The river first flows south from Ham to Péronne, then westward toward Amiens. A few miles before it reaches that city it is joined by the Ancre River, and the country between these two rivers became the Blood Bath of the Somme. It consists of pastoral uplands, broken by shallow valleys, and to make up a nominal landscape nature has provided a number of great wells around which are grouped small villages and towns. Dotted here and there are many woods and copses, most of which were to win grisly fame—Mametz, Railway Copse, Fricourt, Bernafay, Trônes, Delville, Bazentin, and High Wood.

Had Max been provided with a map he might have been able to identify the tragic triangle, the base of which stretched from Hebuterne and Beaumont Hamel in the northwest to Péronne in the southeast. The Ancre cut it roughly at right angles, after passing through the village of Hamel and then turning northeast through Beaucourt and Miramount. This area afforded a wide series of natural defenses, including Thiépval, Mouquet Farm, the Leipzig salient, Ovillers, and La Boisselle. All these points were heavily entrenched and stoutly defended, and many of the key positions were on high ground, enabling the enemy to overlook the British lines. Added to all this was a complicated network of roads that linked important villages.

It was against this complex system that on Saturday, July 1, 1916, the British Army hoped to go to glory and set the stage to end the war.

The Strutter flight took up its introductory patrol at a point south of Méricourt where Major Grimshaw turned north to give his pupils a wide circuit in order to avoid midair collisions. It was ragged, but they were soon back in a V-formation. The major went up to 6000 feet and called to Max. There was no need for Gosport sets since their cockpits were close and convenient. "I want you to notice the balloons just below." He rammed his arm out and pointed to two bulbous gasbags that swung in the wind. "That battered town is Méricourt, the southern end of our line at present. We'll fly along and above the balloon line until we reach Beaumont Hamel. That will be the extent of our battle zone, but of course we shall be expected to range—well, perhaps as far east as Cambrai. That's Cambrai out there. That reddish splotch at the end of that long straight road. Anywhere in there will be our responsibility, so try to remember it."

Max absorbed that and began looking for the balloons as they came within sight. He wondered if the Germans had balloons up on the other side of the line. He peered about, but could see none.

Suddenly, the formation seemed to lose its shape. Max warned his pilot, and then something above caught his eye. Another formation of aeroplanes was streaking past, heading east, and he tried to identify them. They had British cocardes on the wings, but he did not know what they were.

Grimshaw barked, "They're D.H.2s. Single-seater pushers. They're the boys who put an end to the Fokker gunships. I was out on them for a time, but I had a nasty crash." It was the first time the major had intimated he had ever been out at the front.

The aircraft interested Max for he was able to note that they were neat biplane pushers in which the pilot sat in a snug nacelle with the engine at his back. Apparently he had a fixed, or semi-flexible, gun that fired along the line of flight.

There were more aircraft in the air now, all going about their business in a methodical manner, but all keeping smart formations. The landscape below had lost some of its pastoral neatness. Many of the villages had been leveled. Orchards no longer offered their neat rows of blossom-decked trees. The poplars along the main roads had been slashed down to splintered stumps, and here and there the green patches were dotted with patterns of white bursts where shells had bored through the lush topsoil and erupted in the belt of chalk. The effect looked like giant blossoms of cotton wool.

Major Grimshaw made a right turn north of Beaumont Hamel and Max smiled when he saw that instead of completing the circuit and flying back south along the British lines, the major continued on until he could see the swaying outline of a balloon, one with a black Maltese cross on its flabby nose. From this angle, too, he could see the wicker basket that hung below the bag.

"Are we going over the German line?" he asked.

Grimshaw turned his gargoyle face and winked. "Keep your eye on everyone in case one of them panicks when we get some Archie."

Max back-heeled his seat up, and began swinging the Scarff back and forth. He hoped the gesture would warn the other gunners, and he saw the subleader's man carrying out the same preliminaries.

Three thudding explosions burst directly ahead. There was some splintered flame and the lead Strutter danced through the waves of concussion. The major ruddered through the smoke of one and then turned and held his nostrils. He was right. Archie smoke certainly stank.

Max watched for the reaction among the rest of the formation. He saw Laidlaw waving one arm. Then the pilot on the other corner of the back row hoicked over hard, as if trying to avoid colliding with the ball of stink. It was instinctive with Quirks. They always did it during their first few patrols. Max waited for the pilot to recover and rudder back into formation. Instead, he swung wide and barged into another burst of Ack-Ack, and panicked again. This time he banked hard and shot away at speed, passing directly under the main group.

Max slapped his pilot's shoulder. "We've lost Number 4 plane, sir. That is, he has broken off and is heading back toward Beaumont Hamel."

Grimshaw turned and saw the situation. He nodded grimly, and moved to take his formation to the rescue. Max wheeled to check the rest, and then saw to his amazement a monoplane streaking down in a sharp dive with its gun muzzles sparkling. He wondered why Laidlaw hadn't opened fire, but like everyone else Bert was following the runaway Strutter. Max froze stiff. He tried to slap the major's shoulder, but his hand couldn't find any part of the pilot. There was a sharp clatter aft and he saw the taut fabric of the fuselage lose its gloss. White triangles of linen suddenly appeared just forward of the fin, and fluttered in the slip stream. With that, he finally reacted.

The monoplane was very close now, and he could take in the detail of the single wing, the guy wires, the knock-kneed wheels, and the definite flapping of each wingtip. Involuntary action brought his gun into play and Max found himself peering along the black barrel-casing and fingering for the trigger. The Strutter formation was badly disorganized by Grimshaw's sudden turn, and the Fokker came through unchallenged. Then Max fired a long burst while aiming at the engine, and to his amazement saw one wing fold up, flutter wildly, and then remain perpendicular. The Fokker continued on like a flying billboard, then swung madly and skimmed its broken wing away. Max gave it another burst and turned to bellow at the pilot.

Before Grimshaw could react, there was a sharp, nerve-shredding screech and the monoplane exploded and threw a flame-barbed design around what had been the cockpit. Then the Fokker nosed down and began to spin.

"I torched a Jerry!" Max was bellowing. "Look! I torched . . ."

The major took one look, banked over hard and went after the bundle of spruce, linen, and three-ply. He nosed down sharply, fired a long, spraying burst, and almost collided with the hulk of flaming Fokker. Finally, he pulled out, turned and grinned at his gunner. "We certainly put 'Paid' to that bastard, eh?"

"I shot his wing off, sir, and then my next burst made him explode," Max tried to explain.

Grimshaw ignored that and peered about for his patrol. "Where the hell . . . ?" he screamed. "Why didn't you keep track of the others? Where are they?"

For a minute Max peered about, but couldn't see another Strutter anywhere at their level. Then he looked up and saw several were re-forming above, apparently led by a Strutter carrying one streamer.

"Why didn't they stay with me?" his pilot raged. Then he turned and grinned. "Well, never mind. We certainly finished off that bloody Fokker, didn't we?"

Kenyon wanted to clout him with the dual-control joystick handle.

9

Number 70 was lucky on its first familiarity patrol. With the guidance of Bert Laidlaw, Lieutenant Bolithow collected the rabble of Strutters deserted by Major Grimshaw and, with Dame Fortune at the helm, led them safely across the British line. Still gloating over his unexpected encounter with a Fokker E.1, Grimshaw also headed for sanctuary and quite by accident came upon his Number 4 Sopwith floundering around, totally lost in the vicinity of Beaucourt Hamel. Its pilot was much relieved to find another Strutter in the area and quickly tagged on to the twin-streamered tail and breathed a sigh of relief. Major Grimshaw thanked his God for this favor for he was still torn between the thrill of his "victory" over a burning monoplane and the shock of the disorganization of his formation.

"Who is that chump?" he demanded of Kenyon, once the duo had started back toward Fienvillers. "I'll scrag him when we get in."

"I don't know, sir. He is flying Number 4. He has an officer observer."

"Number 4? That ought to be Garland . . . and Tomkins, a misfit from the Royal Engineers. Both of them should be digging ditches with a Pioneer regiment."

Once they were inside their own lines, Max snapped his seat down and pondered on his engagement with the Fokker. He sensed the patrol had been a complete washout and that downing the Fokker had been plain luck. He knew that Grimshaw intended to take full credit for the success, although he could not have put one bullet into the tumbling hulk. It would look good in Grimshaw's report to claim a Fokker on his squadron's first training patrol. He would need something to leaven the report if Bolithow failed to bring the rest of the flight home safely.

Bolithow did his best, but became lost somewhere between the Somme and Ancre, and floundered about over Bray before Laidlaw could identify a route that would take them to Fienvillers. As a result, the bulk of the formation did not get in until minutes after Grimshaw and Garland had landed. By the time they all had run up to the cab rank, the major was fuming and inarticulate.

"We got a Fokker—in flames," he babbled to the recording officer, "and then this cove Garland has to panic when he sees a couple of Archie bursts. God only knows where the rest of them are. I was engaged with the Fokker and by the time it was going down in flames, my whole bloody formation had deserted me, and was kiting back for our side of the line."

"You got a Fokker, sir?" Arundal, a Boer War veteran who had signed up again to get away from a shrewish spouse, inquired timidly.

"No question about it! Went down in flames. Perhaps we can get a confirmation from one of our balloons in the Beaumont Hamel sector. Will you take care of that?"

"I'll do my best, sir."

"I saw him first," Max interposed, despite a glare from his pilot. "I fired one burst into his engine just as he was diving on us. We have a lot of bullet holes down near our tail." That was a revelation to Grimshaw who raced back to find the evidence. Max appealed to Arundal. "He was in flames and with one wing off before Major Grimshaw saw him. Then he went into a dive and fired a wild spray at the burning mess. There was no need to. The Jerry was already going down in flames."

Arundal, a weary oldster who seemed to be held together by his Sam Browne belt, blinked his watery eyes. "Never mind," he concluded, "some of the others will have seen it, I suppose. It won't be well for you to dispute the major's report, you know."

Grimshaw returned, delighted with the evidence in the fuselage fabric. "That swine really put a good burst into us."

"I don't know why gunners in the rear rank didn't see him in time and head him off before he fired a shot," Kenyon said to Arundal.

"I'm glad you tipped me off," Grimshaw added with fake concern. "Gave me a chance to finish him."

"He was finished," Max argued. "I had clipped one wing with my first burst. It was my second that set him on fire—made him explode."

"You leave it to me, Kenyon. I'll make out a proper report on it. You get on to the balloon people, Arundal, and see if they saw the action or have any idea where it fell. Smart, now!"

The old soldier nodded uncertainly, straightened the front of his tunic, and said, "Yes, sir. Immediately, sir."

Grimshaw went off to scrag Garland, as he had promised, but then noted the rest of the formation coming in behind Bolithow. He watched each Strutter make its landing, and then left an order for everyone to report to the recording office.

Max turned his gun over to an armorer with the explanation, "I fired two long bursts at a Fokker, and the drum should be replaced."

The armorer who looked like a small edition of Major Grimshaw, grimaced at the idea of having to clean the gun barrel and check on the ammunition. He grumbled, "I suppose Grimshaw fired his, too?"

"One long burst. About fifteen or twenty rounds."

"Cor! Waste of bloody good Kynochs."

Max started to follow the old sweat to the recording office and then heard Grimshaw bellow, "You get a rest, Kenyon . . . and a light lunch in the cookhouse. I'll take care of the report. We'll be taking off again in an hour or so. I shall want you again."

"Sure he wants me," Max grumbled to himself. "The swine is going to snaffle me out of that Fokker. I just know it."

He slouched off to the gunners' shack, threw off his helmet, goggles, and jacket, and picked up his dixie and an enamel cup. The cookhouse sergeant listened to his request and the reason, grumbled his response but gave the gunner half a can of salmon, a couple of slices of bread, a mug of tea, and slopped a glutinous mixture he called treacle-and-custard into the lid of the dixie. "There you are. That ought to hold you together until you get back. I suppose you'll want another dollop by then. Bloody gunners have jam on it, you do!"

Max glared down at the mixture and retorted with, "Reminds me of the gum-and-gristle poultices my mother used to concoct for ringworm," and then went back to his shack.

When he had settled down, Dougherty came in and started to

sort out his flying kit. "How was your show?" he inquired, and sniffed at Max's meal. "Christ! What's that stuff?"

"We took some slugs from a Fokker, and they use this offal to plug up the holes."

"You saw a Fokker?"

"Only one. I shot it down in flames." Max tried the salmon. Dougherty dropped his jacket. "You had a shot at a Fokker? What was it doing on our side?"

"It wasn't. We went over there, and . . . oh what's the use? I nailed it but Grimshaw's going to claim it."

"Sounds like you all got into a mess. I hope it will be better than that when we go. He's taking the rest of us, you know. I'm down with some bloke who claims he has only done seven hours solo on a Strutter. But what a bloody ramp for Grimmy to do you out of that Hun. That's Grimshaw all over."

Laidlaw came in and tossed his helmet on his bed. "Christ! What have you been up to?" He grinned at Max. "Bloody fine row in the recording office between old Arundal and Grimmy."

"What about?"

"Arundal called a balloon company up the line somewhere. They said they'd seen someone shoot down a Fokker in flames. I take it Grimshaw tried to claim it, but one of their balloon observers said it was shot down by one of the gunners and is reporting it to Wing that way. Grimshaw was nagging old Arundal for calling them up."

"But he ordered Arundal to call the balloon people."

"That's what Arundal said, but the fat is in the fire somewhere. By the way, who *did* shoot it down? I never saw a Fokker anywhere. I was watching our Number 4 plane slithering off for the line."

"I did," Max explained quietly. "I don't know how I did, but there you are. I put two bursts into him, and one wing came off and then he blew up in flames. I showed it to Grimshaw and he went after the burning mess and tried to put a burst in from his front gun. All he did was waste ammunition. When we got back he tried to claim it."

"He hadn't better. The balloon men have already sent in the report with the co-ordinates, and some gunner on the show will get full credit."

"So that was a simple familiarization flight, eh," Dougherty said and picked up his jacket again. "My God, if we ever go offensive."

The orderly corporal kicked open the door, strode in, and bellowed, "Where's Kenyon? Oh, there you are, Max. You're on patrol again with Major Grimshaw in thirty minutes." He stared about the shed. "Who's Dougherty?"

"Here I am, Corporal."

"Same for you. Thirty minutes."

In the next few days Number 70 Squadron gradually worked into the general routine and with two flights carrying the burden until a third could be flown in from England, everyone learned fast with some commendable success. At the same time the friendly association between Grimshaw and Kenyon deteriorated and the American was assigned to the commander of "A" Flight, Captain Ivor MacPartland, who had had some previous experience through 1915 with a photography squadron that had flown B.E.s and Vickers Gun Buses. He was a short, stocky man who favored a comic opera series of uniforms obtained from various unnamed sources. He sported Scotch bonnets, King's Royal Rifles' green trousers, a tunic he claimed was provided by the Lovat Scouts, and various portions of NCO khaki of the Boer War period. He seemed to take any measure to avoid wearing Royal Flying Corps gear.

Kenyon liked him immediately for his unorthodox ways. He was a good pilot and gradually taught his gunner many tricks Grimshaw had never heard of. Together, they became a good team; so capable, in fact, Grimshaw "borrowed" Max whenever he decided to get in more flight time, or to lead a special patrol. All this, despite the fact that since the unpleasantness concerning the Fokker, the major still showed his animosity and treated his gunner like a pariah.

But in due course the cogs of Wing administration geared into train. One afternoon when "A" Flight had returned from an escort patrol between Pozières and Montauban to provide protection for a brace of photography planes, the flight sergeant intercepted Kenyon and growled out of one side of his mouth, "The major wants to see you. Orderly room, Kenyon. Better hop it. He's bloody mad about something. What have you been up to?"

"Who knows? I must have gone on patrol without a shave."

"Well, hop it. Don't say I didn't tell you."

Still dressed in his flying gear, his helmet tucked in a pocket, Max walked through the hangars and clumped up the steps of the orderly room. A corporal clerk looked up and stifled a grin. "He's in there . . . expecting you," he explained, pointing to the door of Grimshaw's office.

"What's this all about?" Max asked in a husky whisper.

"You'll find out. Better knock before you go in. He's like a bear with a sore head, today."

Kenyon took a deep breath and knocked.

"Come in!" the bear in his cave barked.

Kenyon entered and for the first time saw where his CO carried out his ground duties. He was sitting like a khaki statue behind a deal table that was cluttered with the documents and details of his administration.

"You sent for me, sir?"

Almost instantly Grimshaw's mien changed. He grinned, showing his dentistry. "Ah, Kenyon. There you are. How did the patrol go?"

Max was puzzled with the unexpected change of attitude, but reported, "We found the camera planes, sir. A good contact, right on time. We covered them and saw there was a lot of Archie smoke which may blot some of the negatives, but we helped them make a good run over the prescribed area. Once we got them back over the line, we carried out an offensive patrol between Combles and Bazentin, but there was no opposition. Nothing much more than that to report, sir."

"Good. I knew I could rely on you."

"Is that all, sir?" Kenyon wanted to get away from this martinet.

"Well, no." The major tried on another Cheshire cat grimace. "It's something else entirely. About the Fokker we, er, you shot down while flying with me."

"The squadron has been credited with it, I hope, sir."

"Oh quite. I made sure of that . . . and that you received full credit. The balloon chaps weren't quite sure who shot it down, but I made it clear that you had been the first to see and fire at it. I made that quite clear, Kenyon."

"Well, thank you, sir."

"And what's more, I called you in to congratulate you on being awarded the Military Medal for that action. It has just come through from Wing. It will be up in orders tonight. I just wanted to be the first to . . ."

"You put me in for a decoration, sir?"

"Well, not just that way. It was Wing that sent in the recommendation . . . after they had read my report on your smart work on that occasion," the major said with an oily smile.

"Well, thank you, sir. I never expected anything like that. I feel I was very lucky to have seen him in time and to have gotten in a good burst. I was lucky, you know."

"Yes, of course," Grimshaw agreed. "That's the proper attitude to take in these situations. Never try to show how brave you are. Luck always plays a big part. I can tell you . . ."

"Yes, sir. What do I do now . . . about the medal?"

"Oh, of course we do not have the medal here. It will be awarded formally later on, but here's a strip of the ribbon to wear under your wing. You can put it up right away. That's all, Kenyon. Good luck!"

The bewildered gunner took the two-inch strip of ribbon and remembered what Laidlaw had said about the Military Medal. Still, he had something to wear—to show for the experience.

"Thank you, sir. I'm very pleased and proud to have brought this honor to our squadron." He backed away and tried to click his rubber heels, and then saluted.

"Goddammit, Kenyon," Grimshaw raged. "Don't you know any better than to salute an officer when you are not wearing a cap? This is the British Army, not some bloody Hungarian comic opera. The salute is the traditional gesture of the knights of old. It represents the raising of the helmet visor to show you are a friend. If you're not wearing a helmet, how the bloody hell can you raise your visor? It's sufficient to come to attention. That's all. Dismiss!"

"Yes, sir. I'll try to remember."

There was some mild enthusiasm that night when Kenyon's decoration was announced in orders. Laidlaw showed him how to mount and sew the ribbon in its proper place on his tunic, but much of the thrill had been blasted away by the major's unpardonable outburst. At mess that night one or two mechanics slapped him on the shoulder as they passed, but there was no riotous celebration. Laidlaw assured him that everyone would soon get used to it. Dougherty said they ought to give him one so the aerial gunners would all look alike.

"Military Medals," Laidlaw scoffed. "When this bloody war is over they'll be so numerous, civilians will think military tunics were made with the ribbon already sewn on. Same with the officers' Military Crosses."

It was nothing like anything Max had expected, but he went back to his bunk and wrote a letter to his parents, giving some details of his exploit. When he had finished and was licking the envelope, Laidlaw, who was filling in his "Time" book, asked, "Who are you writing to . . . your mother and father?"

"That's right. I think they'd like to know . . . that I'm all right."

"You telling them about your M.M.?"

"Well, something about it, in general. You know . . ."

"Better find out who's the orderly officer first."

"What's that got to do with it?"

"You don't think you can write letters out here and not have them censored? Especially you, after getting a decoration. Old Grimmy will make sure the letter contains nothing about you shooting down a Jerry. That's considered 'secret and confidential.'"

"Jees! Don't you think the Germans already know one of their Fokkers has been shot down?"

"Of course they know, but to us it is 'secret and confidential.' Grimshaw will warn whoever has the orderly dog job to make sure you write nothing of a revealing nature in any of your letters for the next week or so. You must be bloody simple, if you don't know that."

Max tore the letter in two and stuffed it in the stove. "What the hell can you write about? I got a medal, but I can't tell my parents about it. They won't get this news for more than a month."

"Use the standard formula," Bert said, and began brushing his boots.

"What's that?"

"'Dear Mother, please send me two pounds and the *Christian Advocate*. Don't forget the *Christian Advocate*, and tell Dad I won the Military Medal. Your loving son, etc.' That's the only way you'll get it past the bloke who censors *our* letters."

"How do you know all this?"

"How do I know? I once wrote a letter home to my bit of fluff and told her what a bloody fool my pilot was . . . that he didn't know which side of the line he was on, and shouldn't be trusted with a kid's rocking horse. You know what happened?"

"I'm beginning to suspect."

"Right! My bloke was orderly officer that day and he read every bloody word I'd written about him."

"What happened?"

"Two weeks confined to barracks. But of course I still had to do two patrols a day. Two weeks on night guard, after two hours a day of pack drill with full marching order. Wore my feet off almost to my knees."

"But what were you charged with?"

Laidlaw enjoyed a quiet laugh. "Sending improper suggestions through the post—to a young lady. All I said was that I expected to be home on leave in a couple of weeks, and that she'd better get her French drawers washed and ironed. There was nothing about how I'd shown up my pilot."

Max thought that over, and came back with, "Too bad you had all that on your crime sheet. You might have gotten the Distinguished Conduct Medal instead of the M.M."

Laidlaw sniffed and spat at the stove. "Don't you think of anything but medals?"

"What else is there to get out of this goddam war?"

"Write another letter and tell your people what a wonderful bloke your CO is, and how he put you in for a decoration . . . for doing hardly anything. You can catch more flies with sugar than vinegar, chum."

Within another week Number 70 was brought up to strength with the arrival of "C" Flight led by Captain Stuart Saunders. The formation came in neat and tidy, putting on a smart breakaway at the end of the field with each plane taking its place in a tight line-astern, and coming in, one by one, with hardly a machine's length between them. It was a sterling display, and Grimshaw stood fuming, for he fully expected someone to become entangled in a slip stream and rub a wingtip or two away. Nothing of the sort happened. They all touched down smoothly, rolled up to the cab rank and swung into line with no help from the ground crew.

The skipper came up and saluted smartly. "Captain Saunders, sir. Delivering 'C' Flight as ordered. All present and correct, sir."

"You're damned lucky," Grimshaw bellowed. "Don't you know you could have crashed the whole bloody flight, coming in that way?"

"We'd practiced it for more than a week, sir . . . while our front guns were being fitted with the new interrupter gear. I knew the possibility of slip stream, but we actually came in a foot or two wide of its effect. It's hard to notice from this angle, sir."

"Well, don't try it again. I insist on tight formations, but once we get back from a patrol we do not ass around like that, or put on any bloody stunting shows. How do you know whether you have a chunk of old iron through a main spar? Tell me that!"

"I understand all that, sir. I was out here before with Number 7 Squadron, sir . . . Vickers Gunbus."

Grimshaw had to swallow his next outburst. "Oh . . . good work, Saunders. Glad to have you, but for God's sake don't try that nose-to-rudder landing again. You'll have all the other bastards trying it, and there'll be Strutters all over the blasted field. Get your chaps over to the recording office at once and report to Mr. Arundal there. I'll see you later . . . in the mess." By that time Captain Saunders had slipped out of his jacket, displaying a D.S.O. beneath his wings. The major saw the ribbon and turned sharply away.

Number 70 Squadron, now in full strength, did more than its share over the next few weeks to set the stage for the Battle of the Somme. There was plenty of hard fighting, long hours of flying, but less than their share of casualties, although all patrols were carried out well inside the German lines. The new Strutters with fixed front guns and with a well-trained gunner were more than a match for the German Fokkers. Even the new Albatros single-seaters were held at bay. In fact, the aerial gunners more than earned their keep and were most important in gaining the command of the skies in the area of the Somme. The Sopwiths were fast and comparatively nippy in maneuvers, and for the first time British aviation authorities decided to keep records of enemy aircraft destroyed. Previously, such air action was considered to be only part of the day's normal activity.

Envious of the continuing success of the airmen of his three flights, Major Grimshaw felt compelled to lead a patrol at least twice a week, and whenever he became belligerent he always chose Kenyon as his gunner, and the young American's flying time increased much faster than that of anyone else in the squadron. For the same reason, too, his patrol experience mounted for he and Captain MacPartland carried out many "sticky" shows, escorting and guarding the photoreconnaissance teams, or stopping enemy aircraft from taking countermeasures. Considering the few squadrons that faced each other during the early months of 1916, there was much air fighting, and the weather was fairly clement. There was action of all kinds, and Max had engaged dozens of enemy aircraft, but none of his exchanges was as total as his first with the Fokker. At MacPartland's behest he concentrated on keeping enemy aircraft away from the photo or Art-obs planes, and did not always press the fights to their conclusion. The safety of the British aircraft that were providing the information for the Somme show was much more important than an individual victory which could lure them away from their basic assignment.

In contrast, the French and Germans were making the most of the battle victories of their fighting scouts, and the competition in this type of war news was carried to ridiculous lengths. Individual air heroes were dined, feted, decorated; becoming the idols of the Parisian boulevards, or the linden-lined streets of Berlin. They were good copy, not only in their own countries, but in the press of the neutral nations where the dreary details of trench warfare, the frontage of barbed wire that had been breached, or the factors of the day-by-day slogging, no longer interested the reader. A debonair airman, with rows of clanking medals, and the box score of his daily accomplishments, was far more interesting and identifiable, although he was contributing very little to the outcome of the war. The daily progress of the high scorers had no pattern, no vital goal. Millions of other men were engaged in the muddy slots of static warfare, and hundreds of them performed epic deeds of valor daily. They were awarded their country's highest honors, but seldom made important appearances in the world's press. By mid-1915, a winner of France's Legion of Honor, Germany's Pour le mèrite—a decoration established by Maximilian Frederick who could converse only in French—or Great Britain's Victoria Cross, was hardly noticed. But whenever one of these premiere honors was given to an airman, the country's press revolved and delivered column after column of acclaim, praise, and full details of his aerial victories. He may have won the honor while his country's military fortunes were at their lowest ebb, but little of that was included in the citation.

Early one June morning, Wing telephoned that a special photo-reconnaissance was to be carried out by Number 23 Squadron, and insisted they were to be provided with the best of protection. Major Grimshaw promised to lead one of the formations himself. All watches were synchronized between Wing and Numbers 23 and 70 Squadrons, and a memorable day was set in motion.

The commissioned airmen were treated to a typical Grimshaw lecture before he took "B" Flight on the first element of the escort patrol. Captain Melton Standish, "B" Flight's leader, was relegated to the subleader's post, carrying Laidlaw as his gunner. MacPartland and his "A" Flight were ordered to stand by and be ready to take off and relieve Grimshaw's formation at an appointed time. Kenyon and Laidlaw were already out on the line sharing a chocolate bar, when the major led his coterie from the recording office. The two gunners knew, in a general way, what was on the book through a pompous orderly room corporal who usually appeared and slipped them the information from behind the back of his hand.

"You're picking up two camera flights of Number 23 over Mametz," he explained. "They'll be covering a straight line from there to Pozières for a map of the reserve trenches and some new artillery emplacements. It'll be bloody hot, because the area has been given several new Ack-Ack batteries. Don't tell anyone I told you."

Laidlaw tossed his fag away, and spat. "A few more weeks and that bloke will be taking over "Boom" Trenchard's job. He always knows more about what's going on than anyone else on the field. Must have a private line to one of our balloons."

Kenyon snickered. He knew Grimshaw would give him a fair appraisal of the patrol before they climbed aboard, if only to display *his* self-importance. He was right. The major strode up, carrying his flying coat over one arm. It was a new one with a raccoon fur collar and a great display of straps and buckles. He had disposed of his prehistoric crash helmet, having obtained a more modern one with padded earflaps, a fur-lined chin piece, and a brand new pair of Meyerowitz goggles. When he decked himself out in this giddy uniform he looked like a chorus boy out of *Going Up*.

"Well, Kenyon. Here we are again. Probably hoping to pick up another medal, eh? Well, let's see what we can do for you. Should be bags of Huns about." When his gunner made no reply, the major glared and switched to a new tone. "Bloody funny, but the only chaps who get decorations in this squadron are the aerial gunners."

"We seem to fly more patrols, sir."

"Laidlaw has a Military Medal, too."

"He got his before he came to Number 70, sir."

"I don't care where he got it. The point is, he has one."

"He has probably done more front-line flying than any man among us."

"But only as an aerial gunner."

Having spat that jet of venom, Grimshaw took up the matter at hand. "We're covering a photo flight of Number 23. This is a very important show, so keep awake, and let's keep our mob together if we run into any opposition."

Kenyon refused to be drawn in, and climbed up into his cockpit. "Don't worry. You can rely on me. I'll take you up there . . . and I'll bring you back."

"You're the driver, sir."

"Well, don't forget that. What Captain MacPartland can do, I can do equally as well, and perhaps better," Grimshaw said and turned up his fur collar and settled himself while the engine was being started.

"Oh, so that's it," Max reflected, realizing the CO resented the general impression that he and MacPartland had become a very tight team; that MacPartland was a first-class flight leader and was certainly on his way to a majority as soon as an opening permitted his posting back to England.

While they were waiting for all pilots to signal their readiness, Max allowed himself the pleasure of wondering whether he would ever get enough time to be considered for a commission and pilot training. He had heard of such heavenly arrangements, but only by hearsay, or concerning some unknown in another squadron. There was a fellow named McCudden, for instance, who had gone out in 1914 as an engine mechanic, but who could also handle a wireless set, and was said to be able to blow the bugle for reveille. Someone had said McCudden was a sergeant pilot now, but who wanted to be a *sergeant* pilot? A commission was the thing. Along with his yearning for medals, Max was also developing a concealed air of snobbery. To get anywhere in this war, one had to be an officer and wear an officer's uniform. As far as he knew only officers had been awarded the Victoria Cross.

10

The patrol got away with little trouble and assembled over the aerodrome. The weather still held, contrary to general experience when clear, balmy weather that marked the take-off would turn into a sudden rain-slashed tornado the minute they approached the lines. There was some watery sunlight, but it was clear enough for photography; a few wispy clouds and very little wind.

"All right," Major Grimshaw barked over his shoulder. "Whip 'em all together, and let's give the B.E. boys a show."

Max stood up, glanced back at the rest of the flight, and swung one arm in a circular motion. One by one, the Strutters moved in tighter until they presented a picture-book formation.

"Very good, sir," the gunner reported and sat down again. He kept his eyes open and his mind alert and saw they were heading for the open country between Méricourt and Mametz. He caught the movement of men and transport in the Allied area below, and between glances back at the formation tried to examine the hostile ground beyond the stylized design of trenches. He studied communication lines and searched for any indication of activity prior to the dawn. This usually could be traced by the wheel tracks or evidence of foot streaks through the dew-laden grass. These tracks often betrayed earlier activity involved in digging new gun pits, strong points, or temporary storage dumps.

Maxwell Kenyon was becoming progressively clever at noting and reporting these tracings, and he was encouraged to make out his own patrol reports which went to Wing along with those of the commissioned airmen.

"Here we are!" the major yelled.

Max stood up and looked forward. Ahead, in a neat three-plane

V, the photography B.E.s hovered together like weary geese, searching for a lake shore on which to settle for the night.

The gunner turned back to his formation and held his hands out to catch the attention of the pilots, and then swung one arm over and pointed downward to the machines of Number 23 Squadron. He completed the message by cupping his hands around his goggles as a photographer would drape a black cloth about his head to peer into a camera. When he turned back to the aircraft below a white Very signal streaked up from the lead aeroplane and spluttered its welcome.

He next turned his attention to his gun, assured himself it was loaded, checked the exact position of each extra drum, and flipped the Norman wind vane sight to make certain it would respond to any change of aim he made against the direction of flight.

His pilot flung one arm over his cockpit coaming and once more caught his gunner's attention. "They're starting their photo run. Let's give them plenty of cover."

Kenyon nodded and turned back to his rear. He waved one arm back and forth until the five Strutters spread the V wider. His pilot eased back on his throttle, fingered the air-adjustment lever to compensate for the reduction of petrol, and in that manner reduced his speed to keep station above the slower camera planes.

Remaining on his feet, Max kept a sharp lookout to his rear. These escort shows were always dull, since the camera aircraft were seldom harried while the defense aeroplanes were in position. He received a wave from Bert Laidlaw and turned his attention toward the other side of the V.

The B.E.s were maintaining a steady run almost due north toward Pozières on the Albert-Bapaume road. The lead aircraft would photograph the first strip and the observer in it would fire a green Very signal when his run had been completed. They would then turn, traverse a parallel strip with a second plane taking up the assignment, and in that manner cover the required ground, and have the third plane on hand for any emergency.

As soon as the two formations began to run north, it was obvious to observers on the ground or aboard kite-balloon baskets what the intention was. In opposition, Jerry Ack-Ack guns began to belch and flash their venom. Oily blobs of smoke appeared, spat splintered flame, and the concussion made the photo planes dance, the intent being to cause them to tilt left or right, thus throwing the lenses of the cameras off line . . . as much as half a mile or more, depending on their altitude.

Grimshaw watched the gossamer-winged B.E.s waver and flutter. He shook his head in mock despair, knowing that someone would later have to return and pick up the missing segments of the mosaic. Max also noticed this and pondered on the possibility that they might have to go out again later in the day. He had no objection, knowing that every patrol he flew would add valuable hours of time over the line. A complete reckoning would be most important if he ever got a chance for a commission and to take pilot training. He'd have a posh flying coat, one with a fur collar, and the absolute latest in flying helmets. Not one of those old bags dished out to aerial gunners.

Despite the opposition, the B.E.s plodded along, and the Archie fire suddenly died down, leaving only stringy designs of soot across the pattern of the landscape below. Automatically, Max turned to his brood and to his astonishment saw the Strutters had broken their V and were carrying out a wild exchange of machine-gun fire with several fish-tailed Albatros C-III biplanes. He was dumfounded for an instant, but took up the cause and fired a short burst at one of the enemy two-seaters. The clatter aroused his pilot.

"What's going on?"

Kenyon saw Bert Laidlaw pouring a long burst into the engine of a C-III, and was rewarded by a long plume of smoke pouring from the cowling. Kenyon picked it up as it shot past his own wingtip, and the smoke scarf became a tattered pennon of flame.

"Watch out! Watch out!" Grimshaw screeched. "There'll be single-seaters in the area somewhere. These buses are only blinds. Keep your eye on the B.E.s."

The gunner understood little of what his pilot was saying; he was too busy swinging his gun from side to side, and triggering short bursts whenever a target came into view. He saw Laidlaw pouring a splintered streak into the nose of an oncoming Albatros until his pilot yanked their Strutter up in a tight turn. Kenyon saw something flash below the melee and decided it was a Fokker monoplane that was diving for the photo-plane formation. He slapped Grimshaw's shoulder and pointed down past their own leading edge. "There goes a Fokker, a single-seater! You take him and I'll watch our tail."

The Strutter nosed down hard and Kenyon was slapped back against the Scarff ring. Tracer bullets were making a silvery pattern of geometric designs, and there was an unfamiliar vibration somewhere in the fuselage. Max stared about and saw the rest of the formation engaged in short duels with the Jerry two-seaters. There was no discipline or order. Nothing but confusion. Nothing definite to pass on to his pilot. Then suddenly, the lead Strutter jerked into a more frantic dive, but so far Grimshaw had not fired his gun although they were screaming past the Fokker monoplane.

Kenyon turned to his front, still handling his gun and swinging the mount. With that, his goggles began to fade and when he rubbed the lens he realized he was being sprayed with a dark fluid. He flipped them up and sensed that a scarlet liquid was being scattered over his chest and one glove. He sought the source and saw that Major Grimshaw had fallen forward, and there was a short perforation across the back of his flying coat.

Still, the steep dive continued, and they shot through the photo formation. Two stark faces peered at him from one of the outer B.E.s What in hell was Grimshaw doing? He couldn't be diving away from the Albatros group. Like a thunderclap Max realized what had happened. Grimshaw had been hit from somewhere off to the side. Some Jerry gunner had caught him with a deflection shot. That accounted for the torn flying coat and the blood. But they were still in a wild dive and in a few minutes . . . seconds . . .

"Got to get him off that joystick," Kenyon resolved, amazed at his sudden calm. "That's all I have to do. Get him off the joystick, and keep him off it."

He curled one hand under Grimshaw's head and hauled him back in his seat. As the wounded man was steadied against his seat cushion, the Strutter came out of its dive and assumed a normal flight line. Max decided the pilot was still holding onto the stick.

"Don't let him fall back," he continued with Laidlaw's ritual, and holding the pilot with one hand he unbuckled the belt of his own flying jacket and looped it about Grimshaw's neck and then through a fuselage strut. He stared into Grimshaw's face and realized he was out cold. He was snuffling and twin spurts of scarlet mist spread across Max's sleeve. Even then, he felt no immediate concern, although he was alone in that smoke-streaked sky. He carefully bound the major into a secure sitting position. Blood was seeping through his scarf and there was a small trickle from one corner of his mouth. His feet were stamping on the three-ply flooring of the cockpit. Max was relieved to see he was not jamming the rudder bar.

"I wonder how badly he's hurt. I know he's been hit, but where and how badly?" Laidlaw came to his assistance again. "You find the stick and try to get it in the socket, and pull the bloody ship out of its dive." But the Strutter was flying perfectly level, all by itself. "I can't stay up here like this, just flying anywhere," Max concluded. "I'd better get her turned around for our line. Let's see, where are we?"

He lowered his seat, sat down and fumbled for the dual-control lever. He jammed it into the floor socket and immediately sensed that any forward or backward movement brought a response from the nose. But what should he do next? Off to his right he caught the gray ribbon of the Albert-Bapaume road, and directly ahead was the battered spread of Pozières. "I've got to make a turn there . . . somehow," he whimpered, but when he moved the stick the Strutter only nosed down or climbed. He wished Grimshaw would come out of his unconsciousness and take over. He, at least, could use his rudder. Rudder? That was it. What was it Laidlaw said? He peered about the interior of his cockpit and his eye caught the piece of doweling bolted to one of the rudder cables. He snatched at it anxiously, and the Strutter began a flat turn to the left . . . in exactly the right direction. The shuddering turn continued until he could see the Albert highway racing along under the leading edge of the lower wing. When it began to swing too wide, he moved the dowel handle forward again and the aircraft nosed around once more until the road below took up its earlier sweep and flowed straight under the wing.

Max released a sigh of relief and then suddenly saw that the plane was much lower than he had ever been on this part of the front. Now, there was plenty of antiaircraft fire to remind him of his altitude, and he wondered if he should climb to a safer level. Strangely enough, he felt secure and unconcerned about his height and decided to stay where he was until he had passed Albert, now only a few miles ahead. By that time Major Grimshaw would probably pull out of it and take over.

He looked around in the manner of an aerial gunner, but there were no enemy aircraft nearby. He could see the smoke trail of an aeroplane of some kind twirling down toward the ground, and he wondered . . . and hoped Captain Standish would have realized what had occurred and have taken over with his single streamer. He also hoped the smoke trail didn't mean one of the B.E.s had been shot down, but it could be . . . either that or a Strutter.

The thought did not come to Max that he was aboard an aircraft that was plunging on to its own destruction; that when the wreckage was found no one would have the slightest idea what had happened. If it was not totally consumed by fire, it would cause wonder why the pilot had been shackled back clear of his controls and the gunner had seemingly been trying to put the dual-control gear into operation. But if it burned . . .

Max sat there, one hand on the metal tube used for a joystick, the other on the small piece of doweling that actuated the rudder. Just what was he expected to do from here on? He got to his feet and had another look at Grimshaw, but the pilot was still snorting, wheezing, and showing little evidence of returning to consciousness.

The flattened profile of Albert with its cathedral on which the statue of the Virgin still stood erect, passed by and he was able to peer over the edge of the cockpit and view the activity below. The streets were alive with military traffic and men in khaki. He could see the waterfall of the Ancre and the narrow-gauge lines that ran from the west side of the town toward Doullens and eastward toward Peronne. It was the proximity of this battered town that aroused his first shudder of fear. The nearness of the streets, the church of Nôtre-Dame-Brébieres, and the distinct banks of the Ancre reminded him that he somehow had to get this Strutter down . . . unless Grimshaw regained consciousness and relieved him of the problem. Terror jerked him to his feet again and he tried to arouse his pilot, but he was still limp, and his cheeks had taken on a distinct pallor. While he shook and tried to appeal to Grimshaw, the Strutter, with no hand on the stick, began to nose down and flounder into a shallow turn. He left the wounded man, sat down and took over the two-handed device and brought the aircraft back on an even keel. His lips and mouth were dry, and he twitched with the tightness of his viscera. He half-believed Grimshaw was dead, or certainly dying, leaving him in midair to work out some manner of getting the Strutter down safely.

"What do I do?" he bleated, and peered about for an answer.

"When do I shut off the engine to make a landing?" In his confusion he felt deserted; that Grimshaw was playing a macabre trick on him. But in the link motion of his mind he felt his responsibility for the major. There was no way of deserting him, but how was he to get him down safely? "Where should I land? If I try to get all the way back to Fienvillers, he might die from loss of blood. Perhaps I'd better try to get down somewhere where he can be taken care of, a field hospital or even an advanced dressing station. If I can only find something with a red cross on it."

Max pondered further as the Strutter approached the British balloon line. "It would be easier to get down at Fienvillers," he said out loud to himself. "I've always sat in this seat and would be remembering every turn, the glide angle, and the relationship to recognizable objects . . . the edge of the wood, the height of the trees, and those two moldy haystacks. I could use all those to guide me in, and if I can only . . ." But getting down was still the killer.

He continued in this disturbed frame of mind for several minutes, and then spotted an area he recognized, but couldn't remember the name. A mile or so ahead was a collection of marquee tents, a long wooden shed and a park of ambulances. The whole complex was dotted with red crosses daubed on white-circle backgrounds. On the other side of this road ran a reasonably wide stretch of turf. A perfect haven to deliver Grimshaw for there would be doctors, nurses, medical and surgical aid. The major, bastard that he was, was entitled to that. But Max had no idea how to slow down the Strutter, and he had never realized before how beautifully the Clerget engine ran. How the hell did one stop it?

He fumbled and tried to remember what Laidlaw had told him. His thumb came in contact with the small throttle lever partly hidden on the rudder-control side. He had forgotten about that little gadget. He twiddled with it and discovered it moved back and forth. "But where's the air-adjustment lever? There's only this throttle. The blasted engine will conk out completely if I try to run it on the throttle alone," he argued with the unconscious Major Grimshaw.

He knew there were one hundred ways of killing himself, or winding up a basket case. But something had to be done. He experimented by forcing the little lever forward and the rotary eased down to a more subdued tone. The propeller sheen broke into blurry segments of brown and yellow. He watched this magic wrought by the tiny throttle, and jerked when the engine gave off a series of staccato pops. He tried to remember what this popping-back indicated, but by the time he had come to the logical conclusion, the propeller slowed to a halt, went into some silly business of wigwagging back and forth, and finally stopped completely. Before he could draw back the lever he sensed he was gliding past the field hospital layout, so he instinctively rammed the stick forward with the idea of landing as close to the hutments as possible.

The Strutter was floating along like a gull heading for a spit of sand, making no noise of any kind. Then, for no reason, she stuck her nose down and went into a steep dive. None of his pilots had ever approached a landing strip at such an angle, so he drew the stick back and the plane took on a more reasonable attitude. While he wondered what to do next, there was a slight rumble below, a modest bounce, and the Sopwith settled down to a gentle roll along the grass, but still stayed parallel with the road-way.

Kenyon could not believe his eyes. He looked over the edge of the Scarff mounting. There was solid earth—grass, some early daisies, and a flutter of birds. The Strutter was standing stock still. He had somehow brought it in and made a safe landing. Taking no further chances, he stood up, reached into Grimshaw's cockpit and snapped off the switch. He shook the major's shoulders, and with amazement in his voice half-whispered, "We're down, sir. I got her down . . . somehow."

The wounded man made no reply, so Max reached down into his cockpit and found his Very pistol. He selected a red cartridge, aimed the blunt-nosed gun skyward and pulled the trigger. The sizzling ball arched up, spluttered its warning gleam and broke up, but it was enough to arouse the screech of a Klaxon horn mounted on top of the long wooden shed. Max unbuckled his belt that was restraining the wounded man and belted it around himself. He climbed out on the wing root and once more tried to get a response from the snuffling pilot.

"Come on, sir," he begged. "We're down at a hospital. They'll take care of you, but you've got to climb down, sir." He shoved up the major's goggles, and the gesture caused him to open his eyes.

"There you are," Max said with mild cheerfulness. "You frightened me, sir. I thought . . ."

Grimshaw blinked twice, shook his head lightly and allowed streaked saliva to drool from his mouth. He muttered, "What's . . . matter? You're all blood, Kenyon . . . You hurt? I didn't . . . ?"

"No, sir. It's you . . . your blood. You've been unconscious all the way back."

"Bloody lie!" the major whispered and struggled to a more erect position.

"Positive, sir. I had to land us with the dual-control gear."

Grimshaw shook his massive head again. "No! No!" he gasped and choked on another gush of blood. "You can't fly . . . a . . . Strutter . . . with dual-control gear. What are you trying to . . . ?"

"But I did, sir," Kenyon was saying as a voice from below the gun mounting broke in. "What's wrong here? Someone wounded? Let's have a look."

A Crossley tender was chugging nearby and several Royal Army Medical Corps men with Red Cross discs on their sleeves were unfolding a stretcher and opening a bag of first-aid supplies. One of them climbed up on the other wing and stared across at Max. "Which one of you is wounded? You're a fine-looking mess."

"It's not me. It's my pilot. His blood sprayed back over me."

The RAMC men seem puzzled and then saw that Max was struggling to get his hands under Grimshaw's shoulders to hoist him out of the seat. One of them unsnapped the safety belt, and wasting no time or tender care, dragged the inert pilot over the edge of his cockpit and manhandled him down to the stretcher.

"Where'd you stop this lot?" a medical sergeant demanded. "He's got half a dozen slugs through his back and shoulder. Christ! What a packet!"

"We were escorting photography planes just beyond Mametz."

"Are they still doing that?"

"A flight of Albatros two-seaters barged in, and we had to drive them off, but my pilot was hit and fell on the joystick. We went down in a steep dive, but I managed to pull her out . . . and bring her in. I was lucky, I guess."

"You know, sir," the sergeant said as he cut Grimshaw's coat to ribbons to get at the bullet punctures, "they give out Victoria Crosses for shows less than that."

Max sensed the RAMC sergeant took him to be an officer, and grinned his pleasure. "I suppose you can have our squadron advised and explain the extent of my pilot's injuries."

"Happens all the time, sir," the sergeant said and bared the major's shoulder. "We get one of these twice a week, but it's usually the other way round. The pilot brings in a wounded observer and leaves him with us. We've buried half a dozen of them, just over there behind that . . ."

Grimshaw struggled under the blanket thrown over him. "Can't fly a Strutter . . . with the dual-control gear," he tried to argue. "Shoulder pained, but I brought her in. Told him I would."

The sergeant soothed the patient, dabbed at his wounds, looked up and winked. "We'll see your squadron is advised, sir."

One of the medical men bathed Kenyon's face with a wad of gauze, and sloshes of witch hazel. "You sure you're not hit?" he asked again. "Christ! We get some lovely smashups at times, but we've never had an observer bring a bus back after the pilot was knocked out. How did you manage it?"

"I can hardly remember now, but I got it down, somehow."

The medical corps man grabbed Kenyon's shoulder and poked him in the chest. "You'd better. You heard what your pilot said. He's not responsible, of course, but he thinks he landed the bus. You'd better start putting it down on paper—full details—while you can remember. He'll argue that you were pulling a dummy. If you expect to get credit for bringing him in, you'd better have it all down in black and white."

Max felt faint. "But I'm only an aerial gunner. He's my CO. Major Grimshaw of Number 70 Squadron. He'll explain the whole thing when he feels better. He'll have to make out a report . . ."

"You're an aerial gunner?" He unbuckled Kenyon's flying jacket and saw he was wearing a ranker's tunic.

"Just a corporal."

"You poor bastard. If your bloke lives, he'll swear he brought *you* home, although he was badly wounded. He'll make a hell of a story of it. You don't think he's going to let you get all the glory while he lies in bed . . . losing his seniority, do you?"

"Climb up on that step and take a look. You'll see I had used the dual-control gear to fly it back. I had to tie him up to keep him from falling over the stick. He didn't come to until I landed and unbuckled him."

"He wasn't buckled when we got here," the RAMC man said, as though talking to himself.

"I unbuckled him. Look, here's my belt, still out of the loops. It's covered with blood. How would his blood spread all over my back?"

"I believe you, chum, but if your bloke lives, there'll be some hanky-panky."

"I wouldn't be surprised. The first time I went over the line with him, I shot a Fokker down, but he tried to claim the Hun. He almost did me out of my Military Medal. When it came through, he claimed it was his report about me that had persuaded someone at Wing to recommend me for it. That's the kind of man he is."

The RAMC man became confidential. "One of those, eh? There's one on our lot. Can't get enough ribbons up. He'll take them from the French, Russians, Belgians, and even the Italians—after some poor bloody stretcher-bearer wins 'em. The bastard would wear the Iron Cross, if he could pinch one off a Jerry prisoner."

"Do the other Allied armies give out decorations . . . like that?" Max allowed his mind to wander.

"Never mind them. There's only one worth having. If there's an investigation, and anyone asks me, I'll tell 'em what you said, and how you said it. But you're a poor bloody NCO, and you won't stand a chance if your pilot tells his version of what happened. If you've got your napper screwed on right, you'll write down every detail just as it happened, and keep at it until they send for you. Write it down, and *remember* it word for word. You'll be questioned over and over until you won't know whether you were flying or poling a punt at Maidenhead. You put on a V.C. show, chum. Don't let the bastards do you out of it!"

11

The RAMC orderly brought Kenyon a dixie of stew, a large mug of tea and news that his squadron was sending a pilot over to fly the Strutter out. By late afternoon Captain MacPartland and two mechanics arrived aboard a light lorry. Kenyon was leaning on a lower wing, industriously writing out the details of his terrifying patrol with Major Grimshaw.

MacPartland was arrayed in a pair of tartan trews, heavy rubber galoshes, a dark-blue turtle-necked sweater, and a peaked cap that bore the badge of the Argyll and Sutherland Highlanders, although he had been gazetted from the Royal Scots Greys. "Well, what happened to you?" he inquired, first with some concern and then with a grin when he saw that the aircraft seemed to be in fair condition. "Anything for a picnic, eh?"

"Major Grimshaw was wounded. We were on the photo-escort show, you know, sir."

"But what happened?"

"He stopped a packet, and fell on the joystick—unconscious. We went into a steep dive and I had to pull him off . . . tie him back with my belt, and get the dual-control gear together."

MacPartland went to the side of the fuselage and peered into the rear cockpit. "You mean to say *you* flew it—with the dual control?"

"I had to. He was unconscious all the way back, and didn't come to until I had the bus down on the ground, here."

"You flew it back and landed it?" the captain squeaked in disbelief.

"Max started from the beginning, telling exactly what had happened. He showed his bloody belt, his book of notes with most of the time brackets.

"But we were told he had been wounded during a fight with

two-seaters. We lost one of the photo-planes, by the way, and another Strutter flown by Ken Branscombe. They went down in Hunland."

"Major Grimshaw didn't fire a shot. He was hit early in the mix-up. He didn't come to until I unbuckled him. I suppose I brought him around, but he had no idea what had happened. When I tried to explain I had flown back on the dual control, he went into a rage . . . and well, practically called me a liar. But I did, sir. I flew it back and landed it here because I saw all the red crosses."

MacPartland shook his head and glared toward the field hospital. "The trouble is, his version has already gone to HQ. Let's get aboard. I think we can fly out of here. But when we get back to Fienvillers, leave everything to me. Don't talk about any of this to anyone. You understand?"

"I think so, sir."

"Don't even think. Leave it to me."

The mechanics were pouring a few five-gallon cans of petrol into the tank and beginning the engine-starting sequence. Chocks were set in front of the wheels. MacPartland climbed up and gave the Clerget a good test run-up. Quite satisfied, he signaled to Max to get aboard.

"Leave that dual-control stick in just where it is, but don't touch it when we are in the air. Don't touch anything, and when we get in remember what I said. Leave the explanation to me. I'll do my best, but we may be a bit late to head off Grimshaw's report."

Max got aboard, set out his cockpit in shipshape order, latched the gun down secure, and made certain the one spent drum was tucked away where it would not interfere with anything. The chocks were removed, and MacPartland turned the Strutter around and taxied back as far as space would allow. A mechanic held an outer strut while he spun her again and faced down the full stretch of turf. Making the most of the Sopwith air brakes to increase the incidence of the wings, and with judicious use of the adjustable tail-plane, the pilot got her off the ground in a comparatively short run and headed for Fienvillers about twelve miles away.

Max sat ruminating all the way in. He sensed he had been out-rageously lucky to have brought Major Grimshaw back without in-flicting further injury on him, but there was a leaden dread that none of his claim would be believed, and that the word of a pilot of field rank would be accepted as gospel. The maddening part was that he had no idea whether Grimshaw in his pain actually thought he had heroically brought his aircraft and his gunner back to their own lines, despite his serious wounds. Max knew that was possible, and that men under great physical stress accept their hallucinations as solemn truth and insist on their acceptance. If that was so, he had a degree of compassion, but there ought to be some way to bring the actual truth to light.

He had no answer for the problem by the time Captain MacPartland was circling the field at Fienvillers, and when they were down and running up to the hangar's tarmac, his morale and trust in luck were at their lowest ebb. Several pilots and observers were on hand, including Bert Laidlaw who moved out and waited until the armorers had removed Max's gun and collected the drums from their brackets.

"Don't touch that dual-control gear," Captain MacPartland warned from the wing root. "Everything about it is to be left as it is, until I order otherwise." He joined Kenyon who was leaning against the side of the fuselage, because he suddenly felt limp, weary, and on the fringe of complete exhaustion.

"I want you to go straight to your digs. The cookhouse if you're peckish, but don't talk to anyone until I give permission." The captain turned and saw Laidlaw approaching. "Ah, Laidlaw, I want to talk to you. Get into the recording office and wait until I can round up Captains Standish and Saunders. I'll be acting CO until someone comes along to take over. You, Kenyon, buzz off to your quarters."

Bert listened to it all, looked puzzled, and spoke directly to Max, "You all right?"

"I'll be all right." Max moved away at a weary pace. For the first time in his life he wished he had a glass of something strong, something like the hot whisky-and-lemon his mother used to make when he had a cold. He could go one of those right now. Once inside their shed, he slipped out of his flying coat, threaded his gory belt back through its loops, and hung the coat on its peg. He took off his helmet and was almost nauseated when he saw how much of Grimshaw's blood was still streaked along both earflaps. He looked around for Dougherty, but the dog lover was nowhere in sight.

In the recording office Captain MacPartland was interrogating Bert Laidlaw. The aerial gunner stood like a prisoner in the dock.

He glared from Captain Saunders to Captain Standish who had also been tagged for the conference.

"That's your general opinion of Corporal Kenyon," MacPartland said as kindly as he knew how. "What we want is an unprejudiced view, the one down deep inside you. Objectively, what do you think of him?"

"May I ask what this is all about, sir?" Bert parried for time. Both Saunders and Standish shared his discomfort, for neither hardly knew Kenyon.

"I'll explain when we get some idea of what you, and any other gunners, think of Kenyon as a man, as a member of a Strutter team. We've got to get to the bottom of a very unusual situation that may mean a lot to him—one way or the other. Now then . . ."

Laidlaw tried again. "As a corporal, sir, he is senior gunner, but he doesn't take advantage of his rank. But there're only three of us, and we get along very chummy."

"Go on."

"When I first knew him I didn't really like him. I think I expected he'd be one of those American blusterers, but he wasn't, and after a week or so we forgot he was an American. But, of course, his father and mother are English like us, and I suppose it comes through, like."

"Does he have any distinct likes or dislikes for any of the officers?"

Bert hesitated, and then in a burst of explanation said, "He likes you, sir. He thinks you're a bit ragtime and easy to get along with. I don't mean to insinuate . . ."

"Quite all right. He has me down pat." The captain chuckled. "What about the CO, Major Grimshaw? You needn't be afraid to speak out. None of this goes down on paper."

Laidlaw cleared his throat. "Well, while we were organizing at Farnborough he seemed to like Major Grimshaw. They had flown together on anti-Zeppelin patrols with Number 19 Squadron. Grimmy, that's how we know him, had a crash one night and Kenyon came out of it with a broken arm. Still, he was pleased to know Major Grimshaw had arranged for him to join him in Number 70 Squadron. Max seemed quite proud about that."

Saunders and Standish took an interest in the proceedings with its minor revelations, and both lighted cigarettes.

"But when he felt that Major Grimshaw had tried to do him out of that Hun, and then declared it was he who put Kenyon in for his Military Medal, Max said he was glad he was flying with you, sir. What he meant was . . ."

"We see your point, and remember the incident."

Laidlaw suddenly remembered Max's interest in decorations. "I perhaps shouldn't say this, sir, although it's nothing against the man, but Kenyon is a bit of a pot-hunter. He craves medal ribbons. Most of us can take 'em or leave 'em. Still, he was done out of a decoration when he was wounded at Neuve-Chapelle and his machine-gun officer, who was nowhere near the action, got the DSO. Max wound up with a Mention in Dispatches. He sold out about it several times."

MacPartland glanced at Saunders and Standish, then turned back to Laidlaw. "It's nothing against him as long as he doesn't overdo it. You know that Major Grimshaw was wounded today and lucky to get back into our lines."

"We heard about it in a roundabout way in the hangars, and I was wondering . . ."

"It has aroused an interesting . . . well, a very knotty query. The major was badly wounded. So much so, Kenyon claims he fell on the joystick, putting the aircraft into a steep dive."

"So Kenyon used the dual-control gear, and pulled her out!" Bert broke in. "He's always been interested in that wonky gear, and the possibility of flying the plane if his pilot was ever wounded. Is that what happened?"

"We don't know. When Grimshaw was brought round at the field hospital, he claimed he had pulled himself together, determined to get Kenyon back safely, put the bus down near a field hospital, and then he passed out."

"What does Kenyon say?"

"Just the opposite. He claims he put the dual control together, got the plane out of its dive, turned it for our lines, and managed to land near where he saw a lot of red cross sheds. You can see what we're up against."

Laidlaw frowned. "If Kenyon said that, I believe him."

"You mean you'd sooner believe Kenyon than Major Grimshaw?"

"In this instance—yes, sir."

"A few minutes ago you said he was a pot-hunter. Couldn't he have used Major Grimshaw's condition to make up a story of his own heroism?"

Laidlaw rubbed his chin reflectively. "I see your point, sir. It is a knotty problem. Major Grimshaw once tried to do Kenyon out of a Hun, and a medal. Now we have a reverse situation where Max could do the major out of a decoration, for devotion to duty, and bringing a plane back safely. I wouldn't like to have to decide a situation like that."

"Well, whatever happens, bear with me. I've got to drive to Wing and explain this situation. I believe Kenyon brought the bus back and landed it. If I can make Wing believe it, he'll get a V.C. No question about it."

Laidlaw looked as solemn as a bloodhound. He wagged his head. "But they won't, will they, sir?"

MacPartland clapped Bert on the shoulder, but avoided the aerial gunner's eyes. "I wouldn't like to make the decision, either. I think I'd be deciding for the squadron, not Kenyon. Well, get along with you, and remember none of us repeats what was said here. Thanks for your help, Laidlaw."

"But you'll do your best for him, won't you, sir? I believe Kenyon brought the Strutter back, and I hope he is given the Cross. I don't think I could have used that silly dual-control gear and brought her home, but Kenyon would have done it, just to prove to old Grimmy he could. That's the sort of bloke he is, sir."

When Laidlaw kicked the door of their shed open, Kenyon was stretched out on his bed, his tunic and flying boots were off, and smelled of cheap perfumed soap. Dougherty had gone out with "C" Flight to help Number 23 finish their interrupted photo patrol.

"Any news on Grimshaw?" Max asked.

"Not much. He'll probably be all right. In the meantime your bloke, MacPartland, is acting CO. Sounds like you had quite a tea party over the line."

Max sat upright. "You didn't think that dual-control gear would work, did you? Well, it did . . . lucky for me."

"You tried it?"

"Didn't MacPartland tell you?"

"Just told me to make sure you got a rest, and some supper, in case you had dossed off. He's going to Wing to talk about running the squadron until someone else comes out from Blighty to take over."

Max looked puzzled. "He didn't say anything about me bringing the bus back and landing it near a field hospital, so I could get aid for Grimmy?"

Bert wagged his head, went over to his bed, took out his towel and soap box preparatory to washing up before supper. "Nothing about that. You'll probably be off flying for a couple of days . . . to get your breath."

"I'm telling you, Bert, I flew that Strutter back. Grimshaw was out, all the way. I did as you suggested and tied him back with my flying-coat belt. Take a look at it. It's still covered with blood. Grimmy's blood. I don't know how I landed it, but I didn't even burst a tire. When Grimshaw came to he didn't know where he was, but he swore he had flown the Strutter back and landed it, to make sure I got back safely. He's either out of his mind, or a blasted liar."

Bert waited at the door to hear Max out. "If I were you, I'd forget it. Would you put your head on the block for eighteen pence?"

"What are you talking about?"

"That's all it's worth. The Victoria Cross is made out of old bronze cannon captured in the Crimean War, and with its ribbon and clasp is actually worth one and sixpence. Don't expect too much, and remember R.F.C. blokes usually have to snuff it to win one. Be satisfied you got back alive, no matter who flew the bloody bus."

The next morning turned up dud, and no jobs were listed until early afternoon. The orderly officer made his rounds and found Kenyon rewriting and revising his patrol notes. Admiring the comfortable quarters, he made a passing remark on how lucky Max was to have gotten back from the photo-escort show the day before. "I note, too," he added, "that you're off flying for three days, but you may have to pick up machine-gun instruction later this afternoon if the dud weather continues. The orderly room clerk will advise you."

"Thank you, sir," Max responded tonelessly and sat down again.

Dougherty arrived with a pooch he had bought for five francs in the village. It was a pure mongrel with several breed lines of rare disparity. Still, it was a lovable animal and tried to climb on Max's lap.

"What's new out in the hangars?"

Dougherty shook his head and retrieved his pet. "Nothing much. They're going over your bus, checking the spars, and replacing some of the engine wiring, and chiefly swabbing it down to get all the blood cleaned up. Old Grimmy must have bled like a stuck pig."

"Gallons of it."

"Then someone has had to go to Saint-Omer, or somewhere, to pick up a new Strutter. We lost Mr. Branscomb, you know. No one seems to know what happened, except that he went down in a spin and didn't pull out."

"So did we, almost," Max said glumly, "but I managed to pull Grimshaw off the stick and get everything straightened out."

Dougherty stroked his pet for almost a minute, and then said, "Yes. It's all over 'A' Flight's hangar. That is, they're all talking about it under their breaths and saying you ought to get a V.C., or at least a D.C.M."

"Who the hell wants a D.C.M.? Distinguished Conduct Medals are given to bakers if they turn out enough loaves and the Maconochie stew doesn't poison anyone above the rank of lance corporal."

"I'll take a dozen. There's a grant of twenty pounds with the D.C.M."

"What do they give with the V.C.?"

Dougherty pondered on that. "As I remember reading somewhere, you get an extra sixpence a day pay and a pension of ten pounds a year—as long as you live, but it will be continued to your widow until she remarries. But, of course, you're not married, are you?"

"C" Flight, led by Captain Saunders, a former London bank clerk, streamed away to carry out an offensive patrol between Courcelette on the Bapaume road and Combles to the south. At about 8000 feet they came upon a flight of Albatros C-III two-seaters, and a rare old battle ensued. Saunders handled his flight well, and instead of immediately turning to work his way toward his own lines, he banked boldly and went deeper into Hunland as if to cut the Albatri from their own reserve area. The German leader became suspicious and presumed Saunders had offered his flight as bait and that a formation of de Havilland 2s would be lurking above.

While the Jerry leader was making up his mind, Saunders struck and broke up the enemy formation, and with that, the fight became a series of individual scraps in which the British gunners, using the efficient Scarff mounting, played havoc with the Albatros machines. Two were torched and another went corkscrewing down with one wing bay folded back over the tail assembly.

Bert Laidlaw got the first flamer, and Jeremy Louden's Vickers gun torched the second. Bruce Headley, a religious Canadian who used ammunition as though he personally was paying for each round, fired the burst that fractured a Jerry's wing panel, and then followed it down until it crashed on the sugar factory near Montauban.

There was quite a celebration when "C" Flight returned, and even Bert was invited into the officers' mess to have a drink to "wet" his first Hun. When he returned to the gunners' shed, he found Max morose, and little inclined to talk.

"They're having quite a free-and-easy over there," he said to Max. "Wouldn't be surprised if they all get drunk. Somebody handed me a whisky that almost took the top of my head off. I'm a beer man, myself. Couldn't stand much of that Charlie-Friskie."

Max made no reply.

"Oh, and when I was leaving, your bloke, MacPartland, said he wanted to see you—orderly room, first thing in the morning."

"What's that about?"

"How the hell do I know? He has been up to Wing, so I suppose he has something to tell you about old Grimmy."

"I've heard enough about old Grimmy."

"I must say you're in a pleasant mood. You'd be better off going on patrol instead of moping here. What about a walk down to the village? It's not too muddy, and we're running out of candles."

"Better than nothing. Let's go."

Captain MacPartland was standing over the corporal clerk's desk, dictating something official when Max walked in. The clerk looked up with a blank stare, and as enthusiastic as though he had been typing his own obituary.

"Ah, good morning, Kenyon," MacPartland said with even less enthusiasm. "Pop into the major's office there, will you? Be with you in a tick or two."

The cubicle was austere, lifeless, bare of comfort, and typical of most office accommodations on the front. There were a trestled table covered with an army blanket, and a seat made out of a spare-parts crate. A field telephone occupied one end and the rest was taken up by fans of flimsy forms, logbooks, a Crossley hub cap used as an ashtray, and a shallow cardboard box that served as a file for official papers. The four walls had little to offer but a row of rusty tenpenny nails which could be used as coat pegs. A map of the 1914 front, published by the *Daily Mail*, and given to subscribers, was tacked on a side wall. On the opposite side a part of a Haymarket Theatre poster, filched from God knew where, hung dismally with an upper corner curled down. A dusty window with one pane replaced by a sheet of tin looked out on the row of hangars; as dismal a scene as one could imagine. There was nothing in the office to encourage daydreaming or inspire memories of seashore holidays or breath-taking views from a mountain pathway.

Kenyon had just enough time to wonder whether attaining field rank in the Royal Flying Corps was worth such a hovel, when Captain MacPartland slouched in with some papers and an envelope in his hand.

"Sit down, Kenyon, will you? I won't keep you a minute. Take that ammo box there, eh? We don't go in for luxury, as you can see."

Max drew the Kynochs box up in front of the table. The captain scrawled his name to the bottom of two orders, shuffled the papers together and slid them into a buff-colored envelope.

"Well, there you are. That's it," he said and tossed the wad toward the aerial gunner.

Kenyon waited for further explanation.

"Well, I have some good news for you, and some I know you will resent. And I'll have to agree with you, Kenyon. I think we, the squadron that is, have been treated deplorably."

"What's the good news, sir?"

"Well, you're going back to England . . . Oxford, I presume, for a commission and pilot training."

"Already? But I've been out here only . . ."

"You'll see it is Wing's idea of making you feel better. Here are your warrants, leave papers, and five hundred francs which I must list in your Pay and Mess book. You have it with you?"

Kenyon looked bewildered. "I'll get it, sir. It's in my kit."

"Now, about the other business . . . about bringing Major Grimshaw in. I did my best, but Grimshaw's word was accepted against yours. I believe you flew the Strutter back and put it down where he could get immediate attention, but someone at the field hospital filed Grimshaw's garbled report, dressed it up considerably, and signed it. All we had was your claim that you had . . ."

"But I did, sir. On my honor, sir. I used the dual-control gear and flew the Strutter back." Kenyon protested.

"I know, I mean, I believe you Kenyon, and I think it unpardonable to deny you—and your squadron—the highest award that could be proposed. But my hands were tied. What could I do?"

Max lunged at the opening. "That's what I wanted the Cross for, sir. To encourage all other gunners. As for myself, it really doesn't matter," he heard himself saying, and wondered what had inspired such a deceitful statement. "It would have been wonderful to have been written into the squadron's history. Still, I'm glad about the commission, and becoming a pilot, sir," he said dolefully.

MacPartland wished Kenyon hadn't given himself away in that manner, but it concurred with what Laidlaw had said. He *was* a pot-hunter. He continued half-heartedly, "I retrieved some of it. You're getting a D.C.M., if that is any satisfaction. We don't have the ribbon here, but you can buy a strip when you get to London. They have all that sort of stuff at Burberry's in the Haymarket. Put it up as soon as you get home."

Kenyon listened to all this verbiage, positive Wing had used Grimshaw's mendacious claim of self-sacrifice—heroism—in bringing his gunner back safely, although seriously wounded himself, and had ignored his report that he had accomplished the unbelievable; had done his best to get immediate aid for his unconscious pilot. He figured the squadron would get its V.C.—old Grimmy would get the blood-red ribbon.

MacPartland was saying, "It's not much, but it's another ribbon to go alongside your Military Medal. We're all proud of you, and no one out here can ask for more. We can't make public what you did, and the D.C.M. and its citation will carry the usual 'Devotion to Duty' . . . no actual details of valor or heroism. It's too bad, but there you are."

"What did they award Major Grimshaw, sir?"

MacPartland shook his head. "Nothing. They couldn't palm you off with a D.C.M. and then give Grimshaw the Cross . . . or even the D.S.O. He'll get a wooden one. Major Grimshaw died last night. He was badly wounded."

They sat looking at each other in silence, and finally Max said, in order to get to his feet, "I'm really very sorry. Poor old Grimmy never did have much luck, did he? I would have liked to have gotten that Zeppelin for him, but it wasn't our night."

"I know what you mean. Better get your gear packed. There'll be a tender outside at ten o'clock. I've arranged to have you taken direct to Boulogne which will avoid a tiresome train journey. All I can say now is 'Best of Luck!' We'll be watching for you when you come out again. I think you have a bright future . . . and there's still time to get that V.C."

Kenyon shook hands with the captain but could not think of an answer.

12

The trip across the Channel was fairly comfortable and more gratifying than the previous one, after he had been wounded at Neuve-Chapelle. He was unencumbered by injuries or a heavy kit bag as all his NCO gear, including his British warm, had been turned in to the quartermaster. He carried his merest necessities in a haversack. Also, he could preen with his observer's wing, the ribbon of the Military Medal and a wound stripe of gold on his sleeve. He felt as much a fighting man as any aboard the steamer, regardless of rank or length of service. In contrast, it never occurred to Corporal Kenyon that he was being spared what proved to be one of the bloodiest campaigns of the war, and that while the infantry and a handful of R.F.C. squadrons were slogging through the blood bath of the Somme, he would be basking in his first taste of university life at Oxford, wearing K-boots, Fox puttees, Bedford-cord breeches, an officer's tunic, and a stripped-down Sam Browne belt. Only the starched white band on his cap would reveal his intermediate status as a Cadet.

But before this military finery could be obtained, there were certain formalities and tangles of red tape to unravel. On his arrival in London, he had first to exchange his French currency for British. His next stop was at Burberry's where he had the red-and-blue ribbon of the D.C.M. stitched in its rightful place on his jacket. He decided on a military haircut, a swagger stick, and a pair of pajamas, a luxury he had not enjoyed before.

At the Hotel Cecil, which had been taken over for Royal Flying Corps administration by the Air Board, he reported in and was turned over to a supercilious sergeant who appeared to have little time for aerial gunners who aspired to commissioned rank. He was a tall, anemic grouch who dabbed continually at his needle nose with a soggy khaki handkerchief. His uniform showed nothing that would indicate he had ever been more than two hundred yards from the Thames embankment. He spoke to Kenyon as though the aerial gunner were at the other end of some telephonic connection.

"Your train got in several hours ago, didn't it?" he demanded while staring out a nearby window.

"About two hours ago, to be exact. I had to get a bed and something to eat at the Ensign Club. I came straight here from there."

Dewey-nose ignored the explanation. "Slack . . . very slack. Now let's see, you're Corporal Maxwell Kenyon, M.M., I presume. By the way, why are you sporting the D.C.M. as well? Nothing in your papers here about a D.C.M."

"It came through only yesterday, and I was ordered to put up the ribbon on my arrival in London. I just obey orders."

"Highly irregular. Can't put up decorations without proper authority. You may have to take it down until written authorization comes through."

"It should be in my papers somewhere. I had to leave in quite a hurry."

The sergeant took to his handkerchief. "Typical of those ragtime squadrons out there [sniff, sniff]. Improperly dressed most of the time, wear anything they like and put up decorations [sniff, sniff] of any sort."

"Not much money, either," Kenyon commented.

"This is no time for levity. You're posted to Number 1 T.D.S. at Christ Church College, Oxford. That's a ground school. You're due there July 16th which gives you two weeks' leave. A ridiculous waste of time, that. I shall want your address in the meantime."

"Make it the Ensign Club. I have nowhere else to pack in."

"Ensign Club will do as long as you stay there. When you get to Oxford you will take down your corporal's stripes, wear a white band on your cap—they will be supplied—and as soon as possible order a Cadet uniform. All the best tailors have representatives in Oxford, and that should give you no trouble. But remember you do not wear the shoulder strap of the Sam Browne belt until you are actually commissioned. That clear?"

"What do we use for money to buy this gear?"

"You will get a twenty-five pound allowance which should cover all necessities."

"Twenty-five quid will just about buy a tunic, a pair of breeches and a trench coat. It won't cover a British warm, or non-issue flying kit."

"You'll have to make the best of it. You're only a Cadet. Now here's your railway warrant . . . Third class . . . and you'd better get to Oxford early enough to report before 10 A.M. There's no ragtime procedure at Cadet school. You'll have to smarten up."

"See you on the barbed wire," Max quipped and backed away.

"You bloody aerial gunners! More cheek than a wing commander."

"There're no decorations for the meek, Sergeant."

"Bugger off!"

The next two months at Oxford provided another facet in the colorful career of Corporal, now Cadet, Maxwell Kenyon, D.C.M., M.M. His tuition absorbed amid the towers, spires, and quadrangle of Christ Church College was a startling change from the grim, explosive battlefields of the Western Front. He was berthed in what a few months before had been the halls, private rooms, and dining areas of young gentlemen of the upper class. While not so comfortably furnished as during the early years of the century, they were luxurious to one whose martial education had been obtained in the dugouts, trenches, and field kitchens of Neuve-Chapelle, Sutton's Farm, and Fienvillers. Oxford still offered the atmosphere of prewar academics. Dons and professors cycled from class to class, wearing caps and gowns. The streets were alive with students determined to complete their terms before donning khaki of the Officers Training Corps. There was a youthful social order in which young ladies decorated the tea shops, reclined in punts poled into secluded backwaters of the Thames, or added summer gaiety to The High, or the bosky dells of the countryside. All this keyed Maxwell to what he had missed by being denied the pleasures of Princeton.

Some of his companions swotted diligently at their studies. Some, who had transferred from regiments on active service, made the most of the semi-scholastic life, but managed to squeak through when examinations were faced. Kenyon resented the ease with which Cadets, who had volunteered from Canada, Australia, New

Zealand, South Africa, and even the United States, had obtained their commissions. Few had seen active service of any kind, but had applied for Cadet rank in the Royal Flying Corps while civilians. They had arrived in England bearing expensive luggage, tailor-made uniforms, polished field boots and luxurious foot lockers to note with disdain that their British cousins who had already served many months in infantry regiments, or had done a stint as aerial gunners in the R.F.C. still wore the service khaki, hobnailed boots, and made the best of their haversacks or shoulder packs. This class distinction, set up by the Empire troops, had to be endured until Cadet allowances were forthcoming, and little could be done about it until the flight-training courses established equitable leveling processes.

Kenyon was quickly bored with the first few weeks of Cadet training, but had sense enough to slog away at what seemed unimportant subjects, such as map reading, Morse Code, aircraft rigging, interior economy, and muscle-wearying hours of physical jerks. He showed keen interest in aero engines, and handled that subject with ease. His skill at drawing was a great help, but most classes were typical of the "parrot fashion" formula for learning, and he gradually realized that what he had learned in grade school in Newark had been more fundamental than what he would ever learn in a university. In the primary grades, instruction was based on continual drill, not listening to a teacher repeat details that were copied in notebooks, and later recited and remembered only long enough to get a marking.

He was only mildly respected by his instructors, most of whom were "windy" NCOs who had evaded active service on various pretexts and felt uncomfortable trying to instruct a young man who had been through a period of trench warfare, and had been awarded two decorations in air action. He made few friends among his Cadet associates, for none was of his original social level, and most of the Canadians and Americans seemed to have volunteered direct from college or university campuses. The British youngsters huddled in clannish groups, as had their forebears in Norman or Saxon days. They seemed uncommunicative and impassive, but over the weary weeks of training, proved to be most substantial in their friendships, and intensely eager to learn the background of the others.

At first Kenyon spent most of his few evenings off exploring the college town, and browsing in the bookshops on the side streets. Then he gradually adopted the habit of dropping in at certain pubs or modest hotel bars where he savored a gin-and-ginger, a fairly innocuous mixture of Hollands and ginger beer. Drinking for the sake of fitting into a social circle, or to assuage an inner craving in no way interested him. He had seen enough of those doubtful pleasures and their influence on his parents. Sitting in *The Mitre* with his tall foamy glass, he reflected on his slatternly background and quietly rejoiced in his escape from South 10th Street. He heard only now and then from his parents whose letters were pointless comments on what little information about himself he had been able to write them:

> We are glad to know you are fine and well.
> So you are now in the Royal Flying Corps.
> Yes, it must be very cold up at that height.
> We do look forward to your letters.

Never anything more; no details about how they were doing; whether work was plentiful; whom they had met and talked to. Just wearying confirmation that they had received and read his last letter.

In his glummest moments Max tried to envision a future where there was no war, no military service, no uniforms, no steady income. The idea of being relieved of his enlistment oath and resuming civilian life oppressed him. Assured by his youth, he no longer considered the possibility of being killed or seriously maimed. His secret fear was that of being taken prisoner, for since leaving home he had enjoyed a comparative freedom. He had no routine job to perform or stern taskmaster to demand he complete all chores for a stipulated wage. His parents no longer had a voice in his comings or goings, and what was paid to him was completely his own. According to his present viewpoint, his service life had relieved him of all family responsibilities, provided a life of epic adventure, and had rewarded him handsomely—even though he had been scuttled out of the Victoria Cross. Taking everything into consideration, he was enjoying a degree of freedom that would have been out of the question, had he still been slaving at Milligan's. Freedom had became something of a fetish, and he dreaded the possibility of being restrained behind Jerry barbed wire.

While considering this doleful future, he riffled through several theater programs he had kept among his "souvenirs" and suddenly remembered the dancer he had admired in *Chu-Chin-Chow*. He discovered her name was Dido Maitland, and he found himself repeating it over and over and with it a desire for female companionship.

Max's Cadet training was carried out during the late summer of 1916 when the British Army was still slogging on the Somme. He had no idea what to make of the news from France, for the scope of the campaign was too much for his imagination. He still had no concept of the length of the fighting line, or how many men were involved. Like so many others of his age and intelligence, the overall war news as presented in what newspapers had been available at the front was beyond comprehension. He knew only what the headlines stated, and was incapable of interpreting the reason for the ebb and flow of battle. What war news he read, related to the heroics of certain regiments, the description of a bayonet charge, or the puffed-up details of how the latest V.C. had won his decoration. The tactics and strategy of battle, the organization of divisions, or the political background of certain military decisions were just lines of type. As many others of his stripe and youthful concept, he was interested only in his own particular organization. In France he had had no idea to what Wing Number 70 Squadron was assigned, or what Army Corps they were supporting. He had never heard of General Sir David Henderson, "Boom" Trenchard, or Captain Murray Seuter. As for the opposition, they were simply labeled Huns. Baron von Richthofen had not as yet been identified, but a blustering character, known only as Immelmann, was being credited with every epic event on the German side. He was even honored for conceiving an aerial maneuver that had been standard in all air shows several years before the self-styled Eagle of Lille had even learned to fly.

Kenyon ignored the reports of a new military vehicle, cryptically known as a "tank," and the contradictory stories of its success at a place called Flers. This report was soon erased by rumors of new aircraft that were being produced for promised campaigns planned for 1917—if the war lasted that long. One was said to be a new Sopwith that would replace the darting Pup. Another was being built around the Hispano-Suiza engine, and would be used for high-altitude fighting—something unique in the fighter field—which would replace the Sopwith 1½-Strutter. These vague reports left him in a perplexed frame of mind, for it had not occurred to him that he might have a choice of mounts, once his training was completed. Would he apply for single-seater scouts, or two-seater fighters? Even when he had completed his gunnery course at Grantham, he still had no idea what he wanted to fly.

Early in September a small contingent of Cadets was selected from the group that had passed the Grantham machine-gun course, and ordered to pack their gear and be ready for posting to a Training Depot squadron being organized at London Colney. The field was a few miles southwest of St. Albans, and not too far from the Radlett golf course. On the way down from Grantham, Max realized he had been included in a particularly industrious group that had shown up well at Oxford, and during the gunnery course. They arrived about midday one Saturday, and were accommodated in wooden barracks which had been hurriedly constructed early in the war. They were soon assigned to special flights and placed under three or four instructors. The aircraft used were chiefly B.E.2c's that had seen considerable service during the early days of flying in France and Belgium.

There was another group of trainees, said to be "Colonials," but proved to be a mixed bag of Canadians and Americans who had volunteered in Toronto. It was also rumored that most of them had been through a flying course aboard something called a Curtiss Jenny, a mysterious American aircraft few Britishers were acquainted with.

"I've heard of a spinning jenny," Max reflected, "but isn't that something used in the weaving industry? Seems my father used to talk about spinning jennies."

"No telling what the Yanks will come up with," a disinterested Londoner said, and began flipping the pages of his *A.B.C. of Aviation*.

After the initial period of getting settled, Max decided to make contact with this North American contingent in the vague hope he might come across someone from New Jersey. Most of the Americans in the group were a few years older than he, practically all were graduated from Yale, Harvard, or Princeton, and their class distinctions were immediately made clear. Some showed mild interest in him because of his wound stripe that denoted some front-line service. His decorations, however, drew a complete blank. None could grasp how a non-commissioned man had been allowed to fly and earn an observer's wing with an active-service squadron. They had not heard of two-seater fighters, or the role of aerial gunners. With this bewilderment only mildly settled, Max's association with his upper-class countrymen was ended.

Only one, a heavy-set Canadian of untidy appearance, noted Kenyon and caught his background. The interest was not particularly friendly or sympathetic, for Ralph Wallington was something of an outcast himself. But he made the most of the fact that he was already commissioned, a point he thought would impress a lowly Cadet. Wallington had had difficulty in making friends in the R.F.C., chiefly because he was congenitally a clod. It was not so much his personal appearance and careless dress, but his social behavior. Although he had been under the eye and discipline of half a dozen drill sergeants, none of them had been able to make an impression on this uncouth man. His American associates had early booked him as a "slob," a derogatory term not so lightly used as today, and most held him at arm's length.

But the flabby-mouthed Canadian had one quality that erased all his liabilities. Ralph Wallington could fly. In his teens he was allowed to own a motorcycle, and his family always had several automobiles which he soon learned to drive with youthful skill. At his father's plant there were trucks of all types, and Wallington, Jr. could tool them about the logging camps as well as any of the teamsters. In the Wallington timber empire there were horses to be broken and ridden, while the streams, lakes, and waterways of Alberta gave Ralph every opportunity to develop his skill aboard canoes and light sailing craft. These activities gave him that enviable touch deemed necessary for the handling of military aircraft, particularly fighting scouts. All of which explains why this uncouth, untidy young man was to become the most skilled airman of his group.

Ralph Wallington adopted Maxwell Kenyon with no questions asked the minute he realized what Max's decorations represented, and there were a few days when he actually tried to "posh up" his uniform and ape the American's daily turnout. Then too, Wallington noted that this young aerial gunner was drawing considerably more pay than any of the Cadets from Toronto.

"Ah, but you see I now get six shillings a day flying pay, in addition to the base Cadet pay of ten shillings a day," Max explained. "My flying pay continues whether I am with a front-line squadron or not."

"Jesus Christ!" Ralph gasped. "You're not yet commissioned but you're drawing nearly twice as much a week as we who are."

Max enjoyed the situation and grinned. "Well, I *am* a trained observer, and I had to gain my observer's brevet over the enemy line. You can't get those in a flying school."

Ralph mulled that over, and decided Max would be well worth cultivating. Money was always an important item in Wallington's life.

"That extra dough must come in handy when you go on leave. By the way, what do you do about leave, here in England? Your home's in the States, isn't it?"

"Newark. That's in New Jersey. I have been using the Ensign Club in London, but that is only for noncoms. I shall have to find a hotel that is open to officers when I get my commission. As a Cadet, I'm neither one thing or the other."

"I was given to understand Flying Corps guys can move in with any of the chorus girls from the threatical crowd—no trouble at all," the Canadian said with a broad leer.

"I wouldn't know. I've never had any close associations with chorus girls. All that has to wait until I put up my first pip," Max said, but thought Wallington might have a point, and he wondered about that dancer . . . Dido Maitland.

"When do you expect your commission?"

"In my case, as soon as I'm properly settled here, and show any ability in the elementary training school. It can't come too soon for me."

"Swell! We'll go up to London together and have a binge to wet it, the day your pip comes through. What do you say?"

"It's a deal," Max agreed.

13

As a training depot, London Colney was decidedly unlike most other instruction establishments in that those men who planned the complex and laid it out seemed to have lost track of what was intended, shortly after the first hangar had been erected. By the same token, the various groups of trainees who, for the previous few months had been restrained in tightly knit wings and squadrons, discovered on arrival at any TDS that most shackles had been severed, and they now moved about under the impersonal type-written directives tacked up in their mess, lobbies, or lounges. Gone were the bellowing NCOs and screeching instructors. No longer did the students move from lecture to lecture in strict military formation, at the double.

In smaller, loosely knit parties they sauntered to the hangars for dual-control instruction, or attended lectures on related subjects. Some classes were devoted to the Wimperis bombsight, the gun-interrupter gear, map reading, aerial photography, or the identi-fication of enemy aircraft. In odd hours fragmentary instruction in the observation of infantry and artillery ground movement was given to fill in free periods between flying hours, lunch, or when inclement weather interrupted the aerodrome routine.

All this flexibility of instruction was pleasantly new to Kenyon, and it was refreshing not to have to conform to the apoplectic demands of a sergeant major or a disciplined time schedule. It required several days for this simple program to have any effect on his earlier training, but he gradually relaxed and enjoyed the casual tempo. "You live and learn," he said philosophically. "I had no idea how I had been regimented."

The routine orders pinned up in the Cadet mess lounge every evening showed that Kenyon and nine other Cadets were slated for flying instructions at Hangar "A" every morning. There were three instructors commanded by a light-duty major who had, so it was said, been shot down in enemy territory, but had escaped by slipping through the barbed wire into Holland. No one seemed to know any of the details, but had to be satisfied with watching Major Jillick limp about with a glossy blackthorn stick. However, he sported a dingy D.S.O. ribbon, so it was generally accepted there must be something to the story.

Major Jillick addressed the group once and urged them to have confidence in their instructors; by all means learn how to remedy a Number 3 gun stoppage; and stressed the importance of having their visiting cards properly embossed and of the correct dimensions. He then dismissed them and resumed his hourly trudge up and down in front of the hangars with a droopy-eyed basset hound at his heels. That apparently was the extent of Major Jillick's responsibility at London Colney.

Two months later he was cashiered out of the service for establishing carnal relations with a young chambermaid at the George and Dragon Inn in Radlett.

The Cadets were given their first logbooks and shown how to enter their flying time. Next, they were introduced to a B.E.2c biplane, and had their memories refreshed concerning the joystick, the controls, and then shown a general layout of the field, and had the rules of the air explained for the last time.

Kenyon, Wallington, and a young English Cadet, Christopher Roland, were turned over to a Lieutenant Brasenose, a veteran of the 1915 campaign. A cadaverous, hunched-shouldered man, he was even more disreputable in his general appearance than Wallington. He gripped a Congo briar pipe in one corner of his mouth with determination, but never bothered to light it. He apparently drew comfort from the well-chewed stem.

"Well," he opened, after introducing himself in what had once been a cultured university accent but had become a pit-bull growl, "so you temporary gentleman want to learn to fly. So did I once, but I have gotten over all that, and for your information, I have applied for a transfer to the new Tank Corps. There's no future in flying. See that broad mossy area up on that hill?" He turned and pointed across the aerodrome. "Most of you will wind up there long before you learn to put a B.E.2c back on the ground. That's our cemetery. However, it's up to you. Do as I tell you and you may live long enough to get it over Douai or Poperinghe. I know. I've been there, and I was bloody glad to get back. For my nine months of service, I was rewarded—not with a Military Cross but with a sentence of six months of instructing Quirks how to fly a B.E.2c. That I'll do, but once you go solo, you're on your own. Then I wash my hands of all of you."

By this time he noticed Kenyon standing at ease, still wearing his noncom R.F.C. uniform. He strode over to him, peered at his gunner's wing and ribbons. "Well, what have we here?" he said as though he had caught an offensive odor. He removed his pipe and spat. "What the hell are you doing here?"

"I was assigned to you for flight training, sir."

"Where did you get those?" Brasenose growled and shoved the salivary stem of his pipe against Max's decorations.

"I was an aerial gunner with Number 70 Squadron, sir."

"I didn't ask that. I know you must have been an aerial gunner. Where did you get those two ribbons?"

Max had no idea how to answer the uncouth question. "They came through in squadron orders, sir."

Brasenose appealed to Wallington and Roland. "You see what instructors are up against? I asked a very simple, reasonable question, but in reply I get a most revolting example of false modesty." He bellowed at Kenyon: "What did you get them for? What valorous action? How many bloody Huns have you shot down? I want a straight answer. You're wearing the goddam ribbons. Tell us how you got them!"

Inwardly seething, Max tried to compile an answer to the outrageous questions. "I don't exactly know, sir. I didn't write the recommendations. I downed several Huns during my time out there . . . and I was able to bring my pilot back—he was badly wounded —from well behind the lines, using the dual-control gear of a Strutter. My flight commander recommended me for . . ."

Brasenose removed his pipe again and glared into Kenyon's eyes. "You flew a Sop Strutter back on the dual-control gear? You must be Jesus Christ. Have you tried walking on water?"

Max wisely refused to be drawn.

Brasenose strode up and down again before his three students. He had worked himself into an unjustified rage. His eyes flashed and there were flecks of saliva at the corners of his lips. He clenched one hand and pounded the palm of the other. "What am I supposed to do with one so naturally gifted, so gleaming with gallantry and valor? I'm not sure I'm capable of teaching such a paragon the fundamentals of aerial navigation. Goddammit! What is expected of me?"

"I suggest you turn me over to another instructor, sir." Max had found his voice again. "I suppose it could be done this early in the course."

"Oh no you don't! You're my pupil, and you're staying on my list. Who knows, you may be able to teach me something," Brasenose bellowed and wiped the saliva across the back of his hand. "By the way, what's your name?"

"Kenyon, sir. I was Corporal Kenyon before I became a Cadet."

"I see. Not only had you won two decorations in the field, and gained your observer's wing, but you had attained the lofty rank of corporal. We *are* among the mighty!"

"Is that all, sir?"

"It's more than enough for one morning. I'll take someone of lesser prestige, first." He glanced at Wallington. "You're one of the Canadian contingent, I take it."

"Second Lieutenant Wallington, sir. I've had nine hours on a Curtiss JN-4, but that's all."

"Oh, my God! There must be someone I can teach something. What about you?" he growled, poking his pipe stem at the slim-hipped English lad. "What is your particular forte?"

"I'm straight out of Charterhouse, sir. Only a short period of O.T.C. My name is Roland, sir. Christopher Roland."

"Thank you, Roland," Brasenose said, and bowed. "I may be able to cope with a Charterhouse boy. Get your helmet and goggles on. We'll see what a public schoolboy can be taught. You other two sit on that bench. I may be able to face up to you later."

"What a bastard!" Wallington remarked as he and Kenyon made themselves comfortable on a rustic seat outside the hangar.

"I seem to attract that type."

"He's the sort who makes the rest of the world hate all Englishmen. Christ! I thought he'd fawn all over you and have you in the air before you could buckle your helmet."

"He's going to rag the guts out of me every chance he gets. I'll be lucky to get through this course."

"Who knows? Maybe this is his way of showing he respects you. There are guys like that."

"Not likely. My squadron commander at Number 70 was exactly the same. He was the one I brought back," Max went on and told the details of his effort to bring Major Grimshaw in safely. "But before he died he swore *he* had flown the plane back—to save me —and some ass at Wing believed him rather than me."

"If he doesn't want to instruct, he shouldn't be allowed to."

"I'm going to put up with him for about a week. If he still clobbers me, I'm going to ask the major to have me transferred to another group—or even another course. I've been through too much of this sort of thing."

They considered the situation pro and con for several minutes, watching the gyrations of the training aircraft above, and wondering how the English kid was making out. In due course Chistopher made his way through the ranks of training aircraft and joined them on the bench. He still wore his helmet and looked particularly pleased.

"He wants you next," he said to Wallington. "He's in plane Number 970. No rush, he's having a smoke."

The Canadian shrugged his shoulders and pulled his helmet from his tunic pocket. "Well, here goes nothing—nowhere," he said sourly. "What was it like?"

"Fine. I really enjoyed it. Nothing like what I expected. He was as nice as pie." The English lad sat down.

"He's saving it for Kenyon," Wallington said with a grin. "Well, let's see what the viper has in store."

Max watched the Canadian shuffle off and for the first time saw what an unkempt figure he was. His uniform, once expensive and smartly tailored, hung on his unsoldierly frame like a potato sack. His cap had been pulled down dead center on his head and his uncombed hair stuck out on both sides like the fringe of a well-worn cocoa mat. Like so many others of the overseas contingent he had not learned how to wrap on puttees. Wallington's threatened to coil down over his slovenly shoes.

In contrast Christopher Roland was extra smart, although he was wearing the regulation NCO gear and hobnailed boots. He was enthusiastic about his experience, his cheeks flushed with the pleasure.

"I dreaded it for a minute," he went on, carefully replacing his service cap. "The way he taunted you, I felt he was . . . well, I wondered if he had once had a bad crash. But he'd never be put on instructing if there were anything like that in his medical history."

"What's the routine? Just a couple of circuits of the aerodrome and then a simple landing?"

"No. He had me keeping my hand lightly on top of the stick right from the minute we took off. He talked to me through the Gosport tube which he fitted inside my helmet flaps. It was very interesting."

"Cripes! I've never done that in all the time I've been flying. Did he let you try the rudder bar?"

"Yes, after we were up a little way. I don't know how high we were, but he told me to rest my toes lightly on the rudder business, then he made a series of right and left turns to give me a chance to see how the rudder and stick worked together for banking. He even let me try it on my own, but I forgot to keep the nose down, and he just laughed at me."

Kenyon gripped Roland's arm. "Don't forget to book your time in your logbook. You must have been up twenty minutes. That's important."

"Thanks. I dreaded that first flight, but now I'd love to go again, right away. It was nothing like I had expected," Roland rattled on, and then subsided and looked at Kenyon. "But, of course, all this must be nothing to you . . . all the flying you have done."

"It's going to get me in trouble, I am afraid."

"Ignore him. I have an idea all instructors have some such opening speech. Remember your first day at prep school?"

Kenyon avoided Roland's eyes. "I hope you're right."

The English lad rubbed the side of his nose. "I have an idea he's a bit miffed that you have two decorations, and he has none. Remember how he bleated he'd been out there nine months without even getting a Military Cross?"

"He never got a wound stripe, either. You have to earn decorations out there, just as you have to work for good marks in school. They don't come up with the rations."

"It was childish of him. I suppose Brasenose was a good workmanlike pilot, but could not carry out anything with the verve and dash that marks the popular hero."

"Probably something like that," Max agreed and watched a couple of trainers making simple S-turns at the far end of the aerodrome. He wondered if Wallington was up there showing what he had learned aboard a Curtiss Jenny.

"Still, I can appreciate your situation," Roland was saying. "All the aerial-gunner flying anyone can do may have little effect on how quickly you learn to pilot an aeroplane by yourself."

Kenyon was thankful for the schoolboy appraisal. The theory had not occurred to him, and he sat ruminating on the days when he had hoped to go to a prep school. He was beginning to like the youth.

"Well, there you are," Wallington croaked when he returned to the bench. "The savage beast is a mere butterfly when he's aboard a B.E.2c."

"Am I next?" Max asked with some dread.

"Of course. He's busy with some business in the hangar, but you're to report with your helmet. Number 970, out there. Better hurry out and have the Gosport phones hooked in. One of the mechanics will help you."

"How was he with you?"

"Not too bad. Talks too much over the tube, but he let me feel out the bus myself to note the difference between a Jenny and these B.E.s I told him the B.E. was simpler—easier to fly than the Curtiss. He seemed to like that. Actually, it's a goddam good ship for teaching ham-fisted Quirks. Still, I'm glad I had some previous instruction in Canada. It makes it that much easier."

Kenyon unrolled his helmet. "I'll get right out there. It'll give me a chance to go over the bus and remember how the cockpit is laid out. I suppose he instructs from the back seat, eh?"

"You never heard of an instructor sitting in the front seat, did you? If they wipe off an undercarriage, the poor bloody student gets the engine in his lap," Wallington said with a wry grimace.

"Don't let him put the goad to you," Roland said with some concern.

"I'll do exactly as he says," Max muttered and bowed to pull his helmet over his head.

Brasenose was nowhere to be seen when Max reached B.E. 970, but by the time he had inserted the Gosport phones inside his earflaps and had climbed into the front seat of the trainer he saw his instructor coming from the hangar row and zigzagging through the machines being serviced for further flight training. A mechanic helped Max fasten his belt, and hooked in the Gosport tube to the speaker unit that lay on the cushion of the back seat.

"You can't talk to Mr. Brasenose," the mechanic explained, "but he can talk to you. That's all that's necessary. You just listen to what he says, and there you are. Here he comes now."

Brasenose walked around the tail and came up on the port side of the machine. He stood rubbing his palms against his temples and staring at the oil-stained turf. Meanwhile Max tried the rudder bar and worked the stick back and forth, checking to make sure the elevators and ailerons responded correctly. The mechanic standing near the propeller smiled at him and then winked.

The instructor climbed up on the wing root beside the front cockpit and checked to be sure his pupil was properly buckled in and that the earphones were correctly inserted in his ear flaps.

"You comfortable, now?" he asked.

"Yes, sir. Quite comfortable."

"I saw you checking the stick and rudder bar. That's good. Shows you learned something."

"I haven't been in a B.E. for several months, sir. I thought I should take advantage of the time. It's quite different from the back seat of a Strutter."

"Quite," his instructor said pleasantly. "Well, let's get aviating."

"One other thing, sir. You must remember that the dual-control gear on a Strutter is nothing like the dual control aboard a trainer like this. I've never tried using regulation dual control, sir."

"I suppose you had to put the Strutter gear together before you could fly it . . . after your pilot was wounded."

"That's what I mean, sir. The stick was on the right-hand side and the rudder was operated by the left hand by pulling on a piece of doweling bolted to the rudder cables. There was no aileron control."

"I know, I know. So flying a B.E.2c should be much easier than handling a Sop Strutter. However, let's see what we can teach each other."

"Yes, sir," Kenyon said, half-believing Brasenose was going to be amiable.

"All right. We'll take off, fly two circuits of the field and then I'm going to see what you can do on your own. While I do circuits I want you to keep your right hand lightly on the stick and the toes of your feet on the rudder bar. In that way you'll get some idea of what it takes to fly straight and level, and do simple turns. Is that clear?"

"Yes, sir."

Brasenose slapped him pleasantly across the shoulder, climbed down and went back to the stirrup beneath the back seat. He got in, nodded to the mechanic, and set the controls for the engine-starting sequence."

"Switch on! Contact!" the pilot ordered.

Kenyon stared ahead at the mechanic, wondering about the pleasant change in Brasenose. The prop was snapped sharply and the RAF engine caught at once. There was some husky sound in the Gosport phones and then Brasenose's voice came through. "Do you hear me?"

Max nodded, watching the mechanic pull away the wheel chocks.

"Good! I'll try to explain what I am doing all the time. You just listen and go through the motions with me. Off we go."

The instructor increased the engine power, the prop took on a glossy sheen and the B.E. began to rumble away and taxi along the side of the landing turf. "We begin to look out for incoming aircraft," Brasenose was saying, "and be sure to give everyone plenty of room. That's most important."

Max nodded again and saw that the sky ahead was clear, and that there were no planes on the ground in the immediate area. He was beginning to enjoy his experience.

"As you probably know, we always take off *into* the wind so we'll turn into it as soon as we reach the end of the landing area. You'll see the wind sock fluttering on top of the hangar. It gives a general idea of the strength and direction of the wind." Brasenose spoke clearly. "Take one more look for incoming aircraft before we make the turn. Right! We're in the clear. I'm going to take off and I will aim our nose at the steeple of that church you can see in the distance."

Kenyon wagged his head and felt for the rudder bar and placed his fingers on top of the control stick. His instructor eased the throttle up the quadrant, and the B.E. seemed to stiffen like a mustang under the quirt. Then she started to move ahead and pick up speed. The tail came up and the RAF engine screeched through the bare exhaust tubes.

"Here we go," Brasenose said again. "Note how I have to apply some slight rudder to counter the torque of the prop. I'm keeping her nose on that steeple, remember. She's showing forty mph on the air-speed indicator and she should be trying to get off the ground on her own. I'm keeping the tail up only slightly, you will notice, but as soon . . . Here we go. We're off the ground. I won't pull her into a climb until we're well clear and certain the engine is still giving the required revs. I want you to watch that tachometer closely. It's a trick you must learn on take-offs."

Kenyon nodded and followed instructions. In a minute the instructor's voice came through again. "We're now clear of the field and I'm going to make two circuits of the area. Keep your eye open for other aircraft, for there are many of them going through the same school instruction. Now notice how I make the turn. First I put the nose down slightly, just below the level of the horizon. Then I apply proper bank with the ailerons and start the actual turn with the rudder. Don't put too much pressure on the rudder—use just enough to learn how much it takes to make a simple turn. Now we're back doing a straight and level flight down the long side of the field."

Kenyon tried to remember what he had done with the Strutter on that memorable day. None of this was anything like it. Brasenose then went into a second turn and as the machine banked Max looked down and could see the area from where they had started their take-off. "We'll go through the turn," Brasenose was saying, "and then I want you to take over and fly her in a straight line. Remember, the stick is for raising or lowering the nose, and as a secondary control it actuates the ailerons for banking. You know what the rudder is for . . . just as in a boat. All right. You take over and fly her."

Max sucked in his breath, sought a marker to steer for, and rammed his insteps against the rudder bar. The B.E. tried to get her head around, but he brought her back with some slight over-control. Then a wing decided to go down, but he remembered to use the ailerons.

"Not bad," his instructor said. "Now keep her heading in that manner until I take over the next turn. Watch your nose now. She's heading left . . . Good! Now let me have her."

Max was in mild ecstasy and turned to grin at Brasenose who nodded pleasantly and began another turn. Then, when the 180-degree turn was half-completed, he banked in the opposite direction and eased the machine into a right-hand curve. Kenyon felt the rudder go over and the stick pivot in the same direction.

"I'm going into an opposite turn to get out of the field circuit," Brasenose explained. "When we get a little more height I'm going to have you make a number of turns where you'll have no traffic. That clear?"

Max responded, and saw they were flying away from the landing area, and that the altimeter showed they were reaching 3000 feet. He wondered why his instructor was giving him this extra time and certainly plenty of opportunity to use the controls himself. What a change from the attitude shown on their introduction. He was beginning to like the man.

"All right! We're flying toward Radlett, just ahead. We'll keep clear of that area and try out a few more turns and stretches of straight flying. I'm turning her over to you. Let's see what you can do on your own. Understood?"

Kenyon jerked his head and took a full grip on the stick. He put the nose down slightly and aimed for a brownish Norman church a few miles ahead, and practiced straight and level flight. He then realized they were getting well away from the area of the aerodrome, and decided to make a turn and fly back over the same route. He lowered the nose gently and then tried to combine rudder pressure with movement of the aileron. The attempt was not properly co-ordinated and the plane went into a slight sideslip before taking the full effect of the rudder. He tried to remedy the mistake and, like all beginners, overcontrolled and felt himself in a flat turn in the opposite direction. The brown Norman church had completely disappeared and the smear that had been Radlett was now somewhere behind them.

"Never mind. Never mind," Brasenose said brusquely. "Keep trying. You haven't put us into a spin yet. Keep trying."

Kenyon wisely started another stretch of straight and level flying, and when his poise had returned, began all over again to work rudder and aileron together. He managed two fairly accurate turns and then found himself heading straight for Radlett again. Looking around, he located the layout of the aerodrome and went into a half turn with the intention of going back to the field. As soon as the turn had been completed he twisted in his seat and looked at his instructor.

14

Y̲ou're doing very well," Brasenose said. "I suppose you feel you could take over and fly us back to the field. Even make a solo landing, eh?"

Kenyon held both hands up and shook his head. He had had more than he had expected for the first session. He was beginning to perspire and the backs of his knees were trembling. He sat with his head bowed toward the instrument panel.

"You're supposed to be an intrepid, dauntless air hero. You are supposed to have flown a Sop Strutter on its dual-control gear. Now you've had one lesson on a B.E. biplane it should be simple for you to take me back to London Colney and set me down, as you claimed to have done with a wounded pilot out on the Western Front. After all, what's the difference?"

Max was shocked, but tried to grin at the ridiculous suggestion. He shook his head negatively and wished he could talk back and reason with this hateful man.

"Look at me, Corporal Kenyon, D.C.M., M.M." Brasenose screeched over the Gosport. "Watch carefully what I'm going to do." He leaned forward and fumbled with something on the floor of the cockpit. He came up with his control stick and waved it over his head. "Look, Kenyon! I've unfastened my joystick from its socket. I'm going to toss it away. See that, Corporal Kenyon, D.C.M., M.M.? I'm tossing my life away," and with that he flipped the glistening control stick into a twirling arc. Kenyon watched it flashing in the brittle sunlight until it disappeared behind their tail assembly. "You see that, Kenyon?" his instructor screamed. "You're on your own. I can't take over now, but remember you're sitting in the front seat and if you pile us up you'll get the engine in your chest. All you have to do is fly us back and deliver me safe and sound to London Colney. I believe you make a practice of that sort of thing." Brasenose's tirade gurgled to a close and he leaned back and threw both arms over the sides of the cockpit coaming to show he had relinquished all control of the aircraft.

"But, sir," Kenyon tried to yell back. "I've never tried to . . . I mean, sir, I can't . . ."

But Brasenose was fumbling with his Congo briar and leaning back in an attitude of contentment. Max turned back to his own cockpit and wondered how much petrol was in the tank. There was no fuel gauge on his instrument panel and he had to give immediate attention to the attitude of the aeroplane. He leveled off and then looked around for the field. It was about five or six miles away and seemed to be arranged in an opposite manner to how it had been laid out when they took off. He treadled the rudder gingerly and tried to get the nose around in the required direction. He wondered if Brasenose had actually thrown his stick away, or did he toss something out that looked like a joystick, just to test him; to see how he would react to such a frightening order. But he remembered the discarded stick had a large cotter pin swinging from a short length of chain near its base. This was to fasten the stick to the brass socket pivoted to the floor. There was one exactly like it at the base of his control. Then there was the black ring where the blip switch was set in the top of the stick. His stick had that, too!

"When are you going to start your heroic act, Corporal Kenyon?" his instructor was nattering over the Gosport. "I wouldn't want to stay up here until I starved to death."

Max took another quick glance at Brasenose. He was still leaning back with his arms outside the cockpit, staring up at the azure sky above, but the pipe was missing and Brasenose was acting like a man who was suffering an epileptic fit. Max recalled seeing a young woman so stricken on a sidewalk outside a pawnshop on Market Street in Newark. He wondered if Brasenose had . . . but surely it would have turned up in any of the several physical examinations he had undergone before he had reached this stage in his flying career.

A series of maniacal, violent oaths, screeches, and unintelligible jabbering came over the Gosport, and Kenyon feared he was the victim of an insane man's behavior, and that he had better make some effort to get the aeroplane down somewhere as safely as he could. There were breathless instants when he hoped Brasenose had indeed thrown his control stick away. In his present condition he could put the B.E. into a headlong dive and hurtle them into Eternity.

"He can't be doing this to frighten me," Max said to himself. "No man in his right mind would think of playing a trick like that."

Right mind? Was Lieutenant Brasenose in his right mind? He certainly had acted like a man mentally unbalanced when he had taunted him before Wallington and young Roland. There was an infinitesimal period of time when he tried to remember who Wallington and Roland were. Where had they come from? Which one was the Canadian and which was the English schoolboy from Charterhouse? Where the hell was Charterhouse?

The London Colney field was now skimming toward them, and he knew he had to take some measures to get the B.E. down before every ounce was drained from the fuel tank. He went into a wide left-hand turn and carefully studied the topography below. Gradually, the details of the field moved themselves into their correct position, and he could see the white tube of the wind sock fluttering toward the take-off end of the field. There were three rows of trainer aircraft lined up before the hangars and antlike men moved about among them. He could also discern the rustic bench on which sat Wallington and Roland. At least there were two figures in khaki there. It then came to him who Wallington and Roland were, and he wondered if they could see what was going to happen.

Going to happen? What was going to happen? Would he remember what he had learned in those few minutes when Brasenose was rational and most friendly in giving his instruction? Would he be able to remember it all and correlate it into a safe landing? Would he be able to time a glide that would put him over the touchdown end of the landing strip? If he was that lucky, what would he do about throttling the engine? Brasenose had told him nothing about that. There was a regulation throttle near his left hand, but he didn't know whether to move it forward or backward to cut the power. He tried to remember what he had done about the engine on the Strutter. Something about pulling it back, but he had pulled it too far and the Le Rhône rotary had conked out—at exactly the proper moment. What was the proper moment with a RAF air-cooled engine?

He maneuvered into a straight and level flight parallel to the long side of the field and gradually worked into another 180-degree turn, but the altimeter showed he was still flying at about 2500 feet. He was a long way above the level of the landing spread. Then Brasenose began a recital of indistinct poetry and broke off into a series of snorts and choking coughs. Kenyon risked another quick glance back, hoping to note evidence of the cruel joke he felt this was, but the instructor was still twisted in his seat, and now had both arms and his head hanging over the starboard side of the fuselage.

Max decided he was truly on his own, and knew it was neck or nothing. He risked experimenting with the throttle, and discovered it was very flexible, giving him plenty of leeway in lowering or increasing the power. He started a long, shallow power-glide toward the aerodrome, completely ignorant of the stalling speed of the B.E., but his weeks in the back seat of a Strutter had given him some sense of safe flight, and he tried another half turn which put him dead on for the landing strip. He attempted to look about for other planes, but dared not risk taking his eyes off the church steeple Brasenose had used in taking off.

As the anxious seconds ticked away, Max realized that flying a B.E. with regulation controls was simpler than putting a Strutter down, as he had done a couple of months before. By the time he was gliding in for his touchdown, he felt reasonably sure he could get in with not too much damage. He found himself dreading the mischance of a severe crash and the prospects of having a red hot RAF engine slamming back into his cockpit.

He throttled back farther and felt the controls go slack. He reset the throttle and the B.E. seemed to tighten up again. He rammed the stick forward and managed to keep his glide straight, and there was a second or two when he felt he was going to get her down safely. There was an instant when he was positive it would be no worse than an initial bad bounce which might blow a tire or fracture an undercarriage strut. Nothing any worse than that.

Then, as he sensed the wheels were zipping over the low weeds at the near end of the landing strip, and that it was fifty-to-one he would get down safely, he heard a low scream in his earphones. He felt the rudder bar rammed over hard, and before he could compensate for the sudden switch in direction, the B.E. had swerved awkwardly. Kenyon realized that Brasenose had twisted in his seat and had rammed the rudder bar over in his final convulsion.

The B.E. hit while in the start of a flat spin. The starboard wheel dug in, collapsed, and the lower wingtip went down. The rest of the aircraft pivoted on the main spar and flipped over on its back. The starboard wing was torn apart, the propeller blades hacked the turf and then broke away in glistening splinters. Strips of fabric and portions of wing structure fluttered in all directions. There was dusty smoke, a dull gush of flame and Kenyon, hanging upside down in his belt was thankful the engine had stayed in its bearers. But a fuel line had fractured and was spraying raw petrol along the banks of cylinders. There was a high stench of hot varnish, lubricating oil, and torn linen.

Again, experience and instinct came to his aid. He looked around for the safest side to make his escape. He flipped his belt and lowered himself and got free of the cockpit. By that time flames were curling up from the inverted engine and clawing toward his cockpit area. He scrambled out, protecting his face with his crooked arm and crawled over the underside of the top plane. He could hear the screech of a Klaxon horn above the increasing roar of the fire that by then was blossoming into a gigantic scarlet carnation. He stood ashen, and smudged, brushing embers and splintered spruce from his tunic. He then realized Brasenose had made no attempt to get clear.

"Mr. Brasenose! Get out!" he yelled. But there was no sign of his instructor. "Mr. Brasenose!"

Racing around the inverted tail, he could now see the pilot still hanging below the coaming of the cockpit. The high fin still held that portion of the fuselage clear, but it was difficult to tell what Brasenose was doing because of intermittent gushes of thick black smoke. "He's still belted in," Max decided. "He can't get out. He may be pinned down by the edge of the cockpit." Still slapping at the portions of his uniform that were singed by burning embers blasting from the nose of the biplane, Max flung himself at the area where he had last seen his instructor.

"You've got to get out, sir. We're on fire. I'm sorry, but we rolled over just as . . ."

He found the release snap of the pilot's belt and flicked it from its catch, and the inert man flopped to the ground on the back of his shoulders. He began to scream again. It was unearthly. Then, his arms started to flail and Kenyon was struck across the throat and almost choked. Still, he shielded Brasenose from the smoke and long fingers of flame licking along the framework of the fuselage. He struggled to get him clear so his legs could be drawn from the rim of the cockpit. Working in a suffocating cloud of smoke, he could hardly control his own actions, but he clung to Brasenose's shoulders and was able to drag him a few feet clear of the flames that were now enveloping the frontal half of the fuselage. He struggled to his feet, grabbed the unconscious man by his armpits and dragged him still farther away.

That was the last Kenyon remembered of his efforts to free Brasenose. The Klaxon roared into his last measure of sanity and he sensed he was being hauled clear.

When he regained consciousness someone with a Red Cross insignia on his sleeve was sponging his face and giving him sniffs from some kind of a nose cone. He could see men in khaki directing streams of whitish liquid at the burning biplane. There were faces he seemed to recognize but could not put names to. There were officers, wearing Sam Browne belts, and air mechanics in greasy coveralls. Wallington came out of the mist and asked if he was all right. He tried to remember who Wallington was. Then a man who wore a tunic of the Machine Gun Corps and had wings above his left pocket, kneeled beside him and asked how he felt, and could he get up and walk to the ambulance?

"What about Mr. Brasenose?" Max asked in a faint voice. His throat still pained and there were bandages on both hands. "I tried to get him out, but the smoke and flame. It all happened so quickly."

"You probably saved his life, but he's still very bad. We've had to put him in what might be called a strait jacket. Quite violent, he acted. What happened?"

"He threw . . . tossed his control stick away and ordered me to take him back to the aerodrome and land the plane myself. That's how it happened. What was I to do? Then, when I was bringing the plane in, he must have kicked the rudder over hard just as we were approaching the landing strip."

The man who had captain's pips on his shoulders looked puzzled, and then called a flight sergeant and gave him a sharp order. "Find out as soon as you can get a look at the rear cockpit."

"It was my first instruction flight," Max said. "He nearly choked me, too, swinging his arms about while I was trying to get him out of his belt. My uniform's all burned."

"We couldn't understand why you went into a flat spin just off the turf. Someone thought it was a student freezing and jamming the rudder. It has happened before. Until then it looked like an instructor's normal three-point landing."

There was more questioning while Max was helped into the ambulance, and the captain made a few notes as they bumped across the turf and onto the paved roadway.

"I can't understand why he suddenly acted so . . . crazy. He had been very friendly and had me doing straight and level flying as soon as we were off the ground. Then he let me fly all by myself, to do as I liked. Suddenly he began to taunt me about my decorations and being a war hero. He told me to look back, and it was then he threw his stick away and ordered me to take him home. Has Mr. Brasenose been in a crash . . . something that might explain his actions?"

"We won't know until a panel of doctors can make a complete examination. Are you certain he really threw away his stick? Instructors used to play an old trick with what looked like a joystick to frighten students into believing they had actually tossed their control sticks away, but that was stopped. We shall have to make sure he threw his over the side. It doesn't sound like Brasenose. He's been a reliable instructor."

"I'm positive he did, sir. I saw the cotter pin dangling from its chain. I remember that very well. If he hadn't kicked the rudder when he did, I'm sure I could have gotten the plane down without too much damage." Max was still patting the burned portions of his tunic.

"I've ordered the flight sergeant to inspect the rear cockpit, and if the stick has been removed, we'll have to accept your story. If it's still in there, I don't know what we can do but assume Mr.

Brasenose went insane in midair. You will, of course, get some credit for pulling him out of the crash."

"Here I go again," Max muttered to himself. "I'll never get full credit for anything I do. Now I have a madman to contend with."

Two days later Kenyon was up and about, but still in hospital pajamas and dressing gown. His hands were in tannic dressings, and there was a painful burn across one shoulder. His helmet had protected his head and face, and all in all, he was not too uncomfortable.

One afternoon Wallington and Roland were permitted to see him. Roland brought two chocolate bars and a package of Peek Frean's biscuits. Wallington contributed a couple of age-old Canadian magazines, and the information that they now had an instructor named Crankshaw, Lieutenant Bartley Crankshaw.

"You'll like him." Roland said. "He has a Military Cross *and* a Military Medal. He was once a gunner with Number 5 Squadron, and shot down a Taube with just a Belgian carbine. Can you imagine that?"

Kenyon looked at Wallington. "What's he like in the air?"

"Swell! There's no arsing about with him, but he knows what he's doing."

"He showed me how to get into and out of a spin," Chris added with enthusiasm. "Tomorrow we're going to do falling-leafs."

"This kid will be going solo any day now," Ralph said moodily. "I've made three landings already. You better get the hell out of here, or you'll have to start with another course."

"But look here," Chris broke in anxiously, and stared at Max's bandaged hands. "How are you coming along? I mean, your hands?"

"I feel all right, but I can't tell how long I'll be in here. They just look after you here, but you can't get a word out of any of them."

"What happened? I mean, what caused that flat spin?" Ralph said petulantly.

Max related his experience and closed with, "But no one will tell me whether they found a stick in the rear cockpit. All I can get out of anyone is that the fuselage was so badly burned they can't tell whether there was a stick in there or not."

"But," Chris argued, "the whole stick couldn't have been burned. The base of it would have been left in the socket. What sort of yarn is that?"

"You tell me. I'll probably be blamed for the crash, when it was caused by my instructor who had gone off his head. It's a wonder we both weren't killed."

"Jesu! What an experience," Wallington half-whispered.

"We'll have to talk to Crankshaw and see if he can't get you out of here. You two should get on well together. Your hands aren't crippled, are they? Probably just first-degree burns," Roland said to reassure Max.

"But the lousy crash will go down in my logbook when it wasn't my fault."

"Don't book it as a crash," Wallington muttered and winked. "Just record it as a dual-control instruction flight. Forget how you wound up. I don't think anyone will argue about it too much."

"By the way, is Brasenose in this hospital?" Roland put in.

"No. He's been taken to some loony bin in London."

"This sounds like a nice exoneration deal," Ralph Wallington said, and lit a cigarette. "They're not going to let any yarn like this get out in the papers."

Roland broke in. "Well, we have to go. We'll try to see you again on Friday. There's some talk about our commissions coming through by the end of the week. We ought to celebrate."

"Let me know as soon as they do. I can't wait to get that blasted white band off my cap."

"Get those bandages off your hands, too. You'll be days behind us, otherwise." Roland rubbed Max's head.

Max went back to his cubicle and began munching on a chocolate bar and flipping the pages of a *Jack Canuck* magazine, but the contents did not hold his interest. He was despondent about being delayed in his course. Roland and Wallington would be on single-seaters before he could go solo on a B.E. What rotten luck!

"I'll be lucky if I'm not dropped from flight training and sent back to France as an officer observer," he ruminated.

He was roused from his melancholy by the approach of a young V.A.D. "You're wanted in the lobby. Captain Wandsworth wants to see you," she explained. "You know, the officer who brought you in."

"Oh, him. I want to see him, too."

Wandsworth was the ex-Machine Gun Corps man who had transferred to the R.F.C. He greeted Max mildly and led the way to two pillowed wicker chairs.

"Well, I must say you're looking a lot better, and not so well grilled. How are the hands coming?"

"The bandages are the biggest trouble, sir, but I can use all my fingers."

"That's good. I suppose you'll want to be getting out as soon as you can to get on with your course."

"Yes, sir. I hate losing time this way. I'm sure I can handle a stick again."

"Well, I'll see what I can do for you, but there's one matter I came to discuss."

"Have they found anything about Mr. Brasenose's control stick?"

"That's what I want to talk about. We're about ready to believe your explanation, although his cockpit was pretty well destroyed. But, I want you to understand our position—I mean the position of the instructor staff, and the responsibilities of the Central Flying School which turns out our instructors. If Mr. Brasenose did suffer a mental, er, aberration, and as you insist, did take out and throw away his control stick, there will be some unpleasant investigations. First, why his physical condition was not studied more fully, and second, why he acted as an instructor for so long before his mental condition was suspected. All this not only can take time, but will embarrass the whole Central Flying School organization which in turn will slow up the flight training program just when we need to set it into high gear. I hope you understand what I am getting at."

"I understand clearly, sir. Just as long as I am not blamed for the crash. I don't want that in my logbook. But, again, I insist Mr. Brasenose removed his stick, tossed it away and left the plane to me to bring back and land."

"I believe that's about what happened, Kenyon, but there's no point in keeping the incident in circulation. It could mean a long, drawn-out investigation, and you'd be dragged from one meeting to another, all the while losing instruction time, and I know you don't want that."

"I'm willing to forget the whole thing, sir."

"We're ready to take your side and make certain it will in no way blemish your training record. As a matter of fact, we have been considering you for an Edward Medal as a reward for getting Mr. Brasenose out of the crash. That was a stout effort, Kenyon."

"An Edward Medal? What's that?"

Wandsworth shook his head wryly. "It's not quite clear to me, either. It was established by Edward VII about 1907, and is given for heroism or gallantry—*not* in the face of the enemy. I also understand it must be worn on the *right* breast of the jacket, not with your front-line awards. There ought to be something better, but there you are."

"Captain Wandsworth," Max appealed. "I'll do or say anything you like, sir, about the crash, but don't put me in for any more medals. Please, sir. It was the two ribbons on my tunic that first inflamed Mr. Brasenose. I believe he was on the front for nine months and was never once decorated for his services. I think he felt some inner resentment against me right from the start when he saw me, a corporal aerial gunner, wearing the D.C.M. and the M.M. No more medals, sir."

"I think I understand, Kenyon. Then we'll leave matters as they stand and I'll see whether we can get you out of here in a couple of days. I'll sign your logbook and get you back on the field as soon as those bandages can come off. I'll also see about a new uniform." Wandsworth grinned and added, "but I don't know what good another noncom outfit will do you. I think you'll be commissioned by the end of this week."

"That's what I'd sooner have now than another medal, sir."

"I'm glad you'll co-operate, Kenyon. I assure you, you won't lose anything by it. I'd better get along now . . . and thanks!"

"Very good, sir. I'll see if I can get the head nurse to relieve me of these dressings. I'm sure I can handle a joystick."

15

Within a week Kenyon was back on the course and fretting to catch up with Wallington and Roland. His new instructor, Lieutenant Crankshaw, a pleasant-faced Midlander from Rutlandshire, tried not to show his partiality to the former aerial gunner, but it was evident the minute Max turned up at the hangar. He was a compact man who had played Rugby at Cambridge and had been studying to become a civil engineer. He had russet-brown hair, cropped close but still showing it had once been a tightly curled mop. He had dark brown eyes, good teeth, and small ears close to his head. When the dual-control sessions were over he had an attractive smile and a billowing laugh, but in the air he was a disciplined tutor who spoke slowly but with distinction.

Kenyon was introduced to Crankshaw by Wallington.

"Oh, of course. You're the chap who was in Brasenose's crash. Understand you're an old aerial gunner. Good show."

Max held out his hands which were still lightly bandaged, and grinned.

"Forget all that. Let's aviate and see how much you learned during that horrible experience. Get your helmet on and if your hands bother you, give me the tip and we'll just go joy riding and tour the countryside."

"As you say, sir."

On the way to the trainer, Crankshaw explained that he knew all about Brasenose's insanity that had resulted in the crash. "It must have been a fearful experience. We've had students go wonky and freeze on the stick, so the instructor had to biff them over the head with the Pyrene extinguisher, but we've never had an instructor go off his onion like that. He was damned lucky you kept your head."

"If he hadn't been in some sort of spasm and squirming all over the cockpit, I'm sure I would have gotten him down safely. All I needed was a bit of luck. But that's how it goes with me."

"I told you to forget it. Erase it from your mind. You'll get nowhere chewing on old adversities. None of us does. You have a whole new career ahead of you, and remember you've had the advantage of several weeks of active service. Take it from me, I know how much that means, but I can't stress one point too much. What you try to learn here will be more important to your future than anything you may have learned during your first five years in school. There's one other thing I want to make clear."

"What's that, sir?" Kenyon was enjoying every word his new instructor was saying. It was the first time in years anyone had taken him into his confidence with the idea of teaching him something. It was a warm, rosy experience and he couldn't take his eyes off the face of the man who was bestowing this kindness.

"Don't think that because you have been a bloody good aerial gunner you'll have no trouble learning to fly. There's no assurance of that. We've had damn good gunners come here, and they turn out to be complete duds when they get into the back seat and fly solo. A few, a very few, become bloody good, but what they learned as gunners in no way made them good pilots. Their war experience put them furlongs ahead when it came to meeting Jerry over the lines, but it added little to their chances of becoming great pilots. I'm not telling you this to discourage you. It's for your personal information, and I'm telling it to no one else on the course, so you needn't brood on it. Make the most of the time you'll get here. Don't be in a bloody rush to get back to France. Get in as much training as you can. Then, when you're ready, make sure you select the right bus to fly when you get out there. Don't pick scouts, hoping you'll run up a big score. Pick the best available whether it's a scout, two-seater fighter, or bomber. There are some real posh machines coming out, and most of them should be ready by the time you are posted overseas again."

"Do you have anything special in mind, sir?"

"No! I can't tell you what will be super pukkah six months from now. It all depends how the war goes, but for God's sake don't concentrate on the Hun-killer role. That's not particularly important from any point of view. We're on the offensive, remember. Jerry is simply trying to hold on to what he has grabbed. Our job is to fit military flying into the ground situation. We're developing what will be known as tactical aviation, and everybody will have a special job to do. There'll be no place for the glory boys, or pot-hunters."

"This is all new to me, sir. I thought . . ."

"I know what you think. If you do get picked for scouts, however, you'll be better equipped for the job than any of these poor buggers who are just coming out of school, or joining the R.F.C. to dodge the gamble of conscription. Between the two of us, only about thirty-five per cent of today's Cadets will be worth their place in a formation."

Kenyon was tightening his helmet over the Gosport earphones while Crankshaw was speaking, but he was listening with an absorbed mind. He sensed that what the instructor was saying was right, and he was grateful for he knew that at this point he was no better equipped for flight training than young Roland who had no previous misconceptions to overcome.

"Well, there it is," Crankshaw was saying. "Let's get off the ground. Is there anything special you'd like to do when we get upstairs?"

"Yes, sir. I'd like to learn how to fly."

"Good man! Let's start from the beginning. You stand on one wing root, and I'll take the other. In that manner we'll learn the rules of the cockpit. I'll tell you about the engine, the controls, the instruments and how to make the most of what the designers have given us. I'll tell you how to taxi, how to take off, how to gain height, and at what speed to get down again. Once you learn that you won't need me ever again. That is, if you're as knowledgeable as I think you are."

Lieutenant Crankshaw was as good as his word, for he spent more than an hour teaching Kenyon the fundamentals of flying without leaving the ground. When both of them were tired of leaning over the rim of the cockpits, he ordered Max to climb in and go through the engine-starting sequence. Then, as the RAF coffee-grinder ticked over he ordered him to taxi out and put the nose down the runway.

"All right. Now we're going to take off, climb to fifteen hundred feet and made two circuits of the field. That is to say, you are if you wish to. It's up to you. I've told you all that needs to be done. What do you say?"

Max just nodded his head, and with a final look around eased the throttle up the quadrant.

During the next four days, Maxwell Kenyon really learned to fly. He went solo with less than seven hours of intensive dual-control instruction, and made four almost perfect landings while Lieutenant Crankshaw sat on the bench with Roland and Wallington observing the performance.

"I think we're watching one of the most natural pilots to come out of the system," the instructor said as Max worked the B.E. up to its space on the cab rank, "but if either of you tell him I said so, I'll wash you out and made kite-balloon observers of you."

Max climbed down and grinned at the mechanics who rammed the chocks up against the wheels. He walked up to the bench and gave Crankshaw an appealing grimace.

"Not bad. Not bad, at all. The first one was the best, but they usually are. The second was a trifle slow and you should have taken a bad bump, but you got away with it. From now on don't be afraid to come in fast in case you get some low turbulence. You can use all the speed you can get in situations like that. On the whole, however, you did fairly well. That'll be all for today. You can start your solo program on Monday. Let's see. Today is Saturday, isn't it? I suppose all three of you have bunged in for weekend leave and want to get away. Well, off you go then."

Wallington said, "Their commissions have come through and they should be properly celebrated."

"Never mind the rank. Make sure you put those ribbons up on your new square-pushing tunic, Kenyon."

"Yes, sir. Thank you, sir."

"And don't forget to fill in your logbook!" Crankshaw bellowed. "You go solo only once, remember."

"Yes, sir."

While Wallington and Roland waited for Max to fill in the details of his first solo time, Roland eased up and said, "Are you going up to London?"

"I promised Wallington I would. It was his idea to wet our commissions up there. Why don't you come along!"

Roland wagged his head. "I'm not too impressed with Ralph. He's not my sort."

"Anything wrong?"

"No, not really, but I'm going home and I hoped I could persuade you to come along. My parents would love to have you for a weekend. It's not far. Just outside Chelmsford in Essex. Plenty of room."

"I'd like to, but I've promised Wallington. He hasn't been up to the big town yet. Too bad. I would have liked . . ."

"It'll keep. We'll make it another time, perhaps when we get our wings," Roland said to hide his disappointment.

"Sure. I'd like to see the inside of an English home and meet your family, Chris."

"Nothing fancy, just comfortable. We're in an old village where life is a little less hectic. You know, duck ponds, old mills, cricket on the green, and everyone knows everyone else."

"We'll make it next time." Max tucked his logbook into the rack. "That is, if your parents will have me."

"I've told them about you. I mean the kind of person you are. Not the war hero with the medals. They speak for themselves. They're anxious to see you."

Max appreciated the understanding, and said, "I wish you would come along with us."

"No. Mother can't wait to see me buckled into a Sam Browne belt and a pip on my shoulder. You know the *Priceless Percy With His One Pip Up,** and I have to go through with it."

"Remember me to your mother," Max said soberly.

Chris nodded and bit his lower lip.

"Come on, Max!" Ralph bellowed from the hangar door. "We have a big afternoon and night ahead of us."

"I'm glad you got your first solo over with no trouble," Chris said hurriedly. "You'll soon catch up with us. We're doing all sorts of stunts, and we should be moved along to Sopwith Pups in a few days. They say Pups are super."

Max and Ralph packed their haversacks carefully for their trip to London, selecting pajamas, shaving kits, extra socks, shirts, and tooth brushes. Their standard uniform demanded no more.

"Well, here we are," Wallington proclaimed once they were aboard the train. "What are we going to do about some girls?"

"I've been thinking about it, but we'll have to wait until we get in town and make some precise observations."

* A line in a popular song of the day.

· 169 ·

"And there may be a little matter of money," Ralph added, staring out the window. "By the way, where are we going to stay?"

"I don't know yet. I suppose it depends on whom we pick up. Perhaps I can bung in with you if you can get into the Canadian Club although I'm not a Canadian."

"How are we off for money?"

"What do you mean 'we'?"

"I had a bad night on Wednesday shooting craps—dice. I'm a bit short and hoped you'd have a few extra quid on you. I'm just asking."

Max knew that he'd picked a grafter, and wished he had accepted Chris's invitation to go home with him. "Look here, Ralph, I don't lend, or borrow, money. It's a mug's game. If you are short you shouldn't have left the aerodrome." Max took another look at his reflection in the compartment window and liked what he saw. No more white band, a full Sam Browne belt, and a gilt pip on each shoulder. With the rest of his military glory in gaudy array he looked the bold, intrepid young airman of the day—and knew it.

"Five pounds would tide me over."

"Five pounds! That's more than we get a week, even with flying pay."

"You're commissioned now and should have your kit allowance to your credit and could draw on that. Cox's will be open today, for military officers."

Max looked out the window again, watching the outskirts of Hampstead flash by. He had forgotten that from now on his pay would be issued through Cox's bank, and that he could draw on it by check as he wished. "That's right," he muttered audibly. There should be at least twenty-five pounds—his kit allowance—and his pay for the past few days. It was difficult to figure, but he'd planned to find out when he got to London. That, and what he had left over from his few weeks as a Cadet. "I should have at least twenty-five quid there."

"That's what I'm telling you," Ralph broke in with enthusiasm. "We'll hop a taxi from the station and go straight to Cox's. It will take but a few minutes to be identified and get a checkbook. They'll tell you how your account stands."

"If I get any money, I'll lend you five pounds. No more, and you'll have to pay me back within a week."

"If your full kit allowance is still in there, will you make it ten?"

Max let out a sigh. "You're a real blood sucker, aren't you?"

"You get a commission only once, Max. You get twenty quid out of Cox's and we'll have a weekend we'll remember for all time."

"Oh, so now I'm supposed to finance the whole damned weekend. What are you contributing?"

"It'll be my turn next time, when you get your wings. The whole deal will be on me. What do you say?"

"I say we wait until we see what I have at Cox's."

Ralph Wallington's hopes produced a small bonanza. To Max's amazement he learned his account at Cox's amounted to well over forty pounds. Once he had identified himself with his Pay and Mess book, backed up with his fiber identification disc, he was provided with a folding checkbook and a small card of instructions which advised him how to withdraw funds, his daily rate of pay, and a warning in scarlet type not to overdraw.

"Now what can we do for you, sir?" said the amiable cashier who recognized Kenyon's decorations and what they represented. "I presume you wish to replenish the exchequer, eh?"

It was the first time Kenyon had been addressed as "sir" since the day he had flown Major Grimshaw back. He was mildly spellbound for an instant.

"He wants twenty-five pounds," Ralph explained from one side of the window. "In one-pound notes."

Max suddenly found his voice. "Wait a minute. I want to know how this much money is being credited to me. I haven't been commissioned very long."

"What do you care?" Ralph argued in a stage whisper. "Don't ask too many dumb questions."

The cashier placed his fingertips together in the manner of a benign preacher. "Ah. Here we have the legacy of heroes. I note in your account that the twenty pounds bounty awarded with your Distinguished Conduct Medal has been added to your kit allowance, sir. I assure you, your account here is accurate, er . . . correct."

"Give him twenty-five pounds," Ralph repeated hastily. "He'll make out a check."

While Max was trying to grasp the full details of the cashier's explanation, Ralph was unscrewing his fountain pen and fluttering the pages of the new checkbook. "Will twenty-five pounds be enough?" he husked but filled in the necessary details and crossed out the revenue stamp embossed on the check. "Here, sign this on both sides."

Kenyon stared at the slip of bluish paper, wrote his signature carefully as ordered, and Ralph shoved it through the cashier's window. A stack of one-pound notes was passed back in return, and he grabbed them, selected the top ten for himself and handed the remainder to Max.

"I still don't understand it," Max said plaintively as they headed toward the door.

"You don't have to understand it. He told you that some bonus money for one of your decorations had come through and added to your kit allowance. You're a war hero, and remember you had already paid for your new uniform out of your own money—Cadet pay."

As Max stood counting his wad of pound notes, Ralph interrupted with, "Let's try Leicester Square. I hear there's plenty of gash in that area."

Max pocketed his bank notes. "You would know about Leicester Square. That's your speed. It's not for me. I'm going to the Savoy and start out clean."

"You're leaving me on my own?"

"You've got ten pounds of mine in your pocket. What do you want?"

"Look. We came into town together. What's the Savoy?"

"A good hotel in the Strand. I had planned to pick up tickets for *Chu-Chin-Chow*."

"A Chinese restaurant? Here's a cab. You tell the guy where you want to go."

When they were settled in the taxi Max explained, "*Chu-Chin-Chow* is a musical comedy. Very popular. Everyone goes to see it over and over." He wondered how he could get rid of this oaf.

"Why?"

"Well in my case there's a girl dancer. Her name's Dido Maitland, and she's a stunner. I got the glad eye from her the last time I was in town on leave. I'm hoping to pick her up."

"Where do I come in?"

"There are dozens of girls in the show and she'll probably ring in one of her friends. We'll take both of them to dinner, eh?"

"You're financing the deal, and you seem to know what you're

· 172 ·

doing. I'll go along with anything you say. I hope they have a bar at this Savoy."

"They have what they call an American bar. Wait until you see the crowd that goes there. Dozens of Flying Corps guys."

Wallington considered that and rubbed his knuckles across his mouth. "Perhaps we should have taken out the whole forty pounds," he said, studying the taxi meter.

"Never mind the 'we' business. You've had all you're going to get out of me. Stay off the liquor. That can be expensive in more ways than one, so take it easy. This is a posh hotel, and we're supposed to act like officers."

"Oh, my God! Where do you carry your handkerchief?" Ralph taunted.

Max parried, "At least I own one—and use it."

The lounge at the Savoy was filled with young officers of every service, most of whom were escorting frilly young girls in their best frocks and fashionable hats. Off to one side was a dance floor from which thudded the music of American negroes, and the girls in their Scheherazade skirts led their escorts through the intricacies of the tango, the bunny hug, the turkey trot, and the maxixe. The hotel staff in morning coats and striped trousers moved through the groups of khaki and navy blue, hoping to maintain standard decorum. The men laughed heartily, but spoke in mellow tones. The girls trilled to the stories and explanations. There was the perfume of hair pomade, Jockey Club scent, smell of leather polish, starched dresses, and tooth powder. There was the creak of wicker furniture, field boots, Sam Browne belts and the tinkle of empty glasses being rushed back to the scullery. All this provided the undertone of wartime London, particularly at the Savoy. It would be repeated thirty-four years later.

Kenyon guided Wallington through the swaying groups, through a corridor and into the American bar, where the ubiquitous George (all bartenders were George in London, Jack in Paris) stood fondling a silver cocktail shaker. Wallington homed on him like a carrier pigeon.

"Good morning, gentlemen." George said, beaming. He splashed out two Bronx cocktails for a brace of Canadian artillerymen, and then gave Wallington his attention. "What's your pleasure today?"

"What are you having?" Ralph asked Max.

"Just a shandygaff will be enough for me."

"What's that?"

The bartender grinned. "It's just a mixture of light beer and ginger beer. Very good, if you're thirsty."

"For Christ's sake. He brings me into an American bar and then orders a temperance drink. Give me double Scotch and soda. I gotta celebrate."

"Yes, sir." The bartender turned to his task.

"Where did you get that shandygaff line?"

"Someone told me about it when we were in Oxford. Everyone drank it at *The Mitre*. I don't want to get blotto. We have a long day ahead of us, remember."

"I've got to loosen up. Always do. I'm no good until I get a couple of whiskies under my belt."

"You've got only about ten quid to last you until we get back tomorrow night. Money goes fast in London."

The bartender brought their drinks and took a pound note from Max on his shandygaff. He stood squinting at Wallington. "Take both out of that," Ralph said. "I'll buy the next round."

The barman looked stricken. "I'm sorry, sir. We're still under DORA (Defense of the Realm Act). There's no treating at bars during the war."

It was Ralph's turn to look stricken. "You mean to say he can't buy one drink for me, or I for him?"

"The law has been in force for months, sir."

"Christ! Is that what we've been fighting for?"

The bartender placed his hands flat on the bar and leaned forward until his face was close to Wallington's. "It's what your friend has been fighting for, and he seems to have done his share."

Ralph sheepishly peeled off a one-pound note, and changed the subject.

Max tried a diversionary move. "You wait here. I'm going into the lobby to see about some tickets for that show."

"While you're at it, see if this Dido chick is in the telephone book. You can make time that way. Make sure she has a friend, too. We got to stick together, pal."

16

By good fortune Miss Maitland was listed in the telephone book which also gave her address in South Kensington. She was aroused, and by the time she had shaken off some of her woolly-headedness, Max explained who he was, that he had seen her in the show some weeks before, looked her up in the program and hoped she might be in the phone book. He then suggested a dinner before her evening show, and hoped they could get together for an after-theater supper.

"It sounds topping, and you have an interesting voice," Dido responded. "Are you by any chance an American?"

"Oh, that. I was born in the States, but my parents came from Lancashire. I'm a lieutenant in the Flying Corps. Been over here since 1914, but I'll explain it all when I meet you. Now what about tonight?"

"Tonight. Let's see, this is Saturday, isn't it? We have a matinee today, but we might manage a little dinner before the evening performance. I think that would be top hole."

"Good. I'll get seats for this evening, and we can see you after the show. Stage door, eh?"

"We? You have someone with you?"

"I have a Canadian friend. He's an officer, too, and we were wondering . . ."

"What's he like?"

"A rugged lumberjack, but I'll vouch for him," Max said with a restrained sigh.

"Ooo, a Canadian! And you're both in the Flying Corps?"

"Drawing flying pay, so don't worry. We'll have enough to finance a night or two."

"Oh, yummy. In that case, you name the restaurant and we'll

be delighted to join you. I think my friend Winnie . . . Winnie Winspeare will be available. If not, we'll cope somehow. Lots of nice girls in our show."

"I'm calling from the Savoy. Let's agree to meet here for dinner at your convenience. How's that?"

"Dinner at the Savoy? Jolly Gosh! I've never dined there. Just walked through the lobby. Never even had tea there."

"Well, we must make up for that."

"Corks!" Miss Maitland squeaked. "We'll see you there at five-thirty. That should give us plenty of time. Ta-ta!"

Max was delighted with his success. Miss Maitland sounded like a young goddess, and he was glad he had the wherewithal to finance the party. He hurried back to the bar and noted that Ralph had ordered and was well into another double Scotch. "Take it easy," he admonished. "We're in. They'll meet us here for dinner and we'll gather again after the evening show."

Ralph put on a lopsided grin. "You mean you got two of 'em?"

"Dido says she'll cope somehow. You'll have to take your chance, but I think she'll come up with something lively."

"Where are we having lunch? I'm getting hungry."

"Let's try Simpson's. It's right nearby. It specializes in roast beef and massive lunches for men."

"You sure have been around. Roast beef is my middle name. Let's go!" Ralph tossed the rest of his drink down, slopped much of it on his tunic and slid off his stool. "Roast beef of old England! Whoopee!"

"Take it easy."

"Where are we staying tonight?"

"I suppose we ought to think about that, but I warn you, we're not staying here. Too expensive for my purse."

"Where does this Dido live?"

"She has a flat in South Kensington. We'll probably wind up there, unless . . ." Max explained uncertainly, "but don't count on it. I have an idea she's in a respectable place. We won't know until we get together and become cozy."

"Whatever happens, I'm staying with you."

"Remember you have enough money to cover one full night whether we stay together or not, and for God's sake stay sober."

For a century Simpson's had been known for the finest in old English food. The main room was massive, comfortable, well-lighted and designed for men who knew what they wanted. The chairs were roomy and generously padded. The tables provided elbow room, gleaming cutlery, service plates, and spotless napery. Amid it all swirled aromas of meats, hot pies, cheeses, and sauces that would have satisfied Henry VIII. The staff was Old World in its pace, quietly concerned for the patrons' desires, and impeccable in serving the meals. Simpson's provided exactly the style of dining that would assure any young subaltern he was finally on his way up in the military escalade.

There were appetizers in profusion, a turtle soup that would have shamed any French chef, served with a goblet of nut-brown sherry. A flagon of ale preceded the main course—a baron of beef brought to the table on a serving cart with a uniformed waiter to slice off any thickness or special portion his patron desired. There were vegetables to suit any man's choice, and a rack of condiments that would have sent Mr. Pickwick into raptures. All this and the luxury of a dozen aromas that would have tempted the most jaded of tastes.

"My God! Where are we?" Wallington appealed, and rubbed his great hands together. "I haven't seen fodder like this since my old man took me out to British Columbia. Let's see. It was in the Empress Hotel in Victoria. But this is even better."

Max kept silent. He was taking in every feature of the meal, the moves of the waiters, the manner of serving, and the general behavior of the other diners. He retained every factor of the ceremony, which it was, and resented Ralph's crude manner and loud speech. No one else in the great room raised his voice. No one else acted as though this was his first meal in a week. Everyone was at ease, calm, enjoying the lunch with the air of men who had ordered a thousand such repasts. This was the life! South 10th Street was a million miles away.

"What are we having for dessert?" Wallington broke in, and wiped a streak of gravy from his chin. "Jees! This is the place for me every time, Max, old boy."

"Devonshire junket is one of Simpson's most popular sweets, sir," a straight-backed waiter had come forward and whispered. "It was a great favorite with King Edward VII, bless him, sir."

"What the hell's Devonshire junket?" Ralph demanded. "I never heard of it."

"It's a very old Devonshire dish, sir. We put warm milk in a bowl, turn it with rennet, then put some scalded cream, sugar and cinnamon on the top—without breaking the curd. At Simpson's we serve it with strawberry sauce. I'm sure it would delight you young gentlemen."

Ralph appealed to Max. "What's he giving us?"

"Sounds wonderful. I'll try that, waiter. I have a good idea what it is," Max said quietly."

"Make it two," Ralph said with anticipation, "and a cup of coffee. I always gotta have a coffee to swill down my meal."

Max nodded to the waiter, again wishing he had accepted the invitation to Chelmsford. He was becoming outraged with his companion's behavior and hoped he could get rid of him for the rest of the afternoon.

Back on the street, his inner man satisfied, Ralph was anxious to try something else. "What do we do now?"

"First, we're popping across the street and see what we can do about the theater tickets. There's a booking agency in the Waldorf just around the corner."

"Yeh, sure. Then what?"

"Why don't we break up and kill the afternoon in our own way? We can meet back at the Savoy, get a wash and brush-up in time to meet the girls at five-thirty. You ought to see some of the sights, Buckingham Palace, Westminster Abbey, or maybe do some shopping at Harrods, Gamage's, or even Burberry's."

Ralph winced. "What would I be doing in such places? What do I know about London?"

"Hop a taxi and get the driver to take you anywhere. That's the best way."

"I got a stinking idea you're trying to dump me."

"As a matter of fact I was hoping to get up to Foyle's Book Shop in Charing Cross Road. I like to browse there."

"You come to London just to mope around in a book shop? With all the hotels here available where you can pick up a judy, just like that?"

"All right. You go for a judy. I'll look over the books."

"I don't trust you. You got some special idea in your noggin, and you're shunting me out of the play. I'll go with you."

"Just as you say, but you'll be bored stiff."

The afternoon was a melange of Foyle's where Max purchased a secondhand copy of John Buchan's *Prester John*, a thrilling adventure story; a foray into a tea shop; a brief rest at an Oxford Street picturedrome; and a breather in a bar of the Regent Palace Hotel, after which they made their way back to the Savoy where Wallington found time for another double Scotch.

"You really should get a shave," Kenyon protested. "The one you had this morning was little better than a lick and a promise."

Wallington rubbed his chin as they returned to the lounge. "Ah, what the hell. Chorus girls aren't that particular. They like to know they're snuggling up to a real man."

"You're not out in the Canadian lumber camps now."

"All tarts like to be roughed up. They're used to it."

Kenyon gave up and led the way to get a seat from where he could watch the hotel lobby. He was determined this would be the last time he would share his leave with this crude oaf. Ralph slumped down and began unbuttoning the collar of his tunic. "You sure you'll know this Dido frill when she comes in?" he asked, spreading his legs wide.

"Of course. I've seen the show, and I know I'd recognize her anywhere . . . Here she is now, right on time—both of them." Max stood up, glanced at his watch and turned his smile on two girls who were standing in the entrance to the lounge.

Ralph remained seated, but put on a porcine grin when he spotted the two girls. Kenyon saw immediately that they were standouts even in the swirling Savoy crowd. Both wore dresses that were fashionably short and showed fairly generous lengths of well-turned calves. He also noticed that both had been careful with their make-up which had been applied with skilled restraint. He approached them with both hands out.

"Well, here you are," Miss Maitland said, and assumed a professional pose. She darted forward and took one hand. "Amazing, but I would have known you anywhere . . . just speaking on the telephone." She was garlanded with smiles, excited gestures and flashing eyes. "Oh, this is Winnie, Miss Winspeare. She's in our show too."

"Great. It was good of you both to come."

Dido wore a popular toque of jade green and gold topped with a green feather. The varied lights of the lounge highlighted her amber-yellow hair and accented her eyes. Her dress was a bronze-green gabardine, trimmed with cut fringe and a touch of fur around the square neck. "Wouldn't have missed it for the world," she said, glorying in their luck and looking around the high-arched lounge. There were girls in dance frocks, uniforms of khaki or blue, sterile gowns of the nursing services, and hats that had been designed on those being worn by women in the military services. Everyone wanted to be considered to be doing his bit. There were half a hundred different regimental uniforms, cap badges, Scottish trews, a few dress kilts, and gold-ringed sleeves of the Silent Service.

Max grabbed her upper arms and studied her for several seconds. Then he remembered his role and turned to Winnie. "Hello, Miss Winspeare," he said cheerfully. She was an inch or two shorter than Dido but had a beautiful figure and the movements of a showgirl. Her hair was spun bronze as were her eyes which by now had caught the sprawled figure of Wallington, and were showing their disdain. She, too, wore a toque—one of black velvet—crowned with a spray of white feathers. Her dress was two shades of gray flannel, trimmed with brick-red and black embroidery.

Ralph finally floundered to his feet, and stood buttoning his tunic collar. Max moved the group together and completed the introductions. "This is Lieutenant Wallington . . . Ralph. He's a hulking Canadian lumberman, Winnie, so you'll have to expect some backwoods' behavior, but he's really a jewel beneath it all."

"Winnie'll be able to handle him," Dido warned. "She just loves Canadians."

"Well, hello!" Wallington boomed, and threw a massive arm across Miss Winspeare's shoulder. "We got the makings of a great evening."

Dido broke it up with, "Did you get tickets for the show?"

"Did we get tickets for the show?" Ralph barked. "We got a whole roll of 'em! You girls can prepare for anything tonight."

Miss Maitland and Miss Winspeare were puzzled by Ralph's brash manner and the inference of his words. Max knew they were in for a difficult evening, and tried to soothe the situation by announcing, "At any rate we have reservations for the dining room, and you're right on time." He took both girls by the elbows and led the way. Ralph stood mumbling. "Jees! I didn't know we had to make reservations. How'd you think of that?" Max was thankful for the instruction he had learned from the Reverend Mr. Rushton. At the time he did not know he would be using it in the heart of London.

The headwaiter took over long enough to get Ralph in a quieter frame of mind. The room was already well filled with guests, and a hidden orchestra was giving forth with several of the standard chamber music numbers, and then suddenly swung into *The Cobbler's Song* from *Chu-Chin-Chow* at which both girls sat up straight and began to clap with enthusiasm. Their response caught the eyes of several diners and one or two immediately recognized Dido and applauded in return.

"What's all the excitement about?" Ralph asked, looking up from the menu.

"They're playing music from our show."

"Why? Hey, maybe they know you girls are in it, eh?"

Max said, "It's just a coincidence. It's a very popular musical. Now, how about wine? Anyone have a preference?"

The two girls showed interest, but Ralph growled, "Who the hell wants that belly wash. Let's get some real stuff. I say, Bronx cocktails all around."

Winnie Winspeare frowned and appealed to Max. "But we have to give an evening performance. Just light wine for me."

"Quite right. A good dinner and some suitable wine," Max said and beckoned the wine steward.

"You have your grapeade. I'm having a double Scotch and soda."

"Could we have a bottle of, well, something along the line of a good sauterne?" Max asked, keeping one eye on Ralph.

"May I suggest, sir, as a wine suitable for almost anything you may order, a good amontillado."

Max nodded uncertainly. "I'll leave it to you, but a good sherry might be just the thing."

"Very good, sir."

Dido took up the subject. "Well, since we're ordering sherry, a light meal will be ideal."

"See what I mean?" Ralph interrupted. "Order lousy wine and you have to order the fodder accordingly.

"Not at all," Max replied, remembering something his vicar had taught him. "That's a fallacy. Generally speaking, good wines can be served with fish, meat, or fowl. Only rank purists insist on white wine with fish."

"I love sherry," Winnie said. "It has everything—color, bouquet, and flavor. I'm going to order a creamed fish."

"I'm taking chicken à la king," Dido said. "Be quite enough before the show."

"A good idea," Max contributed. "Steak and kidney pie for me."

Ralph managed a disparaging grimace. "Why order grub like that here? You can have your wine and slop. I'm have a double Scotch and a steak. I hope we *can* get a steak in this beanery."

"You can get almost anything you want, as long as you pay for it," Max snapped back, "and this is no beanery, chum. You'll find out when you get back to Calgary, or wherever it is you came from."

The orchestra broke into *Beware of Chu-Chin-Chow*, a piece from the show, and the applause was renewed from other corners of the dining room.

"Good heavens!" Dido pealed. "We're being treated like stars. I thought only Oscar* or one of the principals of the show were recognized in this manner." She turned and raised her eyebrows at Max. "I swear you must have put the orchestra leader up to it. This has never happened before."

Max held up his hands and wagged his head. "I would never have thought of it. Someone must have recognized you as you came in."

"You're a darling," Dido said and leaned over to rub her fingertips lightly over his ribbons. "I'll bet you think of everything."

"I assure you," Max protested and kissed her cheek. "I had nothing to do with it. It would never occur to me."

"Where the hell's my double Scotch and that steak?" Ralph bellowed, and began to unhook his tunic again.

"And when they are brought," Max said with his jaw locked, "I want you to wolf both down and leave our party. We've had enough of your disgusting behavior."

"Yeh? Well what about Winnie here?"

"I'll take care of both Dido *and* Winnie. You can buzz off and find someone of your own stripe. I mean that, Wallington."

Ralph Wallington was big enough and ugly enough to have taken Max's tone as a slur, but the American stared him down. "No need to get sore. I'll pay you the ten quid back. Let's forget it and carry on, Sergeant Major."

But Max was in charge. "You're leaving the minute you finish guzzling and gorging your meal. If it can be arranged, we'll have you moved to another table by yourself. I will not have my friends

* Oscar Asche, author and star of *Chu-Chin-Chow*.

insulted by your manners." He turned to Dido. "Sorry, Miss Maitland, and you, Miss Winspeare. He's on his own from now on."

And in that manner the dinner at the Savoy became another turning point in Maxwell Kenyon's career. He knew the evening had tested him in several ways. He had annealed his courage by his handling of Wallington who was inches taller and pounds heavier. It had stiffened his moral fiber, and he knew that no man, no matter how big or offensive, would ever immobilize him with fear. For the first time he realized the power of words and the manner of their delivery, for they had stopped the lout in his tracks. He had had to slink off on his own the minute the foursome left the dining room. On the way to the main doorway, Max took one of the theater tickets, tore it in shreds and dropped them into a wastebasket. Wallington, who watched the gesture mark the end of his short acquaintance with Maxwell Kenyon, strode through the twirling doors.

Miss Winnie Winspeare allowed time for Ralph to head toward the Strand, and then left by a rear entrance. "I'll see you back at the theater, Dido. Thanks for the dinner, Max," she said with a friendly smile. "Don't worry about your friend's behavior. We get all sorts, don't we, Dido?"

"Better luck next time, Winnie," Max said, and flicked her a sad salute. "What now?" he said to Dido.

"I have a little time before we have to report in. Let's go back to the lounge. It's quiet and comfortable. We can talk there, and there's a lot to talk about."

Max agreed and found a settee beside a drooping palm. "I'm sorry that oaf behaved like that. He's been like that all day."

Dido moved in closer and he caught the scent of her Golliwogg perfume, and felt strangely at ease with her. "I hope I never behave like that," he said thoughtfully. "I wasn't cut out for this level of society. I have a pretty shoddy background to live down, and it's going to be hard enough behaving like a gentleman, now that I'm commissioned. To me, this is a world of luxury, but perhaps if I manage to hang on and keep drawing my flying pay I'll be able to bring myself up to some respectable level."

"You're doing splendidly, but I know what you're talking about. I came from the gutter, too, and am still wondering how I got up here," Dido said in a low voice.

"When I was out in France, I had a lot of luck, but with one medal I became greedy and wanted more . . . more important medals. I once thought I was entitled to a Victoria Cross, but got only a D.C.M. I realize I behaved badly about it, but what can be expected from a guttersnipe. Now I'm commissioned, I'm afraid I shall want higher rank before I've earned it. There's some ingrown greed in me, but if you knew my parents, that is, my mother, I think you'd understand. I'll tell you about her sometime, but not today. You've had enough of my kind for one evening."

Dido patted his knee. "Never mind, old sport. Perhaps I can take some of the pressure off. We're both from the lower classes and we both know where we stand. I like you . . . Maxwell. You're trying to do the right thing."

Max responded with a dismal smile. "It'll work out. I'm looking forward to seeing you dance. You're the lovliest person in that opening number, and you twirl about like a vision."

"It'll be wonderful, knowing you're out front," Dido said reflectively. "By the way, are you staying in town tonight?"

Max stiffened and stared about. "Good Lord! I'd forgotten all about that. I had planned to drop in at one of the officers' hostels and see what accommodation I could get. Ah, well, I'll probably have to find a room at one of the hotels."

"Where's your gear?"

"We checked our haversacks at the station. How are you set up . . . Where do you live?"

"What do you mean?" Dido flushed and looked uncomfortable.

"What about your flat? Or does Winnie live with you?"

"Winnie? Good heavens no! Winnie lives with her family out Wimbledon way. Very respectable, and all that. I'm quite on my own."

"Well, I was wondering . . ."

Dido looked pensive, and then made her momentous decision. "I suppose you could stay with me, although I've never gone in for this sort of thing before."

"I might be able to get into the Strand Palace or the Regent Palace. Practically all the R.F.C. crowd goes to either when they're on leave."

"But you might run into Wallington again."

Max tried on a grin. "Well, what about it? What's your landlady like?"

"No questions asked," Dido said and looked down at her hands. "I've plenty of room . . . if you'd like to try it. I'm just inviting you. I'm not soliciting . . ."

"I can't think of a nicer way to take the taste of that unpleasant dinner out of my system."

17

That evening with Dido Maitland was an experience of comfort and content, such as Maxwell Kenyon had never known. It had its moments of passionate delight, blissful exhaustion, scented slumber, and whispering wakefulness. Wholesome satisfaction came when Dido gave every indication this was how they would share each other at every opportunity, a prospect that also aroused somber reservations.

"You can come here every time you get up to town," the siren crooned in his ear. "If my landlady makes a fuss, I'll move elsewhere, my love. Remember, we've got to make the most of every leave. You'll be sent back to France as soon as you put your wings up. Oh God! I'll go off my head when that time comes."

"I'll be months completing my course," he assured her. "You mustn't let too much of this sort of thing interfere with your job . . . your work. We've both got to stick to the grindstone, at least while the war's on." He was talking through the ennui of relaxation, and figured once a month would be often enough to curl up like this.

Dido snuggled in closer and tweaked his ear.

"You're on your way up now," he warned, "so don't throw your chances away. I'll see you as often as I can, but your career is too promising to risk with too much of this sort of thing."

"Dancing? The theater? What does any of it matter? I've seen, or heard, of dozens of girls in the same situation. You're on top only a short time, and the ones with any sense get out and marry the boys they grew up with. Their own class. The others burn themselves down to a faggot trying to stay on top. Look at the Florodora Girls! They all married well, got out of the theater tanglefoot, and they're all happy as mudlarks. Let's not waste what we know we've got. There's a war on, love. Who knows whether we'll be here when the church bells ring out and the lights go on again. You can get it out there—like thousands of nice chaps—and I can get mine right in the middle of the second act if a blasted Zep bomb comes through the roof."

Max nodded sleepily and admitted there might be something to it.

But once he went through the guard gate at London Colney, the high stench of Castrol immediately erased the bewitching scent of Golliwogg perfume, and he took an evening shower with relish and gusto.

"Well, how was it?" Christopher Roland greeted him when he returned to his cubicle. "Have a good time?"

"Not too bad."

Roland vetted him carefully. "You look like you could do with a good night's sleep. I hope you two behaved yourselves."

"Well, one of us did," Max said, unfolding his pajamas. "How'd it go with you?"

"Oh, you know. Two dozen relatives were dragged in. Mother put on a spread, heaven alone knows how, but we had a glorious feed and a family singsong. Father plays the piano, and before the table was cleared half the village came in and tootled away with the old-time choruses. In half an hour most of us could hardly speak. Even the village policeman barged in, took off his helmet and sang:

> 'I'm P.C. 49
> Anyone can have this little job of mine.'

It had about twenty bawdy choruses, one or two of which made the vicar ask for another glass of sherry. We had a lively time."

"Sounds wonderful. You must include me next time."

"You'd love it. It's such a change from military life."

"Oh, well, here we are back to reality again. Anything special up in orders?"

"We're all back, continuing the motion. I suppose you'll be in for a week of heavy solo time. Wallington is to be passed on to "H" hangar to take up the Sopwith Pup. Once he gets in a few hours on that, he'll probably be sent to one of the Fighter Training

Schools for aerial gunnery, or so I understand. We'll probably be out with a service squadron within a month."

Max pondered on that. "Still, it's not too much time, considering he has never been out to France. I wonder how he'll take that."

"I should think he'd jump at the chance," Chris said with sheer enthusiasm. "Wouldn't you?"

"I'm not quite sure at this minute. When I was an aerial gunner I never thought too much about piloting. I always hoped I'd become one, but I never thought much about the training, the effort it takes. I'm still not quite sure."

"Um. I see what you mean. It must be something like being a reserve on a cricket team, wishing you could go in to bat, but when the captain suddenly points at you to go in, you realize you know absolutely nothing about it. That's the way it was with us at Charterhouse."

"Well, let's forget about Wallington. I just hope they move him well away from our course. He's not our kind, Chris. Crude and a complete clod in company. Sit down, and tell me about Charterhouse. I've never been to a prep school."

"Really? I would have taken you for . . ."

"No. There wasn't the money in my family, and my parents looked down on too much education. I'm beginning to realize what I missed. Did you like Charterhouse?"

Christopher considered the question. "I can't conceive of anyone not liking a good prep school, its traditions, sports, discipline, and the friendships one makes. But just as here, there were clods who hated the place and behaved dreadfully, term after term. I don't know what they could have gotten out of it." He looked quizzically at Max. "You know, I suppose some of us will look back on the R.F.C. with the same warm feeling when it's all over. Don't you feel that way?"

Max sighed, squatted on the side of his bed. "I'm beginning to. I've had some hard knocks, but I've also been quite happy in a way I had never known before. I like the R.F.C. and, I suppose, as you say, we shall look back on these days in much the same manner as do fellows who come out of good universities. I've read how they go back, year after year, for class reunions, wearing their class colors and renewing old companionships. I wouldn't be surprised if we develop a spirit of that kind. And, of course, it would be in a very good cause, I suppose."

Chris got to his feet. "You're to be admired for your courage in the face of so many setbacks, Max. I hope you never lose that faith. I hope you'll be among those who see this war through. I thoroughly believe that evil things and swinish people are put into this world to try us, to test our mettle. I suppose God knows what's good for us. None of us can take the easy way out and discard moral principles."

Max listened with numb amazement. Mr. Rushton never voiced a sermon like this. Was this what a good prep school did to a young man?

Chris was continuing, "I don't suppose any of us will ever do a better thing, no matter how long we live, and somehow I don't particularly fear *not* coming out of the war, and if that happens I shall expect nothing in return from England."

Max could stand no more of this, and he interrupted with: "I'm not worrying about not coming out of the war. That should be easy. What worries me is the prospect of having to go back home— from what I came from. I can't stomach what I left, the stinking home, two sodden parents . . . well, they were half-drunk most of the time. We lived in a squalid tenement, like a brood of pigs. I never knew the fragrant smell of laundered shirts and underwear, unless I did my own. Our meals were revolting offal, and could have been served in a trough. The kitchen was usually a shambles unfit for monkeys in a zoo. The lavatory . . . bathroom, reeked to high heaven, and there was never a chance for a sluice down, because we kept the coal in the bathtub. My old gaffer was too bloody lazy to haul it up bucket by bucket from the cellar, so we dispensed with the bathtub. That's how I lived all my life until I joined up—and got my first taste of living like a human being. Right! The Army to me was what your prep school was to you. Plenty of decent grub, my clothes washed at regular intervals, and money in my pocket. Why should I go back?"

Roland sat staring at the palms of his hands. Finally, he said, "I must take you home next time. Father will keep you up all night answering his questions. My days at Charterhouse will be nothing compared to what you've been through . . . from all accounts."

"Buzz off," Max said, and pulled his bedcovers down. "I'll see you in the morning. Perhaps we can both clear off and tootle about over St. Albans and practice stunts."

"Once you get out of Mr. Crankshaw's hands. He's very interested in you, and has some special plans, as I understand it."

"Just as long as he doesn't make an instructor of me. I've had enough of that with machine guns. Good night, Chris."

"Well, how did your weekend go?" Lieutenant Crankshaw asked Max and Roland when they met outside the hangar. "Never mind. Don't tell me. I have a pretty good idea. Now let's get down to work."

"May I ask what has happened to Wallington, sir?"

"Wallington? Oh, the big Canadian. We've shoved him along for a spell on Sop Pups. He's a very good man and is ready for some single-seater time. Pups are just the thing. If he wasn't so bloody big, I'd have sent him on to D.H.2s, but he didn't seem too keen about flying a pusher, having had nothing but tractors. However, I think he'll do well on Pups."

Chris agreed. "He picked up B.E. flying fast and was throwing his bus all over the sky whenever I saw him stunting over Radlett."

"I'm glad to know that," Max said without further explanation.

"All right," Crankshaw decided. "I want you two to take separate planes and go off toward our reserve 'drome and practice school stunts; tight turns, both left and right, until you know you can do them without sideslipping. It's all a matter of using the rudder as an elevator once you get the wing well down. Then I suggest trying falling leafs, but not side by side. Keep one behind the other and try to make each sideslip the same distance and retain as normal an attitude as possible. Then go down for a few landings at the reserve field. If neither of you wipes off an undercarriage there, you may make a short cross-country flight up toward Hartford, flying side by side with about two wing lengths apart. That'll be enough for this morning. All clear?"

"Could we practice cross-wind landings at the reserve field, sir?" Max asked.

Crankshaw smiled. "A good idea, but make sure you know what you're doing, and keep your wind-side wing under control until you are actually down. I'm glad you brought that up, Kenyon. Off you go . . . and I'll want to see you before you clear off for lunch."

Kenyon and Roland thoroughly enjoyed themselves over the next hour, carrying out the instructor's orders, and Max soon realized that the young English lad was a natural flier who carried out his practice maneuvers with artful skill—probably without knowing just what he was doing—whereas Max found that while flying the same figures equally as clean he had to put his mind on every position of the controls. He learned later that by these means he was unconsciously teaching himself the true fundamentals of flying, an inborn skill that was eventually to turn him into a highly proficient pilot.

The two fliers returned to London Colney, bright and breezy, and exchanged quips with the mechanics before they went into the hanger to fill out their logbooks. Crankshaw caught up with them there and glanced over their notations. He nodded his satisfaction and then guided Max into his sheltered office. "I want to have a few words with you, Kenyon. You've plenty of time before lunch. It's something personal, so I brought you in here."

"I hope nothing's wrong, sir."

"Just a friendly chat. By the way, I met an old friend of yours on Saturday. Captain Horace Drage. He told me he came over from New York with you and wanted to be remembered . . ."

"Drage! Horace is a captain now?"

"He's with a new Sop Pup squadron, one just being organized. He has one of the flights. Damned good man from all accounts. He has been out on D.H.2s, and picked up a bar to his Military Cross."

"Good old Horace."

"He asked about you and how far you were on your course."

"Do you think he was considering asking for me?"

"I'm pretty sure he would, if you finish in time."

"What's my chance, sir?" Max asked, hoping to join Drage again. "I'd love to fly Pups. Not much time, but perhaps I could join him after they get out to France."

"There's a good possibility, but I don't like the idea of rushing your training. In fact, I'd rather keep you here and have you take instruction on several types. Who knows, we might be able to make a test pilot of you. You have many of the natural attributes for such a job, Kenyon. I want you to think it over."

Here I go again, Max reflected, but asked, "Are you trying to create a soft berth for me, sir? I mean, is there anything wrong—physically—with me?"

"Nothing like that. You came out of hospital with a very good medical sheet. It's nothing like that, but we have had instructions from Central Flying School to look out for students with certain qualifications for these special, and most necessary tasks. I want you to think it over. There's no real rush for you to get back to France. You've had your share of it."

"Just what does a test pilot do, sir?"

"It's rather an exciting job and damned important. Some fliers are assigned to the factories where they test-fly the aircraft as they come off the lines. A few are posted to the development people, testing all types of new machines, others remain at the schools checking out aircraft that have been given major repairs after crashes. There're a dozen good posts for chaps who can test-fly many types. I should think you'd like it. It offers good prospects for after the war."

Max became thoughtful, but showed his lack of interest. "I'd rather keep on as I am with the idea of going back to France, sir."

"Well, don't turn it down now. Take time to think about it. They wanted a youngster named Sergeant McCudden to take test pilot-ing, but he was like you. He'd been out at the front as an aerial gunner, picked up a Military Medal and couldn't wait to get back. I believe he's out on D.H.2s. He would have made an ideal test pilot."

"I know the feeling. All gunners want to become pilots. They've been hauled about by all sorts of ham-fisted Quirks, and feel they can do ten times better, but I'll think about it, sir." The risks of test flying had no place in Kenyon's thinking; the only dread he had known was fighting as an infantryman in the trenches. Flying with the R.F.C. was a cakewalk compared to that.

"Good man."

"Just as long as they don't try to make an instructor of me."

"Not a chance. You don't have the temperament for that," the lieutenant said, and laughed.

Max soon realized his routine training was being slowed up, or extended with added features of flight training, and he was un-able to keep pace with Chris who, within another week, was posted on to an instructor who soon had him making school flights on Sop-with Pups that already were being used as first-line scouts at the front. On the other hand, Max was persuaded to fly other models of the B.E., still carrying out routine exercises, such as normal and short circuit-landings, steep turns with and without the engine, take-offs and landings cross-wind, sideslip landings, and various types of approaches to land on fixed marks. As time went on, he was encouraged to try more advanced maneuvers, such as looping, rolling, spinning, making stall turns, and carrying out fighting tactics against other students.

"You're doing well," Crankshaw insisted, "and I hope you appreciate what this extra training is making of you."

The week sped by on many types of wings. He flew every morning when weather permitted, and attended lectures during the afternoons. Gradually, he became philosophical about becoming a test pilot, although he wanted to keep up with Chris. He had come to like the English lad who was so unassuming and rational in his behavior and views. He usually sat with him at lectures, and went to meals with him, chiefly to study his attitude, vocabulary, and to adopt some of his school pattern. He noted that Chris read the more respected London newspapers, the two chief aeronautical weeklies, and usually had the latest book tucked under his arm. Being an avid reader, he could usually take part in any nominal conversation pertaining to the latest political or military situation. One thing Max noted in particular was that Chris never made dogmatic statements, but always prefaced his remarks with, "Well, in my opinion, and from what I read I feel Kitchener should have taken a more immediate interest in the Dardanelles affair, and given it his full support. Of course, I may be wrong, however . . ." He thereby usually disarmed his opponent in any argument, and certainly never aroused any bitterness during such discussions. It was a knack Max hoped to acquire.

There was no weekend leave that Saturday, at least for any of the group of trainees, and Max decided to enjoy his stay on the field, make the most of the lounge, the billiard room and bask in the late summer weather by taking a long walk toward Watford. It would be not too heavy a drain on his pay, and might give him another opportunity to broaden his study of Chris.

But the early planning was suddenly disrupted on Friday when Max received a hastily scribbled note from Dido Maitland, explaining she would be in London Colney over the weekend, and would be staying at one of the convenient theatrical boardinghouses near the center of town. She hoped he would try to see her.

"What the devil now?" Max said, reading the note over a second time. "How can she slip out of her part in *Chu-Chin-Chow?*"

"What's wrong?" Roland inquired.

Max explained with limited enthusiasm. "You've heard of Dido Maitland, the dancer in *Chu-Chin-Chow?* I saw her during last weekend. She's coming here. Looks like I shall have to give up our walk, Chris."

The English lad looked disturbed. "I don't think you can bring her on the field . . . unless there's a dance or some station program to which civilians are invited. But perhaps she could get in for Church Parade on Sunday. That's usually easy."

"That's out! I'm supposed to lead the Cadets. I'd forgotten about that."

Max's experiences with infantry drill while serving with the London Scottish had given him a certain prestige on the parade ground, where he barked, "Form Fours! By the right! Quick march!" to the complete satisfaction of all flight sergeants on the aerodrome.

"It is a bit of a nuisance, and I can't understand how she's able to get out of the two Saturday performances."

"She's something of a featured dancer, isn't she?"

"Her name's well up on the program. She'll get to the top if she sticks to it, and I don't see why she would duck two important performances."

An inner voice warned Max that all was not well with Miss Maitland, and with certain misgivings he borrowed a bicycle to get into town. Why the devil did Dido have to traipse up here?

He located her in a neat, comfortable boardinghouse, one that for years had accommodated cyclists who had pedaled down the Great North Road into London on Bank Holidays. It was owned and managed by Mrs. Eliza Clines, a widow of a Boer War veteran. "Oh yes," she cooed when Max inquired if Miss Maitland was staying there. "If you'll wait in the parlor here, I'll pop upstairs and tell her."

"No need, Ma'am. I'll save you the steps. Just give me the number of her room," Max said in all innocence.

Mrs. Clines halted in her righteous indignation. "She'll come down to the parlor, sir. This is a respectable house, I'll have you know."

"I'm sorry. Will you please tell Miss Maitland that Corporal . . . er, Lieutenant Kenyon is calling?"

"That's more like it." Mrs. Clines sniffed and straightened her mauve-colored house smock. "I'll see if she is available."

Max retreated into the parlor, a cell that looked as though it had been set out for the viewing of a corpse. A bunch of faded straw flowers had been arranged in the fireplace and above the mantel was a gaudy lithograph showing a tabby kitten with one paw in the top of a bowl of goldfish. It was titled *The Culprit*, copies of which were on view in thousands of British homes of that day. The velvet-cushioned furniture was protected with white starched antimacassars. The floor was covered with a well-waxed spread of linoleum that was garish with sprays of tropical foliage, and an oval puce rug was before the fireplace fender. Scattered about the walls were framed postcards of Skegness, Bournemouth, and the ubiquitous Blackpool Tower. One dreary section bore the "marriage lines" of Mr. and Mrs. Clines, the birth certificates of two daughters, a faded telegram announcing that Private Bosworth Clines of the King's Royal Rifles had been killed in action at Magersfontein, December 11, 1899. A bewhiskered man in loose-fitting khaki squinted from a frame constructed of cork discs cut from the stoppers of ginger beer bottles, and a *Prayer for Our Men in Africa* was pinned up at an angle just beneath. In some contrasting relief was a colored picture of Zena Dare in theatrical tights, neatly stuck in one corner of a discolored mirror.

Max was fascinated by the general display and was examining a small case of mounted insects when he heard Mrs. Clines making a stately return down the stairs.

"Miss Maitland will be with you—presently," she announced pertly, but still maintaining her monolithic guard at the bottom of the stairs.

"Thank you."

Within a minute Dido appeared, bringing a zephyr of perfume, illumination and gaiety into the funeral chamber. She wore a heather-mixture suit and her hair was brushed until it produced its own glints. Her eyes were agleam with anxious anticipation. She swept toward Max, glanced back at Mrs. Clines and through her delight said, "Thank you. We'll be quite all right here."

Mrs. Clines peered down her beak and said. "I shall be nearby if you need me."

"I shall be all right."

"I'll be the one to decide that," the harridan declared and slowly mounted the stairs.

Dido flung herself into Max's arms. "Darling! I just had to come."

"What are you doing here? Is anything wrong?" Max snapped.

"I just had to . . . Aren't you glad to see me?"

"Well, yes, but what about the show?"

Dido glanced back toward the hall stairs. "What does it matter? I begged off hoping my sub, Wendy Notting, can take over." She was making a pathetic appeal about something that eluded Max. He took time to stroke her cheek and kiss her forehead. "I thought you'd be glad to see me. It's been almost a week, and I hadn't heard from you. How did I know? You might have been . . . in a crash."

"Don't be silly. You'd have heard somehow. It would have been in the casualty lists."

"That's what I'm afraid of. I never dare look at the papers."

"If you lose your job in the show, what will you do? You can't go barging off like this."

"I simply had to come. You didn't write, or anything. I just had to know you were all right. I dread you knocking about in the Flying Corps. You're such a wild devil . . . all those medals."

Kenyon was puzzled, but wondered why all this sudden panic. "Are you all right? I hope nothing happened after last week," he said in a lowered voice.

"Nothing happened, but it shouldn't."

Kenyon exhaled with relief. "Well, what are you doing here?"

"Don't you understand? I just had to come see you again . . . and make sure you were all right." She stood with her hands on his shoulders, a tear glistening in one eye. "Can't we go somewhere for a place to sit down and perhaps have a cup of tea?"

"There isn't much in this place, as far as I know, but I haven't seen much of it, except from the air. Perhaps we can find a tea shop nearby." He was still puzzled about her appearing here.

"Wait until I get my hat."

He drew her close to him again. "You certain you haven't lost your job? I mean, bunging off like this. This is Saturday. Don't you have two performances today?"

"What does it matter? I can always get something else. My agent,

Solly Weinstein, says he can get me on at the Palladium any time. I just had to see you. Don't you understand?"

A frown deepened on Max's face. "Who's Solly Weinstein? You never mentioned him before."

"He's my agent—like a manager. He helped me get started, and takes care of the business end of my work."

This was new to Kenyon. "I don't understand. Who pays him?"

"I do. Out of my pay packet. All people in the theater have agents. They get you jobs and take a percentage of what you earn."

"How old is Solly, er, what's-his-name?"

"Solly? I don't know. He must be in his fifties. What are you getting at?"

"Nothing, but we've got to work out these visits better than this. I'm not entirely free, you know. I have to take Church Parade tomorrow, and we're supposed to be available most of the time. It's all part of the training. After this, I think we'd better keep it to meetings in London . . . at your place."

Dido was wringing her hands, her eyes reflecting her anguish. "But you may be going off—back to France any day. That mess on the Somme . . ."

"Stop worrying about me. I haven't got my pilot's wings yet, and there's some talk of my being kept here on some Home Establishment duty. I can't talk about it, because there's nothing definite to say."

Dido's eyes glistened again. "That'll be wonderful! I could come down and stay here . . ."

"Don't jump to conclusions," Max said, and frowned.

18

That afternoon and evening were hours of anguish and frustration. Unable to find a convenient nook or sheltered byway where their pent-up emotions could be unleashed, Dido and Max had to wander up and down the streets of London Colney where Max sensed they drew unwanted attention from the townspeople, to say nothing of the leers of military men who were attracted by the unusually smart girl. Today, she was a type seldom seen in provincial towns, and there were instances when Max wished he had never been commissioned. He returned salutes by the dozens, many snapped by mechanics who serviced his machines and swung his props. They all gave Dido the glad eye. No question about it, Miss Maitland was a standout. She wore a jaunty beret with an R.F.C. badge pinned where it caught the eye. Her suit was perfect for the autumn afternoon, but instead of standard fringed brogues and ribbed stockings, she flaunted silk hosiery and medium-heeled pumps that caught every eye.

Still, both would have settled for a quiet parlor in some modest hotel where they could have had a private hour or so to themselves, but London Colney offered no such conveniences. Instead, they had to make the best of a third-rate cinema, the local Picturedrome.

"We've got to give up this idea," Max grumbled as they left the moving picture theater. "There's nowhere to have any time to ourselves. Everyone's gawking at us, just as though they knew what we're up to."

"But there must be . . ."

"All these towns where troops are stationed are being run like a regimental barracks. It's not like 1914 or '15. There are Military Police and Provost Marshals all over the place. I don't want to be picked up by any of them, and you can't afford to. We'll have to be satisfied with weekends when I can get to London."

Dido nodded glumly. "I suppose so. Well, let's pop in somewhere and get some supper. I'm famished."

"You really ought to go back tonight. Tomorrow I shall have to take Church Parade and won't be able to get away until well after lunchtime. Then it will be the same damn' thing all over again, wandering through a park, sitting on benches, and being stared at until we're both ready to scream."

"What about the Church Parade? Civilians are let in, aren't they?" Dido clutched at a straw. "I'd love to see it with you up front. Can't I do that, Max?"

"I'll try to find out, if I see one of the officers of the instruction staff."

They found a small quiet pub where, after ordering port wine, Max learned the proprietor could serve a veal-pie supper in the Ladies' Lounge, and would be glad to oblige.

"Splendid!" Max beamed. "And could we have a bottle of stout with it?"

"I think I can manage a bottle, sir," the publican said and darted to the other end of his counter.

As they sipped their port, Lieutenant Crankshaw appeared and made his way to an open space at the bar. Waiting for attention, he turned and saw Kenyon and his companion. He raised one eyebrow, grinned, and then decided to move in.

"Well, good evening, Kenyon. Never expected to see you in here. What's the occasion?"

Max was delighted to make the introductions. "Dido is a dancer in *Chu-Chin-Chow*." he added.

"Of course. I should have recognized the name. What a capture you have made. You'll be the most popular chap on the aerodrome. Delighted to meet you, Miss Maitland."

Dido ran through the eye-flashing business, cocked her head properly and made the most of her theatrical charm. "Won't you sit down?"

"We're going to have a supper here in the Ladies' Lounge as soon as it can be prepared," Max explained. "Why don't you join us?"

"Oh, no. Three's a crowd. Besides, I have a bit of fluff waiting for me at the station. Some other time."

"Naughty! Naughty!" Dido taunted and pealed with laughter.

"Not in London Colney," Crankshaw said. "We're quite chaste and fragrant. Mrs. Grundy, the Wesleyan chapel, and the Salvation Army rule here. We have to go up to town to kick over the shafts." He took another glance at Dido. "You're not hurrying back for to-night's performance, are you?"

"No, I begged off," she said, giving Max one of her stage winks.

Max said, "I'm taking Church Parade tomorrow. Is there any way Dido can get on the station and attend the service? I believe a few civilians are allowed in. What's the routine?"

"Easy. She reports to the Guard House, gives your name and she'll be allowed through. You may even take her into the Officers' Mess for lunch. Just sign a chit for her meal. You can show her around the hangars afterward. There may be some routine flying . . ."

"Wonderful!" Dido and Max cooed together.

"Speaking of flying," Crankshaw went on, "have you made a decision about the matter I brought up the other day?"

Max said quietly, "If you still favor the idea."

"I certainly do. Listen to me. The R.F.C. is expanding so much, a special Testing Squadron is being organized at Upavon in Wilt-shire, near Salisbury Plain, a bleak, inhospitable place, but you'll have a certain amount of freedom."

Dido listened with eager concern. "Will he be able to get up to London often?"

"The routine is nothing like a training field. Then there's Salis-bury, Andover, and of course Southampton quite convenient."

"Dido will love that," Max said hurriedly.

"Anyway most aircraft offered to the R.F.C. are checked out there. You'll get a chance to study design, control systems, arma-ment, and the way each one handles in the air. You'll get all sorts —dozens of new types and old types that have been modified for further use. It will be a wonderful opportunity for you."

Max pondered over his port, then glanced at Dido. He found the answer in the appeal of her eyes. "If you think I'd qualify after I get my wings, I'll make a formal application. I think I'd like that sort of thing."

"I'll put you in for it, myself. You're the perfect type for the Testing Squadron. You have a certain attitude toward flying, and I know from your experiences with that Strutter in Number 70 Squadron, and your handling of Brasenose's B.E. you have the perfect reaction to emergencies. That's what a test pilot needs most of all." Crankshaw glanced at Dido. "You know, Miss Maitland, you have picked a young man with an interesting future. Don't let him get away."

"What do you think she's doing *here?*" Max said with a faint smile.

"We'll consider it settled, then." Crankshaw got to his feet. "I'll just down a quick one at the bar—and I'll see you both again tomorrow at Church Parade."

To make up for the shortcomings of the night, the next day gave promise of better things. Dido changed into her bronze gabardine dress, clapped on the saucy toque and walked to the guarded entrance of the aerodrome. She encountered no trouble there for Lieutenant Crankshaw had found it convenient to be on hand when she arrived, and proudly escorted her to the lounge of the Officers' Mess. He explained, "Max usually has to take the Cadet group for the Church Parade. He's had plenty of infantry drill somewhere, probably in the London Scottish, and he turns them out beautifully."

"I'm dying to watch him."

"He's going to make a fine young officer," Crankshaw predicted. "I know he wants to get back to France where he thinks there's more chance for promotion—and honors—but he's wrong. He can come unstuck fast if his luck runs out. With a Testing Squadron he can get all the rank he can take—and just as many decorations. Not the V.C. of course, but who would turn down a D.S.O.?"

Dido listened intently. "Please make him heed you. I'll go mad if he goes back to France. He's such a thruster . . . probably can't help himself, but I don't know what I'd do if anything happened to him. I'd go all to pieces."

"Here! Here! That won't do. You've got to consider your work in *Chu-Chin-Chow*."

"None of that matters much now," Dido said quietly. "I've known him only a week, but . . ."

"You're talking rot!" Crankshaw snapped and grabbed her elbow. "These are war times, and we all have to face up. Your job is just as important as mine or Max's. London, and what it means to servicemen on leave, is just as important as a new gun, a faster aeroplane, a bigger bomb, or the comfort of a military hospital.

This is a lousy war. We all know that, and anything that adds a bit of charm or gaiety is as important as the munitions. You stay on your job."

Dido nodded thoughtfully, but did not answer. She was taking in the trappings, the discipline, the military glamour of her surroundings.

A peal of reed and brass raised Lieutenant Crankshaw to his feet. "Well, there goes the band. We'd better get out and find a place somewhere up front. We hold our church services in the gymnasium and there will be reserved seats in the front for visitors, and there seems quite a lot this morning. Let's pop along." They hurried around the barracks square and took a position near where the regimental band was stationed in front of the gymnasium. Crankshaw had to leave her to join the group of Staff officers who had formed up behind the CO, a colonel who would take the salute from each group as it passed and then turned to march into the cavernous building.

The band was giving forth with *Murray's Welcome*, a popular Scottish march that had every foot tingling, and Dido found herself keeping time and swinging her hips until she caught sight of a company of Cadets emerging from an area of wooden barracks. She first noted their caps and the white Cadet bands and then her eye spotted Max striding along in front, chin in, chest out, and swinging his arms in the exaggerated style of the drill master. As the group approached the low dais on which the colonel and his aide stood, he let out a bellow that would have more than satisfied Kipling.

"*COMPANY! . . . EYES . . . RIGHT!*"

With that off his chest, Kenyon gave a salute, smart and prompt.

Dido had to look twice to make certain the ramrod-erect company leader was the same man who had been so warm and tender the night before. She caught her breath, felt an inner titillation of pride that is aroused by such an experience, and then she heard Max bark:

"*EYES . . . FRONT! . . . COMPANY . . . RIGHT WHEEL!*"

The Cadets responded and turned into the wide doors of the gym. The band continued its martial strain until the small group of civilians and the colonel's staff had moved inside. A young air mechanic, brushed, shaved, and pomaded for the occasion, acted as an usher and conducted the visitors to their reserved section and saw that they were provided with a hymnal and a Book of Common Prayer.

Sitting amid a well-dressed group of worshipers from nearby villages, yet completely alone, Dido knew this was the life for her. The theatre need never have been built. Neither had His Majesty's. The atmosphere of the military building with its waxed and polished floor, the hundreds of young men responding to the service, the restrained strings of a Cadet orchestra, the echoes of the hymns, the dignity of men in khaki, and the security of this companionship assured her that all was well, and that her whole future rested in the capable hands and arms of Maxwell Kenyon. She had no intention of being turned back at this juncture.

"Onward Christian soldiers
Marching as to war!"

The training program continued at London Colney in spite of periods of inclement weather, crashes, unreasonable demands by the Air Board, and requirements from the front. New groups of Cadets marched in, took up their courses, and before they were fully acquainted with the depot, were posted away as subalterns and deposited with other Depot Training Squadrons. Christopher Roland packed up and went off to Lilbourne near Rugby where he received further instruction on scouts and began his air-fighting and deposited with other Depot Training Squadrons. Christopher tactics. Max saw little of Ralph Wallington but heard indirectly that he had gone on to Yatebury on the Marlborough Downs near Swindon.

Kenyon completed his basic training at London Colney, but was kept on for several weeks carrying out various flying duties, such as ferrying trainers from the factories, giving repaired planes the required engine and control tests before they were turned over to students. He feared he would be inveigled into some minor instruction work, but no such suggestions were brought up. During this time he had several weekends in London with Dido; leaves that were more wearying than any period of flying at London Colney. For one thing, Dido had been given notice to leave the cast of *Chu-Chin-Chow*, and Solly Weinstein had not been able to get her hired as a dancer anywhere in London. He could have placed her with one of the provincial touring companies, but Dido wanted none of that, with the result she had to give up her comfortable flat in Kensington and take something far less luxurious in Golders Green. This was disturbing for Max who had looked forward to another nuzzle down Sheet Lane with his paramour. Still, he managed to be philosophical. "Oh, well, we'll have to make the best of where you are, I suppose."

"But I can't take you there, Max," she wailed. "I just can't. It's a blasted bear's nest and so awfully out of the way, but what can I do."

"Go back to work. There must be hundreds of jobs, the way all the theaters are jammed every night."

"You don't understand. I'm looked on as a dancer only."

"Damn it all. You can do anything, can't you? In *Chu-Chin-Chow . . .*"

"I know I can, but producers are hard to convince."

"We can't afford to lay up at posh hotels every night on my pay. We spend quids every time I come to town. You don't contribute anything. I have expenses at the aerodrome, now that I'm commissioned. There are mess bills, wine chits, and I have to buy my uniforms, etc. now."

Dido pondered on these pressing problems as they sat in the lounge of a second-class hotel in the Bloomsbury area where she was known. She had given the manager to understand that she had been secretly married to the handsome Flying Corps officer, and as long as they paid their bill he was willing to share and keep their "happy secret."

"I'm sorry, darling. Just this weekend. I'll try my best to get something." She brightened a trifle.

"You'd better. I'm to be sent down to Upavon next week to begin my test pilot training. I probably won't be able to get to London for perhaps a month."

"Couldn't I come down there? It would, or should, be cheaper."

"No. I'll be involved in all sorts of things, besides flying. Lectures by the dozen. Also, you ought to get back to work."

Dido stared into the melancholy across the lounge. "I suppose so," she said plaintively, "still, it will soon be Panto time, and I'm sure Solly can get me into something."

"Panto?"

"The Christmas pantomimes. Musicals for the kids. They put on all sorts through the holiday season. I'll be able to fit in somewhere." Her face took on a new light of interest. "You'll be able to get away for some of the Christmas holidays, won't you?"

"I hope so, but I don't know how a Testing Squadron is run. What's more important is that you get back to work. I don't like you hanging about, doing nothing, all by yourself. You can get into trouble dragging about London . . . with everybody home on leave."

"Don't worry about me. I know how to take care of myself. You're the one we should worry about. All that crazy flying and the sort of things you get up to."

"Let's see what we can think up . . . upstairs," Max said and pulled Dido to her feet. He ran the tips of his forefingers around the points of her breasts, and when she responded, he added: "Now you're on the gong. We have only two nights here, and then I go back to the other grind."

With that reflection they moved toward the creaky elevator, giving each other the hip as they crossed the lounge.

19

The Testing Squadron, organized at Upavon, was a natural off-spring of the Central Flying School that had been created in 1912 simultaneously with the Royal Flying Corps, to train young men to become military pilots. Originally, the school layout was, for some mysterious reason, set on bare land on top of a mountain where it was open to "every wind that blows," as the famous C. G. Grey, editor of *The Aeroplane,* once observed. The officers' quarters were situated on the northern slope of the hill with a 200-foot drop to be seen from their rear windows. The mess had been set up below the personnel quarters, so all who were taking the various courses had to climb a steep slope every time they moved from their meals or quarters to any part of the hangar-workshop area.

The hilltop, providing the landing area, was halved by a road that ran east and west between Andover and Upavon. Almost a dozen sheds were erected on the south side of the road, and in front of them was spread a narrow, flat landing space, quite satisfactory to experienced fliers, but which gave faltering Quirks space for thought. There were other landing areas of various sizes and slopes, and in the early days clumps of pine trees provided annoying updrafts or dangerous obstacles. Drops, dips, and unexpected depressions were innumerable and often trapped the unwary. However, the official selector of military properties obviously had no intention of transferring to the R.F.C., and argued that petrol engines always ran better in pine country. The problems of landings and take-offs had never occurred to him. The site had to do, however, and in fact contributed certain problems that fitted well into the training curriculum, particularly where a full program of landing situations was required.

One midafternoon in late November, Lieutenant Kenyon arrived at Upavon, was booked in, given reasonably comfortable quarters, shown around the shops and hangars, and almost immediately assigned to a class that was to be given short courses in instructor training.

"I understood I was to be trained as a test pilot," he complained to the adjutant, a spare, steely eyed man who had recently transferred from the Northamptonshire Regiment. He wore three gold wound stripes and carried his left arm in a light leather sling.

"You are, but the instructors' course is all part of it." He considered Max's two decorations and quietly envied him. All he had was the Mons Star, indicating he had gone out to the front early in 1914. "Don't worry, Kenyon. You'll never be banished to instructing. We understand you're not the type."

"What is meant by that?"

"In the first place you are too young, and well, your ribbons give you away. It takes a mature man with a mature attitude to make a cool instructor. You'll be just right for testing. There are few war heroes on the instructing staff."

There was no argument with that appraisal and Max submitted to an advanced course of flight training, a two-week period devoted to more explicit detail and a list of precision maneuvers Lieutenant Crankshaw had been unable to teach. Learning a more professional manner of flying an aeroplane seemed to come naturally to him. He passed out on many of the early types, including the comical, but amazingly stable, Farman Shorthorn, an early type of pusher that had been the work horse of the training system during the first two years of the war. The Shorthorn was a standard biplane with the cockpit mounted between the upper and lower planes. The tail assembly was carried on a pair of skeletal outriggers, and the under-carriage consisted of two pairs of wheels—and ash skids—set wide beneath the lower plane.

Kenyon found this comical contraption amazingly easy to fly, and handle in the air at a very modest speed, of course. He was then re-introduced to the B.E.2c and ordered by his instructor to carry out a series of turns, with power off, and power on, until he was ready to revolt. When they arrived back on the ground, his instructor just said, "You must use more top rudder on your right-hand turns, but otherwise you're coming along rather well. That's all."

This was how his first week passed, moving from one type to

another, being given a few minutes of ground instruction as to the quirks of each mount, how to get the most out of every engine, and the peculiarities of pusher or tractor controls. He enjoyed the comparative freedom of the station, and answered only to the typed orders that were posted every night in the lounge. Some days were devoted to a clearer understanding of all instruments, and again Max's skill in drawing stood him in good stead. To his satisfaction, several of them were commandeered and mounted on the walls of a classroom for others to study. He took part in the development of a bombsight which employed a number of nails, some copper wire, and the use of a stop watch.

Max was also credited with an idea that should have been obvious during the first few months of the war. In flying about the Salisbury Plain area he was amazed to note how easily aircraft were spotted on the ground, but became indistinct when they were in the air above. It was clear that the clean Irish linen used to cover the airframes took on a decided whiteness when it was doped. Thus, on the ground they stood out in sharp detail, but in the air were vague and indistinct.

"What we ought to do," he suggested, "is paint the upper surfaces of the wings and fuselage with a brown or green pigment, but leave the undersides in their natural color. That would make them more difficult to spot against the ground, or in the air."

The idea was passed about and, whether through Kenyon's suggestion or whether the idea had filtered through by other means to someone in authority, the first S.E.5s to come off the production line for active service were doped in just that manner.

Max was next ordered to check the instrument arrangements of every type he flew, and at the same time was advised that a new type of Avro, known as the 527, one fitted with a 150-horsepowered Sunbeam engine, was to be given an airworthy test.

"They hope to develop this one to replace the Sop Strutter," a captain of the Experimental Flight explained. "You've had time on the Strutter, haven't you? Go aloft for half an hour or so and see how it strikes you, particularly in the instrument panel layout."

"I can't imagine an Avro replacing the Strutter, sir."

"We can never tell until we try one out. Avro seems very zipped on this one. However, have a go and let me know."

Unquestionably, the machine was a typical Avro. It had the Avro fuselage, but the pilot's cockpit was well aft, compared to the

504s of the 1916 period. The eight-cylindered Sunbeam engine was water-cooled and had upright exhausts trunked above the top plane. The undercarriage used the same oleo boxes as had Avros before it. By now Max had developed an interest in new types, and he took over the 527 with no qualms. The engine fascinated him, and he had no trouble starting it, but he was bewildered by the panel layout, for the standard instruments were not in the expected positions, and he was disturbed by looking at what he thought to be the altimeter which proved to be the tachometer. He made a note of that, and then took off to enjoy himself over Andover. He put the aircraft through several routine figures, including figure eights, and then checked the rate of climb and control at low speeds. He decided the 527 would have to provide better than 103 miles per hour, and certainly *two* fixed guns for the pilot if it was to take its place on the Western Front.

He made his report, and the Experimental Flight skipper smiled and agreed. "Of course, if it is taken on, it'll have to have an up-to-date armament. As she stands, there is only something bolted on to make up for the proposed weight. Still, you are right about the instrument panel. Was she docile, otherwise?"

"Handles very well, even at slow speed, sir, but I think her name is against her. Everyone will remember learning to fly on an Avro —or how they were used as reconnaissance machines early in the war. The engine doesn't make that much difference."

"A good point, Kenyon."

"Anything else, sir?"

"Not immediately, but this afternoon I'd like you to take up one of the new F.E.2ds. They seem to be doing very well across the Channel, and there is talk of providing even better engines than the Beardmore. This model, the F.E.2d, has a Rolls-Royce Eagle I engine. You have flown the old Shorthorn, so you won't have too much trouble with this experimental model. See the flight sergeant before you go aboard. He'll set you straight and make sure you have a couple of sandbags in the front seat, or she'll fly tail-heavy."

"What am I to look for, sir?"

"Anything. You've never flown one, and we want to know the reactions of a pilot who is suddenly taken off one bus and told to fly another. The difference between the Avro and the F.E.2d might turn something up."

"I shall certainly have a dizzy logbook by the time I'm through here at Upavon, sir."

"Make the most of it. You're very lucky. Few men appreciate what they learn here. We had a Canadian, a lout named Wadding-ton, before you came. He was a damn' good pilot . . ."

"Do you mean Wallington, sir? Ralph Wallington?"

"That must be the bloke. A Canadian. Could fly anything damn well, but when he realized we were preparing him for further teamwork, he suddenly 'forgot' how and ran up three crashes in a row."

"Was he hurt?"

"Hurt? No. He knew how to fly—and crash. He wiped the under-cart off a Pup, cartwheeled a B.E., and then pancaked a Morane Parasol in the tops of those trees down there. Not a scratch in any of the write-offs. Amazing—but a tinker of the worst kidney."

"I knew Wallington, sir. A real clod."

"Damn shame. A good . . . great pilot, but he's ducking any-thing that requires a tinge of courage."

"What are you going to do with him?"

"Do with him? We packed him off to a squadron being formed to take the first S.E.5s out to France. We think Major Bloomfield will whip him into shape. He has a knack for it."

Max wagged his head. "I doubt it, sir. Wallington is an un-believable type. We'll hear more from him."

"Ah, well. Things average out. Wallington turns sour, but we get a few like you who make up for that."

When Max had washed and tossed his flying gear into his cubicle he walked over to the lounge where he found a couple of letters in the pigeonhole rack. One was from Christopher Roland up in Lilbourne.

All goes as usual. We're getting plenty of flying on anything that will get off the ground. We fly single-seaters most of the time and try to carry out scout squadron routines. The present rumor has it we are being trained for S.E.5s, and I surely hope so. That will mean a wild period of Fighting School somewhere in Scotland. I've never been across the border and shall look forward to it.

Then again other rumors have it we are to be held back for

something called a Bristol Fighter, a two-seater bus, I believe, but we hear it is something priceless and super.

How are you making out at Upavon? Hear it's a pilot's paradise, and you can fly anything from a Blériot monoplane to a Liverpool ferryboat. Must be fun. By the way, do you see anything of Wallington down there? I believe he was put on that test pilot course. Well, you're still welcome at the Roland estate (Pip! Pip!) any weekend we can make it together. Let me know what your leave schedule is and we'll try to cope.

All the best, *Christopher R.*

Kenyon smiled and wished he could write a letter in that breezy style. He wondered if he could get away for a weekend with Chris and his family, but the idea was dissipated when he opened the second letter which was from Dido Maitland.

Dearest Max,

I miss you dreadfully. When are you coming to London again? So far, no job in any of the Pantomimes. I have a feeling the theatre management has put a black ball on me—whatever that is. I keep trying all the agencies, but they act as though they never heard of me.

Yesterday I ran into your friend Wallington. I was sitting in the lounge of the Regent Palace, mainly to rest my trotters when up walked your Canadian friend. I didn't want to make a scene, and I did try to ignore him, but he sat down, asked about you, in a friendly way, and then asked me to have tea with him, bleating that he was all alone. I actually felt sorry for him and I must say he behaved fairly decently. We talked about you, of course, and he said you're going to be one of the Flying Corps' top heroes—if you don't get killed trying to win medals. He made my flesh creep but the tea came in handy, as I was stony broke. I do hope you never go back to France. He also told me he had had a couple of bad crashes, but he didn't look too bashed about, so I didn't ask too many questions. He think's he'll be going to France shortly with some new squadron. Do you know anything about it? Please let me know what you do in your new job. I mean the kind of flying. When will you be in London again? I'm so lonely and very broke, but you are not to send me any money. I'll get along, even if I have to go back to my mother's. I brought all this on myself, and you are not to try to buy me out. I love you so much, so please bear with me and let me know just what you are doing, and what the work is like. Lots of love and kisses.

                                                                    Dido.

Fuming and swearing under his breath, Max read the letter over and over. In his self-tortured mind it was a stunner. If she was that much in love with *him,* what the hell was she doing having tea with that swine Wallington?

"Hanging around the Regent Palace. Probably hoped she'd run into Wallington. It's always cluttered with R.F.C. guys." He shook his head like an ill-tempered bull. "She didn't have to have tea with that clod, no matter how hungry she was. Doesn't she have any pride?"

Kenyon had no idea what the hunger for companionship coupled with the hunger for nourishment could do for an outcast. He had never experienced either pang.

Bleak as the war was, the 1916 Christmas season afforded short leave periods for the troops. There was no immediate offensive in Flanders and furlough was still available, particularly to flying men because of the seasonable inclement weather. The infantry and other ground forces were provided with mended or even new boots, reasonably clean uniforms, and greatcoats that had been through steam baths set up in deserted breweries. Thus, they were able to go home for another Yuletide completely deloused, relieved of tin hats and rifles, and no longer appearing as though they had just crawled out of the trenches before Ypres.

Kenyon received another invitation to visit Chris's family for the holidays, but that was canceled out by a pathetic appeal from Dido Maitland. She had been taken on in a holiday Pantomime, *Dick Whittington,* which had saved her from having to crawl back to her mother's home in Shoreditch. She explained she had pawned some of her clothes and had even considered taking a Christmas-time job with Marks & Spencer.

Max tucked three one-pound notes into an envelope along with a letter explaining he hoped to be in London from the Saturday before Christmas and probably would be able to spend a week with her.

Dido was at Waterloo Station an hour before Max's train pulled in and spent the time striding up and down the spacious entrance hall, going over the steps and dance routines she had assumed in the legendary story of Dick Whittington—and his cat—who twice became Lord Mayor of London. Between these mental exercises, she read the prewar excursion posters, the war-news placards, and studied other anxious women who awaited their husbands, or sweethearts. A few had the avaricious look of those who expected no one, but were willing to take up with any man on leave who yearned for the glint of a "glad eye."

She tried to vet her appearance while walking past the dusty windows of the tea shop, but the reflection had been kindly subdued. She was wearing a blue serge suit much in need of a sponge and press. Beneath the jacket she had pulled on a fringy cardigan. Her gloves were scuffed, and one was minus a button. She had tried to draw the ruffled sleeve of a starched blouse below the sleeve of her jacket, for effect, but the result was hardly noticeable. Her hat was a narrow-brimmed straw, more suitable for midsummer, and the shapeless crown was trimmed with a yard of rusty grosgrain, and a pathetic spray of artifical cherries.

Her few weeks out of the cast of *Chu-Chin-Chow* had brought Dido Maitland to the level of a despondent streetwalker. She wore no make-up, her hair was lusterless and plainly dressed. She had the complexion of one who had fed well, but from the wrong menu.

The instant Max saw her, he was reminded of his mother, who managed to dress and look like that every time she went to a funeral. The decline in her appearance made him quake. When she rushed up to embrace him, he held her off and demanded, "What are you supposed to be? Are you on the stage again? I mean, is this something . . ."

"It's all I have, Max. I didn't spend any of the money you sent me. I know we'll need all you have." She stood off and looked him over. He was slimmer and trimmer than ever. There were hollows in his cheeks, and his tunic had taken on the look of a garment that had seen rough treatment. His wings were stained, and had lost their original silken sheen. Only his ribbons retained their pristine gleam. He had thoughtfully purchased and sewn on a new set.

"Darling, you look tired. What are they doing to you?"

"I'm all right. I like what I'm doing. I love it."

"Is this why you haven't been coming up to town? You don't know how I've missed you, Max."

"Are you still working?" he asked with a tone of command.

"I'm still in *Dick Whittington* at the Palace. It's not much, but it keeps me in stockings. Several top stars are in it—just for the fun—and the kids pack the theater."

"Well, come on. Where are you staying?"

"With three other girls in Lambeth Road near here."

"Oh, my God! That means we'll have to dig in at that bloody awful flop house in Bloomsbury. I won't be able to stay a full week at this rate. Do you have a bag?"

"Not with me. We have a matinee today, so I'll bring one from the theater afterward. In the meantime we can go somewhere nice for lunch. I'm starving for something, somewhere respectable."

"How long will this Panto thing run?"

"Until just after the New Year. That's all. Then I'll be back where I was. I may have to go home and get a job as a shopgirl."

"Have you seen Wallington lately?"

"Only once. Quite by accident."

"Of course. He must be living in London. What was he up to this time?"

"Oh, the poor devil. I felt sorry for him. He was supposed to go to Fighting School, but he had a physical breakdown."

"Probably a dose of clap."

"No, darling. Please believe me," Dido pleaded, unable to keep control of her hands. "He was in a proper hospital for about a week, and was told there was nothing the matter with him. It wasn't what you think."

"I wouldn't bet against it. He's a filthy clod."

"He thinks they're going to make a ferry pilot of him, whatever that is."

"That's about his level. How long did he hang around here, sponging on you?"

"How could he sponge on me? I haven't had a wage packet in weeks. I had to pawn most of the clothes I had bought when I was in *Chu-Chin-Chow.*"

"So he *was* paying the bill," Max persisted, and punched a fist into an open hand.

"It was only a dinner. Nothing else. He didn't have much money, or so he said. I wouldn't do anything like that . . . not with Wallington."

"Why the hell does he seek you out every time he's in town?"

"I don't encourage him. He just seems to turn up."

"Well, give him the push after this," Max grumbled but took her arm. "Let's go somewhere where we can talk things over. We'd better make it somewhere cheap in Fleet Street. I'm only a Second Louie, remember."

"Darling, I'll make it up to you. If we didn't have a show this afternoon, I'd say let's go straight to the hotel, but we don't get paid for rehearsals, and Pantos always hold back one week's pay. I won't get anything until next week, and most of it will go to pay back . . ."

That Christmas leave was expensive, in spite of Max's efforts to live cheaply. Their Bloomsbury hide-out was packed, and they had to settle for another where the rates were somewhat higher, particularly when the manager detected their illicit alliance. Short associations were made with other couples and these led to added drinking and impulsive decisions to have dinner in the West End. There were unnecessary tea dances at popular clubs where Dido hoped to be noticed—hours that could have been more profitably spent walking in the parks or simply enjoying the Yuletide displays in the shopping areas. Renowned museums, galleries, and free exhibitions held no attraction for Miss Maitland. She'd visited most of them under duress as a schoolgirl.

"I know we have to buy at least one drink, Max," she explained, "but you never can tell whom we might run into. All the most important people in the theater are to be seen there."

They took the gamble whenever possible, but no important people recognized Dido Maitland.

During the afternoon of Christmas Eve when funds were worse than low, Dido came up with a last-ditch idea.

"Look, sweetheart. Let's face it. I'd better go home and see what my mum and dad can do. They'll be in a proper holiday mood, I'm sure. I can pay them back when I get my Panto money."

Dido's parents could afford only a few shillings, holiday or no holiday, and she returned to their hotel with failure in her face and hopelessness in her posture.

"It's no use," Max said when she showed him the few half crowns she had borrowed. "I'm nearly broke. My account at Cox's is so slim, I'm not sure I can pay my mess bill which comes due at the end of the month. We can't go on like this. It's not worth it."

"I'm not worth it?"

"I mean, for what we are getting out of this miserable sort of thing. Don't misinterpret everything I say. If we were married as some of the fellows are, we'd probably have a little home somewhere. You'd either be working, or getting an allotment and we could provide our own living."

"I'll marry you any day," Dido peeped.

"Nothing doing! I've seen enough of that continual struggle . . . back home with my parents. Marriage is not for me—yet. I wouldn't go through that sort of thing. What I have seen in my own home has cured me of any of that life. Marriage is nothing but a nonstop argument, a daily flareup, arguments and quarrels that go on for hours. Who the hell wants that sort of thing?"

"My parents don't go on like that. They're lovely to each other."

"My God! You should see how mine carry on. All I remember, as a kid, was hiding under the bed, beneath the table, or tearing out of the door to get away from it. I used to think they would kill one another. Too bad they didn't."

"Maxwell! How can you talk like that?"

"I've got to go back to Upavon. What else can I do? I'll see Christmas Day in with you, but I shall have to clear off right after that—on Boxing Day. I'm sorry Dido, but we're really down on our uppers."

"I'm sorry, Max. It's all my fault," Dido said and fingered a tear from her cheek. "I should have stayed in *Chu-Chin-Chow,* but I thought only of you. You go back to your station. It'll be all for the best, and I know you don't want to take any chances with your . . . what you want to do in the Flying Corps." She brightened for an instant. "For two pins, I'd blasted well go and join up myself. They're taking girls to work in the Officers' Mess, I believe. I can't drive a motorcar, but I could become a waitress. It would be better than nothing, and who knows, I might get posted to your station."

"Talk sense. Your place is on the stage. You had no right to throw all that away, and who knows what this Panto job will lead to?" Max growled.

"If I joined up, I'd be *somewhere* near you, and I know you need me . . . stony-broke, or with packets of quids."

"You listen to me. In the Flying Corps, the Army, or any service you have to obey orders. You don't go fluttering about just as your feelings move you. The way you go on you'd be doing pack-drill fourteen hours a day!"

"I suppose so," Dido agreed listlessly.

20

Upavon on the tag end of Christmas was a dreary place. Everyone who could be spared had deserted the aerodrome. Those who were still on duty, lolled or lurched about with little interest in what they were supposed to be doing. There was plenty of extra food, but none of it was particularly palatable, so Max made a supper of a plate of Stilton cheese, a few thick slices of bread, and a glass of port wine. Reflecting that he could have been enjoying himself as the center of conversation at Chris's home, only added to the dreariness of the day. He wandered about the living quarters but could find no one he knew to talk to. Back in the lounge he curled up with the last few chapters of *Prester John,* knocked the billiard balls back and forth, and finally returned to his cubicle where he decided to write a letter home to let his parents know how he was, and that he was now a commissioned officer. He reached the point where he had scrawled out his new address, complete with his rank and had added D.C.M., M.M. to his name when he lost interest and tore the sheet of paper into shreds.

"Why should I bother to write to them? They're not interested in me. Have never mentioned anything about what I've done, or what decorations I have. I'm not going back to that murky hole. I'll apply for a permanent commission—and stay in. I don't know of a better life than this, and there'll be a pension of some sort when my time's up. All I've got to do is to stay out of trouble—and stay single. I'm not getting involved with anyone after what I've been through. These English girls are bad news. I'd be a damn' fool to give up this life. Test pilots will always be needed as long as there are aeroplanes to fly."

And with that contrived decision he decided to look up Daily

Orders, a copy of which would usually be in the lobby. He learned that the next day, for those available, there would be several new machines to be checked. On paper, he was still on leave, but he knew that if he turned up at the hangars the next morning someone would be glad to accommodate him and put him to work. He returned to his cubicle, pulled on his pajamas, picked up a copy of *Flight* and read until he was drowsy, trying to understand why President Wilson was so concerned with getting the belligerents to consider something called peace negotiations. "What's he trying to do? Bugger up the war completely?" he grumbled, and flicked off the light.

After a leisurely breakfast, Kenyon, wearing a pair of Castrol-stained breeches and his noncom tunic over a soccer jersey, walked out to the hangars with his helmet and goggles under his arm where he was greeted by a technical warrant officer who was delighted to see a pilot still sober after England's Boxing Day, the most hilarious time of the Christmas season.

"Mr. Kenyon, sir. I thought you were among the missing. Aren't you supposed to be still on leave?"

"I was, but I became bored, so came back last night and decided to come out here to see if I could get a flip on something, if only for some fresh air."

"You're on, sir. We've got a number of B.E.s that have been modified for Zeppelin fighting. You can give us a hand on any of them."

"Are these Home Defense buses?"

"Most of them. Some have been converted to single-seaters and provided with experimental armament. Number 8407 over there is fitted with eight Le Prieur rockets. First, we'll be staging a ground-firing test to make certain the ignition system is properly wired in, then we'll want someone to take her up and fire a set from the air."

"Ought to be interesting. I've never fired a rocket."

"There's more to it than that. We'll want some details on how it behaves if you fire the bank on one side, and then on the other. She may swerve badly, but we don't know. We'll want a full account of how she behaves with the rockets in the brackets on the interplane struts, and how she pulls out after both banks have been fired. It might be very important. Want to have a go?"

"When will the ground firing be completed?"

"Any minute. In the meantime, perhaps you'd like to take up Number 1688 at the end there. She's carrying two Fiery Grapnel weapons which they hope to drop on Zeppelins. It's a bit Heath Robinson* but a test has to be made."

The two men walked over to Number 1688 and Max noted that another single-seater version of the B.E.2c was carrying two four-pronged grapnels, weighing about forty pounds apiece, beneath the front end of the fuselage. They could be released from the cockpit, but still retained on light cables. The basic idea was to drag them across the top of a dirigible until built-in igniters caused them to explode.

"What sort of test am I supposed to do with her?"

"You take off, get up to about fifteen hundred feet, and you'll spot a simulated Zeppelin set out on the firing range. It's made of poultry wire and loose hay. The wire should hold the grapnels long enough to ignite the explosive. At any rate, take the contraption up and see what you can do with it. Once you release them they will be lowered about one hundred feet. In fact, you'll be able to see them below you as you approach the target. It's got to be carried out, and it's all yours if you want to have a go. It might be a bit of a lark."

"Has anyone tried this grapnel business against a hay bag?"

"Well, no. You see, they want to know whether they will actually explode on contact with something as fragile as a dirigible's framework."

"Suppose they don't."

The warrant officer folded his hands on his belt buckle. "In that case, I suppose you keep on trying until you pull the bloody things off. There's no suggestion on the work sheet."

"Well, anything to enliven the holiday season," Max said morosely and pulled on his helmet and goggles. "I hope the altimeter has been calibrated recently."

"I wouldn't know about that."

Mechanics were summoned, the engine started and Max settled in his seat. He was shown how to lower the grapnels and given a test sheet to fill out while climbing for the required altitude.

"I'd give it a couple of tries to make sure you've hooked into something fairly solid," the warrant officer repeated over and over.

---

* Heath Robinson was an artist who specialized in cartoons of ridiculous aircraft being used in unbelievable situations.

"Frankly, I don't believe the bloody thing would work if it was hooked into a tombstone."

"Well, let's go," Max said, chuckling mildly. "Will you call the range officer?"

"Right away. He'll fly a green flag for you to indicate the target is ready."

The Home Defense machine was in good order, and the engine unusually responsive. Number 1688 took off like a swallow, and before Max had completed his initial records concerning take-off, climb, and degree of lateral control, he saw the altimeter needle flicking back and forth over the 2000-foot marker. He curled back in a wide sweep and sought the simulated target laid out on the firing range on the south side of the aerodrome. A green flag fluttered from the concrete shelter where the range officer was established. He cut his power, dropped down a few hundred feet, fired a red Very light toward the range and received a green flare in response. He continued his circuit, losing height with each mile, and then brought the grapnel ship down to about 700 feet. As he approached the edge of the range he released the two "sky hooks" and heard the whine of the cables over the pulleys. Then he felt a slight jerk when they ran out to their full length. He looked back and down and saw the two ugly pronged grapnels streaming behind him. He glanced at the altimeter again and saw that he was gliding in at about 300 feet. Then he wondered whether he should make his attack across the target or along its full length. Since he was already approaching what was meant to be the stern section of the Zeppelin, he decided to continue on.

Maintaining a straight approach, he gradually lost more height and suddenly saw that the firing range was guarded by a tall hawthorn hedge. It was risky, but he was so involved in getting at the "Zeppelin" ahead he paid little attention to the possibilities. The dangling grapnels slashed through the hedge, and the delayed shock caused the B.E. to be snubbed in her flight. The braking created a stall and the biplane plunged down on the simulated target. At the same instant both grapnels snapped out of their entanglement with the hedge and came looping up in a low arc toward the tail end of the target. At that point both exploded and set fire to the stern of the wire and straw marker.

Kenyon was too engrossed in getting free of his cockpit to sense what was taking place behind him. Fortunately, the hay and straw used to form the general shape of a dirigible was not too dry and did not immediately burst into flame. There was some smoke, a low chug of ignition and gradually the covering responded with coils of yellow fire.

By that time Max had seen the full extent of the experiment, and he took immediate action. He vaulted out of his cockpit, slid down a fairly substantial portion of the form and landed in a pile of straw that prevented any serious injury. When he got to his feet and divested himself of much of the cover, he saw that the whole target would be consumed, taking the B.E. with it. He stood off, appreciating what was meant by Fiery Grapnels. Why the target had been erected close to the bordering hedge was not clearly explained by the warrant officer.

But it was just another day in the life of a test pilot. Another "secret weapon" had come to nothing, and the remains were stacked in the field knacker's shed. Kenyon was driven back to the hangar where he filled in his logbook, was given a mug of tea, and asked to make the Le Prieur rocket test before he broke off for lunch. Compared to the grapnel fiasco, Number 8407 provided an enjoyable time, and Max was tempted to fly down to Bournemouth to give some unsuspecting antisubmarine blimp a dash of excitement, but on second thought he completed the task, remembering that he hoped one day to obtain a permanent commission.

Day after day, the engineers, armament men, Home Establishment designers, and ranking Hun-killers with ideas for something more offensive, contributed new and more fantastic brain waves to the manufacturers. They conceived B.E.s that delivered a storm of Rankin darts and incendiary bombs. Others mounted guns that sprayed Brock and Pomeroy ammunition in all directions. Those who bruised easily persuaded others to provide armor-plated cockpits that weighed more than 400 pounds, restrictions that made it difficult for the underpowered biplanes to get off the ground.

The temporary success of the Fokker E.1 had created a demand for a competitive weapon, and the armament men had to rely on more and greater calibered guns, while they awaited a suitable interrupter gear. Further experiments were made with deflection blocks bolted around the blades of the propeller after the manner employed by Roland Garros who had first devised a front-firing gun months before Anthony Fokker knew there was such a contrivance. The Royal Aircraft Factory's experiments and in-air results were comparable to those enjoyed by the Frenchman, but not widely accepted by British pilots who rightly argued that the D.H.2 pusher was employing the same theory of firing along the line of flight without the hazard of deflected bullets spinning off in all directions.

Guns were mounted everywhere to fire in any direction. One armament enthusiast bolted five Lewis guns to the spreader bar of a B.E.2c's undercarriage which, when fired against a ground target, created such shrill thunder, a flock of dairy cattle was stampeded. The owner put in a claim for losses, arguing his cows were so terrorized they had not given milk for seven days. Another B.E.2c was fitted with a Lewis gun mounted behind the pilot, and intended to hold off enemy aircraft moving to "get on its tail." The arrangement seemed to work so well, the first aircraft thus armed was flown out to France to be tested under active-service conditions. Unfortunately, the ferry pilot who delivered the machine became lost in a layer of mist and landed by mistake on a German aerodrome, and in that manner handed over to the enemy Great Britain's secret weapon.

In another instance the British Admiralty, feeling responsible for the continuing Zeppelin attacks, adopted the American Davis gun and made plans for a special aircraft to take it into the air. The weapon was difficult to handle because of its length, since it was necessary to use a recoilless mechanism. When fired, a compensating charge was forced along another barrel facing aft. The shell used was highly explosive, and it was believed such a weapon would be most suitable against raiding dirigibles. It was tried out on several types of aeroplanes, and the Admiralty then ordered a special plane from a firm known as the Robey-Peters Company. This was a large three-seater biplane powered with a 250-horse-powered Rolls-Royce engine. Two Davis guns were mounted in gunners' nacelles built into the undersides of the upper wings. Photographs extant show the position of the nacelles, but no indication of how the weapons were mounted. On its first experimental flight—without the gunners in the nacelles—the Robey-Peters stood on its nose when the undercarriage skid dug in on take-off. Three days later, suitably repaired, the big-gun bus got off the ground, did a half circuit of the field, and then crashed on a nearby insane asylum. Upon examination it was noted that the test pilot had taken off with his aileron controls crossed. That ended the short career of the Robey-Peters, and its air cannon. What was left was allowed to burn and blot out the harrowing experience.

Lieutenant Maxwell Kenyon was actively involved in many of these ambitious and frantic schemes, and he gradually became philosophical with the experiences—comic or hazardous—that were crowding his logbook. Following the demeaning affair with Dido that broke up his Christmas holidays, he found himself becoming more interested in the work, and he willingly volunteered to take up any contrivance the manufacturers or testing authorities offered him. The hazards played little part in his thinking. He gloated in the number of flying hours he was recording week after week. Had he had a better educational background, especially in mathematics, he would have been pushed along to more important work, perhaps in the designing field, but he was never able to express clearly his findings or offer figures that substantiated his claims or suggestions. He could fly practically anything with wings and sufficient power, and by now had developed the inner instinct that enabled him to control a fractious aircraft and bring it down with little, or no, injury to himself. But when attempting to explain his theory of why the aeroplane had behaved in any peculiar manner to men with engineering minds and backgrounds, he was at a loss and frustrated. Simple arithmetic was the limit of his expression, and higher mathematics with their bewildering formulas and symbols left him seated with his hands dangling between his knees.

Yet, there were those who realized that when Kenyon took his time and related his findings in basic English and simple arithmetical tables, he was clearer and more rational than the engineers who relied on their slide-rule nomenclature and airy mannerisms when explaining the same problem. Although Max had a few friends in the Testing Squadron, it was obvious that the educational class system was more important than practical ability and man-to-man fraternity.

Through the winter and early spring of 1917 while continuing his service with the Testing Squadron, Max began to realize he was thinking and acting as an adult. There were periods of thought that flipped through his mind like short chapters in a book. By day he was engrossed with aeroplanes, air speeds, landing procedures, stall problems, and the possibility of pulling off a set of wings. At the end of his working day he put the many problems in his logbook, ignoring the hazards, risks, and law of averages. None of it compared to the risks he had taken at Neuve-Chapelle. Today's gamble was nothing more than the odds faced in a game of Inner-Hinder-Pitcher in the middle of South 10th Street where the Kinney trolley cars clanged their relentless attack.

After a bath or a stripped-down wash, he would change his undershirt and replace his old noncom tunic and breeches for his Burberry jacket and Bedford cords and saunter into the lounge where he would exchange the events of the day with the other scrubbed and polished pilots. From that point on a mental metamorphosis took over, particularly during dinner with his peers when he was waited on by truckling orderlies who were supervised by a kiwi mess president. He ate contentedly to a background of chamber music offered by an NCO string quartet. It was then Lieutenant Kenyon figuratively draped himself in the trappings of a modern cavalier and allowed his thoughts to gather up the loose ends of his gaudiest plot and counterplot.

He would volunteer for an active-service squadron. After all, with only the D.C.M. and M.M. he must be considered little more than an aerial gunner. It would require a Military Cross to prove he'd been out to the front as a pilot, flying a military aeroplane. True, a few officer observers had been awarded the M.C., but their ribbon had been tainted by the single-wing brevet . . . the flying ass-hole, as it was known in the trade.

He could remain on Home Establishment just so long. Eventually, he would have to return to France and take up where Horace Drage and probably Christopher Roland were already in the thick of it. He had no idea where Bert Laidlaw or Dougherty, the dog lover, could be, but they obviously must have been relieved and sent back to England for flight instruction. It was time to begin making his moves to get back where he could pick up his glory road.

Once the meal ended and the airmen had dispersed in groups to their various interests, the old loneliness set in. There were a few minutes when he wondered whether it could be possible to get leave to go back to America. A few Canadians had been so rewarded, but Canada was not America. The United States was still neutral, although the news in the *Daily Mail* had it that President Woodrow Wilson was becoming exasperated with the behavior of the Kaiser's government. Count von Bernstorff had been handed his passports, whatever that meant, The *Californian,* an Anchor liner, the *Laconia,* a Cunarder, and the *Afric* a White Star liner had been sunk and a number of American citizens had been lost. The United States government had made public a communication from Germany to Mexico proposing an alliance and offering as a reward the return of Mexico's lost territory in Texas, New Mexico, and Arizona, but little of this made an impression on Max Kenyon. He simply rose every morning, had a leisurely breakfast, and reported to the hangar for his next test. The activity in France through most of March when Bapaume and Peronne were captured by the British, when the Germans evacuated Roye, Lassignay, Chaulnes, Nesle, and Noyon in no way attracted his attention.

Early in April when the United States declared war on Germany and Austro-Hungary he was completely unresponsive. He could not imagine America being at war with anyone. Her history on a battlefield was half a century in the past, and he hadn't the slightest idea what an American soldier would look like. Navy bluejackets, yes. But he couldn't remember seeing an American soldier, except those who had been in the old G.A.R. parades on—what was it? Decoration Day? It was at this point that most of his questions became muddled. None would compound an answer. He rephrased them in his mind, but it wound up an annoying conundrum. The only solution was to be found in France where so much of his present character and military importance had been formed.

Dido Maitland? He couldn't understand Dido. Why a girl with her charm, grace, beauty, and professional skill would throw it all away for a dud weekend at London Colney was beyond his comprehension. The answer there never occurred to Maxwell Kenyon.

The Northamptonshire Regiment officer received Max with unexpected friendliness. He stood up and offered his free hand. He had a natural rapport for the young lieutenant, as he himself had come up from the ranks.

"How do I go about requesting a transfer to a service squadron, sir?"

"What a coincidence. We've just had a chit concerning you. They want us to send you to Martlesham Heath. A rather important test station, I might say. Your work here has been well done, and I'm sure you are to be given a second pip and put on a lot of important jobs. It's a splendid opportunity, Kenyon."

"I appreciate what you say, sir, but I feel I've given more than my share of time to testing. I'd like to go back to France with a scout squadron, sir."

"I can understand your impatience. That's what it is, wanting to get back into the thick of things, but you must remember that no one out there today would have anything reliable to fly had it not been for earlier test pilots."

"I know all that, sir."

"At Martlesham you'll be testing prototypes of machines that will come into service late next year, and I don't think I need stress how important 1918 will be. All new equipment, new engines, and a new concept of fighter aircraft; you'd be ill-advised not to jump at the opportunity. It's a lovely part of the country, too."

Max was not to be placated. "I'm losing all interest in test flying, sir. I've been on it long enough. I'd sooner get back to front-line service. Everyone who started the primary course with me is out there, and I'm beginning to feel left out of things. Whenever I go up to London I meet fellows who have about half as many hours as I, and they're—some of them—already flight commanders. I'm still where I started."

"But look at the varied experience you have."

"Only test-flying experience, sir. I want to go out to the front and see how good a pilot I really am. Please see what you can do for me, sir."

"I'll do my best, Kenyon, but I wish you'd think this over. However, there are openings for experienced pilots with one or two of the new S.E.5 squadrons. You haven't had a chance to try the S.E.5, have you? That is, we've never had one here, but from all accounts they're not all that was expected. I suppose, though, some test pilot will straighten them out."

"I'd rather try it out in France, sir."

"Good lad! No one should be discouraged from volunteering for France. Not too many do."

"I'd go out today, sir. I feel I've done my bit with the Testing Squadron."

"I'll do my best, Kenyon."

21

As always in the Royal Flying Corps, only the new aeroplanes moved with any particular speed. Max's request for a posting to an active-service squadron proceeded with the velocity of a strolling slug, and as a result he continued his routine work on the test field and found time to read a new John Buchan adventure novel entitled *The Thirty-Nine Steps*. Then there was the day he received another letter from Dido, asking when he would get up to London again. The plaintive note was flipped into the fireplace of the lounge, and with that Max hoped to dispose of the former dancer in *Chu-Chin-Chow*.

Presuming he had completed an emotional release he, to some extent, became a changed person. He mixed more with various groups in the mess. He played poker for small stakes and tried to learn the fundamentals of bridge, but admitted cheerfully that he had no head for the mental discipline and mathematical factors of the game. He was a better than average billiards player, and around the green baize table was accepted by other airmen who previously had known him only as a determined pilot with a one-track mind and limited subjects of conversation.

The change, not immediately apparent, evolved gradually as he picked up acquaintance with others he had not noticed, or for some personal reason had ignored. Early in his military career he had avoided the brash, noisy, blatant groups, just as he had done at Fourteenth Avenue School. Now he enjoyed the horseplay, the incessant chatter, and learned to contribute to the badinage. He joined groups that gathered at the bar to exchange technical talk of their day—what they had flown, their opinions of certain types, and their general denunciation of back-stagger design. He was now sharing the comradeship inspired by the pleasures of malt, hops, and whisky, taken in what he considered moderation. He joined small groups for weekend walks through the countryside, stopping at pleasant country inns for rustic meals and pots of foaming ale. He enjoyed the conversation the various scenes, winding lanes, and old coaching houses aroused, as compared to the continual discussions of promotion, enemy aircraft, the casualty lists, and someone's latest boudoir escapade. Along with these changes in his day-by-day activities, Kenyon noticed with inner satisfaction that his pay was going farther, and his modest living resulted in a respectable bank balance at Cox's. So smoothly was his life flowing at Upavon, it came as a slight shock to learn that his request for a transfer to a service squadron had been acted on.

He had just landed after working out a new two-seater pusher, fighter-reconnaissance craft, known at the time as an F.E.9, which was powered with a 200-horsepowered Hispano-Suiza engine. Although by now the British had several gun-interrupter gears, there was still considerable hope that the pusher's field of fire for the observer could, in many instances, be retained. In two short hops Max found that its climb performance left much to be desired, and the large ailerons caused unpleasant handling characteristics. Yet, he would have liked to have finished the general test. He frowned when he was handed the message concerning his transfer, and hurried across to the adjutant's office with mixed views.

The captain of the Northamptonshire Regiment greeted him warmly. "Well, I finally managed it for you, although I thought I never would. You're getting ten days' draft leave, after which you'll report to Pilots' Pool, Number 1 Aircraft Depot, Saint-Omer, France."

"It was very good of you, sir," Max said with little enthusiasm. "Can you tell me what I shall be flying out there?"

"No. All that is decided at Pilots' Pool. You'll be farmed out to whatever squadron needs a replacement. That's the way it goes."

"But I'll be on scouts, I hope."

"I'm pretty sure of that. Probably one of the new S.E.5 squadrons that are being organized."

"I'll like that, sir, although I've yet to see one."

"I understand everyone likes them, as far as flying is concerned. However . . ."

"But there's another thing. I don't want draft leave, sir. I wouldn't know where to go. I have no home, or relatives in England. I'd rather go straight out if you can frame my orders that way."

"You don't want your leave?" The adjutant was mildly surprised. "That's very unusual. We'll have to see about it. I'll get in touch with Mason's Yard in London, but if you change your mind, please let me know."

"You can rely on it, sir. I want to go straight out."

"My word, but HQ will be upset. I don't suppose it's ever happened before—a man not wanting to go on leave."

"Just make out my warrant for Saint-Omer, sir. I'll be packing my kit."

The decision imbued Max with new enthusiasm, and he hurried to his quarters to sort out his belongings which by now, early May, had become part and parcel of the furnishings. It was reminiscent of leaving home in 1914 but in this instance his future was in clearer focus. He'd be back on the front in a few days, flying over the lines, no longer a lowly aerial gunner, but a scout pilot. He would be completely on his own. He secretly hoped—and believed —he would be posted to an S.E.5 squadron, one located on the Arras front where he understood the heaviest air action was; where something called a Jerry flying circus was said to be operating. That's what he wanted most of all, for by now Maxwell Kenyon believed he was a first-class scout pilot, or would be in a week or two. He had no idea he had just missed the aerial butchery that was a few years later referred to as Bloody April.

He was so enthused about his prospects, he forgot his bitterness about Dido and scribbled her note.

Dear Dido, I have perhaps neglected you, but I have been kept busy down here. I may be able to see you any day, as shortly I am going back to France. Don't worry about me. I shall be all right. I hope things are going better for you, although I have seen nothing of your being back in *Chu-Chin-Chow*, and I suppose you can use a fiver, which I am enclosing and hope it comes at a good time, I mean when you don't need it too badly. I'll let you know my address when I get settled out there.

All the best, *Max Kenyon.*

He felt even better when he sealed the envelope. Dido wasn't such a bad sort, and she probably would appreciate his gesture. He wanted to write to Horace Drage and Christopher Roland, but had no idea where they were, but he hoped to have the luck to tie in with one or the other. It would be like old times.

He mailed Dido's letter in the mess lounge when he went to lunch. He asked whether there was an S.E.5 in any of the hangars which he might try his hand on. A technical captain shook his head. "We've been hoping, but so far no luck. They're still rasping off the rough edges on her at the Royal Aircraft Factory. The Hisso engine gives cooling trouble, and they're trying to fit a Lewis gun behind the hollow crankshaft of the engine. No one thinks it will work."

"But I understand Number 56 Squadron is already out in France with them. They're at Vert Galand Farm, aren't they?"

The technical man shook his head again, and pinched his nostrils. "They're not too satisfied with them. Captain Ball put out a personal report that the S.E.5 is a real dud, and he's still flying his old Nieuport."

"Not cheery news, is it, sir?"

"If I were you, Kenyon, I'd get in as much time as I could on one of the Sopwith Pups. We have a couple in Number 3 hangar. You can't be certain you'll make an S.E.5 Squadron."

"Sop Pups? They must be about through as service planes."

"They're still damn' good buses below 12-thou. They'll be kept until they can be replaced by the S.E.5, or the new Sopwith Camel. I'd at least get in a few landings. You never know."

"I've never flown a Pup. I know everyone likes them, but I thought Pups were about ready to be scrapped, or whatever is done with them."

"Take my tip. Get some time in on the Pup."

But Max was too ecstatic about going back to France, and never considered the idea. Also, another bid to the adjutant's office advised him he could leave for Saint-Omer in three days' time. In the meantime he could pack up, go to London for a night and make any final arrangements he deemed necessary.

With most of the day ahead of him, Max arrived in London and put up at the Imperial Hotel in Russell Square, went over to the Army & Navy Stores on Victoria Street and bought a new short flying coat, a pair of gloves, and a very modern flight helmet. Looking in the shop mirror he couldn't help recalling Captain Grimshaw's last turnout, but quickly erased the memory and hastened out to look up Solly Weinstein to find out how he could get in touch with Dido.

Mr. Weinstein had no idea. "I'm beginning to worry about her, mister. She's a blasted fine girl . . . a real artist, but she seems to have lost all interest in her work. I get her jobs, but she somehow forgets to check in."

"She *is* a puzzler. I'm on my way back to France, and just thought I'd call and find out what she's doing. Nothing important."

"She is to me, but I can't imagine what's got into her. Dido was on the way up, and we both could have made some quids, but once they get the love bug, you never know what they'll do next. I've got another in *Going Up* at the Gaiety. The tales I could tell you, mister."

"She's not in any real trouble, is she?"

"Nah! Dido's too smart for that. It's just that she'd not thinking straight. That's all."

He asked no more questions, thanked the agent for his trouble, and hung up. He wondered how he could get in touch with Winnie Winspeare. He wandered into the Coal Hole for a light lunch, and pondered on the Dido situation but could find no answer. So he settled for another visit to Foyle's where he found a copy of Philip Gibbs's *The Street of Adventure*, a story set in Fleet Street. He had started to read it while at London Colney, but the owner had moved on taking it with him before Max had finished it. While lounging in the Cave Tea Room, another popular hangout for flying men, he resumed reading where he had left off.

No one of interest interrupted him, so he returned to his hotel, had his hair cut, repacked his valise with the additional clothes, and still feeling rather flush, took a taxi to Les Jacobins in Regent Street. An expensive dinner in no way reduced his loneliness, but he made the best of it and decided to end his last evening in London by seeing the American star Doris Keane in Edward Sheldon's play *Romance*, which had been running successfully in London for months. It proved to be a rewarding change from the interminable list of war plays, and he especially enjoyed the closing scene—a Thanksgiving Day dinner in a New York apartment, for it reminded him of his magazine-loaded trudgings around Newark's Lincoln Park only a few Thanksgivings before.

He awoke the next morning feeling fit and secure, and looking forward to another trip across the Channel, although the weather promised to be muggy and threatened rain. He had a hot bath, a good breakfast, packed his toilet articles and the new book in his haversack and checked out. The boat train from Victoria Station was to leave at 9:45 A.M., and he was at the terminus a half hour early. He placed his valise in the luggage van, bought a morning paper and found a seat beside a window that looked out on the platform. He watched the movement of troops and decided that most of them were going back to France, for the majority looked like seasoned servicemen. There was a certain air about them, the way they handled their gear, the professional manner of getting aboard, and the minimum of effort in everything they did. The neophytes were well-washed, their uniforms comparatively new, and they made anxious inquiries of everyone from the Station Master, through the Railroad Transport officer, down to the lowliest porter.

"Is this the boat train for Folkestone? How long do I have? I'd like a cup of something. No time for breakfast. Can you . . . ?"

Gradually, Kenyon's compartment filled up with other officers representing the various services. One glance around and he saw he was the only Flying Corps man in the lot. Most were members of Territorial infantry regiments; lean, spare, and still weary. One or two were being seen off by young women or elderly gentlemen. There were husky artillerymen who immediately shucked off their Sam Browne belts, caps, and loosened their tunics.

There was little conversational intercourse. No one knew, or had any interest in, anyone else, but all adhered strictly to the rule of the road. No one trespassed on anyone else's luggage space, or crowded his seat area. Regimental badges and divisional patches were inspected, and that was that. An Army Service Corps captain took a letter from his breast pocket and read it over and over. Kenyon picked up his newspaper, skimmed the headlines and learned that General Henri Petain had succeeded General Robert Nivelle as Commander-in-Chief of the French armies, and that someone called General Ferdinand Foch had been appointed Chief of Staff. He also noted that the British were still slogging away on the Arras front, and had captured Bullecourt. He was about to turn to an inside page when the train began to move in that smooth silent manner of all British rolling stock. He glanced out the window to make sure they were actually under way.

Dido Maitland, her hat askew and her hair fluttering its signal of anxiety, was hurrying along the platform, staring into each compartment window.

Max snapped to his feet, intending to lower the window and catch her attention, but some adverse force compelled him to sit down and take up the newspaper again.

"That young woman looking for you?" the Army Service Corps captain asked solicitously.

Kenyon shook his head. "No, but for an instant I thought I recognized her. Not the same person at all."

France looked much the same, only more crowded with men in khaki. At Boulogne there was a tender awaiting R.F.C. officers who were heading for Saint-Omer. There was no one he knew, but through casual conversation he learned that all scout pilots hoped they were going to S.E.5 squadrons, and that most two-seater blokes were praying they would wind up on Bristol Fighters. One smart-looking captain admitted he was going back to a Pup outfit, but hoped it would be the second squadron to get S.E.5s. He seemed to like the idea, and ignored all references to latrine rumors concerning them.

"They're bloody tough since the former-ribs have been strengthened," he argued. "They'll outdive anything on the front, and if you know how to use the Lewis gun mounted on the Foster-Cooper rail, you can play hell with Jerry two-seaters. You just get below and behind where the gunner can't get at you, draw the gun back and tilt it upward, and you can drill plenty of ammo into them. Nothing to it."

On the way to Saint-Omer, Kenyon pondered on that possibility. Using the wing gun in that manner fascinated him, and he determined to specialize in that method of attack. He knew that two-seaters could be dangerous if you let the gunner get in the first burst, but hiding below and getting into a position where he could not bring his gun to bear would be a profitable method of attack. He mused on the prospect all the way to Saint-Omer.

There was no time for chatter, or for looking up airmen he had once known, amid the swirl of men and piles of baggage at the

Number 1 Aircraft Depot. There was no time to be patient or impatient, for he had no sooner checked in with the NCO at the Pilots' Pool, than he was told to stand by.

"Sit down over on that form, will you, sir. You've arrived just in time." The NCO did not look up from his papers. "Now, let's see, you're Kenyon, M. E., Second Lieutenant . . . Right?"

"That's me," Max said and tried to look over what the man was reading. "Will there be time for a spot of tea?"

"No, sir. Keep your gear handy, too."

It was puzzling to Max who had expected to be dawdling about Saint-Omer for a few days. That was the usual way. Hang around, fly spare machines from Number 1 Aircraft Depot to Number 2, or air-test aeroplanes that had been repaired at the aircraft park. Some tales had it that pilots had been delayed at Pilots' Pool for weeks but, of course, it was all rumor passed on by the gloom merchants. Max loosened his gear, sat down on the assigned bench and wished he could go around to the bar and listen to the conversation. The best he could do was catch snatches as men passed by in twos and threes. "Of course, it was bloody rough. We still have to go over too bloody far to do what GHQ expects us to." "You won't believe what you'll see when you get back to the squadron. You won't know half of them, Skipper." "I'll swear that Albatros D-III is twenty-five miles an hour faster than anything we have." "I pity the poor bastards who are still flying Pups. Imagine Pups against Albatri." "Ah, but wait until we get S.E.5s—or Camels." "Did you see the casualty figures in *Comic Cuts?* We lost 302 killed or missing during April, and they thought the Somme spilled some blood."

"Mister Kenyon!" the NCO bellowed from behind his counter. "Mister Kenyon, sir."

"Right-o, Sergeant," Max cried and rushed from his pile of gear.

"Ah, there you are. You can't ask for faster service, can you, sir?"

"I've been posted already?"

"You'll be leaving in a quarter of an hour. Here we are. You're posted to Number 66 Squadron. They're at La Grange. At least that's the way we say it."

"La Grange? Where's that?"

"Somewhere between Merville and Estaires. On the River Lys, I think. Anyway, the driver will get you there, sir."

"But I thought I'd be here for a day or two."

"Not after last month, sir. We bung them off as fast as they report in."

"What are they flying—at Number 66 Squadron?"

"I don't know, sir. The last I heard they were still on Pups, and we're still delivering Pups to them."

"Pups? I've never flown a Pup."

"You can't pick and choose. There's a war on, but I wouldn't worry. They say anyone can fly a Pup."

"Can you?" Max said grimly.

"Your tender will be on the line in ten minutes, sir. Best of luck."

"But can't I talk to someone . . . in authority?"

"This morning you could have talked to the adjutant, but they jerked him out of here to go fly F.E.2bs with Number 22 Squadron about an hour ago."

"But, I thought I might be sent to an S.E.5 squadron."

"Have you flown one, sir?"

"Well, no . . ."

"There you are then. The way things are, you're likely to be posted anywhere. You can count yourself lucky you're going on Pups."

There was no argument. Max took the order, tucked it in his logbook which he stuffed back in his tunic pocket. Much of his enthusiasm had drained out, and for the first time he longed for a strong drink, a double-something. He was going up to the front on Sopwith Pups. He felt like a skylark sent out to break up a flock of eagles.

During the run from Saint-Omer, Max sat on the back of the tender with his baggage and his thoughts. An RFC major had taken the front seat with the driver. He was a somber man with a small military mustache, pale blue eyes, a patrician nose and the ribbon of the D.S.O. below his wings. He made no attempt to engage either Kenyon or the man at the wheel in conversation. He simply sat erect, arms folded across his belt, and stared straight ahead. As Max's eyes became accustomed to the dim interior of the tender, he noticed a light kit bag on which had been painted in neat script letters:

PHILIP ALLINGTON
ROYAL FLYING CORPS
B.E.F

Kenyon decided that the field officer up front could possibly be his new commanding officer, but he made no attempt to inquire.

The tender tore along the Merville road, a cobbled poplar-lined highway that had seen much of the campaign. There was not too much military traffic at that time of day, and they made good time. Then, rather unexpectedly, the driver turned sharply to the left, slowed down and had a word with a military policeman who didn't bother to salute the major, but pointed down a country lane. In a minute or so the tender swung off into a traffic-hacked area over which loads of industrial cinders had been spread. Beyond were an assortment of the usual sheds, huts, hangars and a rank of Leyland lorries. In an open area in front of the hangars stood several Pups being serviced by the usual number of mechanics. The tender crunched up to the door of a low Adrian hutment and stopped with a jerk.

"Squadron office, sir," the driver croaked over his shoulder.

Max could only see a post with a small board nailed to it on which a torn Daily Orders sheet flapped. There was a slender pole from which fluttered a flag made up of R.F.C. colors, and a gas alarm, contrived from a discarded acetylene tank.

The major unfolded his arms, nodded, and climbed down to the muddy roadway.

"Here we are, sir," the driver chanted over his shoulder.

Kenyon roused himself and began to move his kit to the back of the tender. The major appeared, looked surprised that there had been a passenger inside. Max remembered his kit bag and handed it over the tailboard.

"Is this yours, sir?"

"Oh, yes. I had no idea we brought anyone else along. Thanks. Are you posted here?"

"Second Lieutenant Kenyon, sir. Reporting from Pilot's Pool."

"Well, bless my soul. Let me give you a hand, er, Kenyon. Damned glad to have you." Major Allington reached in and took Max's haversack and appealed to the driver to come give a hand. "Look lively, there. Mr. Kenyon is reporting for duty."

In a few minutes Kenyon and his trappings were deposited outside the orderly room, and Major Allington was chirping through the open door for more assistance. Max was bewildered by all the attention.

"We have Mr. Kenyon here. Where is everybody? Tomkins! Where the devil are you?"

There was some muffled scurrying from the interior and two startled figures filled in the frame of the doorway. One was a captain who wore an observer's wing and a Military Cross, the other, a peaked-looking corporal, decorated with a pen over one ear.

"We've collared a new pilot, Tomkins," Major Allington repeated. "See that he is properly attended to."

"Yes, sir. Immediately, sir."

"And Tomkins, I suggest you put him up with, er, Captain Roland. He *is* a captain by now, I presume."

"In orders last night, sir. He'll buy an extra pip next time he goes into Saint-Omer, I suppose, sir."

Max appealed to the threesome. "Roland? Christopher Roland? I knew him at London Colney."

The man called Tomkins looked puzzled, but explained, "We have Christopher Roland. He's a flight commander now, what with one thing or another. I'll see if he'd like to have you with him. But I'm sure he will."

Major Allington linked his fingers together, as he listened to the explanation. "Of course he will. I want you to see that Kenyon is properly taken care of . . . and when he's settled I shall want him in the bar for a before-dinner brandy. We do have something left to drink, I hope." And with that parting shot the CO disappeared and Kenyon was led inside the recording office by Tomkins who kept glancing at Max's decorations. Finally, as he took his seat behind his desk he could restrain his interest no longer.

"You've been out here before, er, Kenyon?"

"Yes, sir. I was an aerial gunner with Number 70 . . . Sop Strutters."

"Jolly good. We are lucky."

"Well, with reservations," Max said with concern. "You see, I've never flown a Pup—practically everything else at the Testing Squadron, but I've no time at all on Pups."

Tomkins blinked. "Oh dear, but it shouldn't be too bad. Pups are easy, so everyone says. I wouldn't know."

"That's what worries me. I had hoped to get on S.E.5s."

"Everybody wants to get on S.E.5s, but Roland will make sure you get plenty of time before you go on patrols. Leave it to him."

"I can't believe he's already a flight commander. It seems only a few weeks ago we were both going solo on B.E.s at London Colney."

"If things had gone on as they have been, he'd have been a major by now," Tomkins said testily. "Well, let's get on with the paper work. You have your logbook with you?"

Half an hour later Max was spreading out in a roomy cubicle, making himself comfortable with the aid of a batman who explained he "took care of the gentlemen in this hut."

"You take care of Captain Roland?"

"Oh, yes, sir. He bunks in here, too. A very nice chap, Captain Roland, sir. You'll like him."

"He's on patrol now?" Max went to the windows. "By the way, where is the aerodrome?"

"You might well ask, sir. It's out there among the beet root. It's just a few wide paths through the stuff, and we have to make the best of it. Nothing like an ordinary aerodrome, but you'll get used to it. You just have to remember what you're looking for when you come home."

"Amazing!"

The batman went to the window and had a look to see what amazed Kenyon. He was a short, bulky lad with very bowed legs. His face was round, his hair the color of old rope, and his tunic was mottled and stained with what Kenyon assumed to be boot polish, Brasso, soup stains, and streaks of brakish tea. "Ah, you're right, sir. It does take a bit of getting used to. Just a few pathways through the turnips, so to speak."

"I understand Roland is on patrol now, but should be back shortly." Max began to set out his toilet kit on the top of an engine crate that served as a dresser.

"Any minute, now. It's his first show with two streamers, and he's shorthanded. He'll be glad to know you've come to fill out the flight."

Kenyon exhaled with resignation. "I won't be much use to him for some time. I've never flown a Pup."

The batman ignored the remark and stood listening, cocking one ear toward the ceiling. "I think they're coming in now, sir. I'm pretty sure."

"Good! You can finish up here, and I'll stroll out to the Tarmac to watch them come in."

"They'll be coming up to the 'B' Flight hangar. The one in the middle."

22

Five Pups, gleaming in the setting sun, gay with new paint and varnish, displayed large block numerals on their fuselages as they came across the beet field in a trim five-plane formation. Max looked for two streamers on the leader's tail, but none were to be seen. Then as the tight V broke up into a line-astern, landing approach, he noticed that long red-and-white pennons were fitted to the outer struts of the lead biplane.

"That's a new one. Thought streamers were carried on the king posts of the elevators," Max cogitated to himself.

The little scouts disappeared beyond a distant copse and then, one by one, reappeared again and glided into a narrow pathway through the beet field. It was amazing that none of them missed this unusual landing strip. They dabbed down gently, got their tails down and came waddling up toward the limited Tarmac in front of the hangars, where air mechanics trotted out, took over the wingtips and helped guide the Pups up to their cab rank.

Max hurried out to the lead plane and stood where the pilot couldn't miss seeing him. Roland, his face splotched and pitted with oil and cordite, shoved up his goggles and peered toward the newcomer. He switched off, took a second look and then bellowed, "Max! For heaven's sake! Good old Max!"

"Chris! Congratulations on your third pip. How did your first show go?"

Roland flipped his belt and practically vaulted out of his cockpit. He rushed up to Max and took his face in the palms of his greasy gloves. "Damn' good! Damn' glad to see you, Max. Where are you holed up? I mean, what squadron?"

"I'm here. Just came up from Pool and I've been assigned to your flight. I'm billeted with you! Can you beat it?"

Chris grabbed Max by the shoulders. "Not another word. It can all wait. I've got a bit of a problem with Spicer. He's one of my new men. Wait here until I get through dressing him down."

"I can't believe it. You a flight commander . . . dressing someone down, but go ahead, I'll wait for you at the recording office."

"We'll all be there in a minute. Glory, it's good to see you, Max."

Amazed at Chris's new authority and his acceptance of command, Max went back to the shelter of the hangar and watched the byplay that went on when Chris got his pilots together. He had a word with each one, slapped a shoulder, poked a finger and then took one of the oil-stained wretches aside and led him around the nose of a Pup. It took only two or three minutes. The culprit was then released and allowed to wend his way to the shelter of the recording office. Chris then hurried over to Max, and they sauntered arm-in-arm toward Tomkins's office.

"What was the dressing-down about?"

Chris shook his head. "We don't spread idle gossip. I do it the way admonitions were delivered at school. You got it. You accepted it, and it never went past the chancellor's door. It worked at Charterhouse. It ought to work here."

"Am I glad I was posted here," Max said, and tightened his grip on Chris's elbow.

"Same here, but where the devil have you been all these months?"

"At the Testing Squadron—Upavon. It was fun for a while, but I had to get back to France, Chris. I wasn't getting anywhere."

"Tell me about it after we get our patrol reports in, eh?"

"What was the show like? Any luck?"

"Rather! We all got back."

"No, I mean any Huns?"

"Packs of 'em, but we all got back. Spicer was lucky . . ."

Half an hour later, while Roland sloshed and puffed through a wash and a shave, they talked themselves blue in the face, as Max expressed it.

"But I've never flown a Pup, Chris. Practically everything else."

"There's a brand new one out in the hangar. You can start flying it right after breakfast tomorrow, and you can keep on all day long, if you like. But I want you to be ready for a patrol the following day. If you can't master the Pup in one day, you'd better go back to Upavon."

"I've heard they're supposed to be easy to fly, but are they good enough to take over the line against Albatri?"

"I don't know. We took a beating all through April, which explains why I'm a flight commander. Remember what we said back at London Colney, Max. It's all in a good cause. Granted we have only one gun and not too much power, but we can outmaneuver anything Jerry has. The real trouble is . . ."

"I know. You have to go over too far. That's all we hear on the other side of the Channel."

"Engines can conk out or the weather turn sour. It's not always the Huns. Too often we're trying to erase a mistake some damn' fool makes when he ought to know better. That's why I'm glad I got you, Max. You've been out here, and know what you're doing, or should."

Max changed the subject. "I came up from Saint-Omer with Major Allington. What's he like? He was very nice to me when he found out I was coming to Number 66. In fact, he seemed a bit pathetic in the way he went out of his way to welcome me. It was he who ordered Captain Tomkins to have me put in with you. Nothing like the usual CO attitude."

Roland looked sad as he knotted a tie. By now he had adopted a standard G.S. open tunic. "I don't know what to say about Allington," he began and dropped his voice. "We've had wicked losses, and he took it all—well, personally, as though it was something for which he was responsible. At the height of it, he tried to lead every patrol himself, and of course wore himself down to the knuckle."

"Is he any good as a pilot?"

"He wouldn't have lived this long if he wasn't. But no one can keep up the pace he set himself, so Wing ordered him to limit his flying to one patrol a week. He, of course, took no notice of the edict, so he was ordered back there for a complete physical. That's where he had been when he came back with you. If they have found even a hangnail or a gumboil they'll relieve him, ship him back to Blighty and stick him in a swivel chair at the Hotel Cecil. That will finish him, of course. It'll be too bad, but no one can run a squadron and fly two or three patrols a day—on Pups."

"What about the other flight commanders? Are they in the same spot as you?"

Chris lowered his voice again. "You keep your nose clean and don't try to win the war off your own bat the first week, and there's no telling where you will wind up. None of us deserves two streamers. We haven't had enough time to learn what to do as members of a flight, to say nothing of leading a patrol. Donoley of 'A' Flight is a stage character Irishman who thinks he's a Donnybrook brawler. Actually, he couldn't lick my sister."

"I didn't know you had a sister."

"She'll keep until we get home together. Donoley has been lucky, but if he ever gets into a real jam he'll be among the missing."

"Who leads 'C' Flight?"

"Cartwright, Stanley Cartwright, a moody Dorset farmer. He's a pukka pilot, but he couldn't lead a flock of geese to a pond. He has no idea what formation flying is all about, or why we do it, but one day he came back and found himself a captain and was given 'C' Flight. So far he's been so blasted lucky, he thinks that what goes on every day is simply routine. Take it from me, Number 66 Squadron is a squadron of the damned." Chris stopped and squinted at the ceiling. "Let's see. Wasn't there a book of that title? I seem to half remember . . ."

"But has either of them lost anyone?"

Roland screwed up his expression. "Funny thing. With this job-lot trio of flight commanders we haven't lost a plane, or had a pilot wounded."

"Get any Huns?"

"No. We flounder into flocks, put on what we believe are scraps, but we all get home. So far, no Huns since the April debacle. We got a few then but, well, mostly by Major Allington. Since then . . ."

"But why don't they send out experienced flight commanders from the Home Establishment Pool? There must be hundreds of them eating their hearts out, wanting to get back here."

Roland produced a wry grimace, and stood buttoning his tunic. "Are there? You'd be surprised. However, we're back to Major Allington. He argued that he wanted flight commanders who had come up through the flights—pilots who had what he considered the spirit of Number 66. You can figure out the rest. For weeks now three inexperienced flight commanders have been leading understrength flights on difficult patrols deep into enemy country. My God! Some days we go as far as thirty or more miles over the line. Yesterday we were messing about over Roubaix, doing an offensive patrol!"

Max whistled. "At what altitude?"

"Seventeen thousand feet! It's as cold as hell up there, but none of us minds as long as the blasted engines keep turning over."

"By the way," Max interjected suddenly. "What about old Wallington? Ever hear anything of him?"

"Wallington's a proper dose. He was sent out here to a Pup Squadron—Number 46, I think it was—but he did one patrol, went sick, and was never booked again. He was shipped back and for a time he was ferrying planes out to the front. From what I heard in Saint-Omer, he was a charmer and never got lost or broke a tail skid. Last I heard he was being primed again for a scout squadron. Wouldn't be surprised if he didn't come out on S.E.5s. Perhaps that's what he's maneuvering for."

"Wallington is a real dog."

"I'm afraid so. He just doesn't have the spirit," Chris agreed almost kindly. "Well, let's get into the bar. I understand the CO has promised you a drink."

"I'd like to talk to Major Allington," Max said solemnly.

"Wait until he finds out you've been out as an aerial gunner—on Strutters. You won't get to bed tonight."

"A" Flight, under Donoley, had the early morning patrol, a job to escort a flight of camera ships that were to photograph the length of narrow-gauge railway tracks that ran from Orchies north toward Roubaix. Both Chris and Max were up early enough to see them take off, and then went back to the mess for breakfast. The day promised fair weather with nothing much but some early haze, a few stringy layers of light cloud, and a light wind that brought a low whiff of rotting vegetation from the sugar-beet fields.

"My flight isn't due off until just before noon," Chris explained over their bacon and eggs, "so I'll have time to get you started on Pup problems, of which there should be none. You've flown aircraft with the 80-horsepowered Le Rhône, I presume."

"Half a dozen, at least. No problem there, once I go over the throttle and air-adjustment lever."

"Take plenty of time. My mother could fly a Pup, just by reading the book. But first of all get used to this wonky field. Take off, circle it for fifteen minutes and you'll see it lies in the bend of the river. After you've oriented yourself, do half a dozen take-offs and landings to make sure you have solved the trick of getting in. And for heaven's sake, watch the wind sock. It can change every ten minutes here."

Kenyon listened and nodded, quietly surprised how mature Chris had become in a few weeks. "Then what?"

"The gun on Number 12—that's your bus—has been calibrated, so after you have a talk with the armorer sergeant, you can go up again and put in some gunnery practice against the target we have laid out on the firing range, just inside the bend of the river. The target is made of old Pup wings set out in the general arrangement of an aeroplane. The range man will have a green flag flying if the target is available."

"If he has a red one up," Max broke in, "it will mean he's pasting up the holes made by a previous visitor."

"Right! Use up the full belt—about five hundred rounds—and come back and have the rigger corporal make any adjustments you feel are necessary in the controls. But you probably know more about this than any of us. If anything is done, take her up again and do a triangular cross-country, say northwest from here to Cassel, turn almost southwest to Saint-Omer and from there make your way back to La Grange. I'd stay below five thousand feet, particularly if it clouds up. That ought to keep you busy until later this afternoon."

"I would say so."

"Get a good lunch and be ready for a tour of our balloon lines."

"On my own?"

"It all depends. I may be back in time to go along with you. At any rate, wait until I get back. There may be a couple of others turn up, and we'll give them a chance to get some flying in."

"You mean replacement pilots?"

"We need at least four more. Both 'A' and 'C' flights are still trying to fill out. We expect two today, flying in from Saint-Omer with new Pups. By the end of the week we may be up to full strength . . . we hope."

"So that's how it goes."

Chris assumed a schoolboy grin. "If the truth be known, you're probably the most experienced pilot, except Major Allington, in the squadron. But don't dwell on it. Just take your time and learn your front."

Kenyon nodded, finished his breakfast and prepared to return to their cubicle. "I'll get into some working togs and wander out to the hangar. What's the flight sergeant's name?"

"A good point. He's the man to be in with. Name's Hollowell. Sar'nt Hollowell, he calls himself. But a very good man. I'll be nearby to see you get off properly."

Kenyon's first full day with Number 66 Squadron was a memorable one. A brand-new Pup with a large numeral "12" painted on both sides of the fuselage was out on the line awaiting him. He had dressed in a pair of greasy slacks and his old NCO tunic which still flaunted his observer's wing but no decorations. His new flying coat with a raccoon collar, a helmet lined with chamois skin and spanking new goggles gleamed in contrast to his uniform and marked him as a newcomer. A small group of mechanics glanced at him but showed no particular interest. None of them saluted him, so he wisely said, "Good morning. Is Flight Sergeant Hollowell about?"

"He's usually in his office. Other side of the hangar," a fitter corporal said and took up a tool box. Before Max made his way to the designated cubicle, a harsh, flat voice assailed his ears.

"Ah, there you are, sir. Bin expecting you."

"I'm Kenyon. Lieutenant Kenyon, Sergeant."

"Right-o. Everything's all ready, sir. I'm Sar'nt 'Ollowell. Mister . . . that is, Captain Roland spoke about you, sir. Well, everything's just as it should be. Your Number 12's ready for you, sir. Saw to it, meself."

During this announcement Max took in Sar'nt 'Ollowell. He, first of all, was decidedly knock-kneed which reduced much of his self-esteem. He had a round, bloated face, small, close-set eyes and a pair of unusually large ears that fanned out like the mudguards on a French motorcar. His rank stripes were soiled, and the embroidered propeller above one set seemed to have lost one of its blades, all of which indicated that Sar'nt 'Ollowell was used to doing things himself. Because of that Max took an immediate liking to him and insisted on shaking his very dirty, grease-stained hand. From that moment on Lieutenant Maxwell Kenyon had Sar'nt 'Ollowell in his hip pocket.

"I'm to do a few landings and then have a knock at the target. Will you see that I have enough petrol . . . and a full belt of ammunition, Sar'nt?"

"I've anticipated all that, sir. Number 12's full of everything. We'll get you started immediately. If there's anything amiss, you let me know an' I'll scorch a few arses," Sar'nt 'Ollowell promised with a wink that tilted his cap over several degrees. Then he let out a series of unintelligible bellows that brought a number of sleepy mechanics into action.

"There you are, sir. The corporal fitter will go over the engine with you."

Within a few minutes Max was running the Le Rhône while two mechanics held down the tail. Satisfied with her revs, and checking the controls, he nodded to a corporal who removed the wheel chocks, grabbed an interplane strut and helped him turn the Pup into a pathway that led to a cinder-covered space in the center of the field. There he decided which lane provided a take-off closest to the direction indicated by the wind sock. There were drainage ditches on each side of the pathway, so he made sure he was well centered before he pushed up the throttle.

The Pup responded to every demand of the controls, and he swept away, delighted with her behavior. He looked down and saw that Chris and several others were out in front of their hut-ments watching him. He circled carefully and was amazed to see that the area below with its crisscrossed tracks was actually an aerodrome. Only when he identified the three hangars *and* the wind sock was he positive it was from that crazy design down there that he had taken off. He continued to circle and when he came to the river he looked for the gunnery range. It was where Ro-land had explained, and the red flag indicated the range tender hadn't prepared the target as yet. He went back to the area of beet roots and tried his first landing.

It was a perfect three-pointer, and three more assured him that the tricky layout at Upavon had well prepared him for front-line landing strips. He then went back to the gunnery range, circled about, trying various school maneuvers and making sure he could be seen from the La Grange area. He first went up to 4000 and came down in a slow spin. He tried again, spinning in the opposite direction and the Pup responded wonderfully. He was so pleased with his mount he decided to go through the whole test sequence.

He did a succession of loops, pulling out at 1000 feet. Three slow barrel rolls came next, then one of the newest maneuvers he had learned at Upavon—the flick roll. So well did the little Sopwith Scout respond to his demands, he put on several more, thoroughly enjoying his display without wondering whether anyone below was watching.

Perfectly satisfied, he went back to the gunnery range and saw the green flag fluttering. Checking the light wind from the smoke of a farmstead fire, he moved to dive down, first one way and then the other, and pulled up his hydraulic gun-gear handle. The Pup nosed down like a bolt and Max pressed the thumb-trigger mounted on the handle of his spade-grip. A long burst of fire spat from the Vickers, and he could see the tracers spattering into the T-shaped target below. He yanked out a few feet off the ground, zoomed for height and turned back with the wind under his tail. Down he went again, this time in a more shallow attack, and again his burst of bullets danced and sparked dead on the target. Twice more he attacked the laid-out wings, and then saw that his tracers had actually set fire to one of the doped panels. With that, he gave up, banked away and watched the wing engulf itself in a smoky flame.

As Max settled back for his cross-country triangular course, he realized, as had so many before him, that the Pup was the most delightful warplane to fly. He also appreciated what he had learned while serving with the Testing Squadron where he gained experiences on so many types, so many different engines, and had used the various weapons that were being adopted. No rookie pilot had ever come out to France with so much fundamental knowledge of military flying, or such skill and confidence in flying machines through many intricate maneuvers. If he couldn't hold up his end with this background—as Chris had said—he'd better go back to Upavon. He thought of all this as he went sight-seeing as had been suggested. In his mind he realized how fortunate he had been. His eyes looked down on areas that earlier had been important battle-fields. He had seen photographs of much of it but the black-and-white prints in no way conveyed the reality, the vastness of the campaign, the remains of earlier entrenchments, and the graves of the thousands of young men who over the past thirty-four months had fallen in the slaughter staged over a front of more than 300 miles. Similar scenes, closer to the immediate struggle would come into his bird's-eye view of where he, too, would again become part of the carnage; where the trenches, line of battle, sapheads, and miles of barbed-wire would remind him of Neuve-Chapelle. But today, he had once again become a flying man, one completely in charge of the winged weapon he was aboard, who realized that with any luck he could pick up his glory trail where he had left off—a disgusted aerial gunner who had been palmed off with a Distinguished Conduct Medal when he should have been awarded the Victoria Cross.

He passed over the aerodrome at Cassel, the one hidden in the apple orchard, and turned southwest for Saint-Omer. It was a glorious experience, and he carried out sham battles with non-existent Fokkers and Albatri, but still wishing he was flying an S.E.5 with a Lewis gun that could be tilted upward to blast the underbelly of an unsuspecting Halberstadt.

Above Saint-Omer he spotted two Sop Pups taking off from the Aircraft Park and thought they might be the two Number 66 was expecting. He decided to join them, and when it was obvious they were setting their course for the area, taking in Hazebrouck, he dropped down and joined them. He had no idea who they were but felt an immediate camaraderie and decided to help them find La Grande and guide them into the strips laid out in the beet fields. He flew up close, waved a friendly signal, and was soon leading a three-plane formation back to the aerodrome. It was an exhilarating experience, and on their arrival both replacements expressed their gratitude.

Roland's "C" Flight had left for its midday show, but Sar'nt 'Ollowell took over, and guided the newcomers to their correct berth, telling "Leftenant" Kenyon what a bloody fine exhibition he had put on. "The major said he'd never seen anything like it, sir. He also said you'd have to show everyone how you do that flick roll. Ain't anyone here who's ever performed it, I can tell you. You'll liven this place up properly, you will, sir."

"Thanks, Sar'nt." Max returned his wink.

23

More than pleased with his morning's work, Max sluiced off and went into the mess and noticed for the first time that it was composed of two Adrian hutments, insecurely fastened together end to end. One half was furnished as an anteroom, the other was the mess proper. The anteroom, or lounge, offered two windows that looked out on the River Lys, and an unobstructed view of the collection of huts, tents, shops, and an armament shed. There also was a farmhouse on the fringe of all this, but he could see no evidence of its being inhabited. The furniture had been salvaged from a dozen shell-battered homes, but had been repaired, polished, and made presentable by the squadron carpenter. There was an ancient Bechstein grand piano in one corner, as improbable a piece of furniture as one could expect, but it was decorated with a German flag and several spare parts from a dismantled aero engine. A spray of wilted wild flowers leaned over from a vase made from a 9.2 shellcase. Scattered in studied disorder on the walls were a few Bruce Bairnsfather cartoons of Old Bill, and the usual complement of leggy Kirchner prints.

Max was studying one particular young lady who seemed to have been caught *en déshabillé* by a lewd delivery boy, when he was greeted by Major Allington who had entered from the mess.

"Ah, there, Kenyon. You're back, I note. Jolly good show you put on for a man who had never flown a Sop Pup. Seemed to be enjoying yourself. You'll have to teach some of us oldsters how you do that flick roll. It will come in handy against the Albatri."

"She handles beautifully, sir. I thoroughly enjoyed my first flight."

Major Allington looked pitifully relieved. "I'm very glad. We could use half a dozen chaps like you."

"I also picked up a couple of Pups while finishing a cross-country.

They appeared to be coming out of Saint-Omer, and I had an idea they were heading this way, so I joined them, and showed them the field. We now have two more pilots and a couple of new machines."

The major raised his eyebrows. "Jolly good! Whatever made you think of that?"

"It seemed logical. Anyway, they both made it in with no trouble."

The CO considered the explanation, and then said, "Let's sit down here, Kenyon. I want to talk to you. Roland has probably told you we've had a very rough time over the past few weeks. We lost too many men and machines, but we did the best we could under the circumstances. However, it hasn't added any glitter to the squadron record."

Kenyon wondered what this confession was about. "Many squadrons seem to go through rough times now and then, sir."

"No doubt about that, but we don't deserve too much compassion. We just didn't hold our end up."

"Was it that Pups are becoming, well, obsolete?"

"Nothing is obsolete until you have something to replace it. The Pup is the best we have, and we're expected to use it."

"But from what I learned at the Testing Squadron, it appears the Germans have several single-seaters that greatly outperform anything we have on the front."

Major Allington shook his head sadly. "I had a chance to fly a Jerry Albatros D-III, a captured bus, down at Number 1 Aircraft Depot yesterday morning. I couldn't see any real advantage in it. True, it has two guns, whereas the Pup and Sop Triplane have but one. The Albatros is a heavy, cumbersome plane, compared to what we fly. The workmanship is dreadful, but perhaps adequate. The Pup is far more maneuverable below twelve-thousand feet."

"I must admit she handles beautifully, but is that enough?"

"In my opinion, the enemy have the advantage in that they select the battlefield, and you know what Wellington said about that, or was it Napoleon? Anyway, we must go into their territory to make them fight, or to get information. We order our reconnaissance or Art-obs aircraft into their area to get the desired information, and we have to send our scouts to provide the protection. This is the way it will be all the way to Berlin. They have to defend only what they had no trouble taking back in 1914. It's as simple as that for Jerry."

"Do you think there is any chance of our getting—say S.E.5s within a reasonable time, sir?"

"No. Our showing over the last few weeks puts us well down the list. As things stand now, I'm afraid we'll have Pups for a long time . . . or until we are wiped out."

Major Allington had the mannerisms, gestures, and lackluster eyes of a weary man, although he couldn't have been much over thirty. He entwined his pale fingers endlessly, and listened to a Le Rhône being run up out on the Tarmac. "I'm afraid we don't have first-class talent any more. It's men, not machines that make a squadron. We want pilots, not multi-gun scouts. Some commanders have the luck in that the men they select to build up their squadrons fulfill their early promise. Others have the knack, the judgment, the natural leadership. I'm not a martinet, a barracks' square soldier. I'm a bloody good pilot, but probably a complete dud in this job." Major Allington cranked to his feet, offered a wan smile, and said, "Well, have a good lunch." Then he brightened. "By the way, if you feel up to it afterward, why don't you take the two new men up to the line for a look-see? Show them our balloon lines and the area of our front. I'm sure you're quite capable of that, since you've been out here before."

"With your permission, sir."

"Well, see how you feel after a bite. It's just an idea, but don't take any unreasonable risks. I'll see you for a drink after dinner."

"Thank you, sir."

A bowl of soup, a greasy ham sandwich, and a mug of tea put Kenyon in a good mood. Also his talk with the CO had aroused a grim determination to get on with the war. If Major Allington felt he was capable of leading a balloon-reconnaissance for a couple of newcomers, why not make the most of it? No need to wait for Chris to come back. Besides, he probably would be too weary to take on an added instruction flight. He sought out the two replacements who still had to find out the routine of the noon lunch. One was named Thornhill, the other was a sergeant pilot named Evers who Thornhill explained was taking his meals in the sergeants' mess nearby. "He's a very nice chap," Thornhill, a stocky Yorkshireman, said. "I believe he bought his own training at the Grahame-White School and then applied for a commission in the R.F.C.

"What happened?"

"I'm not sure, but it's probably a matter of schooling. He'd been an apprentice in his old man's motor-body works somewhere in Luton, and is a top-hole mechanic. It's the old upper class asserting itself, but he'll soon get a commission if he sticks it out."

Kenyon took a liking to Thornhill. There was no side to him. No reference to *his* schooling, though he showed the marks of good breeding. Another Chris Roland, but a year or two older.

"Well, look here. Would you like to do a trip up to our balloon lines? The major suggested I take you and, er, Evers to get you acquainted with our area. We'll stay well on our side, but we all might learn something."

Thornhill looked perplexed. "Have you been out before?"

Max explained about his time with the London Scottish and as an aerial gunner. "For one thing, I'm pretty sure I'll know which side of the line we're on," he said with a chuckle. "By the way, to which flight were you assigned?"

"We're both with 'A' Flight under Captain Donoley."

"Well, if you can get permission, and a bus, I suggest we make a threesome and do as Allington suggested."

"If you don't make it more than an hour, I'm sure we'll be glad to get in the experience."

"See you on the Tarmac in a quarter of an hour."

"Right."

Enthusiastic about the prospects, Max hurried out and found Sar'nt 'Ollowell in conversation with a sergeant pilot whom he took to be Evers.

"Ah, there you are, sir," Sar'nt 'Ollowell greeted. "What are the plans for the afternoon, or are you waiting for Captain Roland to get back?"

"Major Allington suggested I take the two new men for a look-see up to the balloon lines. Any chance they can get a couple of planes and permission to go?"

Max introduced himself to Evers, a lanky individual who returned a pleasant smile for the handshake. He could not have been more than nineteen, but he was large-boned and moved like a soccer halfback.

Sar'nt 'Ollowell pursed his liverish lips. "Let me see. I suppose

'A' Flight will let them take the buses they just flew in, but I must remind you their guns haven't been calibrated. They're mounted, but the C.C. gear has not been adjusted."

"We won't go too near the lines, and it's ten to one no Jerry will be over or beyond our balloon lines," Max said to Evers.

"I'd love to go, sir. It's just what we need."

"Mr. Thornhill said he would go if we didn't do more than an hour. I take it he's a bit tired."

Evers winked. "He had a big night, winding up his draft leave, sir, but he should be good enough for an hour."

Sar'nt 'Ollowell came back with the news that they could have the two machines, since there were no armament men available to time the C.C. gears. "But they can work on them after you get back."

"Ten minutes," Max suggested and went to get his flying kit. "I'll be here, sir."

While Kenyon was gone for his flying gear, Sar'nt 'Ollowell tied two red-and-white pennons to the rear interplane struts of Number 12. When the rigger corporal raised an inquiring eyebrow, he was told, "Mister Kenyon is takin' the two new pilots up the line for a squint about. They'll be flying behind someone with two streamers and this will be a good chance to get used to them. You leave 'em on there."

"That ought to make Mister Kenyon feel bloody important, if you ask me."

"Nobody asked you."

When Kenyon returned to the Tarmac he tried not to notice the streamers, but inwardly he was elated, and realized that Sar'nt 'Ollowell was plugging the "up from the ranks" tradition. The Sar'nt also swung Sergeant Evers's prop and showed him a new trick with the air-adjustment lever.

Remembering his tuition under Major Grimshaw, Kenyon had a portion of a map in his hand and explained his plan to Thornhill. "We're here at La Grange now. This is the River Lys winding in and out, a good marker to come home on. We're going to fly up to Armentières, a big battered town to our east. From there, I'll take you to our balloon lines as far as—let's say Ypres. You'll be able to identify that by what's left of the Cloth Hall which is about all that's still standing. If the weather holds, we'll continue on north as far as this mess of canals and the River Yser until we see Dixmude off to our right. That'll be far enough, and if there is time we'll come back over the same route. You got it?"

"I think so. You certain you know this front?"

"Well enough, and it's very distinct up in that area because of the chalk that shows where the trenches have been dug. I'll take no chances since neither of you has a gun. No heroics. If by chance some Jerry photography bus is trying to sneak over to work the Ypres-Poperinge area, we'll leave him to the Ack-Ack batteries, or hope someone else intercepts him."

"I see you know what you're talking about," Thornhill said and climbed aboard his bus.

In ten minutes all three were at 6000 feet, following the winding Lys northward. The weather still held, but there was a promise of mist moving in from the Channel. There also was a scattering of cumulus high overhead, but from 6000 feet they could see for miles in every direction. Max reveled in his command and watched the red-and-white pennons flutter from his struts with the pleasure of an admiral who for the first time sees his flag run up the mast. He glanced back now and then and was pleased to note that both Thornhill and Evers were still in good formation position. The river below twisted and turned, and then the front line, marked by its Grecian frieze of trenches and offshoots of communications and sapheads, spread beyond the stagnant areas of waterways and canals. He pointed below to the skimpy row of kite balloons that were straining against their cables and swinging toward the enemy lines with the power of the prevailing wind.

They coursed along in this manner as Max indicated the salient features. To their right there were blobs of white antiaircraft bursts, marking the explosions of British gunners. Beyond that, salvos of black smoke bursts indicated the enemy's war against intruding Allied aircraft. The conducted tour was moving along at a steady pace when Max spotted a four-plane formation speeding toward them. They were tightly knit, and as they approached, he realized they were nose-down for added speed, and he wondered what they were racing from.

A square box of white antiaircraft warned that there were enemy planes somewhere above, and another glance at the speeding quartet told Max they were Sop Pups. As they came closer he saw the block numerals used as identification by Number 66 Squadron.

"That must be Roland's flight," he muttered to himself. "But why the frantic rush, and why only four? 'B' Flight was only one man short this morning."

Max continued north wondering whether it would be wise to turn and join the Pup formation. Glancing back to make sure his charges were still with him he realized that the British gunners below were firing at two German Halberstadt two-seaters. Above them in a neat V were several Albatros single-seaters acting as escort. But why was Chris racing away in that manner? He wondered whether . . . He glanced back at Evers and Thornhill and remembered they were helpless, or would be if the Jerries attacked. He felt he ought to turn and take the same withdrawal measures Chris had, but instead he instinctively banked sharply and began to climb. The two newcomers stayed with him. He wondered whether either one had noticed the Jerries above, or were still blindly following him.

He reset his throttle and drew more revs, and still climbing, kept his eyes on the two Pups behind him. He wished one or the other would have sense enough to turn back and join Roland's formation, but he did not know whether they had recognized that they were Number 66 Squadron's buses. All in all, it was a situation he had not anticipated, and he knew there was a chance of his blundering into a dangerous predicament. Still, he remembered to pull up his C.C. hydraulic gear handle to put the synchronization into mesh. He had no idea of trying to interfere with the Jerries. He was simply responding to the instincts espoused while flying with Number 70 Squadron. He continued to bank and climb, wishing either Evers or Thornhill had the sense to race after "B" Flight's formation, but they were still tagging on to his tailplane.

There were too many possibilities to consider, but he felt no personal concern. He'd seen Jerries before. He'd attacked all types of Huns. There was something familiar about all of it, and he began to relish the exigency, if only he could be rid of these two rookies. He looked at his instrument panel and saw he had climbed to 7500 feet. Then glancing about for the high-level Albatri he suddenly saw he was looking straight up at the muddy-white belly of a two-seater. The revelation made him gasp. He fumbled for the spade-grip trigger and then let out a low cry. "My God! I wonder whether old 'Ollowell had my ammo box reloaded!" He tried to remember whether the point had been brought up. He was positive nothing had been said about his gun, just that the others had not been . . . "Am I starting all this again? Here's a chance to blast a bloody Hun and there may be no ammunition in the box."

While he argued with himself, he was drawing a true bead on the fuselage just above him. When the Aldis sight was clogged with mud-streaked fuselage, he pressed the trigger, still half-believing he had nothing to shoot. Then to his great joy the gun rattled and he saw streaks of tracer race across the few dozen feet of space and crash into the Jerry fuselage. He held the trigger down and almost put his top plane into the wheels of the Halberstadt. He cleared just in time, and as he passed heard a low gushy explosion and knew he had torched a fuel tank. He banked hard and saw that Evers and Thornhill were still tagging on, as though linked by fine wires. It was a wonderful feeling, and he looked about for more Jerries to conquer. Continuing in his climbing turn, he saw his victim was burning fiercely and dropping his nose. He looked about for the other Hun, thanking old 'Ollowell for refilling his ammo box. The second photo plane was turning away, and the gunner was hosing the area trying to hold off the three Sop Pups. Max had to suppress a laugh for it reminded him of one or two more frantic moments of his aerial gunner days.

He moved to get under the Halberstadt, and then heard a frightening crash. It wasn't the brittle crack of an antiaircraft shell, but more like the thud of two man-made masses coming together. His first reaction was that Evers and Thornhill had collided, but when he looked back they were in exactly the same position. He glanced up and to his surprise saw that two Albatros D-IIIs had locked wings and were slithering sideways just above the Halberstadts. A silver V-strut whirled across the sky like a boomerang, and again by instinct, he sensed that both had come down in a tight dive but when the three Pups moved below the two-seater, they had tried to pull out, and had each turned in the wrong direction.

A most astonishing coincidence, but one that had occurred many times. Max banked sharply, praying he could get the two weaponless Pups clear of the mess. He glanced down and saw the bend of the Lys where it swung almost due east for Hallouin. He had to remember that. He headed due west and saw Evers and Thornhill were still with him, but had been forced to fly wider of his tail. He was grateful, and turned his attention to the remaining Jerry aircraft. He checked his C.C. gear and saw that the Halberstadt, followed by four Albatri, was heading back for its own side of the line, encouraged by salvos of white antiaircraft.

"My God!" Max gasped when he realized they had escaped from a hazardous experience. "How the hell did we get into a mess like that? What was Chris doing, screeching home? Wonder what happened."

He decided his little formation had seen enough of the war for one afternoon, so he headed for La Grange. The fact that he had destroyed his first Hun, as a pilot, completely eluded him. He *was* concerned that he had taken two helpless pilots into a critical situation with no justification. He berated himself all the way back, never once glorying in the illogical manner in which they had destroyed three German aircraft. His firing up into the Halberstadt had been just a normal reaction. It did not occur to him he had made a bold and skilled attack. Gradually, as they approached the crisscrossed field, some of the details shifted into clearer focus. He had had no other choice but to fire at the Halberstadt. There was no way—at the time—to order Evers and Thornhill to join Roland's formation and clear off with them. Had they done so, the Albatri would have swooped down on them and they would have been blasted out of the sky with no weapons to defend themselves. By the time he was gliding down into the beet field, Kenyon had his report clearly outlined.

There was no need. Both Thornhill and Evers would provide a very clear and exciting explanation of what happened.

When Max rolled his Pup up to the Tarmac in front of his hangar, a small group of pilots were standing around a man who was being attended by a sick-bay orderly. There was the flash of white bandage, pads of gauze, the whiff of antiseptic and the anguished face of a man who had been wounded. An ambulance crunched over the cinders and swept up to the group. Major Allington fussed like a mother hen, but helped the man into the conveyance, and then floundered up to Kenyon.

"He'll be all right, but we've lost him for a while," he said as though talking to himself, "but Spicer went down, so Roland says. He seems quite cut up about it, but . . ."

"We saw them coming back with two Halberstadts and several Albatros single-seaters, sir. We wondered what had happened when we noted only four Pups. We were doing the balloon lines, and then found ourselves in the middle of the Huns . . . two photography planes. I shot one down in flames, and then two of the Jerry scouts collided while trying to attack us. We came home after that."

Allington stood like a man coming out of an illogical dream.

Sergeant Evers corroborated, "Mr. Kenyon got directly below the two-seater and shot it up beautifully. It exploded at once, sir."

Major Allington stared at Thornhill, "But you were only supposed to be . . ."

Kenyon explained, "We were on our side of the line, but the Jerries were on a photography show. I could see the aperture for the camera. I don't know why Roland didn't do something about it." The instant he said that he knew he had blundered. There was a period of silence.

The major ignored the inference and said kindly, "He was worried about Waldron who was wounded. He wanted to be sure he got back safely. There are times when we have to obey our consciences."

Max did not think a man's conscience had anything to do with how he waged his war. "I suppose so, sir. I take it 'B' Flight has lost two more pilots and another machine."

The group left the hangar and went to the recording office where Max found Chris sitting on a creaky wicker chair drinking something from a milk-white glass. Two other pilots were swigging on mugs of tea that gave off an aroma of issue rum. Chris looked up wearily and managed a pathetic smile. Evers and Thornhill were in two other groups that listened to their excited explanation about their balloon-line experience.

Evers was saying, "Mr. Kenyon piled into the lot just as if the Albatri were not there."

Thornhill explained, "I didn't think about not having a gun. We just tied on and kept our formation together. It all added up to three Huns."

"What are they talking about?" Chris asked Max.

"We got into a scrap. What happened to you?"

"That damn' fool Spicer. Broke off again, just as I had the flight all set for an attack on a pack of D-IIIs. We had height and the sun—what there was—behind us, but Spicer couldn't wait. Down he went, they cut him off and we had to try to get him out. It was then Waldron was caught in a cross fire. There I was, watching

Spicer being shot into bits and getting the signal from Waldron that he was hit. My first thought—which was silly, I suppose—was to get Waldron safely across the line. This is how everything goes wrong. We wondered why you didn't join us."

"We couldn't. Neither Evers nor Thornhill had a gun. We were just out doing the balloon lines. I couldn't understand why you were streaking back when there were Jerries well over our side of the line."

"What could I do? I had to get Waldron back."

"He could have made it alone from there."

"Don't criticize, Max. I'd lost one man, and I wanted to make certain Waldron got back. What would you have done?"

"I would have thought you would have done what any Charterhouse boy would have done. I would have seen Waldron across the line, and then gone back after those two photography planes. It was a wonderful chance to get them on our side of the line for a change."

Chris knew he was being baited for his education, so he switched the subject. "What's this about your shooting down one of the Halberstadts, and taking two men with no guns up that close to the line?"

"Get your drink down and your patrol report made out. I'll tell you about it later. I'll probably get jankers, unless Major Allington lets me off."

Just then Captain Tomkins weaved over from his desk. "It's right, Kenyon. They have your Halberstadt near Number 9 Balloon Company site. Bloody good show!"

"What about the two Albatri that collided?" Sergeant Evers demanded. "They ought to be in the same area. They came down on Mr. Kenyon, but he darted under the second Halberstadt, and in the mix-up they locked wings. It was a wonder they didn't take the other photo plane with them."

At that point, Max displayed his complex character, and said, "Why don't we give both Evers and Thornhill credit for one Albatros each. They were as much a part of the cause as I was."

Captain Roland looked up, completely bewildered.

After tea Major Allington called a special meeting in the anteroom. One flight was out somewhere over Menin, but the rest of the flying personnel were ordered to sit in. "Well, it has been quite a day so far, gentlemen," he began, as he still sipped from his cup of tea. "We have lost Mr. Spicer and Mr. Waldron of 'C' Flight. Mr. Waldron, fortunately, will have a spell in hospital in Blighty, but he'll be quite comfortable. On the other side of the innings we have credit for three Huns, thanks to Mr. Kenyon, who was on a balloon-practice flight. Heaven only knows what he might have done had we sent him on an offensive patrol."

Kenyon arose to interrupt. "Excuse me, sir. I downed only one. The others crashed as the result of a midair collision."

The major put down his cup and produced a professorial glare. "Mr. Kenyon! I resent being contradicted. You have been credited with three Huns. They have been confirmed beyond all doubt. In fact, all three were inside our lines. I won't delve into other recommendations Wing may have made, but I am—for your impertinence—recommending you for promotion to captain, and plan to have you take over Captain Donoley's 'A' Flight."

There was an admixture of underbreath assent, gasping surprise, and a short burst of clapping with small areas of silence.

"Captain Donoley will be posted to Home Establishment for a special course on aerial fighting at Turnberry. You will take over his flight as soon as your captaincy has been confirmed. That, Mr. Kenyon, is what happens to junior subalterns who contradict their superiors, and to confirm further your punishment, I hereby order drinks all round. Mr. Kenyon, will you see that the mess steward takes everyone's order, please?"

In that manner—delighted with his little joke—Major Allington applied the trigger that was to send Maxwell Kenyon on his meteoric career as a scout pilot. Within a week, he was awarded the Military Cross, his captaincy, and had led his flight on his first offensive patrol.

While dressing for dinner that night, Max confided in Chris. "This is how things go for me. When I do the right thing, I get chopped down. But if I blunder into something, and it comes off, I'm a hero. By rights, I should have been cashiered for taking Evers and Thornhill up the line with no guns. Both of them deserve credit for the way they stayed with me, giving the impression we were a three-ship flight. That really took pluck, but they acted as though they enjoyed it."

"They certainly had a front seat for a terrific show," Chris said, smiling for the first time that afternoon. "For a minute I thought

Allington was going to take drastic steps, and give you my flight. He could have done, you know."

"In a way," Max said reflectively, "I wish he had made me your subleader. I don't like being rushed along. I would rather stay in 'B' Flight. We could have a hell of a time."

Chris made no comment on that point. "I knew he was getting rid of Donoley, and you fill the bill. It works out perfectly for Allington. All I can do beyond that is wish you lots of luck, Max."

"That's one thing I never attract," Max said moodily, really believing it.

24

The next morning was fairly peaceful for the clouds were too low for the early morning patrol which would have been assigned to "A" Flight. The lay-off gave Max some time to get adjusted to his new assignment, and after breakfast, following a short talk with Major Allington, he went to "A" Flight's hangar to make himself known to his flight sergeant, a peppery little NCO named Gerrard, who, compared to Sar'nt 'Ollowell, was the epitome of the spit-and-polish timeserving soldier. His boots gleamed, his puttees were wound with precision, and his breeches would have put a Life Guardsman to shame. He had the Mons Star ribbon on his spotless tunic and his cap badge gleamed like a ceremonial order. He was almost too good to be true. He had a sharp-featured face, pale blue eyes, a hint of mustache and a blued chin that marked the man who knew how to shave. The minute Kenyon appeared on the Tarmac, Gerrard quick-stepped from the gloom of the hangar, clicked his heels, and gave a salute that would have passed at Buckingham Palace.

"'Morning, sir. Flight Sergeant Gerrard, sir. All present . . . and correct this morning, sir."

"Good morning, Flight," Max returned. "I'm Lieutenant Kenyon, and I seem to have inherited 'A' Flight, but I suppose you know about that. We're washed out so far this morning, but I may want to look over what equipment . . . Pups, we have on hand."

"We have six completely serviceable aircraft, sir. All other ranks are present or immediately available."

"That's a good start. I hope I can keep everything together for you. I'm new at this job, but we have no choice, do we? I'll appreciate any help, or advice—or even a good ticking off—whenever I need it. I'm not sure what pilots I'll have, but I suppose that will be straightened out in the office. Let's have a look over the machines. I presume I shall have to take over Captain Donoley's bus."

"Number 1 is a very good grid, sir. We put in a new engine only a few days ago. She's pretty well run in by now. I suggest you take her up and check out the controls. Captain Donoley liked them tight—too tight, for my money, sir. I wish you'd check them out for yourself. We can loosen them in a jiffy."

"Then we won the two new Pups flown in from Saint-Omer, I believe."

"Yes, sir, but we had to plug up a few bullet holes after you brought them back yesterday afternoon. Sergeant Evers's bus was properly peppered."

Max restrained a smile. "As long as the main spars are undamaged, he'll be all right."

"Mostly through the fuselage, sir. No longeron damage, but we replaced one rudder cable that had been nicked. I take it you had an exciting view of the balloon line."

"We were bloody lucky."

"Ah, well, sir. We can all do with bags of that. Let's hope you have brought us a good dollop. We've had plenty of the other kind."

"We aim to please, Flight," Max said, feeling quite pleased with himself.

By noon, Max, assisted by Major Allington and Captain Tomkins, began to get his job in order. Looking over his pilot list, he learned he had a young, wiry little Australian, named Griggs, as his subleader. Griggs had been at Eton at the outbreak of war, but at the first opportunity had "slung his hook" as he put it, and worked his way into the R.F.C. He had been with the squadron only three weeks, but had more than held up his end, and was credited with two two-seaters and a kite balloon. Max subconsciously resented Griggs, first for his being an Etonian, and second for having earned his first streamer.

Thornhill and Evers were, of course, retained, much to Max's relief for he felt both would make fine pilots. The other two were leftovers from Donoley's flight—Peterkin, another lad from prep school, and a chunky Cornwall man named Ruskin who appeared to be nearing his thirties, but who had been with the squadron since the middle of April. He had been offered a streamer, but was satisfied to be led, and not assume such responsibilities. From all accounts, he came home patrol after patrol, without any particular damage, completely content with his part, but seldom firing his gun.

"I just manage to fill in the odd space here and there," he admitted. "I don't know why they keep me on."

But young Griggs said, "Take no notice. He's always where you want him, getting in some Hun's way, and he seems quite happy up there. Ruskin's all right."

Cartwright's "C" Flight stood around on the Tarmac for nearly an hour, but was finally washed out, and their Pups tucked away for the night. In the early afternoon Max sat with Donoley, getting a lead on the paperwork a flight commander was expected to take on.

"You have to go through with it, but if it gets heavy, drop it on Gerrard's shoulders. He loves figures," the retiring flight commander said before he set off for the bar. "Well, best of luck. They're having a bit of a binge tonight, seeing me off, and welcoming you in. It ought to be quite a party. We haven't had a decent beano in weeks."

"They won't see me there for long. I'll probably have a big day tomorrow."

"You'll get used to it. It's what makes the R.F.C. what it is."

Max suddenly remembered Evers and Thornhill, and he checked to see whether their guns had been calibrated. Sergeant Gerrard had made sure of that, so he ordered them both to get upstairs and do a routine gunnery test. "We may draw the early morning show tomorrow, and you might as well be prepared."

After tea Major Allington followed Max into his cubicle and sat down with him. "I've been on the wire to Wing. You've been put in for your captaincy, although the colonel argued it was a bit unusual to rush a man like this. However, there was a major in his office who remembered something about you when you were an aerial gunner. You never told me about that Sop Strutter, Kenyon . . ."

"I've been trying to forget it, sir."

"Well, whatever, you've been seconded for a temporary captaincy, but can wear the pips, of course. There's no bother about your Military Cross going through."

"I'll wait until I see everything up in orders, sir."

"Proper thing to do, of course, but I just wanted to assure you that down at Wing they seem to be very glad we latched onto you."

"Are we getting any replacements for Chris Roland's flight?"

"We've put in for two, of course, but who knows?"

"Is 'B' down for an afternoon patrol?"

"Just a routine offensive patrol, if we get any weather."

"If Roland's shorthanded, why not let me do the show for him? We can use some over-the-line practice. We won't be out long, and I'll keep them well in hand."

Allington took a serious view of the offer. "It's good of you, Kenyon, but I wouldn't want to offend Roland. He could borrow a couple of pilots from 'C' Flight. We do it regularly."

"Why not let me take either Evers or Thornhill and fill out his flight, sir?"

"I don't want you substituting for anyone."

"Well let me take my mob up and give Roland a rest."

Allington thought it over. "Would you do that, Kenyon? It would be a help, and in the long run Roland will appreciate it."

"I wish you'd talk to Chris. He may resent my taking his patrol, and I know he'll hate the idea of anyone trying to make things easy for him. Make it sound as though you want us to have the experience, sir."

Major Allington managed a grandfatherly smile. "He'll listen to me. I know how to handle prep schoolboys." He rubbed the side of his nose. "I was a prep school professor before the war."

Max looked amazed. "Good lord, sir. How did you come to join the R.F.C.?"

"I really don't . . . quite remember. It seemed like the thing to do at the time."

Dud days were not all they have been presented in popular literature. Getting out of the early morning show because of rain or fog, could be a happy release, and if inclement weather was promised through the midday there often was an opportunity to go into Saint-Omer or Amiens for some unnecessary shopping, a hotel dinner, or a hot bath. But seven or eight hours of uncertain idleness, bridge-whist, poker, chapters of a book one had forced one's self to read, the continual mawkishness of *Any Time Is Kissing Time*, *Roses of Picardy*, *Three Hundred and Sixty-Five Days*, and *Maid of the Mountains* ground from an asthmatic phonograph would usually arouse any red-blooded man to action and make him wish he could go out and make Fritz expend his antiaircraft shell ration.

Thus, when Max ranged through the anteroom, the armament shed and the hangars looking for his pilots, he had no trouble getting them into flying gear on the prospects of a short jaunt over the line. Even old Ruskin admitted he was going balmy sitting around trying to make up his mind to answer a stack of recent letters.

"It's just a practice show—for me," Max explained, "and I want a full flight. If the weather threatens, we'll come back, but if we can get over at any decent height, we'll try to stir up Jerry. Any arguments?"

"Anything for a change," Griggs said, grinning.

"Take-off in ten minutes. Rendezvous at three thousand over the field."

There were broken streaks of sunlight well in the west when Max took off through the beet-root field. The cloud level above began to break up, and there was promise of an hour or so of fair visibility. He circled and watched his flock take off, one by one, and climb after him. In fifteen minutes they had formed up and were heading for the lines at the 6000-foot level. The golden gleam off to their left was spreading wider and sending brassy beams through the breaks in the clouds. He looked back and saw that Griggs on the outside—coffin corner—was sheep-dogging the others into a tighter formation. Evers was off his right elevator and Ruskin was tagging on to the left. Thornhill and Peterkin were on the back row, lined up with Griggs. It was a perfect formation, and Max felt as happy as he ever had in his whole life. This was living. No matter what happened, he at last had two streamers and five scouts behind him.

But with the immediate satisfaction came the realization that this could last only as long as the war, or as long as he could evade the consequences of air action. He saw the same dismal end to this temporary superiority, this false aura of distinction. There seemed no future, but to return to the slatternly hovel on South 10th Street, the degrading atmosphere of that fetid kitchen, the melancholy spirits of his father and mother and their gutter skepticism. He could never return to that!

He took his flock toward the bend in the Lys where he had first seen Roland's formation the day before. He turned north, but headed for the east side of Ypres, checked his map and saw that Menin farther east had picked up some stray bars of sunshine, and could be clearly seen. He continued north, studying the British balloon line, and tucking away a few salient points to remember when they came back.

At Ypres he circled the old town and then decided to follow the road down to Menin. "I've got to learn this sector, chunk by chunk," he was saying to himself when a dull explosion belched below. He looked and noted they had drawn their first Archie. Three more blobs took up the opposition, but he ignored them as they were well off range. Perhaps the next salvo would be closer. Now he could recognize the telltale scars of trench warfare. There were all the old gashes, craters, sapheads, and shapeless puddles of green slime. The barbed wire embroidery was there in exactly the same designs that he remembered when he was with Number 70. Another belch of antiaircraft fire made his machine dance with the concussion, and he waved the formation to open wider. He smiled to himself, as he remembered the tricks Majors Grimshaw and MacPartland had unwittingly taught him.

He was reveling in the fact that other than the belches of stinking black smoke, this was as perfect a time to carry out formation practice when he caught a red signal flare from somewhere behind. He glanced back and decided it had been fired by Griggs. The Australian was wagging his wingtips and pointing somewhere above and behind. Max turned to look over his other shoulder and saw a V of Jerry Albatri several hundred feet above. He considered the situation, and then recalled the successful ruse Captain Saunders had used with his Sop Strutters of "C" Flight to break up a formation of C-IIIs near Courcelette. He took another glance back toward Griggs, nodded to him and turned deeper into Hunland. "We're not too far over, and they're not likely to expect us to risk going farther, unless we're trying to kid them into something sticky." He thus justified his move, ignoring that Saunders had used the trick with Strutters with aerial gunners in the back seats.

But lightning was to strike twice for Maxwell Kenyon. He continued toward Menin but started to climb. The Jerries above turned with them, seemingly falling for the ruse. However half of the pack stayed at their present level while four came down like fletched bolts.

Kenyon opened his formation, and Griggs turned away, banked hard and came back just as one Albatros jockeyed to fire on Thornhill. The young Aussie had timed it perfectly. His first burst caught the D-III broadside, the interplane strut went out and the two wing panels folded up, slapped together, and the fuselage wrenched itself from the tangle of spars, fabric, and ribs. The two D-IIIs behind held their course, but ran into cross-fire bursts from Kenyon's and Peterkin's guns. A pure white Albatros with a Prussian shield and eagle insignia snapped into a sharp zoom, faltered at the top and went into a tight spin. The other panicked, failed to fire a shot, and kept straight on. Ruskin nosed down after him, and his first burst took the tail clean away from the garishly painted Albatros. So he pulled out and climbed back to where Kenyon was leading a ragged throng around another D-III with a green-and-white design across an earth-brown fuselage. Thornhill darted past Peterkin and took careful aim. In less than a minute a green-and-white plane was jerking about with a great scarf of flame snapping from its engine cowling.

Max then waved the re-form signal and was pleased to see how quickly they were back in tight formation. He looked up for the rest of the Jerries and saw they were making uncertain moves to get into the fight, but the leader's indecision brought about his undoing. Another formation of British biplanes came down the chute and scattered them. In a complete rout, they went into frantic dives and two appeared before Max's flight. He poured a long, deflection shot at one, and to his delight saw it jerk up sharply, stall at the top of the zoom and then begin a long spiral down. Max had used the same laying-off procedure he had learned with the Lewis gun many months before. The last member of the Albatri force was trying to get away from the other R.F.C. formation that was driving it down toward Courtrai.

Max decided his formation had performed well enough for one late afternoon, and he turned back toward the British line. He wondered what type of aircraft had made up the other formation. "I've never seen anything like them. I wonder if they could be S.E.5s of Number 56 Squadron. How they can dive!"

They crossed as soon as possible, for he did not wish to risk the possibility that anyone had taken any damage from the first short attack by the Jerries, but kept them in tight formation all the way back to La Grange. He tried to figure out just who had downed what, but beyond his own deflection shot he was not too certain who should be credited with anything, although he was certain about Ruskin's Hun, and thought Peterkin had put a telling burst into another. He decided to scribble out his patrol in time brackets, the area they had covered, some details of the scrap, and make a mention of the assistance given by a flight of unidentified British scouts.

They broke up, went into a long line-astern and got down without any of them slithering into a drainage ditch. Only the flight sergeant and "A" Flight's mechanics were on the Tarmac to greet them, but as they rolled up to the hangar, Captain Tomkins strolled out, smoking a big briar pipe, and followed by a frisky wire-haired terrier. Thus was the scene laid for the revelation of Kenyon's first offensive patrol.

"Well, I see you all got back safely," Tomkins said. "Bloody good formation coming in, too."

"Thanks," Max said and grinned mischievously. "We had a bit of a scrap near Menin."

Young Griggs trumpeted, "A bit of a scrap? We cleaned up a whole Jerry formation. You never saw anything like it. A flock of S.E.5s joined in, but we didn't need them. We had scuttled the lot. Who says Pups can't fight?"

Tomkins drew out his pipe slowly. "You took them into a Jerry formation?" he demanded of Kenyon.

"They were above us, so I lured them down by making them think we were going all the way to Menin. That is, we lured half of them down, and we cleaned out all three of them. When the rest came down, we put paid to two of them, and left the last one for a flight of . . . you say they were S.E.5s, Griggs?"

"Oh, yes. We've seen them once or twice before."

"Good God, how they can dive!"

But Tomkins was anxious to get it down on paper. "Never mind the S.E.5s. Into the recording office with you, and let's get it straightened out. Major Allington will put on a double binge to-night. Bloody good, Kenyon."

After half an hour of pro and con, Kenyon had given full credit where it was due. Griggs had the first, no question about that. Peterkin claimed and was credited with the second, and Ruskin finally admitted he had shot the tail off the third. After some chatter, Kenyon agreed Thornhill's burst had started the fire that finished the Albatros with the green-and-white scarf design. They all concurred that Max's deflection shot had accounted for the fifth. Sergeant Evers had come back emptyhanded, but he was delighted to have been on the patrol.

"Bloody good!" Tomkins kept saying. He hadn't had such pleasure in weeks. "And no kit bags to pack up."

Major Allington came in, glanced over each patrol report. He was followed by Chris and Captain Cartwright who were as pleased as though all this was being credited to their own flights. Unquestionably, it was a red-letter day in the books of Number 66 Squadron.

"Five bloody Huns in one patrol," someone in a corner of the recording office kept saying.

Major Allington actually lit a cigarette and accepted a whisky-and-soda from the mess steward. He looked a very happy man, but still asked dozens of questions over each shoulder. "We must call up Number 56 and thank them for . . ." He beamed. "What can we thank them for?"

Max gave the accepted answer. "For driving them down where we could take care of them."

Chris cocked one eye at Max and concluded he was learning fast. If he kept that free-and-easy manner, he'd go a long way.

"Jolly good!" Allington agreed, and chuckled. "You'll see to that, won't you, Tomkins?" We thank them for driving those Huns down where we could take care of them. Exactly those words, remember."

Chris Roland was still schoolboy enough to believe that this first offensive patrol of Max's would instill a new jolt of esprit de corps into the squadron; that from now on Huns would fall every time a pilot pressed his gun trigger. They would be considered among the elite squadrons on the front. Number 66 would erase the stigma of their losses through the previous month, and that even he might justify the captaincy that had been thrust on him by the ill fortunes of war.

It was quite a party that night. All agreed the tide had turned, and who knew, any day they might be rewarded with S.E.5s.

To a certain extent much of Kenyon's good fortune and his leadership, bold as it was, improved the work of Number 66

Squadron. Huns were downed and escort shows carried out day after day with considerable success. Whatever the reason, each patrol was rewarded, not only with victories, but when machines took heavy battle damage they were always escorted back to the safety of their own lines. When fuel tanks were holed and Le Rhônes conked out, the pilots always remembered to turn on their gravity feed and zoom a few dozen feet above the enemy lines—to escape and fly again. So spirited did the squadron become, Major Allington led a wild rip-roaring squadron show up and down the balloon lines every Sunday afternoon, leaving a trail of smoking gasbags or shot-up winch trucks. On two such shows pilots were wounded by gunfire, but both reached their own field and were sent to hospital—and Blighty—with sophomoric good will.

Weeks flew by with no serious setbacks. A few men went on leave. Captain Cartwright went home to organize a squadron, after putting up the purple-and-white ribbon of the Military Cross. Major Allington was awarded a bar to his D.S.O., and intimated there were other decorations in the offing, but everyone seemed too interested in running up his score, and such awards were always another excuse for a binge.

But it was the continued success of Captain Kenyon that fired this lively turmoil. He gave his all to leading "A" Flight and was determined never to lose a man. He carried out every assignment given him, chiefly because of the loyalty of his pilots, a point he would not always admit. If he showed immediate willingness to credit a man with a victory or a job well done, it was because he secretly enjoyed the pleasure of being in a position where he *could* extend such largess. It was a form of power or authority he had not known before, and he felt deep satisfaction in dispensing it. In addition to his apparent generosity, he was an outstanding air fighter. His score mounted day by day, and his victories were carried out in a masterful manner. Few realized the bulk of the credit lay in his gunnery, a skill he had learned in the early months of the war, and had never lost. His eye was true, his finger a precision instrument that never betrayed him. Because he was a master of the difficult deflection shot, he used it as often to down his foe, as to keep himself out of the danger segment of any aerial engagement. His days as an aerial gunner had given him more than any gunnery instructor in Britain could ever contribute. He knew to the fraction of an inch how much he must lay off for any type of aeroplane, flying at any speed, or crossing his line of fire at any angle.*

Had Captain Kenyon's war career been brought to a satisfactory conclusion in the early summer of 1917, he would have returned to civilian life a respected serviceman. Had hostilities been brought to a close at that time, he might have returned to his family with many of the attributes of the temporary gentleman with no preconceived notions of how the world should treat him. Instead, the fortunes of war allowed him to continue his ambitious career and redouble his earlier yearning for the premier decoration that had evaded him.

During 1917 four Victoria Crosses were awarded to gallant Royal Flying Corps pilots, two of them posthumously. Max read the citations avidly and compared the deeds with his own experiences. Sergeant Thomas Mottershead of Number 20 Squadron had been flying an F.E.2b with a Lieutenant Gower as his observer. When well over the line they were attacked by enemy aircraft and the fuel tank under Mottershead's seat burst into flames. Gower did his best to douse the fire while Mottershead sat it out, trying to bring his aeroplane into the British lines. The gallant sergeant died of his wounds and burns, and was honored with the V.C. for his effort.

Lieutenant F. H. McNamara, an Australian of Number 67 Squadron, was awarded the famous bronze cross for rescuing a fellow pilot who had been shot down while bombing a Turkish railroad. It was a thrilling story of how one man will risk his all for a comrade. To Max's disgust, he learned that McNamara had been flying—of all things—an old B.E.2c. On that same day, June 6, 1917, Captain Albert Ball of Number 56 Squadron who had destroyed forty-four enemy aircraft before he himself was killed; was awarded the V.C. posthumously.

Max's secret ambition was further inflamed when he read later that Captain William A. Bishop, a Canadian who had started as an observer and had become a Nieuport pilot with Number 60 Squadron, was honored with the V.C. after he had destroyed forty-

* Twenty-three years later, another air hero who had risen from the ranks, George E. "Buzz" Burling of Canada, became famous as the Malta Spitfire, and destroyer of twenty-nine enemy aircraft, using exactly the same system of gunnery.

seven Huns, and sent back to Canada for a rest. (He returned to the front later, heading his own squadron, and ran his score up to seventy-two.) Max could picture himself returning to Newark with the blood-red ribbon of the V.C. If Bishop could be sent back to Canada, why couldn't he return to the United States? After all, America was now in the war.

In July, Max was granted a short leave to Paris, and he was astonished to see the manner in which air aces, as they were being called in the City of Light, were lavishly honored and acclaimed. The Americans he met had no eyes for his three modest decorations. They knew only the French Legion of Honor with its scarlet rosette, or the ribbon of the V.C., flaunting the miniature bronze cross in its center.

He returned from his short leave, determined to remedy the situation. He also had assumed a new attitude of command, and almost overnight became a tyrant, a martinet, an unreasoning bully who treated his men—and his friends—with none of the open comradeship that had marked his joining Number 66 Squadron. Chris Roland, the finest gentleman in the squadron, became Max's chief target.

25

Early in 1917 the German Airship Service lost their noted Heinrich Mathy, along with most of their original nine commanders, and the German High Command was compelled to develop an alternate means of renewing its air offensive against London. Following an ineffectual start with a small force of L.V.G. biplanes, it was decided to build up a special force, using the Gotha—a twin-engined bomber—as its chief weapon. On June 5, 1917, twenty-two Gothas bombed Sheerness and Shoeburyness at the mouth of the Thames. A week later fourteen more reached and bombed London in broad daylight. Seventy-two missiles were dropped in the Liverpool Street Station area, and the casualties during this raid were greater than the total sustained in fourteen months of Zeppelin raids. One hundred sixty-two civilians were killed and 432 injured.

The Gotha raids were a shock to the London defense authorities, who found it hard to believe such a force could blast its way through the defenses and strike with such precision. A new counterthrust had to be devised. Additional aircraft were assigned to Sutton's Farm. Number 39 Squadron was equipped with the new B.E.12, which was only a few miles faster than the old B.E.2c. A few S.E.5s were also added, but when the Germans increased their Gotha raids, striking at a number of diverse targets, it was decided to bring Number 56 Squadron and their S.E.5s back from France and bolster further the Home Defense force. They were accommodated at Bekesbourne near Canterbury. Then, to the surprise of all concerned, Number 66 Squadron was suddenly uprooted from La Grange and moved to a seacoast aerodrome outside Calais.

In this, there was some hope the Pups might intercept the Gothas on their return from raids over Great Britain.

The move to Calais began with a full day of frantic packing, the movement of motor transport, and bellowing and screaming about baggage that had, or had not, been loaded. The coastal field was typical of the seacoast aerodromes. Part of it took in a long stretch of sandy beach, the rest had been gouged out of scrubby grass, gorse, and what had been windswept thicket. A breakwater ran down into the surf, offering shelter for a concrete ramp that had previously served a RNAS seaplane squadron. The living quarters were a conglomerate of sheds, long buildings where fishermen had once dried their nets, two comparatively new Adrian huts and a collection of Nissen barracks in various states of disrepair. There were patches of sand everywhere, but at least it was a change from La Grange.

There was no flying for twenty-four hours, and all hands went to work making the quarters more livable. Once that was completed, as many as could be spared were permitted to take a plunge in the surf, a pleasure that was accompanied with typical horseplay and gales of laughter. As soon as communications were established, conflicting orders, requests, and advice came in from all directions. Someone offered the news that Number 46 Squadron had been sent to England and was setting up shop at Sutton's Farm.

"Why couldn't we go there, too?" was the general complaint. "What can we do on this side of the Channel?"

Major Allington took the obvious view. "We're supposed to get what is left after 56 and 46 have pulled their stingers."

"But Gothas go over at night, don't they? We're not equipped for night flying."

"You'll be surprised how quickly we'll learn if the necessity comes up. The Huns have been attacking at night, but since July 7 they have been breezing over in daylight—and raising hell. We put up seventy-eight aircraft round London regularly, but the Jerries seem to get back safely, no matter how much they are shot up."

This sort of conversation marked each day while the new Bessenau hangars were erected, a livable mess set up, and belts of ammunition were loaded to carry Pomeroy and Buckingham ammunition in the hope the Gotha fuel tanks could be torched with these incendiary rounds. After two days of all-out effort Number 66 Squadron was finally straightened out and ready for their interception program. Their main task was to get off the ground as quickly as possible, once the alarm came through from the Home Defense Group.

It was believed that the Sop Pups would be most suitable for this work, particularly in harrying any of the raiders that had been damaged over England. All pilots were warned that the twin-engined Gothas would be carrying one machine gun mounted to fire through a tunnel in the fuselage. These weapons carried belts of armor-piercing ammunition, interspersed with tracer bullets every fourth round. Both guns were electrically heated to prevent stoppages at high altitude, and the heating elements were made of electric filaments that ran through oil-soaked asbestos shields. Current was supplied by one of the engines.

While most of the pilots of Number 66 Squadron were not too keen to fight Gothas over the English Channel, Kenyon proclaimed that compared with intruding over the German lines every day, it would be something of a holiday. "The only thing we have to worry about is to keep clear of that Hun in the tail turret. We're not shooting down Jerry photo buses now," he warned. "The idea is to go in at an angle, one that will prevent the front gunner from shooting unless he risks clipping his flying wires, struts, or even the propellers. In fact, the front gunner has a very limited field of fire anywhere but forward."

"How does he know all this?" Chris's subleader, a comical character called Jorrocks, asked.

"Don't ask me. He learned most of it while he was at the Testing Squadron; lectures, photos, and all that sort of thing. You can be assured he knows what he's talking about."

"I suppose so," Jorrocks agreed, "but I wish he'd be less offensive when he's dishing out all this top-drawer information. He's getting unbearable lately. Ordering everybody about. I heard the major ticking him off yesterday. Told him straight he was getting too big for his boots."

"Oh, what was that all about?"

"Seems he asked his flight sergeant to let him paint some silly insignia on his Pup. He'd drawn a giddy idea of a three-cornered hat with a red-white-and-blue rosette that had a star in the middle. Supposed to be all the rage down on the French front where some

Yanks had formed a squadron long before America came into the war."

Chris smiled. "I hadn't heard of this."

"Gerrard told him that nothing more than the identifying numerals were allowed, so he went off in a huff and complained to Major Allington. He got a good talking-to, so now the major is in his black book."

"Ridiculous. The CO has been damned good to him ever since he arrived. But you wait, Max will get what he wants, if he has to complain to Wing. But what a silly idea. Childish, I think."

"If he feels so bloody American all of a sudden, why doesn't he relinquish his commission and put in for a transfer to the American forces?"

"He'll never do that," Chris decided. "He's doing too well here to toss away whatever seniority he has piled up. He wants to stay in after the war. He'll wind up a squadron leader one of these days."

"God help everyone under him. He's driving his own flight crazy," Jorrocks said quietly.

Kenyon had suggested that when they went aloft to intercept the bombers on their way to England, a full flight should be sent into the air, if they could be warned early enough. In cases where small groups had been ordered to various diversionary targets, formations of three Pups would be sent off at ten-minute intervals. This would be kept up as long as it was known Gothas were in the air. As it turned out, the latter plan worked best on the French side of the Channel since the bombers were at 10,000 feet and well on their way before Number 66 could be warned, and were over the mouth of the Thames by the time the Pups had reached that altitude.

Drills went on, hour after hour. A new set of signals was devised which enabled flight leaders to direct their attacks with more precision. Some of the signals were given by hand, just as cavalry leaders had done for years. They also employed the various colors of Very cartridges to be used in night formations, should they ever be sent up after dark. All agreed, after several days of this co-ordinated flying, that they had become a tighter knit squadron and had come to know each other better, particularly in their disciplined manner of flying in the smaller formations.

But with all the drills and practices, life at Calais began to pall. After the raid on July 7 when it became evident the Royal Flying

Corps was setting up a network of defense squadrons, there was little further activity out of the Gontrode station, where the bulk of the enemy bombers was located; until the middle of August. In the meantime, understandable impatience set in, and it was pointed out that all this time could have been put to better effort.

"We could be taking conversion courses on S.E.5s, instead of sitting around here doing nothing," Kenyon grumbled, and skimmed an oyster shell toward the surf.

"Better still," Roland said, "we could be carrying out our regulation leave. I haven't been home since I came out here, and there's Dover just over there."

Captain Ludlow, who had come over from Home Establishment to take over "C" Flight, had another idea. "I wish we were back at La Grange doing regular patrols. We'll never get S.E.5s, unless we do something to get mentioned in *Comic Cuts.*" Ludlow was a quiet, self-sufficient man who had won a Military Cross and a bar. He knew his trade, but refused to preen his experience or exploits. In the lounge he left all the flying and patrols behind, and enjoyed good conversation, and had a knack of drawing others out to relate their backgrounds and family associations. Before the war he had been a Second Officer with one of the leading mercantile marine shipping lines.

Then there was the day when Major Allington got the call to go back to England to take a post with the London Air Defense Command, leaving the squadron in the charge of Captain Tomkins. Two days later who should turn up to replace him but Major Ivor MacPartland, Kenyon's old Sop Strutter pilot. Their reunion was none too enthusiastic, for Max still held a latent bitterness over his treatment in the matter of Major Grimshaw. He had long argued to himself that since Grimshaw had died of his wounds there was certain proof that he had at no time been capable of flying the Strutter back. So why hadn't he and Number 70 Squadron been honored with a V.C.?

Once the two men had a word together, Max said, "I suppose you're surprised to see me a flight commander so soon." There was a tinge of exultation in his voice.

"Not at all. In fact, I may have had something to do with it," MacPartland said with an enigmatic grin. "I was at Wing when Major Allington made his appeal for you. I reminded the colonel you were the gunner who brought Major Grimshaw back, on dual control."

Max had no response for that, so he said, "What happened to Bert Laidlaw? He was a gunner with me. Remember?"

"Laidlaw? Haven't you heard? He's with Number 54 Squadron, the first to get the Camels."

"How's he doing?"

MacPartland fitted his grin again. "He's a bit of a disappointment, for an aerial gunner. So far, he's only a full captain with a D.S.O., and seventeen Huns, but give him time."

Kenyon looked stupefied. "But Bert never wanted anything like that."

"None of us gets what we want out here, as you well know. If he keeps his nose clean, he'll have a squadron in three months, the way he's going."

"He was a good chap," Max agreed with little spirit.

On August 16, the German 3rd Bombing Squadron was mustered for a raid on London, but the timing was most unfortunate. On that date a low depression was passing over southern England and the Channel, causing low clouds, rain, and poor visibility. The Gothas ran into this bad weather soon after leaving the Belgian coast, but their take-off was duly noted and forwarded on to London by Allied agents operating out of Ostend. No defense aircraft were sent up in England by the London Air Defense Command, but Number 66 was alerted and ordered to try to intercept in case the Gothas risked the weather and attempted to get through. The Readiness alarm sounded, and MacPartland decided to send his three flight commanders out on a probing flight. He put Kenyon in front, and Roland and Ludlow were content to follow the commander of "A" Flight.

Taking Kenyon aside, MacPartland said, "I'm leaving it up to you. It can be dirty out there, but you'll have to make the decision. Never mind going for glory. Turn right around and bring them back if it looks risky. I don't want you barging about in that muck when there is a chance there might be a score of Gothas in the same murk. If it's that bad, they won't get to London, anyway."

"It might be fairly clear to the northeast," Max said, and hoped he wasn't going to have trouble with MacPartland.

"If you get any Gothas, I want you to shoot them down, not

crash into them. I mean that, Kenyon. I want all three of you back—safe and sound."

"We're wasting time," Max said petulantly, and hurried off to his Pup.

In two minutes the three Pups were streaking toward the murky northeast.

After taking off from Gontrode, a force of thirteen Gothas reached the Belgian coast and encountered the first evidence of threatening weather that already was blanketing the southeastern section of England. Though in wireless communication with his base, the leader of the German raiding formation still had no reliable information on the weather over his course and above the proposed target. Because of this, he blundered on, hoping to find breaks in the cloud cover or an improvement in conditions.

Kenyon led the way to the 7000-foot level and then began to work over a segment of the search while still climbing toward his planned 10,000-foot operating level. At a point about twenty miles northeast of Calais the visibility deteriorated. A swirling pattern of mist presaged what was to come, and both Roland and Ludlow, the former deck officer, realized there was no future in staying up much longer.

But Kenyon, grumbling beneath his breath, doggedly bored on and sashayed back and forth, seeking some magical corridor in the sky, hopefully an open area, where he might find a pack of Gothas heading across his path. There were instances when he disappeared completely, and would as suddenly reappear, his cocardes gleaming through the prop-swirled mist. Roland sensed Max would continue on despite the prospects. Ludlow decided he was following a damn fool. He knew this kind of weather to the last common denominator. "Next thing he'll know, his compass will be spinning like mad and he'll find himself on his back. What the hell's the matter with him?"

Roland could just discern Ludlow a few yards off to his right. The newcomer was wagging his head in anger, or disbelief. It was difficult to tell. Once, Max stared back, and Ludlow raised his gloved hand and jerked his thumb in an unmistakable demand to turn back. Max replied with an open palm, as much to say, "Take it easy. It'll clear any minute."

Ludlow had no idea how Kenyon reacted in weather conditions such as these. He had not flown with him before. On the other hand, Chris knew him like a book and sensed he was working on the premise that any minute a pack of twin-engined Gothas would appear, and . . . he'd go to glory. Max had to do things his way, the hard, or hope-for-glory way. Their leader kept doggedly on, darting back and forth, left and right, seeking the opening he believed had to be somewhere in this murk. After one such sally, Ludlow lost track of him, so he moved in closer to, but lower than, Chris. In that way he could keep clear of him in case he too went into sudden changes of direction.

Then the unexpected happened. Kenyon had completely disappeared into the sable backdrop of the nightmare setting, but coming out of an opposite wall of obscurity, Ludlow saw three, perhaps four, great bombers, each daubed in dull green-and-brown camouflage. For a few seconds they appeared in some detail, and as they turned sharply toward a solid bank of sooty cloud, he saw Roland bank in the same direction and then zoom to fire into the underside of the last Gotha of the formation.

"Look out for that blasted tail gun!" Ludlow bellowed, and tried to get off a burst before the Jerries completely disappeared. He saw Chris pouring a long burst into the underside of the nearest Gotha, one with a black Maltese cross on its rudder. He was admiring Roland's tight burst when he saw it answered by a spatter of return fire that illuminated the underside of the Gotha's tailplane. Roland's gun stopped immediately, the little Pup faltered, dropped its nose and started to spin through the sodden cloud below.

Ludlow swore through clenched teeth, but then let out a deep breath and chuckle. The Gotha Chris had fired at was flaunting a long flame pennon from a wing section below the engine. The fuselage picked it up and the tail was quickly enveloped in a blossom of spiky gold.

"Good! Good!" the "C" flight leader said to himself. Then he saw Kenyon come racing out of a bulbous cloud ahead. Max saw the fading shapes of the Gothas, and took a hasty aim at the port engine of the flaming bomber, although his lone gun could add little to the consuming incandescence. A short burst, and Kenyon hoicked away and disappeared into another cloud barrier.

"My God! This muck must be full of Gothas." Shaking his head in disbelief, Ludlow remembered Roland and started a slow glide down, hoping to find him and make sure he was still under control.

He left the rest of the Gothas to Kenyon, and for several minutes made a breathless zigzag search, but could find no trace. He circled at 6000 feet, pondering on the situation and presuming Kenyon—thruster that he was—would continue to stalk Gothas as long as he had fuel to stay in the air. He wished him luck and dropped into a wider circle until at last he broke through the thickest of the cloud layer. Below, he could see the whitecapped waters off Dunkirk, and then to his concern saw a coastal motorboat racing toward a floating hulk of burning wreckage. There was a portion of panel showing a black Maltese cross, and he knew Chris had downed his Gotha. But less than three chain lengths away floated a battered wing of a British aeroplane, one bearing a distinct roundel. A German tail gunner had taken his final revenge because Roland had forgotten Max's warning about the gun tunnel in a Gotha.

26

Ludlow stayed in the vicinity which he identified as a few miles off Dunkirk, hoping to learn whether Roland had been picked up, but instinctively he knew the young captain had gone to the bottom, still strapped in his cockpit. There were some unreadable heliograph flashes from the motorboat, probably telling him something, but Ludlow was unfamiliar with the message code, so he banked away and took up his course for Calais. He was back within half an hour and was puzzled to note that Kenyon's Number 1 Pup was already on the sand-swept Tarmac. "He must have raced home for some reason. Why didn't he wait and try to get his formation together? A hell of a way to use two streamers," he decided as he taxied up to his hangar.

As soon as he got out of his helmet and gloves he looked around at the various groups gathered on the Tarmac. Kenyon was talking to MacPartland. Captain Tomkins was coming around the hangars with a message flimsy in his hands. Flight Sergeants Hollowell and Gerrard were talking to some "A" Flight mechanics. Another group formed and walked over to inspect Ludlow's Pup.

"Ah, there you are, Ludlow," Tomkins greeted. "What was it like?"

"Bloody awful. A proper pea souper. Why Kenyon persisted in staying anywhere near it, is beyond me. No excuse for it."

"Except that he got a Gotha. Shot it down in flames somewhere off Ostend."

"Ostend? We weren't anywhere near Ostend. Last area I saw was just beyond Dunkirk. Ostend's about fifty–sixty miles from here. We were somewhere northwest of Dunkirk. What the hell's the matter with the chump?"

"Well, whatever, he claims he shot a Gotha down in flames."

"Does he know what happened to Roland?"

"Roland? No. He thinks he got lost in the murk, but he should soon be back. What are you worried about?"

"Roland will *not* be back. He spun in just off Dunkirk. I went down and saw part of his starboard wing floating in the water."

"I suppose we'd better talk to Kenyon and get this straight."

MacPartland was arguing with Max about the weather. "I don't know why you risked that muck. The raiders had turned back, and most of them were over Belgian territory, according to what London heard from Ostend."

"It was thick, I'll admit, but it paid off. I put a long burst into one and it broke into flames immediately." He turned to Ludlow. "I don't suppose you saw anything of it, eh, Ludlow? I lost both of you right after we bored into the weather."

"I saw you firing at the Gotha Roland had torched, if that's what you mean. We were still flying together, and I saw Chris stop a packet from a tunnel gun. He spun in off Dunkirk. When you disappeared again, I went down and saw both the Gotha and a Pup's starboard wing floating in the water."

Max looked puzzled. "Roland got one?" He challenged MacPartland. "So it was worth taking the risk. We downed two of the swine."

Ludlow wagged his head. "Only one. What kind of cross did the one you shot at have on its rudder?"

"That's easy. He carried a black Maltese cross. Not the straight-barred kind most of them are using now. I remember that very well."

"The one Roland shot at carried a black Maltese cross on *its* rudder. By the time you were shooting at it, it was almost completely in flames. That's Roland's Hun, Kenyon, and you're not claiming it. It was the last thing he did. He spun in off Dunkirk."

Kenyon mulled over Ludlow's words, and then turned to MacPartland. "After all the warning about that gun tunnel," he muttered while his lower lip trembled.

The major was livid. "How could anyone remember anything, flying blind through that muck! Laidlaw had you down pat. You're a pot-hunter, Kenyon, and you'll go to any extreme . . ."

Max's tan faded to a saffron yellow and he fumbled with his helmet, but he tried one more tack. "Excuse me, sir. You have my side of the story—and Captain Ludlow's. I think you ought to take time to consider both before you make up your mind. I think I am entitled to that."

MacPartland shoved his face into Kenyon's direct vision. "You listen to me. I've known Captain Ludlow for months. He's a man I'd put my last quid on. I've known Roland only a few days, but I'd back him to the limit, too. Unfortunately, he won't be here to speak for himself. Do you still claim that Gotha?"

"It's down off Dunkirk," Ludlow broke in. "You told Tomkins you were somewhere off Ostend."

Kenyon rubbed his unshaven chin. "I'll have to think about it, sir. Perhaps we should credit it to Chris, er, Roland, since he's down somewhere. Let's credit it to Chris."

"How generous of you." MacPartland was sarcastic. "I hope you also take credit for his being where he is. There was no justification for risking that muck. The Jerries were on their way back, at any rate, and downing one wasn't worth the risk. From all accounts the weather was stuffed with Gothas and Pups. It's a wonder any of you came back. If you ever again put a formation of yours into such a hopeless situation, I'll have you . . . damn it, yes, I'll have you court-martialed!"

"I'm sorry, sir." Once more Max's enigmatic personality took its twist. He turned and offered his hand to Ludlow. "I'm sorry, Ludlow. It was unforgivable of me. I have no excuse, but I am sorry. Please try to forget it."

Ludlow was mildly stunned. He knew he had little choice but to accept, without feeling he was kicking the man when he was down. Avoiding Max's eyes, he shook hands and said, "Sorry."

The London Air Defense Command, accumulating considerable night-flying experience, additional squadrons and new aircraft that included Sopwith Camels, Bristol Fighters, and S.E.5s, became more effective as the weeks dragged by. The Gothas, later supported by the multi-engined Zeppelin Giants, tried persistently to break through and batter London, but the percentages against them soon made the raids unprofitable. Royal Flying Corps squadrons that had been withdrawn from their front-line duties in France and Belgium were returned to their original aerodromes. Number 66 packed up and went back to La Grange and again girded for renewed conquest of Albatri, Fokker triplanes, Halberstadts, and the new Hannoveraner CL.III, a two-seater reconnaissance aircraft that was also valuable as a contour fighter.

By early autumn they were in the thick of things. The front showed much of the action of the previous August. There were days of bad weather that kept what flying was risked down to low levels where the quagmire, so representative of battle areas in the Ypres sector, was clearly visible. There were thousands of shell craters, half-filled with greenish slime. Roads that once had wandered through placid villages, were nothing more than churned-up tracks. The front line could be distinguished only by the craters that had been linked up, the outlines of duckboards, and when infantrymen turned their faces to look up, it could be determined that the trench was occupied and that it was another link in the slime, water and shell holes.

It was into this zone of horror that the battle for Passchendaele would be continued. Above it the Von Richthofen Circus would attempt to hold command of the skies, but by now Bristol Fighters, Camels, and S.E.5s were offering better than they took. The days of Bloody April were forgotten, and were being paid back with an offensive that was taking much of the glamour from the Von Richthofen forays. An entirely new company of British air fighters was coming into its own but, unfortunately, little official expression of their scores was being made public.

Major MacPartland took over the command of Number 66 with a new hand and attitude. He flew two or three patrols a week himself to see how the Pup pilots "stacked up." He switched leaders and subleaders whenever possible to give new men an opportunity of expressing themselves. On one occasion he flew as subleader to Ruskin who was assigned to provide escort for a photography trio sent out to Tournai. GHQ was planning to make a new mosaic map of the area. While making their strip-runs over a heavy railroad concentration, the B.E.s were attacked by a formation of Fokker triplanes that apparently had come up from somewhere over the Douai area. MacPartland did not relish the situation, but half smiled to himself when he saw Ruskin settle down closer over the photo planes like a mother hen guarding her chicks. As the Tripes made their first move to attack, the leader couldn't decide whether first to blast out the Pups or go through and wipe out the camera ships. His indecision gave the major a chance to draw off slightly and then put his Pup up on a wingtip and cut across the oncoming Tripes. He nailed the leader with a short burst, and the others broke up into undecided formations of twos and threes. That gave the Pups another opening, and Griggs came in from his coffin corner to shoot out the single struts of a gaudy Fokker. Again the enemy broke up and the Pups went to work.

The situation was settled in less than three minutes. Ruskin had stayed down with the B.E.s, and when one gallant Hun tried to get through to the camera ships, the temporary leader blocked him off by the simple expedient of blundering into his way. The Hun hoicked hard, and ripped off his wings. The whole action was completely unorthodox, for no Pup pilot did anything the pilots in the Fokkers expected. When it was all over and the B.E.s were on their way back with boxes of exposed plates, Major MacPartland let out a *Whoosh!* and then broke into hearty laughter.

When the Pups arrived back, everyone tried to remember who had downed what. It was learned that Peterkin had been shot through the thick part of his right thigh. His leg had stiffened considerably by the time he tried to get down among the beet root, and as a result he skidded off the rutted runway and landed on his nose in a drainage ditch. He was perfectly satisfied, however, showing no remorse at leaving Number 66 for a few weeks of convalescence in Blighty.

There was another feature to this particular day, one that was becoming a routine affair. After his "A" Flight had gone off behind the streamers of Lieutenant Ruskin, Max Kenyon decided to add to his time and experience with a lone show of his own. It was an idea MacPartland had agreed to whenever Max wished, under such circumstances. Half an hour after the photo escort had landed, Max returned with a shot-up Pup and reported he had brought down two enemy aircraft over Vervicq. One, a Halberstadt, had lost its wings, the other was a Pfalz D-III which had been attacking a British balloon.

"How did you know it was a Pfalz?" MacPartland demanded.

"We had identification photos of it, three or four days ago. I recognized the different interplane struts; otherwise it looks much like an Albatros. If you don't believe me, have Tomkins call one of our balloon people in that area. It almost fell on their winch truck. They must have seen the Halberstadt go down, too."

MacPartland knew when to shut up. He sensed Kenyon had had

a good day, particularly when he'd put one down on a balloon winch. Both were confirmed within a half hour, and Number 1 Aircraft Depot had what was left of the Pfalz to examine and report on.

Kenyon was not a particularly brave man. His courage was founded on the hope of recompense, bolstered by the fear of failure. He was fortunate in that he had never sniffed the acrid breath of Death, but had endured enough pain and injury to recognize that the terminal blow—in his belief—was nothing more than the wound he had suffered at Neuve-Chapelle. Death in no manner taunted him, for by now he felt one of the elite, honored with that youthful optimism which Plutarch saw as a contempt for life.

Armed in this manner and with the determination to carry on, despite Major MacPartland's scornful opinion of him, he added to his score almost daily. True, his arithmetic was not always proven out, for in taking his flight into what at times were one-sided conflicts, he sacrificed the men he was relying on to protect his tail. One afternoon Griggs went down in flames just the other side of Lille, and Ruskin *had* to take a streamer. Thornhill was badly wounded and only just got down inside the British line. Other names were added to "A" Flight's role, and were quickly erased. There was Perkins, a young American who had arrived full of vim and ambition. There was Bircham, Alnwick, and Tonsley. Not all were killed, but were shot out of action for one reason or another.

When Max's score was well into the thirties, MacPartland called up Wing and had them order him back to England for a short period of Home Establishment. "I'm not sure what you can do with him," he explained to the colonel, "but I want him away from the squadron for a time. I need to get everyone settled down again. Kenyon is a disturbing influence, regardless of how many Huns he has. I hope you understand me, sir."

"Thoroughly. He's not the first in that class. Keep him out of the air for a couple of days, and I'll arrange to have him go back and take a course on the new S.E.5s. You'll be getting them soon, and he might as well take the conversion course with the test boys at Farnborough. The new types still show a few rough spots, but they're a big improvement . . ."

"That sounds about right, sir. He'll jib at the order, but it's as good an excuse as any. And another thing. I don't see how we can hold back a D.S.O. much longer. Do you think it could be arranged so that he'll get it while he is at Farnborough?"

"He's certainly earned it, and I'm certain it can be arranged."

"I don't want him here when it comes through. He'd be unbearable with all that glory."

Two days later Max packed, and was called in to have a talk with the major before he left.

"Just wanted to wish you luck," MacPartland said, "and to give you some advice."

"I know why I'm being taken off the front," Max said belligerently.

"Well, then, there's no need for me to tell you. All I can say is that I hope you'll like the S.E.5. You've been blatting about it long enough."

Kenyon was taken aback. "I'm to get an S.E.5 squadron?" he almost squeaked.

"Of course not. You're not ready for that kind of administration yet. You haven't done too well handling a flight."

Max looked subdued. "But Gerrard took care of everything."

"You can't take Gerrard everywhere with you. No. You're to take two weeks' leave, and then join a Royal Aircraft Factory test team at Farnborough to work out the bugs in the new S.E.5a. It has a more powerful engine and a lot of modifications. You might enjoy yourself," the major rambled on, "and when you come back to France you'll be able to show all the boys how to fly them. We should have S.E.5s by that time."

Max kept his thoughts to himself, and heard the major saying, "We're not having anything special tonight in the way of a send-off. We have two very important patrols tomorrow and everyone needs plenty of shut-eye. I'm sure you understand."

"I've never been one for binges, sir."

"They're not for everybody."

"About coming back. Am I to be posted to Number 66 again when I'm through at Farnborough?"

"I don't know. It did not come up while I was talking to Wing."

Max knew he should withdraw gracefully, but he kept on talking. "No one wants a man who is running up a score. We're outcasts. It's a form of jealousy, or envy."

"You're talking rot, Kenyon," the major said evasively. "I don't suppose it occurred to you that this is for your own welfare. You've had a long spell. Too many high-scoring men have been allowed to burn themselves out when they might have been recharging their batteries. You should be thankful someone respects how well you have been doing."

"If I've done so well," Max exploded and got to his feet, "why am I not sent back to organize a new squadron? I'd get plenty of change doing that. I've earned it, but no, I'm posted home to do a job that can be as nerve-racking as anything we get out here."

MacPartland held his tongue. Kenyon waited for an argument, but the major only packed his pipe.

"All right. I'll go back, but I'll haunt everyone in the Air Council until I get a straight answer. I'm not taking this sitting down."

"Good-by, Kenyon." The major lit his pipe. "You've had a good innings, remember. Best of luck. I can't say any more, can I?"

"No, sir. I hardly expected this much."

London seemed much the same, only more crowded. There were a fair number of Americans on the streets, but none who came from anywhere in New Jersey. The war news in the newspapers that were now immediately available was not too promising. Passchendaele had been captured by the Canadians, and the mess in Russia was even more bewildering than ever. The Bolsheviki, now led by Lenin and Trotsky took possession of Petrograd and deposed Kerensky. The Italians were in full retreat and were back to the Piave. There was some satisfaction in the news that the British had captured Ribecourt, Flesquières, Havrincourt and Marcoing. Another report had it that British tanks were threatening Cambrai after capturing Burlon Wood. There was little or nothing concerning the activities of the Royal Flying Corps.

Max put up at the Regent Palace and noting the change in the weather, realized that another winter was only a few weeks away, so he decided to invest in a British warm, since his trench coat was little more than a fleece-lined raincoat. He also took in the theaters, visited the bookshops and spent a long afternoon in the British Museum. *Chu-Chin-Chow* was still playing. Bairnsfather's *The Better 'Ole* was on view at the Oxford Theatre, and a youngster by the name of Noel Coward was a member of Sir Charles Hawtrey's supporting cast in *The Saving Grace* at the Garrick. While dawdling over breakfast one morning, Max glanced through the London *Times*, skimmed the headlines, and then the Gazette column caught his eye. He glanced down it idly, and to his controlled delight saw his name connected with the award of the Distinguished Service Order. He had long hoped for this honor, but had no idea it would come as soon as this.

Once more, he went to Burberry's, and put on a casual approach to the Decorations counter.

"Good morning, sir. Are you back with us again?" the dignified salesman asked. "I remember our putting up your D.C.M. What is it this time?"

"Oh, well, I happened to notice in the *Times* this morning that I'm being awarded the D.S.O. You'll see it in the Gazette section, if there is any question."

"Oh, none at all. Jolly good, sir. That's the stuff to give 'em. Bags of decorations."

"Can you take care of it for me, and please note that my Military Cross ribbon can be replaced. It was a hack job in Dunkirk."

"Immediately, sir. Just step round into our fitting room. It won't take a minute. Not near as long as it takes to win them, eh, sir?" The salesman chortled at his quip.

The addition of the new ribbon and the knowledge that his account at Cox's was better than he had expected made Max decide to enjoy himself. He hurried back to his hotel to rid himself of his battle-stained trench coat. He put on the boxy camel's-hair British warm, and went to the Café Royale for lunch. It was fairly crowded, but after checking his cap and coat, the headwaiter asked him if he minded sharing a table "with another Flying Corps officer."

"Not at all. Be someone to talk to."

To his surprise and delight, he was seated opposite Horace Drage—Major Horace Drage, D.S.O., M.C.

"For God's sake!" Max gasped, almost upsetting his chair.

"Max! I thought you'd be back home showing off your medals . . . like Bishop and the other heroes."

"Look who's talking, and a major at that."

They shook hands over the table.

"I hear you've torched a flock of Huns," Horace said more quietly. "What are you doing in London? Here for a Buckingham Palace investiture?"

Max wagged his head. "No such luck. I've booked thirty-seven Jerries, but I don't seem to have any friends at Wing. I'm on fourteen days' leave, and then I'm to go to Farnborough for conversion to S.E.5s. I don't know what for. I'm never told anything. I just learned of my D.S.O. by casually skimming through the *Times*—the Gazette column. You can see it's brand new."

Horace leaned forward with eagerness. "You're going to Farnborough?"

"That's the order."

"Well, look here. I'm commanding Number 24 Squadron, and we're refitting with S.E.5s right after the New Year. We'll reorganize at Athies. I'll put in for you, that is, if you'd like to join us."

"You just try to keep me out."

They shook hands again.

"Let's show 'em what a couple of Yanks can do when they get together."

"Yes, but you'll not be flying Pups, remember. We'll be on highaltitude shows and will let the Camels take care of anything below 13,000 feet. If we work it properly, we can really punish them. But you will have to take it easy, at first. I can use a damn' good flight commander."

"You got one," Max promised, and ordered a bottle of wine.

Horace looked over Kenyon's strip of decorations. "You have certainly come a long way since we parted at Lyons Corner House in 1914. What the hell was the name of that ammunition ship on which we worked our way over?"

"Damned if I know. Forgot it months ago. I can't remember what the insides of a B.E.2c look like."

"To think," Horace added, as he watched the wine steward pour, "when this is all over, I'll have to go back to school and be expected to remember how to sit still for hours."

Max had no response.

"Which reminds me," Horace continued. "you ought to think about putting some of your experiences down on paper with the idea of writing an instruction book on fighting in the air."

"Me—write a book?"

"Why not? You've flown so many types and have downed various Hun planes. If you tell how you did it, with some detailed illustrations, it would be bloody valuable. There are some important changes coming in the R.F.C. organization, and a book of that sort would give you a chance to get in with the top nobs. No telling where it would lead."

Max agreed that the idea was sound, but knew there wasn't a chance in the world of his completing such a volume, since he lacked the ability to put words together to present a logical explanation suitable for teaching the subject. "I'll think about it over this leave," he said.

"It could be a real boost for you after the war. That is, if you have any hope or desire to stay in."

27

Maxwell Kenyon saw another war Christmas in London, the one everyone hoped would be the last. His conversion training at Farnborough was more a period of rest than a tour of duty. He immediately took to the new S.E.5a with its 200-horsepowered Hispano-Suiza engine that drove a four-bladed propeller, giving a speed of 126 miles per hour at 10,000 feet, and an operational altitude of well over 18,000 feet. By the time Number 24 Squadron was equipped with the new model, he learned practically all there was to know about the machine.

His weekends were still spent in London, although on one occasion he went to Manchester, but could find no relatives or anyone who remembered his parents, so he spent a dreary day or two at the Midland Hotel listening to Lancashire businessmen haggle about prices, stocks, bolts of material, or soccer football. The war was seldom mentioned in Manchester.

He made a half-hearted attempt to get in touch with Dido, after expecting to run into her in the theater district. He called up Solly Weinstein.

"You still trying to get in touch with that crazy jane?"

"I just wondered whether she had gone back to work."

"Now and then she gives it a try. I could have got her in *Peter Pan* with Fay Compton, but I can't hold her interest . . . in anything."

"What about Winnie Winspeare?"

"Winnie? Don't you get any papers out there? She married Sir Walter Edmonds. He's a big pot in the Bank of England, and has a string of racehorses. Leave it to Winnie."

Max was glad to be back in France where he believed he understood what was going on. He found Horace Drage and his

Number 24 Squadron comfortably quartered at Athies, a well-equipped aerodrome a few miles east of Arras, which also meant they were opposite Douai, the area that spawned Von Richthofen's Flying Circus, as some war correspondents were calling it.

To his mild surprise he found Horace Drage to be a most efficient squadron leader. He handled his men as he had handled athletic teams in that New England school, a system that worked under the most trying conditions. He now was a splendid pilot, one who flew as though nature had intended him to, and he selected his men with sagacity—except in the case of Maxwell Kenyon. Within two days, Major Drage realized he had picked a loner—another Albert Ball—a man who did not fit where teamwork was paramount. Like Ball, Kenyon should have been allowed a completely free hand, an aircraft of his own selection, and turned loose, as was Ball in the last few weeks of his career.

Max was given "C" Flight, a brand-new S.E.5a, and another discourse on what was expected of him. This came after he had gone off on his own, instead of attending a lecture in the recording office. His solo foray was not too profitable for he came back with a piece of antiaircraft shell through a lower longeron, and his machine had to be sent back to the aircraft depot for a major repair.

"You listen to me," Horace began when they were alone. "You're not flying Pups now. We'll be operating at well over 15,000 with the S.E.5. What the hell were you doing down where Archie can get you?"

"I was looking for Huns. All we get here is talk, talk, talk. No action."

"You'll get more than you bargained for, any day now. We know the enemy is planning a big push. He's brought dozens of divisions back from the Russian front, and he'll come through as soon as the mud dries."

"We've heard all that since the Cambrai show."

"And I'll tell you something else. Jerry has two-seaters that can tootle around at about 17,000 feet. They'll be doing Art-obs, photography, bombing, and raising hell, hoping we'll waste time with their scouts. But we're not going to, we're going to run high-altitude shows to put these high-flying Jerries out of the play."

"Is that where McCudden has been getting his twos and threes every day?"

"Exactly. He's been concentrating on L.V.G.s, D.F.W.s, and particularly Rumplers and Hannoveraners. The new Albatros D-III can also operate at 18,000 feet. In other words, we're concentrating on two-seaters."

Max looked somewhat dismayed. "They're murder, unless you know how to tackle them."

"I agree, but that's our job, and we're going to do it."

To be fair, Max did more than his share, but he resented being under Horace. He resented taking the responsibility of leading a flight, and running his formation as it should be handled. He obeyed orders, however, and had a good subleader in Bartley Cummings who before joining the Royal Flying Corps had been a divinity student at Cambridge. On the ground he was a quiet, studious member of the squadron, but in the air he was a hooligan and had run up a good score when the squadron was flying D.H.5s.

For a week or ten days, "C" Flight carried out every patrol according to the letter, but no one downed a Hun. Everyone was thrilled with the S.E.5, but most were disturbed with having to handle one Vickers and one Lewis gun. Most of them seemed to forget there was a Lewis mounted on the top plane, and usually forgot to use it in action.

One day, Max wangled permission to fly up to La Grange to visit his old Number 66 Squadron, or so he said. But he made certain there were 500 rounds available for the Vickers and four drums of ammunition for the Lewis. Instead of heading north, he turned due east and circled over the Douai area, but it was noontime and German flying gentlemen were more interested in their luncheon than in continuing their Circus devastation up and down the Western Front. He penetrated about ten miles and by that time was at 16,000 feet. Still, no action until he spotted a Jerry two-seater below and west of him, flying above a canal and heading toward Le Catlet.

Max remembered all that Horace had told him about Jerry two-seaters. He closed his radiator shutters, drew back his throttle, and moving into the sun, went down to the 9,000-foot level and decided it was an L.V.G. The two-seater seemed to be gliding with its prop just ticking over. The gunner was leaning over and staring into the pilot's cockpit, his gun left pointing upward. Max got within one hundred yards and pressed both gun triggers. Pieces of plywood snapped away from the fuselage and the machine went into a tight right-hand turn, jerked twice, and then nosed down in a tight spin and hit the ground near Lebancourt.

Turning back and making for height again, Max saw three V-strut Albatri off to his right. They followed him as he moved toward his own lines, and then tiring of the game, he suddenly whipped around and fired a long burst at the nearest one. The Jerry scout broke up immediately and went down, after tossing away a complete panel, and spinning erratically until it burst into flame. It then went down like a torch.

Max turned north and saw two D.F.W.s being shelled by British Archie. They were at about 8,000 feet. Again, he was unnoticed until he was pouring a burst into one from about 200 yards. This unfortunate torched at once and spun down. The other stayed and fought with the gunner firing timely bursts every time Max put his eye to his Aldis sight. This went on for minutes, or until the S.E.5 was moved into a position ahead and beneath the nose of the Jerry. Then drawing his Lewis gun down on its mounting, Max passed under, firing a long burst which stitched a line of tracer along the belly of the two-seater. Max then dived away, and when he pulled out the D.F.W. was following him down with a long pall of smoke dragging from its engine cowling. He stayed in the vicinity long enough to note that it crashed near Honnecourt.

That put Max in the more-than-forty class of Hun hunters.

The spring of 1918 erupted with the March push that upset Allied plans. The Jerries thundered through between the churned fields of Passchendaele and La Basse, crushing everything before them. The front-line infantry was overwhelmed, the reserve area overrun, and there was little chance to withdraw the big guns. Nothing stopped the enemy until he had outrun his lines of supply. Only the Royal Flying Corps put up any semblance of opposition. In that carnival of carnage, anything that could get off the ground staggered into the fight, and laid the basic plans for tactical aviation. Anything with wings, fuel, and manpower to guide it poured Cooper bombs or streams of Kynochs ammunition into the field-gray columns that marched toward Amiens. Reconnaissance aircraft could offer only vague details of the battle zone. Two-seaters, temporarily acting as bombers, gave everything they had to block the roads, sever the railroad lines, and level any natural cover. Other two-seaters battled German countour-fighters. D.H.4s unloaded anything that would explode and scatter shrapnel. Camels, Pups, Bristol Fighters that had operated previously between 10,000 and 14,000 feet were ordered down to contour level to drop Coopers and whiplash roads and pockets of German troops. This pattern of war went on for two weeks, a campaign that left attackers and defenders completely exhausted.

Only the S.E.5 squadrons seemingly enjoyed themselves. They were given a free hand between 12,000 feet and their ceiling to attack and destroy anything flaunting an enemy insignia. A hundred new aces were admitted to that gallant company during those fourteen days. Dozens more moved into the twenty-plus class, and others were received into the list of the greats, the exclusive class that was to illuminate the undying history of the Royal Flying Corps.

Number 24 played a memorable role in all this. Major Drage led his hawks valiantly and was thankful for the backing of his pilots and ground staff. Hour after hour, tight formations took off and zoomed into the upper levels of the fray. Miles above the hand-to-hand conflict they harried and drove off high-altitude aircraft sent out to photograph or bomb the British back area, while affording support for their own D.H.9a bombers that were concentrating on German munitions cities. They played their role well while suffering grievous losses—losses that were valorous in the glare of the bright flame of aerial victories.

Max banked, turned, and darted through this maelstrom, a cold, determined duelist who felt no fear nor was constrained in any way by timorous nerves. It had been this way for weeks, and he had lost accurate count of his score in his frenzied desire to keep flying, fighting, and returning to report his achievements. Only then, with both feet on the ground, did the effect of his competition make itself felt. Out of his cockpit his muscles became limp and refused to support his frame. He was unable to hold a pencil and had to make his report verbally, steadying himself against the recording officer's counter. What his fingers could not inscribe or relate, his calm mind offered word for word, and he was never betrayed by an inaccuracy. He knew what time each engagement was started and when his enemy had crashed. He knew to the mile where it had fallen, and how many bursts it had taken to destroy him. He could give complete details of every type he had engaged, offer minutiae as to insignia, colors, and at times the actual numbers stenciled on the aircraft. What balloon companies were still in action confirmed every patrol statement Captain Kenyon made, and later on marveled at the completeness of his reports.

There was no time for the formality of promotion, or the ceremonies of decorations. Short rests and hot meals were more important, and there was no time to read and consider Daily Orders. In fact, few were even typed during the push, for there were days when it seemed possible the squadron would have to be moved back toward Doullens.

The gods of war, leaning over their checkered plan, moved their pieces and set the board for Maxwell Kenyon's final war patrol. There had been a lull in the action, first noted in March behind Albert, a lull that puzzled the chiefs of the Imperial General Staff. A special reconnaissance patrol was sent out to determine what the enemy was up to. No particularly reliable information was forthcoming, so new orders went out demanding that the Royal Flying Corps continue its pressure at all levels. An all-out effort was expected of all squadrons. There were plenty of machines. New ones were being brought in daily from the Number 1 Aircraft Depot. War-damaged planes were being flown back by ferry pilots for further use in the Home Establishment training schools.

Early in April, after leading his flight on still another patrol deep into enemy territory, Max racked up another victory. They trapped three Hannoveraners over the Sensee Canal, and hacked two of them to fluttering wreckage, after which they returned mildly jubilant to a rewarding lunch. Max was not hungry, but managed to down a pot of beer and thoughtfully munch a sandwich.

Horace drifted across the mess and sat beside him. "So you bagged another this morning," he said looking kindly into Max's face. "I think it's about time you took it easy."

For no particular reason Max took a new tack. "The Tommies up in the trenches, if we have any left, can't take it easy. Why should we?"

Horace gripped his lower arm affectionately. "That's not the point at all. No one can replace them at this particular time. You can be relieved for a few days, or a month. We have plenty of pilots. I feel you need it, Max."

"Here we go again," Max said with a smirk. "I've run up a few more Huns, so you're going to pull me out and send me back to . . . Farnborough, Martlesham Heath, or some such funk hole."

"A few more Huns? Your score is well over fifty!"

"Who cares? Who takes any notice of it?"

"You ought to take a rest. All the top scorers accept it."

"Well, I'm not. I'm staying here, damn your eyes, until they give me what I'm entitled to. I'm going to get a squadron, or know the reason why."

"What the hell do you want a squadron for? I'd give anything to be just a flight leader and have some part of the day to myself. I'm responsible for every man on this field, and I don't like it."

"So you say, but you're doing damned well at it. That's what I want, the rank and the prestige—I think they call it. I want to wind up my war with field rank. I'm not going back home to the States. I'm staying here—in this new Royal Air Force, everyone's talking about."

Horace stared at Max in bewilderment. "You must be crazy. This is just a war, not a way of life. You're still an American. If you must become professional, why not in the service of your own country?"

"That's all very well for you. You have a home and a respected family to go back to. There's a complete education waiting for you. What do I have, other than what I have here? I'd be crazy to give all this up, and nearly four years of active service. I can be out with a pension in eighteen years. By that time I'll still be only forty. What's forty, these days?"

"How do you know there'll be money left in England for soldiers' pensions? The country is bankrupt now, or so my father writes and tells me. They'll be paying disabled men for the next fifty years. Use your loaf, Max."

"All I want is a major's crown, and some experience running my own squadron. After that, no matter how long the war lasts, it'll be honey and jam."

Horace had trouble deleting a smile. "I thought you were out for a Victoria Cross."

"I've all I need with the D.S.O. Any chump with animal instinct can win the V.C. I have all the medals I need for my future. If you're a pal of mine, put me in for a squadron, and a majority, and leave the rest to me." Max tried to make the statement sound as though he meant it.

"I wouldn't play a trick like that on you, Max. You're not the type. You have no administrative ability, and you don't mix well, even with members of your own flight. No matter how many Huns you down, you're not the man to inspire others."

Max had no answer, so he snapped, "You still owe me ten bucks, remember?"

"I'll pay you back on the way home, in good old Royal American greenbacks." Horace wished he could understand Max Kenyon.

An hour later Max was in the air again on another of his lone patrols where he felt at home in an element that had taken him over and given him his most pleasurable moments. His S.E.5a had been serviced from rudder to prop, for his corporal fitter knew that Captain Kenyon would be off again as soon as he had downed his lunch. The armorer had checked the feed belt of the Vickers and made sure all the Lewis gun drums were in their slots.

With no particular salient in mind, he climbed to 6000 feet and followed the line he believed the British balloon companies had taken since the beginning of the push. He was just south of Ypres when he noticed another lone S.E.5 heading due east. In an unusual spirit of fellowship, Max banked hard, turned and placed himself just behind the tail assembly of the scout. The pilot looked back, but gave no indication of recognition, or pleasure in his company, but continued in an easterly direction until they were approaching Tourcoing. Max was puzzled by the strange attitude of the pilot, and after studying the aircraft for several minutes, he noted certain familiar features. In the first place, it carried a block letter "M" and a black-and-white checkerboard design on the fabric wheel covers. Less than a week before, as leader of "C" Flight, Max had flown this same S.E.5a on a routine patrol. Over Henin-Lietard it had received a tight burst of bullets at the root of the lower wing, and because of the damage to both the main spar and a longeron, it had been temporarily repaired and flown to Number 1 Aircraft Depot for a more thorough renovation.

Max wondered why it had been put back in service and was being flown on a lone patrol. His imagination conjured up all sorts of schemes with himself as the principal figure. From his position he could see where the wing root had received a hurried fabric patch repair, so obviously the damaged wing had not been replaced. But why was it being flown across the Jerry lines? He moved in closer and made authoritative gestures and poked a finger toward the west. The pilot shook his head. Max reached down for his Very pistol, inserted a red cartridge and pulled the trigger. The sparkling scarlet arc spluttered its warning, but the indication of danger aroused no response. Didn't the fact that Max's mount carried the same squadron letter, and wheel covers decorated with black-and-white squares—an obtuse symbol reluctantly allowed by Horace—mean anything to the fool?

Max eased in closer, hoping to recognize the pilot, but that worthy kept his goggles down, and hunched low in his cockpit. Max flipped his up, and grinned. But the other pilot did not respond in kind. Instead, he turned away and looked down over the opposite side of his cockpit.

"If he's a ferry pilot flying my old bus out of Saint-Omer, he's certainly off course for Folkestone. I ought to get him turned around. Perhaps his compass is off."

Still the former Number 24 Squadron scout headed due east.

"The damn fool! What's he going to do if a pack of Jerries tries to head him off? He probably doesn't have any ammo for the guns. There's no drum on the Lewis. Of all the damn-fool situations."

The conclusion was highly optimistic. Before Max could think up another ruse or measure to get the pilot back on a course for the Straits of Dover, streams of tracer bullets cut across his vision from several angles. Instinctively kicking his rudder over, and hoicking for height, he pulled into a sharp turn, half-rolled, and took in the situation. At least ten or a dozen scouts were buzzing all around him. There were several gaudy Fokker triplanes, and as many more Albatros D-IIIs. All of them were wildly decorated in typical Jerry Circus colors, bands of whites and yellows, tail assemblies in direct contrast with the wing and fuselage décor. There was no garish scarlet body the infamous Baron Manfred von Richthofen was supposed to prefer.

Max glanced at his clock and checked the time. It was exactly 1:36 P.M., and he knew he was halfway between Armentières and Tourcoing. He picked out one D-III which seemed to be floundering through the attack with no particular purpose in view. He gave it a good burst and saw the pilot throw up one arm and then

crumple up under his cowling. The Albatros nosed down sharply.
That was enough. He allowed a gaudy triplane to zoom over him,
and then ruddered to stay in the same relative position. He drew
down his Lewis gun, selected the right trigger, and poured two
short bursts into its belly. The Fokker went into a frantic zoom,
stalled and fell into a tight spin. Two twirls and it ripped its
upper plane away and the gaudy panel flipped and flopped through
the streaks of tracer smoke. With that, Max moved to look for
the other S.E.5, but his old scout was still carrying on its jaunt
into Hunland.

"The clod must be crazy. Doesn't he recognize Jerry scouts when
he sees them shooting? Does he think this an afternoon game?"
A sharp rattle along his own fuselage put him back on guard. He
zoomed again, but three triplanes stayed with him. He banked
hard, pulled the stick back against his belt and soon turned inside
the threesome and began firing short bursts as Fokkers came into
his sight. One grouping took out a great chunk of wing and the
Dr.1 went into a sharp sideslip. Max throttled for more height and
took another burst somewhere below. He could feel the jackham-
mer vibrations around his undercarriage, and he knew he would
have to make a thistledown landing if he got back from this
tango. "That damn' fool ferry pilot," he growled.

He took another quick glance toward Tourcoing and realized
the other S.E.5 was still heading east, but now seemed much lower.
Why the Jerries had not spotted him was a mystery, unless they
planned to get him on his return. Max went into one of his whirling
dervish routines. The sky was cluttered with Fokkers and Albatri,
so he made the most of the fact that he had a dozen targets to fire
at, whereas the enemy had but one, and their efforts to draw a bead
on him without hitting a squadron mate, made their task the more
difficult.

Banishing the fate of the other British scout from his concern,
Max concentrated on the task at hand. He was his old fighting self
once more, cool, unhurried, and flying with expert precision, getting the most from his superior mount. He settled back to perform
a workmanlike job and spent the next few minutes taking out struts,
severing tail assemblies, or triggering short burts into engine
cowlings. There were odd moments when he received lashings
himself, and he could see short pennons of fabric flicking from
ragged perforations in one lower wing panel. Still, he felt no

concern, knowing that if the situation worsened he could always nose down, apply full throttle, and no Jerry scout in this pack could stay with him. The line was only a few miles away, and in his combative mood, he was actually enjoying himself.

He cut clear while he changed the drum on his Lewis, and before he rammed it back up the Foster-Cooper rail, he took a long deflection shot at an Albatros that had decided to get altitude should this Britisher climb for sanctuary. Kenyon's gamble-burst caught the D-III cold, and it plunged through the smoke, stench of oil, tracer fire, and swirling scouts until it finally tossed away a wing and spun out of sight.

By this time Kenyon saw the hunting was thinning out. The opposition had lost interest, as one by one the Jerries found reasons to slip away and head back in the direction of Douai. He picked out a green-and-gold triplane, and in two circuits completely outmaneuvered it, cut away an aileron, and watched it slither off, clearly out of control. He then checked what he could see of his own damage and turned for the British line. He scribbled a few details of the action, jotted down the time brackets, and then saw he was skimming over his own balloon lines. Had he looked down he would have seen the men of Number 7 Balloon Company waving and firing salvos of Very lights. But Captain Kenyon was pondering on the behavior of the S.E.5, the one with his old squadron block letter "M" and his checkerboard-decorated wheels. He saw none of the congratulatory display around the winch.

His undercarriage held, although the scout swerved dangerously when he got down at Athies. A tire had been hit and although Max held her off as long as he dared, she dropped a wingtip, tossed the tire away and he ground-looped, but with plenty of room to spare. He sat there and waited until a tender came out with a flight sergeant and a ground crew. They first towed him carefully up to the cab rank while two mechanics held the wingtip clear.

"Cool" was the general comment. "Wot's 'e bin up to this time?"

Max offered no explanation, but hurried to the recording office, unbuckling his helmet and unbelting his coat on the way. Horace Drage sat in the doorway. He had an expression of anger, mixed with surprise and some raised-eyebrow pleasure. "What the hell have you been up to?"

"Get Number 1 Aircraft Depot on the wire, right away!"

"We have Number 7 Balloon Company telling us that one of our scouts shot down at least seven Jerry Circus planes. It has to be you. You were the only one out. Are you all right?"

"Of course. Get Saint-Omer on the wire."

Horace looked puzzled. "What's that all about?"

"We sent my old 'M' bus back there about a week ago, didn't we? After I had a main spar and a longeron shot up."

Horace gnawed on a spear of cuticle. "That's right. What about it?"

"Some ass, some dullard ferry pilot, was flying it completely off course, opposite Tourcoing—that is, if he was heading for Folke- stone. I spotted him and tried to head him off, and get him on the right course. He was flying due east!"

Horace gave his recording officer the nod. "Get Saint-Omer— Number 1 Depot."

Max interrupted. "Find out who was flying our old 'M' bus, and where he was supposed to be taking it. He's probably down in Hunland by now, and bloody lucky if he's alive. I was trying to get him turned around when suddenly we were cluttered up with Albatri and Fokker Tripes. I started to take care of them, hoping he'd have sense enough to head back—at least over our line—but the damn' fool kept straight on toward Tourcoing."

"Leaving you to shoot down more than half a dozen Jerries. What the hell were you using—a howitzer?" Major Drage put on a gamin grin.

"They weren't very bright, any of them. They acted like a bunch of replacements getting some front-line instruction, but with no mother to guide them." For the first time Max managed a faint smile.

"If you downed seven, that's a record. We've had some Canadian shooting down six in one day, but you're being credited with seven —on one patrol! Let's get your report written out. Wing will want it for that reason, and to put in *Comic Cuts*. But there's more to it than that. I'll tell you about it later."

"I suppose they're going to stop me from flying, or some such wonky idea," Max grumbled, and went to the rack for a report form.

The recording officer held up one finger. "I have Number 1

Depot. It *was* your old bus being flown back to the Royal Aircraft Factory. They couldn't handle the full repair right now, so they sent it home."

Kenyon went to the recording officer's desk. "Ask who was flying it."

The request was made, and the recording officer jotted down the information. "Do you have the ferry pilot's name—his first name and rank?"

He looked up at Max. "They say his name is Wallington, Lieutenant Ralph Wallington."

Kenyon turned to Horace. "Do you know Wallington? Ralph Wallington?"

Horace stared down at the splintered floor. "I suppose everyone has heard of Windy Wallington. There was a time when he was the featured joke in all R.F.C. messes. Actually, I don't remember meeting him."

"He was at London Colney with me. A damned good pilot, but he funked out every time he was posted to a service squadron. A Canadian, but a yellow-streaked clod. He ought to have been shoved into the trenches."

The recording officer broke in, "They're saying, this Mr. Wallington was doing his last ferry job, and was going to join a new S.E.5 squadron tomorrow."

Max and Horace exchanged knowing glances. "He won't!" Max said with contempt. "He probably skunked out and handed my old bus over to Jerry. That's why he was flying east instead of west."

Horace took a conciliatory attitude. "None of that, now. You can't prove it, and it doesn't do to make such statements. There's a libel law in England, and the damn' thing works."

"Goddammit! You know that's exactly what Wallington would do."

"Perhaps, but none of us can prove it. Just mention seeing him in your patrol report, but make no comment or give any opinion. These papers will be available for years to come, and you don't want to become involved in any court-martial, if it ever comes up."

Max scowled at the ceiling. "I'm amazed he never thought of it before."

"If he did, as you infer, it probably took a lot of courage to fly into the Jerry lines with no guns or ammunition."

"Courage?" Kenyon raged. "I had to hold off that pack of Huns

· 308 ·

while he made his getaway . . . and the bastard still owes me ten pounds."

"Well, simmer down. Right now, you're more important than a dozen Wallingtons. We have it from Wing that you are not to fly —even an engine test—until they give permission. Now play it sensible. No telling what they have in mind."

Max sucked the end of his pencil and turned back to his patrol report.

For two full days, Max sat around, bemoaning his fate. He stayed away from the hangars, although Horace said he ought to go out and have a last look at his bus. "How you brought it back, no one knows. The Aircraft Depot people have a photographer here, and he says he's never seen anything like it. A couple hundred bullets, but none anywhere near a vital point."

"So what is there to look at?"

"You should be glad you were so lucky. Not that I want to start you off on that theme again."

"I'll consider myself lucky when I get a squadron. Then I'll be able to make my own decisions for a change."

The corporal clerk came into the anteroom and advised Horace he was wanted on the telephone. He gave the clerk an inquiring look, and received, "Yes, sir. It's come through." He saluted and strode off.

"You'd better come along, Max. This may have something to do with you."

Chiefly for something to do and to learn more of the routine expected of a squadron leader, he followed the major across to the orderly room. The corporal stood holding the telephone, and grinned as he turned it over to his CO.

"Drage here, sir. Good afternoon."

There was muffled conversation, and Max sensed that everyone in the office was sitting as if halted halfway through a routine chore, but staring at him with expectant expressions.

"That's excellent news, sir. Yes, I have him right here. Just a moment, sir."

Drage handed the instrument to Kenyon. "Colonel Loraine of Wing wishes to speak to you."

Max took the instrument gingerly and stared down at it. "What's all this?" he inquired.

Drage pointed to the receiver. "He wants to talk to you. That's all."

"Yes, sir. Captain Kenyon here."

A booming voice responded. "Well, well. I want to be the first to congratulate you, Kenyon. We have just received word that the King has awarded you the V.C., the Victoria Cross, and I must say it's an honor well earned."

Max stood cotton-mouthed, but finally said, "I'm very pleased, sir, and most surprised."

"No need to be. You've had it coming, you know. Done a top-drawer job, Kenyon. We're all proud of you."

"Thank you, sir, but could you explain what . . . just what it was I did to get the V.C.?" He saw Horace cover his mouth with both hands.

Colonel Loraine had to think that over. "Well, of course the citation seldom goes much beyond mention of exceptional bravery, valor under fire, or in the face of the enemy. Mention is seldom made of any specific action, but in your case there will probably be a reference to your valorous show the other day when you single-handedly downed seven Huns during one patrol. I really don't know . . ."

"But I presume you put me in for the decoration. What did you stress . . . ?"

But Colonel Loraine had rung off. He had more important matters to attend to.

Max stood holding the silent instrument in his hand until Horace took it from him and hung it in its cradle. He then grabbed Max's hand and shook it warmly. "Bloody good! It couldn't have gone to a better guy. Congratulations!"

"But . . . I wanted to know what I did . . ."

"You don't ask questions like that. There'll be something definite in the citation which will be read out when you go to Buckingham Palace for the award." Major Drage gasped, and added, "My God! The King will have to give you five medals at one time. There's another record. Bishop got only three, and McCudden, if he ever gets the V.C. will have only the D.S.O., the M.C., and the M.M. to receive with it."

"But what can I say if anyone asks what I did to receive it?"

"You'll think of something," Horace said and led him back to the anteroom. "We'll have a real binge tonight, but first I want to tell you that you'll fly no more with Number 24. You're going back to London for Home Establishment."

"Why not a squadron?"

"Will you listen to me? You'll have some leave . . . as much as you want. You can even go home to the States for ninety days, if you want."

"That's out. I'm never going back there."

"Be reasonable, Max. You owe it to your parents and your home country, if only to show what some Americans have already done in this war."

"You wouldn't understand, Horace," Max said, as he tried to remember the details of the South 10th Street tenement.

"Well, take two weeks' leave and then report to whatever is headquarters now, and they'll have something for you. There's talk of organizing a Sopwith Snipe squadron. The Snipe is far superior to the Camel, and you may get one to tool about."

Max brightened. "Golly, I could be out here with my own squadron by June or so, if the Snipe works out."

Horace shook his head. "If you're smart, you'll take it easy. Remember you came out here for Neuve-Chapelle back in 1915. After looking over that S.E.5 out in the hangar, I think you'll see you've about used up your dollop of luck."

Number 24 Squadron's binge to wet Kenyon's V.C. was something of an anticlimax, for the award had not generated any particular enthusiasm in any quarter of the squadron. After all, it had been expected for a month or so, since Max's luck had continued at an unprecedented pace, and it was only a matter of time before someone at Wing, in an undisturbed moment, would make up his mind to try his hand at a recommendation. In this case, although Kenyon was never to know it, his award came about chiefly because Major Ivor MacPartland had persisted in nudging Colonel Loraine at every opportunity. "We'd better give him something before he shoots himself down," he had concluded, and with that remark the rusty cogs at Wing began to grind.

The trip to London was uneventful, but, on arrival at Mason's Yard, Max found he was the center of the new Royal Air Force's planning to put on a publicity campaign, and over the next two weeks, he was dragged from one Home Establishment center to another, either being put on show, or asked to explain "how he did it." To the amazement of Staff, Max responded to their demands and, after one or two tries before Cadet groups, he produced a line of "patter" that had everyone sitting on the fronts of their seats. At the Air Fighting Schools at Turnberry, Marske, Frieston, Sedgeford, and East Fortuner he held forth on the importance of the deflection shot, the flexible Lewis gun, and the proper manner to attack two-seaters. On one occasion, he agreed to write a training treatise and draw his own illustrations, but the good intention was soon forgotten.

He went back to London and found most of the aeronautical and military journals were featuring articles about him, his score, and his theories, all illustrated with interesting photographs. He was shown climbing into his flying kit, talking to his flight mates, checking his own guns, playing soccer with the mechanics, and in some scholarly poses reading Henry James. The Fleet Street hacks were taking over the Royal Air Force's office of public relations. His nights were spent going from club to club, from hotel lounge to night-club dance floors. He drank very little and had not as yet adopted tobacco, but made the most of the other vices expected of war heroes. He also met many Americans, most of whom were on certain inter-Allied staff jobs, but all complete strangers to him. Their stiff-collared jackets which they wore with starched white-linen collars—so impractical, even in London—amused him. He was also interested in how differently they spoke, and he wondered if he had arrived in England nearly four years before with such a strange assortment of phrases, slang, and the various types of speech that were now an indistinct memory. They all seemed to speak much louder than necessary. Several of them asked him why he had not transferred to "his own country's service," and how he came to be over here in the first place. Few could comprehend why anyone would volunteer to fight for a "foreign" power as far back as 1914, which in 1918 seemed a long decade ago. No explanations satisfied their queries.

"But I like it with the British," he informed one who said he was a major, although he had had no previous military service. "In fact, I'm hoping to stay here and get a permanent commission in the new Royal Air Force. It offers a wonderful future, and I have already put in nearly four years."

The well-dressed, polished, and manicured major might just as well have been listening to a Pakistani warrior speaking in urdu.

Eventually, Maxwell Kenyon was called to the Hotel Cecil and first ordered to purchase a new RAF uniform. "You've been gazetted a squadron leader, the same rank as major in the Royal Flying Corps. Don't worry about insignia and rank badges. The people at Burberry's will take care of everything."

"This, of course, comes out of my own pocket?"

"Naturally."

"Does this mean I am to get a squadron?"

"In due course. Meanwhile you report to Martlesham Heath where a number of Snipes are being prepared for active service. You will be in charge and are expected to organize a full squadron of flying personnel and the ground force. You'll find your orders in this envelope. That'll be all."

The new uniform took much of the pleasure out of the promotion, for it in no way was as smart as the R.F.C. tunic or the G.S. jacket he had become accustomed to. The color, still Army khaki, seemed most incongruous. Eventually, the new Colonel Blimps decided to ape the French, and adopted the so-called azure blue with which the RAF became recognized.

The work at the Martlesham test station was arduous, wearying, and beyond Kenyon's limited ability, but he persisted and finally built up a squadron that he felt was ready for active service. The new Snipe was as easy to fly as the old Pup, and the Bentley engine gave it a top speed of 121 miles per hour at 10,000 feet. Its maneuverability was unbelievable, considering its weight of 2,020 pounds fully loaded.

Weeks later when he had his war birds at top form, the whole squadron of Snipes was turned over to an all-Canadian organization and became Number 1 Squadron of a so-called Canadian Air Force, and reorganized at Upper Heyford. To mollify Squadron Leader Kenyon, he was ordered back to London for a special investiture at Buckingham Palace. At the Hotel Cecil he was put through an intensive period of instruction in protocol. "You will appear properly dressed, but will wear no decorations of any kind. Remove your ribbons, leaving the space below your wings entirely clear. This will make it easy for His Majesty to pin on the three . . . let's see, he will bestow five medals at once. Good heavens! How will he manage it?"

"I'll stand perfectly still," Max said, simply for something to say.

"Don't be facetious. You will appear at the left-hand gate of Buckingham Palace, promptly at 11:30 A.M. You will wear gloves, that is, one on your left hand, and carry the other. You will be instructed how to march the ten yards across the middle of the room, turn to your left, and bow. You do *not* salute, since you will not be wearing your cap."

"I know better than that," Max protested.

"You'll be surprised what you'll forget in the presence of the King. An aide will be holding your medals on a purple cushion and the citations will be read out by the King's equerry. You will not speak unless His Majesty asks you a direct question. If he congratulates you in any manner, simply nod, or say, 'Yes, sir.' The King will close by shaking hands with you, after which you will do a smart about-face and march out over the same area by which you entered. Do you have all that clear?"

"I believe so."

"Well, see to it you get to bed early. No pre-decoration roistering tonight, remember. This will be the most important assignment you will ever take on. That's all, Kenyon. Good luck!"

Squadron Leader Kenyon took his instructions seriously. After dinner at the Savoy where he was staying for this auspicious event, he carefully removed the double row of ribbons from his new jacket, trimmed away the loose threads, brushed the bare material clean and went to bed. The next morning he polished his boots and belt buckle, dressed carefully and knotted his tie. He examined himself in the mirror and was shocked to note how naked, how insignificant, he appeared without his familiar ribbons. He glanced down at his left sleeve to make certain his two wound stripes still gleamed there.

Downstairs he was too keyed up to enjoy his breakfast, and sat mentally rehearsing his instructions, and couldn't remember which glove he was supposed to wear and which to carry. He went into the lavatory, washed his hands, and looked himself over once more—and forgot his swagger stick which he had bought for the momentous occasion.

Still feeling improperly dressed and militarily impotent without his decorations, he turned left out of the Savoy entrance and walked toward Trafalgar Square. It was a crisp, bright day for autumn in London, and instead of hailing a taxi, he walked to Buckingham Palace by way of the Mall. As he strode along he wondered why on this day of all days everyone seemed so cheerful as if anticipating an unexpected holiday. Then, to his amazement, for the first time since he had joined up, he heard the peal of a deep-throated bell. It was certainly more massive and imperious than Big Ben. Two young girls who were approaching him, let out a two-toned squeal, waved, and started to run toward Trafalgar Square. The great bell bellowed again and then, as if aroused for some occasion, Big Ben began its eleven o'clock chime. With that, other church bells took up the orchestration and steam whistles began to toot. More people appeared from nowhere and started linking arms. Some children ran across the Mall waving Union Jacks. Two yelping dogs followed them.

Max strode on, wondering what the clangor was about. Then, as if by magic, the Mall, which had seemed deserted when he began his walk, suddenly filled with motley groups of people—mostly civilians—and all were in a holiday mood. He wished he was wearing his ribbons. Someone blew on an old battered bugle, and streams of people ran in aimless routes across the grass in St. James's Park. More church bells were added to the noise. Big Ben finished his count, and a stirring peal of bells took up the gaiety.

A mounted policeman moved along at a brisk walk, the brasswork of his saddlery gleamed in the watery sunlight. Behind him a troop of Life Guards, still in khaki, rode to attention, their equipment jingling to the time of the military trot. The policeman smiled and saluted Max. With that Squadron Leader Kenyon darted to the edge of the turf, and put out his hand. "What's all the merriment about, Constable?"

The mounted man reined up. "God's truth! Haven't you heard?" Kenyon wagged his head.

"*The war's over!* Jerry has packed up at last. He signed the Armistice at eleven o'clock. You're lucky, you know. You'll never have to go out there, young feller."

Max stood transfixed as the mounted policeman's horse pranced away. The shock was not that the war was over, but that the bobby believed he was practically a recruit. No ribbons, or decorations of any sort. He had even missed the two gold wound stripes on his sleeve.

The war was over!

The crowds expanded by the minute, their shouts and laughter rattled across the historic Mall. Some waved to him, others, arm-in-arm bundled him out of their way as they sang, *Jolly Good Luck to the Girl Who Loves a Soldier.* The war-long cry, "Are we down-hearted? . . . Naoo!" echoed through the trees, and packs of released schoolchildren raced in all directions screaming, "The war is over! The war is over!"

Max pressed through the tangle of riotous people as he threaded his way toward the Palace. His mind was awhirl with the implications of the unexpected situation. He continued to glance down at the bare spread of material below his wings. There was an instant when he wished he was back in the gay kilt of the London Scottish.

Ahead, there were thunderous roars that he realized were pealing from the crowds in front of Buckingham Palace. He sidestepped and jostled his way through groups of soldiers, most of whom had thrown away their caps or had given them to passing girls. Every other one seemed to have an uncorked bottle gripped by the neck. Someone shoved a whisky bottle at Max, but he laughed and said, "Sorry, I'm due at the Palace for today's investiture. Must arrive sober."

"Fat bleedin' charnse, mate," a giant Grenadier said in a guard-house voice. "You'll never get within one 'undred yards of the gate. All that's bin canceled for today . . . an' for the rest of all time, we hope."

"Have a drink, chum." An artilleryman with one hand bound up in a gory bandage offered his bottle. "It'll never be this cheap agayne. Don't worry, you'll get your bit of tin. They'll send it to you in a little cardboard box. That's 'ow I expect to get mine."

Kenyon stared at the bandaged hand. "You were for today's investiture?"

"Not 'arf, but they can *send* me my Victoria Cross, an' the postman can pin it on."

Everybody roared.

Max took the bottle and downed a stiff slug. He got his breath, rubbed his hand across his mouth. "Right you are, Gunner!" he gasped, and would have joined them in the festivities, but remembered he was wearing none of his ribbons. His last chance for glory had been denied him. He decided to totter back to the Savoy.

That was the last he remembered of Armistice Day.

Squadron Leader Kenyon's war had come to its end. There would be praise for all from Field Marshal Sir Douglas Haig down to the lowliest conscript still taking rifle drill on some unnamed parade ground, but Maxwell Kenyon would seldom be remembered again—except for the fact that he had once played soccer with the mechanics of his squadron. The Colonel Blimps would remember that when he persistently applied for a permanent commission.

If he only knew that;

War after all's but a flash in the pan.
It's the battles of peace that makes the man.
                            Henry de Halselle.

Epilogue

Squadron Leader Kenyon continued up the steps of the companionway of the *Trigantic's* bridge. Each step was a gesture, a painful effort to play the game as he had observed it in others over fifty months of warfare. At the top he turned and looked down at the girl who still stood at the rail. He studied her puzzled expression, and felt clean and warm inside. He knew she had no hint of what he intended, or that he was capable of such a thought or generosity. He pointed authoritatively and said, "You stay there. Don't move until I call for you. Under no circumstances . . ." He straightened up and looked across the wing of the bridge and tried to determine how close they were to the entrance to the Straits of Belle Isle. Peering through the distant mists he decided that the slate-colored smudge a few points off the bow was Belle Isle itself which guarded the entrance to the strait. It had to be, please God, it had to be. He hurried toward a junior officer who stood at the starboard wing, adjusting the focus of his binoculars.

"Tell me, is that Belle Isle out there?" Max inquired, anxiety in his eyes and hands.

"You're not allowed up here, you know."

"Yes, I know all that, but it is important. Most important. Is that Belle Isle out there?"

The lookout put the glasses to his eyes, studied the indistinct mass for half a minute and then nodded. "Correct. That's Belle Isle. Beyond it is Henley Harbor."

"How long will it take us to pass it, and be in the strait?"

The lookout lowered his glasses. "Well, we have to reduce speed now. It might be almost an hour before we're in the strait proper. Now I must ask you to leave the bridge, sir."

"Right away. What's your captain's name. I mean the commander of this vessel."

The lookout glanced at Kenyon's blood-red ribbon and its bronze miniature. "I'm very sorry, but you can't stay up here. Captain Twillingate is very strict about passengers coming on the bridge."

"He's Captain Twillingate? I've got to see him, immediately. Very important. See that young woman down there standing at the rail. She's in trouble, and only the captain can help her out. Where is he?"

The young officer was taking in more than he could digest. "Wouldn't the doctor, or the sergeant-at-arms be more suitable?"

"It's nothing like that. She's not ill." Kenyon hoped, and looked out toward Belle Isle again.

"Well, look, you go in this side door here, cross the control bridge and the navigating officer will show you to the Skipper's cabin. But don't let on I let you through. Twillingate will have my ticket."

"Thanks. Keep your eye on that girl, please."

Kenyon slid the control-bridge door open and stepped over the coaming. He closed the door carefully and looked around the maze of polished brass, waxed mahogany and gleaming glass. He spoke to the first man who looked at him. He was standing behind a steering wheel mounted aft of the illuminated binnacle.

"Where's the navigation officer?" Max half-whispered.

The man at the wheel nodded toward an officer who was conning the ship through a fixed telescope.

"Where can I find Captain Twillingate, please?"

The man in blue penciled in a neat cross on a table chart, and cocked his head over his right shoulder. "Through that door and first on your left. He was there a minute ago."

Kenyon muttered a silent prayer, flipped a heavy curtain aside and found himself in a dim, narrow corridor. There were three doors on each side, but he was lucky. He knocked on the first and was answered by a deep growl. "Come in."

He thrust open the door with anxiety. The heavy-shouldered seaman was sitting at a narrow table with the residue of a late breakfast on a tray at one elbow. Before him lay a sheaf of type-written papers and a chunky briar pipe.

"Captain Twillingate, sir?"

The monster glared at him and lowered his head closer to his fists. He removed his eyeglasses and took a sidelong glance.

"Oh, it's you, eh? What the hell do you want and who let you up here? These are my private quarters." The bulldog skipper bellowed and started to get to his feet.

"Yes, sir. I know all that, but I have a request of great importance. A very serious matter."

"Get the bloody hell out of here. Go to the purser if you've lost anything. What do you think my sea cabin is for?"

"Captain Twillingate, sir. Will you please listen for sixty seconds? That's all I ask. It has nothing to do with that photography or camera affair. Nothing like that."

"Well, speak up. What the hell do you want? I must be on the bridge in a few minutes."

"Yes, sir. I know. I appreciate your problems of command, but we are still on what legally are the high seas, as I understand it. Am I right?"

Twillingate looked up at the clock on his wall. "For the next forty or fifty minutes, yes." He got to his feet and went to the porthole on the right side of his cabin and peered out.

"That's Belle Isle out there, isn't it, sir?"

"And when we pass it I have to be on the bridge and will be there most of the way in to Montreal. Now get on with your blather."

"That's all I want to know, sir. Now, as the ship's master there is one thing you can do on the high seas, but only on the high seas."

"I can do anything while I am master of this vessel. Don't forget that."

"According to maritime law the master of any ship on the high seas can perform a marriage ceremony. Right?"

Twillingate puffed like a grampus. "You want to marry someone? Someone aboard here? Not that chit with the camera?"

"No, sir. We haven't much time, but there's a young woman on board—another young woman—I want to marry before we get to Montreal."

"Why the hell can't you wait and have a regular ceremony ashore at a church? What's all the bloody rush?"

"Unless she is married, she won't be let off at Montreal. She's aboard with false documents. She got a man named Wallington to bring her aboard as his wife. They're listed as Mr. and Mrs. Wallington."

"And you want to marry a woman like that? After she's been on board sharing his cabin? What the hell is the matter with you?"

"She needs help, sir. When we get into port Canadian Immigration men will pick her up because she has no proof of marriage, and God only knows what will become of her. She'll probably be sent back—deported, if that's the word—but I . . . I need her. I was the first to dirty her name. You know how it has been with young girls in London . . . in all big cities during the war."

"What about the man she's with now?

"Wallington? He's a nobody, a crummy coward who never once earned his rations. He welched out of everything, once he got his commission and learned to fly. You, sir, you would have had him keelhauled within a month. He was a damned good pilot, but tinkered out every time he was posted to an active-service squadron. He finally deserted . . . and landed in the enemy lines."

Captain Twillingate sat down and rammed his great fists out before him on the desk. "I don't understand any of this. What are you trying to do? Does this girl come from a good family, or have any money behind her? Is that what you're after?"

"She's destitute. Couldn't pay her fare, sir. Born in Shoreditch. Was on the stage for a time and seemed to be on her way up, but then she met me, and overnight her career meant nothing to her. She gave up everything, believing I needed her. When the Armistice came and everyone scurried to get home, I was trying to get a permanent commission. I never had another thought for her. I was looking after myself. Marriage was the last of my thoughts. But she was still determined to . . . look after me. When I was nowhere to be found, she had no other choice but to put the proposition to this louse, Wallington."

"And you want me to marry you? Don't you realize what I'll be shackling you to? She's obviously no good, and probably never will be. But you must have a future of some sort . . . a Victoria Cross, and all the rest. Why don't you think of yourself? She can't add anything to your life, but could be a drag for the rest of your days."

"Please, sir," Max pleaded with his palms flat on Twillingate's desk. "Whatever future I had is all behind me. I'm just a war hero. All these ribbons don't tell any of the real story."

"What about your parents? Aren't they entitled to something from you after all your years over there?"

"They've lived their lives, sir, as best they knew. This girl has all hers before her. She needs a friend, a helping hand, and I know my father will worship her. He's that kind. If Miss Maitland is stopped in Montreal, there's no telling what will happen to her. But if I can marry her on board here, she'll have something, a certificate no one will be able to deny. After that, it will all be up to me. I can get something to do. I brought on most of her troubles and it's up to me to remedy the situation."

Captain Twillingate rose wearily from his chair. "She's damaged goods, you know."

Kenyon nodded and stared down at his hands. "True. I had a lot to do with it. It's nothing to do with Wallington."

There was a half-minute pause and Twillingate finally responded. "I can see the war did more than make a decorated hero of you, son. It apparently made a man of you." He went to his bookcase and drew out a Book of Common Prayer. He turned and looked at Max, shaking his great head in disbelief.

"All right. Get her up here. I'm due on the bridge in a few minutes. I wonder where I can find a marriage certificate."

Max smiled, and said, "I used to be a choirboy before I joined up, sir. I believe you'll find one you can tear out of your Prayer Book—particularly if yours is a Mercantile Marine edition."

Captain Twillingate sighed and said, "I learn something new every day."